• • • • • • • ❖ • • • • • •

Rescuing Emmie

Andy Hughes

ISBN 979-8-852007-63-6

This book is a work of fiction and any resemblance to actual events or persons is entirely coincidental

Cover design by Leah Hughes

CHAPTER 1

"How do you know which house it is?" Rebeca's rich Nicaraguan accent pierced the warm Florida night.

"Shhhhh!" Toby put his finger to his mouth, and Rebeca was immediately sorry for her thoughtlessness. "I took a virtual tour, compliments of Google," Toby whispered.

Rebeca frowned, confused, but said nothing. Growing up in a small tribe in the middle of the jungle, many western ways were a mystery to her. Just then, the moon poked its bright light through one of the few holes in the dark, cloudy night sky, and seemed to shine down and focus on them like a spotlight. Immediately, Toby grabbed Rebeca's arm and ducked down behind one of the very few hedges in the neighbourhood. It lined the side of the garden and was the only thing blocking them from view if someone should look out the back windows of the large, L-shaped bungalow.

Toby looked down at the green numbers on his watch – 8:58 pm. "Benito should be coming out any minute," he said, barely audible.

As if on cue, a light turned on inside, and the two teenagers could see the dark-haired boy at the kitchen sink. He looked strikingly like Toby, but with a rounder nose and a squarer chin … a similarity that he had used to his advantage when they had first met.

⸺⊷●⊶⸺

Benito turned on the tap and filled a glass with water. He looked out through the window, but with the darkness outside and the bright light inside, all he could see was his reflection and his dark eyes staring back at him.

"Good," he thought nervously to himself. If his uncle came into the room, he would not be able to see him. He finished drinking the water and put the glass on the counter, wiping his sweaty hands on his jeans and swallowing hard. He turned his ear to the direction of the living room and heard Tadeo snoring loudly in front of the TV. He nodded to himself, took a deep breath, and walked to the back door that was to the left of the sink. Quietly, he turned the handle, and pushed the door open, stepping out into the warm night. He stopped dead as the snoring paused, and his heart pounded against his ribs. Two full minutes ticked slowly by as Benito stood completely still, while the two teenagers, crouching behind the four-foot-high hedge, silently watched him and wondered what he was doing.

As soon as the snoring resumed, Benito slowly shut the door behind him and grimaced as it gave a little squeak just before it clicked shut. He paused a moment before he quickly tiptoed down the path to the little gate that connected the hedge with the wall of the house. It gave a loud squeak as he opened it and the sound made him jump forward, falling over Rebeca who was crouching closest to the opening. Unfortunately, she was just shifting her position and was slightly unbalanced when Benito made contact, and they both ended up in a heap on the decorative gravel.

"Umph!" Rebeca called out involuntarily as she ended up on the bottom and Benito fell heavily on top of her.

"Shhhh!" Toby whispered unkindly for the second time. Then added quietly, "Are you all right, Rebeca?" The moon had shone through the night again and he saw Rebeca push Benito off as she tried to regain her breath. She slowly got up and brushed off the gravel that had become embedded in her clothing and her bare arms. She nodded, and as she did, the moon disappeared, enveloping them in darkness. The house was on a corner, and the side where they were positioned was under a large tree that hid them from the street light. Several seconds later, their eyes adjusted adequately enough for the teenagers to see where they each were, and they drew closer so they could talk in whispers.

"Where is she?" Toby asked anxiously.

Benito handed Toby a piece of paper, then answered, "She's at this research centre for a few days."

"Research centre?!" Toby said, his voice a little louder than he had intended.

Benito nodded, "You can't bring monkeys into the US as pets, so my uncle had to get her into the country pretending she was for research. They have to sort out some stuff, and then he is going to sneak her to his client."

"Benito!" A loud voice boomed out the back door of the house and two of the teenagers ducked. Benito stood motionless, fear permeating his entire body, and hoping with his whole being that his uncle would not be able to see him in the dark. "What are you doing out there?!" Benito's heart sank.

Toby glanced at the wheelie bin by the side of the curb, and whispered, "Tell him you are taking out some rubbish."

"I … uh … I …". Toby rolled his eyes in the dark as Benito sputtered his reply. He was going to give them away. "I was just taking something out to the rubbish bins!"

Benito and the others held their breath as the large, dark-haired man stood in the doorway, deciding whether or not to go get his nephew and drag him inside.

"Well, hurry up! You have two minutes!"

It seemed an eternity as the teenagers waited; then Tadeo gave a growl for effect, and turned back into the house, leaving the back door open.

Toby grabbed Benito as he turned to go. "What if we can't get into the centre before they move Emmie?"

"I'll try to contact you ... I'm doing what I can, Toby! I don't know when or if my uncle is going to let me have my phone back. I gotta go!" Panic overtook him and he pulled away from Toby and ran back in to the house, the fear of his uncle consuming him.

Toby held the piece of paper tight in his hand, and for a moment contemplated his next course of action. He turned to Rebeca and offered his hand to help her to her feet. "Come on! Let's get out of here!"

Rebeca was only too glad to comply, and the two of them trotted back down the alley to the waiting rental car, where Toby's brother sat anxiously waiting for them in the driver's seat.

Toby opened the passenger side door of the midnight blue convertible Mustang, and pulled the seat forward for Rebeca to get in the back. Joe turned to Toby as he got in the front, relief washing over his tanned face. He couldn't resist a ruffle of his brother's hair. Toby scowled.

"I'm not a two year old, Joe! Why do you do that?"

"You'll always be my baby brother!" He smiled, then added, "Did you get the address?"

"Ya, it's a research centre. Evidently you can't bring monkeys in as pets, so they had to pretend Emmie was brought in for research. I guess she will be there for a couple of days before Tadeo arranges to get her to his buyer."

Joe twisted around to look at Rebeca who had sat in the back seat. "Are you all right?" he asked, concerned as she wrinkled her small nose and rubbed her arms which had red marks on them.

"Just brushing the last of the gravel off."

Joe turned back to Toby with raised eyebrows. Toby recounted their meeting with Benito, and Joe sighed deeply. "That kid is such a ...".

"Forget it," Rebeca interrupted, not wanting to hear yet again how much Joe disliked Benito. "Shall we see if we can find this research centre?"

"No," interjected Toby, "let's go back to the hotel and look it up on the internet. We need to plan how we are going to get Emmie out of there. We'll go in the morning."

"Aye aye, captain!" said Joe, saluting his brother mockingly before he put the car into gear and sped off down the road.

"Slow down," scolded Toby, "What're you going so fast for?

Joe patted the steering wheel with a huge grin on his face. "How can I not go fast in a car like this?"

"If you get a ticket, *you* are paying for it! It doesn't come out of expenses!"

Joe squinted his eyes at his brother and let his foot off the pedal slightly, enjoying driving a vehicle he would most likely never own.

⸺⧫⸺

Benito lay on his bed in the dark room, looking out of the window at the few glistening stars he could see in the night sky that was not quite dark due to the lights glowing in Longwood. The house itself, owned by a friend of his uncle, was in the middle of the small city.

He thought of his mom in her hospital bed with pneumonia back in England, and a tear silently rolled down the side of his face. She had looked so pale when he had last seen her a couple of days before he left for Canada. He said a little prayer to Toby's family's God, asking Him to heal her.

He sighed deeply as he thought of the dark night sky at the house in the country, just outside Okotoks, in Canada. It seemed like a lifetime ago, but it in fact, it was only a few weeks since he was lying in bed in the basement of a house owned by a warm couple who thought he was their nephew. It had been the first time in a long time that he had been genuinely happy and content. Okay, so he had managed to get an unsuspecting Toby on a plane to Nicaragua to be met by Benito's nefarious uncle and into a horrific experience in the jungle. Benito had pacified himself with the knowledge that Toby was a smart kid and had had no doubt that Toby would survive whatever he encountered.

Benito still felt it had been fate. He had been waiting in Heathrow airport to board a plane to fly to Managua, Nicaragua, where he would meet his criminal uncle and hand over a package of diamonds that were hidden in the bottom of his bag. Toby had sat down beside him and they laughed as they looked at each other – two amazingly similar looking boys. Toby was going to his aunt and uncle's place in Okotoks to help them move into their new home, and was rather unhappy about the whole thing. They had spent an hour together, and by the time it was near to board their planes and Toby had asked him to watch his backpack while he went to the toilet, the plan had formed in Benito's mind. The icing on the cake was when Toby also handed over his can of pop for Benito to hold. Benito slipped in some sleeping pills he had, then swapped passports and tickets. Ten minutes later, they were heading to their respective boarding gates, only separated by two other gates. They said goodbye, and Benito hung back a bit, hiding in the crowd, as he watched Toby try to get on the plane to Calgary, and was then ushered quickly to Benito's gate where he was put on the plane to Managua. Benito knew that before Toby had realised he was on the wrong plane, the pills would have taken effect and he would be too drowsy to do anything but buckle up. Benito had put enough in so that he would sleep all the way.

Benito had then walked casually over to the plane bound for Canada, and boarded a relaxing flight, where he spent the most blissful nine hours he could ever remember. He had spent a lot of time with his uncle over the previous twelve years, as his mom was single and had nobody else to help her look after him or take him to and from school when she was at work. Tadeo, his uncle, was into all sorts of criminal activity and had dragged Benito into some terrible situations, even using him to be a courier for various things, like the diamonds.

Toby's aunt and uncle had not seen him for several years, so when Benito stepped into the arrival waiting area, they had no idea that the boy they were meeting was not their nephew. After a few days of heaven, working in their garden and going to the Calgary Stampede, his uncle had phoned while they were out and left a message. That was the end of his glorious holiday. A couple of days later, Benito and Aunt Doreen had flown down to Nicaragua to find Toby.

Toby's aunt and uncle had been unbelievably forgiving. They had talked about God and His amazing grace and how because they had been saved from their sins and hell, they felt compelled to show the same grace to Benito. It was still hard for him to comprehend. He did not know anything about sin and hell, and it still was a little confusing to him.

Toby's older brother, Joe, who had met them in Managua, seemed slightly less forgiving than Toby's aunt and uncle, and every now and again Benito thought Joe might pummel him for getting his brother into trouble.

Benito sighed again as Tadeo's voice broke into his thoughts, bringing him back to the present. Benito could hear Tadeo on the phone talking to someone about the monkey, and Benito got up and walked to the bedroom door opening it a crack, so he could listen to what was being said.

"Tomorrow evening?" Tadeo asked, then paused as he listened to the voice on the other end. "Okay, seven o'clock. Yes. At the Peter Briggs research centre?" Another pause. "Yes, of course ... Yes, I know the area ... Okay, fine." Tadeo hung up without saying goodbye, and Benito quietly clicked the door shut and trotted quickly back towards his bed, jumping the last few feet as he heard his uncle turn the handle to the bedroom.

Tadeo poked his head through the door, glaring at his nephew. Benito was starting to cause him more complications: Benito's cowardice was a big problem. However, an innocent-looking boy was still useful to him, and Benito's fear of Tadeo was greater than his cowardice. Perhaps, thought Tadeo, he could put up with his nephew for another year or two. Then, well, then he would have to decide how to get rid of him.

"Benito!" he called out loud, and Benito flinched involuntarily at the gruff voice, but lay still on his bed, hoping his uncle would go away. "Benito! You stupid boy! I know you can hear me."

"Yes uncle," Benito whimpered quietly.

"We need to go pick up some supplies tomorrow morning. Then you can have the afternoon free. I want you to do a little job for me in the evening."

Benito's heart sank. He dreaded Tadeo's 'little jobs'. "Yes, uncle," came an even quieter reply, and Tadeo grunted.

"You ungrateful little toad! I'm paying your mother's rent while she is not working, so you better carry out my instructions precisely."

As Tadeo closed the door, he squinted his blue eyes and smiled sinisterly to himself at his little added 'incentive' to get Benito to do as he was required.

CHAPTER 2

At the Holiday Inn on the east side of Orlando, Toby and Joe sat on the edge of one of the beds, while Rebeca sat in a chair opposite them. She had a room next door, but the three were eating pizza and discussing their next move to rescue the little capuchin. Emmie had befriended Toby during his adventure in Nicaragua, and in several ways she had taken care of him in the jungle. He even credited her with saving his life.

Toby stuffed the last of the pepperoni pizza in his mouth, and after taking a large gulp of his pop, said, "I think we should take a drive to this research centre tonight after all, just to have a look around and …"

He was interrupted by a pinging on his phone. Toby pressed 'answer' and immediately a stunning blond girl with emerald eyes smiled demurely at him. A little quiver raced through him and he smiled broadly back. "Hey Gwen!"

"How is your hotel?" she asked, and Toby found it difficult not to focus on her full, perfect lips. He shook himself and answered,

"Your parents chose an excellent one – pool and everything! Tell them thank you very much!"

Gwen Wentworth had been kidnapped and taken into the heart of the jungle in Nicaragua. The diamonds that Benito had been smuggling had been the ransom her parents had paid. They had never been recovered, but Gwen's wealthy parents were still indebted to Toby and Rebeca for rescuing their only daughter, and promised a bottomless supply of anything that the two teenagers wanted. Their request was to be able to rescue Emmie, and the Wentworths went all out providing everything that would be required, starting with a very comfortable hotel and a rental car.

"Have you found your little monkey yet?" Gwen did not really think much of the capuchin, but she knew how much Emmie meant to Toby.

As Toby relayed the evening's events, Joe glanced over at Rebeca. His heart crumbled as he realised for the first time that this amazing young woman whom he admired with a deep affection felt no returning emotions. She was watching Toby with a sad longing, but looked away suddenly as she became aware of Joe's gaze.

She smiled at Joe, then stood up and walked up beside Toby, "Hello, Gwen!" she called out and Toby turned his phone toward her so Gwen could see Rebeca.

"I, too, say thank you very much to your most generous parents!" They gave each other a little wave, then Rebeca strode purposefully toward the door that joined the two rooms. She hesitated, feeling completely inferior to Gwen and unsure of what to say next. "I am going to get ready to go to the research centre." There was nothing Rebeca needed to do to 'get ready' except grab a light jacket, but she needed to escape the discomfort she felt from the beautiful smiling face and Toby's captivated response. She left the room, closing the door behind her.

Gwen gave a little chuckle as she shrewdly recognised the jealousy which she so easily and often produced in other females.

"Plain polite Rebeca!" Gwen immediately regretted her words the moment they left her lips as Toby's admiring smile was swallowed up by a frown.

"Why do you have to be so unkind?"

"Exactly!" echoed Joe, defending Rebeca despite the recent revelation of her lack of feelings for him.

Gwen sighed deeply, but managed a convincing apologetic smile, unashamedly batting her eyes at the two males. Joe was unaffected, but Toby softened at her demeanour as she spoke, "I'm sorry," with a half smile and twinkle in her eye, and finally succumbed.

"Well, just try to be nice to her. It must be hard on a girl to see someone so stunningly gorgeous as you are."

Joe rolled his eyes and pretended to stick his finger down his throat, gagging loudly. Toby ignored him.

"It is good to see you without all that make-up on that your mom makes you wear."

Another gag came from the other bed. Toby threw his empty pop bottle at his brother with deft accuracy, but Joe ducked just in time.

"Anyway, we have to go. We are going to check out where they are keeping Emmie, and try to come up with a plan of how to get her out of that research centre. 'Bye!"

Gwen blew him a kiss, and before that annoying blood could rush up his cheeks, Toby clicked 'END'. He tossed his phone on the bedside cupboard and launched himself on top of his brother pretending to pummel him as he made loud grunts and groans. Joe was stronger than Toby, and a loud tussle ensued. An elbow knocked off one of the bedside lamps, bringing Rebeca rushing back into their room.

She stood wide-eyed as she saw the two entangled and the lamp on the floor. Rebeca grabbed a pillow and began firmly hitting each of them in turn while she chastised them like children. "Stop it! Do you not have respect for this hotel and these things that do not belong to you? Stop now before you break something!"

She swung the pillow at each of them again, and Joe ended up on the floor with Toby leaning over the bed laughing at him. Joe responded in laughter interspersed with groans as he rubbed his elbow that had landed on the ground first.

"Okay, Mother!" Toby grinned cheekily as Rebeca frowned at him.

"I vote we go and look at this research centre before Rebeca beats the two of us up!" Joe chuckled sheepishly, as he dragged himself to his feet and placed the lamp, which fortunately was still in one piece, back in its place.

Rebeca and Toby nodded in agreement, and in a few minutes the three of them were belted into the Mustang with Toby programming the address into the GPS, as they headed out of the hotel parking lot. Toby punched 'Merritt Island' into his phone and brought up a map so he could have a wider view of where they were going.

"Hey! That is where Cape Canaveral is!" Toby said excitedly. We ought to have a tour around there."

"I doubt they'll let us in to just have a look around at night time," said Joe, only half listening as he looked in his rear view mirror before indicating to get into the left hand lane.

"Don't be stupid!" Toby wrinkled his face at his brother who was too busy focusing on the road to look at him. "I meant in the day sometime before we leave back to England." Then added, "After we rescue Emmie."

Rebeca spoke up from the back, "What is … Cape … Cana … veral?" She pronounced the syllables carefully, leaning forward and touching Toby on the shoulder.

"Oh! Of course! I suppose you have never heard of it in the depths of the Nicaraguan jungle!" Toby's spoken words were more as a reminder to himself than anything. He continued, "It is where all the space shuttles have been launched," he said simply.

Rebeca sat back and nodded her head thoughtfully, "I have heard of these things at my school. How amazing for the people who have been in space, to see the earth and to

14

walk on the moon; to see God's amazing creation from a completely different view."

The three sat in silence as they each imagined what it would be like to be in space. Finally, Rebeca continued, "I think it would make you feel very small, would it not?"

"Oh, for Pete's sake!" Grimaced Joe.

Toby and Rebeca looked at Joe, confused. He pointed to the sign ahead: "Pay Toll". The sign to keep on the main road was for prepaid tolls only, so just at the last minute, Joe indicated right and quickly went across two lanes of traffic to go in the cash lane.

"I guess we didn't program 'no tolls' in when we put in the address," said Toby. "I don't think it is much, I have some change in my pocket. He turned on the interior light and examined the coins. I probably have enough."

Rebeca was frowning again in the back. She did not know what 'Pay Toll' meant, but she hated to keep asking what things were. However, when they got to the booth, and Joe inserted the money without getting anything in return, her curiosity got the better of her. "What are you paying money for?"

"Who needs to explore space when you have all these new things in Western society?" Toby joked, but his grin disappeared as he turned around and saw Rebeca's face. "Sorry, Rebeca, I didn't mean to hurt your feelings."

Joe looked in the rear view mirror and his heart melted. He gave his brother a sharp cuff with his fist.

"Ow!" Scowled Toby, rubbing his left shoulder, "I said I was sorry! You're lucky you are driving, otherwise..." he paused, looking at his brother who, although was the same height as Toby, was five years older and had filled out into a solid frame. He knew when they had wrestled earlier that Joe had held back considerably.

Joe glanced over at his brother and raised an eyebrow, "Otherwise ... what? You might ... slap me? You lanky squirt!"

Toby paused, thinking of a response, "Well," he began, trying to sound tough, "Just count yourself lucky that you are driving, that's all I can say."

Rebeca rolled her eyes as Toby's hurtful joking was forgotten.

"Why do males always have to be so ... so ... full of testosterone?"

Joe and Toby looked at each other, their frowns turning into huge grins as they glanced at each other and laughed heartily.

"Because, sweet 'gentle' Rebeca," Joe mocked her affectionately at the thought of her earlier use of pillows, "That is how God chose to make us!"

They drove in silence for a few miles, then Toby spoke up. "I hope Emmie is okay. She must be frightened being caged in a laboratory. What if they decided to do some kind of tests or something on her?"

Joe shook his head, "There wouldn't be time for tests by the sound of it. Benito said she was only there for a couple of days."

"Oh!" called out Rebeca, "Are we driving over the ocean?" She looked out the window and saw the shimmering water on both sides of the highway.

Joe glanced at the Satnav. "Looks like it is called Indian River." He said as he turned his concentration back to the road.

"It is actually the Atlantic ocean," clarified Toby, "But a row of islands runs down the east coast of Florida, making it look like just a strip of water."

After only a few minutes, they were back on land again and Toby pointed out a sign.

"Ulumay Wildlife Sanctuary!" he called out, then glanced at the satnav. "Looks like we have to drive past it a little way, before we can get off the A1A." Toby helped Joe navigate so he could concentrate on driving. They came south off the main road and began driving through a housing estate.

"Are you sure this is right?" asked Joe as he continued driving.

However, a few minutes later, they turned west up a dark, narrow road, with large trees on either side, and no houses. After 100 metres, there was a blue sign with white writing that read "Peter Briggs Institute". Ahead, the entrance was blocked by a heavy gate with a keypad and a speaker. A tall, thorny hedge lined either side of the gate at front, behind which was a high metal fence topped with razor wire.

Joe and Toby looked at each other with raised eyebrows. Rebeca disappointedly voiced their thoughts, "I do not think we will be able to just sneak in there."

Toby sighed deeply, pausing for a while before answering, "I guess we will just have to ring the bell when we come back tomorrow."

"What will we say? We are looking for our lost monkey?" questioned Rebeca. Toby laughed.

"Why, Rebeca, if I didn't know you better, I would think that was sarcasm!"

"I do not know that word," she said, looking confused.

"Never mind," said Joe, looking over at Toby, "My brother has enough for all of us!" Toby gave him a swift short punch, and Joe was just about to retaliate when Rebeca interrupted them.

"Must you two do that all the time?"

"It's how we show love, Rebeca!" Joe laughed, while Toby just smiled, and answered her first question.

"We will be teenagers doing a school project, wanting some information on monkey research."

"But we are not doing a school project," she protested, then realised what he meant. "I do not like to lie, Toby."

"Well, we can't just ask for Emmie back, Rebeca, they would throw us out. Don't worry, I'll do the talking and you can just smile sweetly and nod your head."

Joe started the car as he spotted the security camera moving in his direction.

"We better move, we look kind of suspicious just sitting here. I think we should still have a look around tonight, but we'll have to park further up the road and walk back down." He did a three point turn on the narrow road, and headed back. "Watch behind me, Toby, and as soon as the road has curved enough for us to be out of view, I'll pull over. I don't want to have to park up by the houses."

A few seconds later, Toby called out, "Clear!"

Joe nodded approvingly. "Good! We are still too far from the houses for anyone to be likely to notice the car."

He pulled onto the grass verge since there was no kerb, and they all got out. Joe locked the doors and they headed back to the research centre. Although there were no street lights, the night did not hide them as the moon was full. They slowed up as they came to the curve in the road that hid them from the watchful eye of the security camera.

"It seems to be just focused at the entrance," Toby said softly. "If we stay right on the side and stick behind the bushes we should be able to go up the side of the property without being seen, and hopefully we can walk around it and have a look to see if there is another way in."

They crouched behind the bushes that lined the side of the road and crept slowly to the chain link fence that appeared to surround the Institute. They got to the hedge that bordered it, and as it was as high as the ten-foot fence, they now could stand up straight as they walked without fear of being seen.

Gradually, however, as they walked along, the undergrowth grew thicker until it was impassable.

"Too bad we didn't have a machete!" joked Joe. "We could hack our way through."

"That would not help," whispered Rebeca, as she stopped to listen and smell the night air. She looked ahead over the vegetation, and the boys waited for her explanation.

"There is much water over there. Can you hear the mosquitoes?"

As if on cue, Toby felt one of the tiny creatures on his leg and gave it a loud smack. "This must back on to the Ulumay Wildlife Sanctuary. Perhaps there is a way in on the other side."

The three of them headed back to the road, crouching behind the bushes until they got around the curve and could cross the road without being seen. They followed the same procedure as before, and this time managed to go a further five minutes before they were halted, this time by the water itself.

"I don't think it would matter if the water wasn't there," said Joe, "This thorny hedge and security fence seem to be a solid wall all around the compound. We are going to have to come back tomorrow with the pretence that Toby suggested.

Silently, they crept back to the car. When they got in, Toby tapped on the satnav screen and entered in the address for their hotel.

It was midnight by the time they got back, and they were all tired. Rebeca said goodnight to the brothers and went into her adjoining room.

It still felt strange to be in this 'civilised' society, as Toby called it. Some things seemed a bit backwards to Rebeca; like brushing their teeth. Toby and Joe's Aunt Doreen had bought her a toothbrush and toothpaste and showed her how to clean her teeth. She had never had to do that before, as the food she ate in the jungle with her tribe did not cause these 'cavities' that Aunt Doreen had described to her. It did not sound good, having holes in your teeth. At first, she thought she could just continue to eat the food she was used to, but she quickly found that this was not going to be possible, especially in a hotel! And the boys seemed to enjoy food that stuck to her teeth and left a funny taste in her mouth. Joe and Toby assured her that she would soon get used to 'western' food, as they called it. Though she felt that an odd term, since Nicaragua was as west as the United States. They assured her that once she *was* used to it, she would not want to go back to her native diet. She was not convinced.

Rebeca picked up the toothbrush and squeezed on a little bit of the minty paste. It tasted like the wild mint leaves that she used to pick and chew in the jungle. When she finished, she stood for a moment, contemplating the odd feeling this paste left in her mouth. It did feel 'clean', but she was not sure she liked that tingly feeling; it felt like she had eaten mala mujer nettle. Perhaps she would get used to it.

She looked at her reflection in the mirror and immediately the image of Gwen's beautiful face on Toby's phone flashed in her mind. Her face seemed quite ordinary in comparison. Her dark eyes and thick lashes felt quite plain when compared to Gwen's emerald green eyes, and her olive skin and round face seemed almost childlike when she pictured Gwen's creamy skin and fine cheekbones.

Rebeca continued to look at the reflection as she undid the single braid at the back of her head and brushed her thick, dark brown hair with the hair brush that Aunt Doreen had given her. She sighed deeply as she thought of the look on Toby's face when he spoke to Gwen. It was obvious that he liked her a lot. The feeling in her stomach was quite unpleasant, and her thoughts drifted to her mom, wishing she could talk to her about these strange emotions.

Putting down the brush, she switched off the bathroom light and climbed into bed, pulling the thick quilt over her. Immediately, she threw it off – it was far too hot. She got up and opened the window, but the noise of the city was too loud and strange, so she closed it, climbing back in the soft bed and wishing she could hear the night sounds of the jungle. All she could hear was the humming of the air conditioning unit under the window ledge.

Rebeca lay there for some time, talking to God as she looked out at the strange sky that was lit up by electric lights that blocked out the stars. She poured out her heart about all the things that troubled her: how much she missed her mom, how she did not know what to do about these strange feelings she got when she thought of Toby, how she missed her father and wondered how much he was missing her. She felt a pang of guilt at her exhilaration of leaving the jungle and heading off to an exciting adventure, knowing she had no way of contacting him, to let him know how she was. All the while wondering if she had done the right thing by leaving her jungle home, but knowing she wanted to help Toby find Emmie and get her back safely to her troop in the jungle.

⸺⸻≫●≪⸻⸺

Toby and Joe jostled at the sink as they brushed their teeth, chuckling about Rebeca's scoldings. Joe tossed his brush on the side and ruffled Toby's hair, jumping back out of the bathroom and leaping into his bed before Toby could retaliate. A gentle beep resonated from Toby's phone, resting on the cupboard between the two beds, and Joe reached out to grab it before Toby could get to it.

"It's from lover girl!" he called out, as Toby wrenched the phone from his brother's hand. "Too late! I saw it – a big kiss and a winking emoji, Miss You!" Joe made a kissing sound and laughed heartily.

Toby shut the light off as the colour crept up his face. He climbed into his bed and smiled at Gwen's message as he said absently, "You sound jealous! I thought you liked Rebeca."

Immediately, Joe's manner changed. He did not want his brother to know how much his heart hurt. Trying to sound nonchalant, Joe said lightly, "I admire her, but nah!" Pausing, he added, "You do realise she likes you? I mean *like* likes you."

Toby put the phone down beside him on the bed as he turned curiously to his brother. "What? You're joking, right?"

"You are such a half wit, Toby." He shook his head. "I kind of suspected, but I caught her looking at you tonight while you were talking to Gwen. That jungle girl is smitten."

"Huh." Toby said thoughtfully.

"Huh. You are so articulate!" Joe jibed. He turned over to face the other way, in case Toby could see his face. "Good night, baby brother."

"Uh, ya." Said Toby, lost in his thoughts. "Goodnight." Toby leaned back down and picked up his phone, typing a simple 'goodnight' back to Gwen. Turning his phone off, he placed it on the bedside table and stared up at the ceiling wondering at Joe's words. Toby had thought she was just being nice to him. What did he know about how girls felt? Except for Gwen – she made herself perfectly clear!

CHAPTER 3

"Get up!" bellowed Tadeo as he opened the door and leaned into Benito's room.

Benito jumped up to a sitting position and blinked rapidly, his heart racing at the sound of his uncle's voice. He looked at the clock that sat on the little chest of drawers by his bed. It was 9:15. He had not slept very well, and had only just drifted into a deep sleep about seven o'clock that morning. He would have to see if he could get his uncle to get him more of those sleeping tablets.

"Okay uncle!" He called out as he threw the blankets off, swinging his feet to the floor. He knew not to keep Tadeo waiting.

"You've got fifteen minutes to get dressed and have something to eat. I want to leave at 9:30," he said crossly.

He was always cross when he spoke to Benito. A picture of Toby's uncle, Derrick, flashed into his mind: his gentle face smiling broadly and his warm brown eyes twinkling. How lucky Toby was to have such a kind uncle. He just did not understand how Toby could not have wanted to go help Derrick and Doreen at their new house in Okotoks.

Benito shook himself as Tadeo slammed the bedroom door shut behind him. He'd better hurry. When his uncle said a time, he meant it to the second.

Five minutes later, after a quick splash on his face at the bathroom sink and changing into his jeans and T-shirt that he had worn yesterday, Benito sat at the little kitchen table with a bowl of corn flakes and a glass of orange juice. He paused for a moment, remembering the times he had prayed with his 'pretend' aunt and uncle before each meal. It had caught him out the first couple of times, as he had never done that before, but he had soon gotten the hang of it. He felt like he should say a prayer now but … on his own it seemed so strange.

Tadeo hovered by the kitchen sink, looking out the window absently while he sorted in his mind what things he would need. He turned and saw Benito looking at his food contemplatively.

"What are you doing boy?!" he called out gruffly, making Benito jump again. "Saying grace??!" He laughed with his face scrunched up at his joke, having no idea that that was exactly what Benito had been doing.

Benito called out "Amen!" in his mind, hoping that Toby's God had heard him, wondering if He listened to everyone, and started shovelling down his cereal. Three minutes later, he washed it down with his juice and stood up sharply, nearly knocking over the table in his haste not to make his uncle wait. His reward was a clip around the ear as Tadeo leaned over and caught the glass as it fell over and started rolling off the table.

"You imbecile! Now get on and brush your teeth so we can go! You want teeth like mine, don't you?" Tadeo grinned wickedly like a fierce dog baring his white teeth, and Benito almost expected him to start barking. It was weird that his uncle always made him brush his teeth. He wasn't sure why Tadeo insisted, but he was not about to argue.

At 9:30 exactly, the two of them climbed into the old, black Dodge Ram – which also belonged to Tadeo's friend – and Tadeo backed down the drive, taking a quick look at his phone to confirm the directions before heading off down the road as Benito was putting on his seat belt.

It was already quite hot and the air conditioning was not working in the truck, so Tadeo pressed the buttons to open both windows. Benito only found it mildly cooler as the air blowing in was still relatively warm, but the movement of the breeze on his skin felt refreshing. He rested his arm on the open window ledge and leaned back, relaxing slightly as the truck rumbled through the streets, while Tadeo remained silent, absorbed with the thoughts of the final touches to his plan.

Twenty minutes later, Tadeo turned off the road into a large outdoor shopping mall. There were plenty of spaces available, but Tadeo drove until he could see the store he wanted, "PetSmart", before pulling into a gap and parking. He pressed the button for the windows without warning Benito, who's arm was still resting on the ledge. He pulled back his arm sharply, scraping it across the rim of the window as he did so. He sucked in his breath sharply, but said nothing, gritting his teeth at the pain.

Tadeo turned off the ignition and climbed out of the truck. He stood frowning at Benito who remained in his seat. "Get out, boy!" he snapped.

Benito fumbled with his seatbelt and Tadeo huffed at him, tapping on the side of the truck door impatiently with his fingers. Finally, Benito managed to unclip his belt and he opened his door, almost falling to the ground as he stumbled out in his rush to appease his uncle. He steadied himself and slammed the truck door shut heavily.

Tadeo locked the doors and headed into the pet shop with Benito trailing silently behind. The doors opened automatically and a whoosh of cool air enveloped them as they entered the large store. Benito shivered at the change in temperature as he followed Tadeo who was looking up and down the aisles.

"Can I help you find something, sir?" A small teenager with long curly red hair pulled up in a ponytail, grinned widely at them, flashing her silver braces. She wore a blue shirt with a PetSmart logo on the right side.

"Dog carrier," Replied Tadeo abruptly, frowning at the girl.

Undeterred, her smile remained fixed, and she turned around waving at them to follow her as she bounced ahead of them with an energetic walk, her ponytail swinging from side to side. Benito had to almost trot to keep up with the girl and Tadeo.

"Follow me, sir! They are just down this way."

She guided them to a varied collection of cages and carriers, and stood for a moment, letting Tadeo have a short scan of them all, before tilting her head slightly and grinning wider, "What sort of dog do you have, sir?" Her blue/green eyes danced as she waited for Tadeo to reply, looking at Benito and then back at Tadeo.

"A small one." Tadeo raised an eyebrow, scowling at her in irritation, but the friendly freckled faced girl didn't miss a beat.

"Oh! A mongrel, is he? I think mongrels are the best! I'd love to have a dog, but I still live with my parents and they don't like animals." She walked to the end and picked up a pet carrier, just the right size for a capuchin monkey. "How about this one?" The grin never left her face as Tadeo snatched it from her.

"That will be perfect," he said and headed back to the front of the store to the tills.

Benito smiled weakly at the girl, "Thank you," he said, before hurrying after Tadeo.

"You two have a great day, now!" She called out with a cheerful wave, before heading off in search of another customer in need of her enthusiastic assistance.

———⟫●⟪———

Tap! Tap! Tap!

Toby squinted his eyes open. Had he just heard something?

Tap! Tap! Tap!

He picked up his phone and sighed as he realised he had turned it off the previous night. He pressed the button to turn it on.

"It's 9:00 little brother!" Joe said, looking at his watch as he stood up beside his bed and slipped on his jeans. Then called out before the tapping began again, "Come in, Rebeca! We are awake!"

"Hang on! I'm just in my boxers!" Toby protested too late as Rebeca opened the door adjoining her room.

She shook her head and half smiled at Toby as she entered wearing a lilac T-shirt and beige shorts.

Joe sucked in his breath slightly as his gaze moved down to her brown walking sandals. He had never noticed what shapely legs she had. He shook himself and coughed, trying to chase unwelcome thoughts away and also hide the fact that he had been ogling her womanly figure. Fortunately, Rebeca was looking at Toby hiding in his bed.

"I really do not understand this need to be in a certain type of clothing before someone sees you. You were wearing shorts yesterday that covered the exact amount of you as your boxers do – what difference does it make?"

Joe chuckled on his side of the room as he slipped on his T-shirt from the previous day. Then sniffed it, wrinkled his face and removed it before grabbing a clean one from his suitcase.

"You gotta admit, she's got a point, buddy!"

Toby scowled at his brother as he slipped out from under the duvet and, grabbing some clean clothes from his suitcase on the way, dashed into the bathroom and shut the door.

Rebeca sat down on the end of Toby's bed, and smiled as she watched Joe fumbling around his messy suitcase looking for some clean socks. She sighed quietly, admiring his solid frame and how handsome he was. His short thick brown hair and thoughtful brown eyes, along with his rugged features would surely make many girls' hearts skip a beat. However, for her, she could just admire him like she admired beautiful scenery. She knew that Joe liked her, but it was just unfortunate that her heart was set on Toby. He was a little on the skinny side, and had rather boyish features that were not overly good looking. However, he had a genuine caring heart and a peculiar, but deep, way of looking at things, that drew her to him. Beauty was indeed, in the eye of the beholder, as her mother used to say. At the thought of her mother, a pang of guilt hit her. Her mother had been a strong Christian and had told Rebeca that she must only marry a man who loved God. Joe, with all his faults including his temper and current bitterness towards Benito, was a man who loved God. Toby, on the other hand, did not appear to know much about God at all. Where did that leave her?

Toby reappeared with dirty clothes in hand, and stuffed them into his full suitcase. It looked like he had just dumped a drawer full of clothes upside down into the case.

"How do you two find things in your bags?" Rebeca looked from one to the other. Toby and Joe looked at each other and shrugged their shoulders in unison, making Rebeca laugh. "Are you ready now?" she asked. "I have been awake for three hours and I am quite hungry!"

Before receiving an answer from either of them, she headed for the door that led out into the hallway of the hotel. The boys followed her, Joe shutting the door behind them as they hurried to catch up. The elevator pinged and opened just as they reached Rebeca.

Rebeca made a slight grimace as they all stepped in and the doors swished closed while Toby pressed the button for the ground floor. Joe could not help himself, and he put his arm around her.

28

"You'll get used to lifts," he comforted her, gently.

She smiled weakly at his attempt to allay her fears. "It is not natural," she said, "to step inside a box that shuts its own doors, locking you in, and let it take you up and down. What if it decides not to open its doors again? We could take the stairs. We are only on the sixth floor."

Joe squeezed her shoulder gently. "There is an emergency button, right there." Joe pointed to the red button on the panel. If the box decided not to open its doors, you press that button and some men will come and open it for you!" He said gently; then added, "But if you really don't like it, we will take the stairs."

"What?" declared Toby, "I don't want to walk up six flights of stairs."

Joe looked at his brother's thin frame and laughed, "It will put some muscle on those skinny legs of yours!"

Before Toby could retort, the elevator stopped and the doors slid open, much to Rebeca's relief. The three of them exited the elevator and turned left into the restaurant. It was a buffet, so they each grabbed a plate and a tray. The boys quickly piled theirs high with everything as Rebeca eyed everything slowly, and decided on just an array of fruit and some pancakes. They grabbed some drinks and then took their trays to a small table in the corner so they could discuss their plans privately.

Rebeca ate her food slowly, savouring the flavour of the pancakes and syrup, and was pleasantly surprised at the tastiness of the fruit, since she had not picked it directly from the ground or trees.

"This is very good fruit," she commented.

"Well, that is because we are in Florida. They, like Nicaragua, grow a lot of their own fruit. Someone else may pick it for you, but it is still quite fresh."

"Now," said Toby, "Rebeca, you have done really well at making yourself look a lot younger with your two braids and ribbons. I think it is best that just you and I go into the research centre. Joe does not look much like a student."

"Not with this well-built body!" smiled Joe cockily as he looked down at himself, before shovelling a large forkful of sausage into his mouth.

Toby and Rebeca looked at each other, rolling their eyes.

"I still do not like the idea of lying," Rebeca pursed her lips thoughtfully.

"Ah, well, you don't have to!"

Rebeca looked at him, puzzled, before Toby added, "You will be the foreign student from Nicaragua who does not speak English very well!"

Rebeca smiled happily, "That, I believe, I can do quite well!"

Benito climbed up into the pick-up truck and fastened his seatbelt while Tadeo put the pet carrier onto the back seat. Tadeo looked at him.

"You don't need that thing on, yet, boy. We are only driving around to the other side of the mall." Tadeo climbed in and started the vehicle. He started to back out, then slammed on his brakes and cursed at an elderly lady in a dark blue sedan who had stopped directly behind him. She had one finger pressed to her lips as she looked around, deciding where she wanted to park. Finally, she spotted the perfect spot, and carried on slowly up the parking lot to a collection of disabled bays nearer to the mall entrance.

Tadeo finished his manoeuvre and headed to the other side of the mall where there was a grocery store. He found a space near the doors, and turned off the engine. This time,

Benito did not wait to be told to get out of the truck. He opened the door and jumped out, shutting it with a slam.

Tadeo scowled. "Why do you have to always draw attention to yourself?!"

Benito looked at the ground, frightened to look Tadeo in the eye, but quickly looked up as he heard Tadeo walk away from him towards the entrance. He jogged to catch up to his uncle, and followed him in like a scolded puppy.

Tadeo grabbed a shopping cart and pushed it quickly through the fruit and vegetable section, tossing tomatoes, lettuce, cucumbers, mangoes, apples, kiwi fruit and other items into it. On the left side of the shop in the far corner, was an upmarket delicatessen/ready prepared food section. There was an amazing array of tantalising cheeses and cold meats and dishes of various meals in ceramic dishes. Benito's stomach growled as he looked at everything. The small bowl of cereal he had had for breakfast was not enough for a growing teenager, but he stepped back when Tadeo turned and squinted his eyes at him.

"I'll have that lasagne," said Tadeo, turning back to the counter and pointing to a large, delicious looking lasagne covered in a mountain of cheese. It must have been just prepared, as the smell wafted over to where Benito was standing and he unconsciously licked his lips.

"One moment, sir, while I find a lid to put on it. It is still slightly warm, so take the lid off as soon as you get home, as there will be condensation on it. As soon as it is cool, put the lid back on and store it in the fridge; unless of course, you are going to eat it straight away!" A large Mexican man who looked like he had eaten far too many lasagnas, placed a clear plastic lid over the dish and handed it carefully to Tadeo. "Would you like some garlic bread to go with that?" He smiled a bright white smile. Tadeo paused.

"Sure, okay."

The man's smile grew wider. He picked up a baguette and placed it in a narrow paper bag.

"You will not be sorry! These are our best sellers. We are famous for our lasagne and garlic bread! I can assure you that you will be returning next week for another!"

Tadeo gave him an irritated smile and took the baguette, tossing it in the cart and heading off across the store. He went up and down all the aisles, putting in various items, and Benito walked closely behind him, eyeing the lasagne and wondering if that would be his lunch. His stomach growled as he thought of it.

At the checkout, Benito clumsily helped Tadeo pack the items in bags and the two of them, laden down and hot, walked slowly back to the truck. Tadeo put the shopping on the back seat beside the pet carrier and Benito got in the truck. When Tadeo finished, he sat behind the steering wheel and pulled out his mobile phone. He mumbled something under his breath that sounded like wig and hat, and Benito wondered what his uncle was planning. Tadeo usually did not tell Benito the details until just before he wanted Benito to do things for him; Benito was glad since he had enough trouble sleeping as it was, without knowing ahead of time what it was that he would be doing. If he didn't know, then he could pacify himself with the possibility that THIS time, maybe, it would not be so bad.

Tadeo turned on the engine and swung the large truck deftly out of the space and headed back out onto the road. Benito turned down his window and relaxed a little as the breeze blew across his arm and face and through his hair. There was not a cloud in the blue sky and the sun grew hotter as it rose higher in the Florida summer sky. For a moment, Benito began day dreaming and he was back in Okotoks, digging in a vegetable patch, when suddenly the siren from a police car blared behind them and jerked him awake. Tadeo cursed and pulled over to the curb.

Benito glanced in the rear view mirror and saw a police officer get out of the car and stride toward Tadeo's window. His heart began beating heavily and Tadeo's blue eyes glared at him, silently ordering his nephew to remain silent. Benito was only too glad to comply and rubbed his sweaty hands on his jeans.

The tall uniformed man came up to the window, and he spoke in a deep voice. "You have a light out, sir." He smiled authoritatively, then added, "AND you were speeding. Five miles over the limit. May I see your driving licence and registration?"

Tadeo sighed but got out the paperwork and handed it to the officer, who wrote the details down in a notebook.

"If you can get out of the vehicle, I will show you the light."

"That's fine, I believe you," Tadeo snapped at him and the officer's smile faded.

"It wasn't a suggestion," said the officer curtly, "Get out of the truck, sir." Tadeo silently cursed himself and begrudgingly got out of the truck, obediently following the man to the back of the truck.

Something on the seat caught Benito's eye. His uncle's phone! He looked in the rear view mirror and back down at the phone. Hesitatingly, he picked it up and tapped a couple of times. Bingo! The address of the man who was buying the monkey! Benito looked in the mirror again and opened up the glove compartment, rifling through the items for a pen and some paper. As he did so, the edge of his phone poked out from the bottom of the pile. He reached out to take it, but stopped just as his fingers touched the precious item. No. His uncle would know. He reached instead, for a small empty envelope and a black pen. Quickly, he copied down the details from his uncle's phone, his heart pounding so loudly he could hear it in his ears. When he finished, he tossed the pen back in and stuffed the envelope into his pocket. He heard his uncle's voice become louder as he walked closer to the door and Benito swiped back to the home screen, tossing the phone back on the seat just as his uncle's face appeared by the window. Tadeo got in and slammed the door shut. He tapped the steering wheel angrily, while the police car pulled out from behind him and drove off.

An hour later, having visited a few more stores and purchased all the supplies that were required, they were cruising back to the house. Benito was looking forward to getting out of the hot vehicle and back into the air conditioned house. His stomach growled again. And perhaps he would get some delicious lasagne for lunch! Perspiration started beading up on his forehead and he wiped it off with the back of his hand. Too bad the air conditioning in the truck was broken – or so his uncle had said. Benito would not be surprised if Tadeo had lied. He enjoyed making others suffer. Benito's Aunty Maria, Tadeo's wife, had left him when Benito was only eight years old, but he remembered the day clearly. She came over to see Benito's mom and was hysterical. He did not remember the details, but he remembered Aunty Maria screeching to Benito's mom that Tadeo was a psychopath, then she had left, and they had not seen her since.

At that moment, Tadeo turned to him and laughed. "You look a bit hot, boy!"

Could Tadeo read his mind?? thought Benito, terrified. He looked over at his uncle who had returned his gaze to the road. *Surely not!* A shiver ran down the back of his spine, and he shook involuntarily. Tadeo looked at him quizzically, but said nothing as he pulled into the drive of their borrowed house.

Benito helped his uncle take in the bags and various items that Tadeo had purchased, dumping them all on the floor as they entered the welcome coolness. Benito let out an involuntary sigh of relief, and Tadeo looked at him, squinting his eyes. An evil grin slid across his face and he turned to the air conditioning dial on the entrance wall.

"I think it is too cold in here, don't you think, Ben?" He laughed, and he turned the dial down to the OFF setting. Benito said nothing.

They carried the items from the entrance into the kitchen, and Tadeo emptied the bags, putting the groceries into the cupboard and fridge. Benito stood and silently watched him, knowing better than to offer help. He eyed the lasagne as Tadeo placed it on the counter beside the fridge and lifted off the plastic lid. He glanced over at Benito who was gazing longingly at the tasty looking dish of food and chuckled wickedly.

"Stupid boy! You don't think I spent that kind of money on food for YOU??!" Benito's face dropped and Tadeo sneered at him. "Sit down, you can make your own lunch." Tadeo grabbed a loaf of bread and tossed it on the table in front of the hungry teenager. That was followed by a pack of sliced ham, some tomatoes and a head of lettuce. Tadeo then banged a plate and utensils down in front of Benito.

"And two slices of bread is enough for you, you greedy boy!" he added as he saw Benito open up the bread and take out four slices of thinly sliced bread. Reluctantly, Benito put two slices back and as he reached for the ham, Tadeo bellowed, "And only one slice of ham!" He paused a moment then said, "You can have all the tomatoes and lettuce you want!" He burst out in hearty laughter, and tears surfaced at the edge of Benito's eyes. Fortunately, Tadeo turned away before he saw, and Benito quickly wiped them away. Tears invoked a hideous anger in his uncle, and he would very likely get a thrashing with his uncle's belt if he saw them.

Tadeo finished putting everything away and joined Benito at the kitchen table with a package of butter. He grabbed six slices of bread, buttering them thickly and filling them with half the large package of ham.

"I, on the other hand, am larger than you and need to replenish my energy!" He winked at his nephew and smiled unkindly.

Benito tried to eat his sandwich slowly, savouring the meagre offering from his uncle, remembering wistfully, the huge steak and baked potatoes he had eaten at Doreen and Derrick's house. His stomach grumbled unhappily as he finished his sandwich with a glass of water, and he carried the dishes to the dishwasher. He started to clear the table, but Tadeo brushed away Benito's hand.

"I might have seconds," he said with his mouth full of food. He paused, then added, "You can have the afternoon to do what you want – as long as you stick around here so I can keep an eye on you!"

Benito rubbed his temples with his fingers. His head was pulsating. "I have a headache. I think I will lie down for a bit." He started to leave the kitchen, then turned at the last minute.

"Could I get some more sleeping tablets, please, Uncle Tadeo?" He tried not to sound too desperate. "I am not sleeping well."

Tadeo studied his pathetic-looking nephew. He was eighteen years old, but he looked fourteen. He was tall, but he was skinny – and sickly looking. Tadeo had already collected some more sleeping pills from his supplier, but had not yet given them to his nephew. He liked the feeling of control over others. He knew Benito had not been sleeping – the kid seemed to live in a constant state of anxiousness. But Tadeo liked Benito being at his mercy. Still, the boy would probably perform his act better this evening if he got a little rest. He stood up and pulled open a drawer. Reaching in, he took out a small bottle of pills with no label on it. He threw it to Benito who, surprisingly to both of them, caught it.

"Only one!" Tadeo commanded, looking at the clock. Benito usually took two before he went to bed. Tadeo wanted him up in five hours.

"Yes uncle. Thank you." Benito smiled weakly, and filled a glass with water, and slunk to his darkened bedroom where his curtains were closed and it was still slightly cool. He shut the door behind him, hoping to keep the heat out as long as possible. He sat on the edge of his bed and opened the bottle, he tipped it and two pills fell onto the palm of his hand. It was tempting to take them both, but he knew how angry Tadeo would be if he was not awake to do whatever it was Tadeo had planned for Benito; so he reluctantly put one of the pills back and screwed on the lid before placing it on his bedside cupboard.

CHAPTER 4

If it wasn't for the fact that he was worried about his little friend, Emmie, Toby would be enjoying the drive along the Florida highway, with the top down and the music blaring from the radio. He glanced over at Joe who was tapping his fingers on the window ledge, singing along to the music. Toby looked over his shoulder at Rebeca, who was mesmerised by all the new sights and sounds. It was hard to believe that it was only just over a week ago that they were all in the Nicaraguan jungle. Now, they were in a people jungle – where one city and town seemed to roll in with another indistinguishably.

This time, they were ready for the toll road, and Joe pulled off the main lanes and along beside the toll booths. Rebeca smiled to herself as she watched Joe put in the money. It pleased her to know that she did not have to ask any questions this time. There was something comforting about things becoming familiar when there was so much that was new and strange.

Soon, they were crossing Indian River again. Rebeca looked on both sides as they drove along the bridge. It looked more like an oblong lake this morning, but she could see how you would not realise it was the Atlantic ocean.

"Just remind me of the final directions, Tobs," Joe spoke as he turned off the radio. Toby duly obliged, and a short while later they were parked where they had been the night before. Joe turned off the car engine.

"I think you should park right by the entrance," suggested Toby. "There is no reason why my older brother who loves his new car would not drive me and my friend right up to the research centre." He smiled at Joe, who promptly started up the car again and drove down to the entrance. The road widened into a kind of turning circle, so Joe pulled up on the right side and put the lever into park.

"Look, they are watching us!" said Rebeca pointing to the camera that had moved to their direction and stopped, pointing straight at them.

"That's fine," Toby assured her. "Let's get out." He grabbed the notebook and pen he had purchased from the hotel shop, opened the door and stood up, pulling the seat forward for Rebeca to climb out. He turned to Joe, shaking his head. "Did you not think about Rebeca when you asked the Wentworths to rent you a Mustang? I'm sure you could have found a sporty-looking four door car."

Joe gave them both a guilty smile. "Uh, ya, sorry about that Rebeca." He gave her some warm puppy dog eyes and she laughed, shaking her head.

"Boys!" Rebeca replied amicably.

Without further comment, the two teenagers walked up to the steel gates and Toby pressed the CALL button on the chrome key pad to the left.

"Yes?" The answer was immediate, startling Toby.

"Oh!" He laughed nervously, "That was fast!"

"Just call me Speedy Gonzolas." The man said sarcastically in a bored sounding monotone. They could hear him heave a great sigh.

"Oh! Ah," Toby laughed again, and hesitated.

"Is this some kind of Knock Knock Ditch game?" The man sighed. "Because if it is, you forgot to run away."

"Huh?" Toby asked, confused, looking at Rebeca who shrugged her shoulders in reply.

"You know, the game where you ring someone's doorbell and run away." He paused, then repeated in a droll voice, "But you forgot to run away."

"Oh!" laughed Toby again, "No, sorry." He cleared his throat. "We're from a High School in Orlando and we are studying primates. My friend and I chose to do our report on monkeys."

"You should have phoned first."

"Well, uh," Toby frantically tried to think of an answer, then caught the sight of Joe doing a selfie as he leaned against the Mustang and it inspired him. "Well, you see, my older brother there, he just got that car, and he's going to drive it across to California tomorrow, and uh, he said he could drive us today or in three weeks time. Our report is due next week and my parents work long hours so they can't drive us. So, we had to come today."

"What about your friend's parents? They work long hours too?"

Toby was unsure if the man was suspicious or just being awkward, but put on his friendliest voice. "Oh, uh, Isabella here is a foreign exchange student, from Nicaragua." He smiled up at the camera. "She is staying with my family."

Rebeca flashed her most charming smile and said pleadingly, "Please, señor! You will help us, no?" She added the puppy dog eyes that Joe had just flashed at her.

The speaker clicked off, and Toby and Rebeca looked at each other questioningly. A loud BUZZ sounded and the gates slowly swung outwards. As soon as the space was big enough, they entered. They crunched along the short gravel drive and up to the glass doors that opened automatically when they got close. A thick dark-haired man sat behind the front desk, his chest stretching to capacity his grey polo shirt with the logo Peter Briggs in navy across the top left side. Toby wondered why he hadn't been given a bigger one. The man squinted his eyes and raised one eyebrow.

"So, you two livin' together, huh?" he asked.

Toby and Rebeca looked at each other, and both shook their heads, embarrassed.

"No, sir, you misunderstood," said Toby flustered and Rebeca added,

"Uh, no, sir. You no understand!" Too late, Rebeca saw the twinkle in the man's eyes. She smiled and laughed, "Ah! You make joke!"

Toby smiled, too, and looked at Rebeca, chuckling to himself at her performance.

The large man stood and came around to the front of the desk, and Toby watched in amazement as he stood in front of them. He must have been over six and a half feet tall. No wonder he hadn't been given a bigger shirt – they probably could not find one in his size.

"Wow! How tall are you, sir?"

"Six foot eight," he answered, trying to pull his shirt down further without success. He crossed his arms over his ample chest and looked down at the two of them intimidatingly. He paused for a moment, enjoying their astonishment for a moment before he dropped his arms to his side and sauntered slowly down the tiled hallway, silently waving his hand over his shoulder at them to follow him. At the end of the hall was a choice of left or right. The man turned right, walked to the end, then turned left, then down another hall way before he went left again. Toby was frantically trying to orientate himself as to where they were compared to outside. At the end of this hall, the man opened a heavy fire door and stood aside to let the teenagers enter.

It was a large room, with several tables in the middle and about thirty cages lining the walls around them. Various species of monkey filled the majority of the cages. Toby scanned them all quickly as he tried desperately to spot Emmie.

"Hey Bob! These kids are doing a report on monkeys – can you spare ten minutes to give them some info?!" Bob, a thirty something man with a thick mop of blond hair and funky red square glasses looked up from his table and smiled warmly at them. The tall man shut the door behind him as he left the room.

Just then, there was a loud "HOO! HOO!" from the far corner. "HOO HOO! HOO HOO! HOO HOO!"

Emmie! It had to be! Toby looked at the little capuchin jumping up and down in the cage.

Bob looked over at the monkey and back at Toby and Rebeca.

"HOO! HOO!"

"Hmmmm." He took his glasses off and placed the tip of one of the arms in his mouth thoughtfully. "That's weird. That is the first noise that little monkey has made since it came here a couple of days ago." Bob got up and walked over to Emmie who was now beside herself with excitement, rattling the cage, desperate to get to Toby. Toby and Rebeca followed close behind the man, who was too absorbed to notice and tell them to stay back.

"Can I hold her?" Toby asked.

Bob turned around sharply, suddenly remembering the two teenagers.

"I think you should stay back." He paused. "How did you know she was a girl?" He asked.

Toby looked at the man innocently, "She just, uh, sounds like a girl!" He burst out with a grin, and before the man could stop him, Toby was standing in front of Emmie, who reached through the wire and grabbed his fingers with her tiny hands and began making faint squeaking noises.

Bob shook his head. "Well, what do you know?" A thought popped in his mind. "You better not touch her, she has not finished her quarantine." He grabbed Toby's hand and pulled it away, and immediately, Emmie started again,

"HOO! HOO! HOO! HOO!"

Within minutes, all the monkeys were making a raucous, calling out with various noises and rattling their cages frantically.

"I'm sorry," said Bob, "You are going to have to leave."

"Oh, please, sir," begged Toby loudly, "Please will you answer some questions? Maybe out front, in the lobby?"

The man scrunched up his face and looked at his watch. "Give me five minutes to finish this report and I will meet you there." He looked down at the table where he had been sitting when they came in, and motioned to some sheets of paper.

"Okay, thank you very much!" said Toby eagerly, and he ushered Rebeca, out of the room. He shut the door behind them and whispered to Rebeca as they walked.

"I'll ask him some questions, and you ask to go to the toilet – the washroom they say here in Florida!"

"I don't understand," whispered Rebeca as they stopped before they got into earshot of the big guardian at the front entrance.

"You'll have to go back and do what I was planning on doing. Emmie probably won't make such a noise if you go to her."

"What were you planning on doing, Toby?" She scolded him, "You didn't have a plan, remember? You were just going to, how do you say? 'wing it!'?"

"Well, it came to me while we were in there. There are a couple of windows high up, which I am certain face that boundary fence we walked around. I want you to open them – just wide enough to draw Emmie to one of them, but not enough for anyone to notice. Then I want you to see if you can unclip Emmie's cage and hang it down lightly so she will be able to open it, but so Bob doesn't see it. I don't know if it will work, but we have to try!"

"Okay," she agreed.

Just then, Bob came around the corner. "Why are you just standing there?" he asked.

"We got lost," said Toby, who was feeling slightly guilty that the lies were beginning to come out quite naturally.

Five minutes after sitting down in the lobby and drilling Bob with various questions about monkeys, Rebeca spoke up,

"Please, sir, may I use your … washroom?"

"Uh, oh, I guess it would be all right. Go down the hall and turn right, then, it is another right, at the end of the hall."

"Thank you, sir!" Rebeca jumped up and walked off, but instead of turning right the second time, she turned left and trotted quietly back to the room that held the monkeys. She turned the door handle quietly and, as Toby had suspected, when Emmie saw Rebeca she made soft purring noises instead of the loud hooing she had made earlier.

Rebeca walked to the cage, her heart beating heavily, and her ears tuned to any noise outside the room. Carefully, she studied the clasp on the cage and saw how she could leave it hanging so it looked like it was closed, but could be flipped up by a little capuchin. Her heart was beating so loudly, she could barely hear anything outside the door as she climbed up on one of the tables to reach a window. She unlatched it, but let it swing gently back down so it looked closed. It was not a heavy window, and a little monkey should be able to open it. She paused for a moment, then did the same to the window next to it. She looked around for a moment, then satisfied, she jumped off the table. Just as she landed on the floor, the door to the room swung open.

"What are you doing in here?!" Bob stormed in the room with Toby at his heels, his face panicked, silently apologising to Rebeca for not being able to stop him. He waited at the door, hiding behind a cupboard in hopes that Emmie would not know he was there.

Rebeca stood for a moment, looking like a frightened child waiting for a parent to dole out some punishment, and not knowing what it would be.

"I ... uh ... I ... am so sorry, sir!" She looked at Toby and then back at Bob, who was angrily waiting for an answer.

"I got lost and ... uh ... when I found myself in here, I couldn't help having another look at all the monkeys. They are so adorable!" She pleaded for mercy from the man with her watery brown eyes.

"Did you take any pictures?" He glared at her. "Give me your phone!"

Rebeca looked confused.

"I do not have a phone, sir."

Bob frowned at her angrily. "What teenager doesn't have a phone?" he demanded, as he walked towards her, determined to find her phone.

Alarmed, Rebeca put her hands up like she was going to be arrested.

"Empty your pockets!"

Rebeca looked down at her shorts and lifted her T-shirt so it was just above the shorts waistband. "I have no pockets," she said softly, looking down at herself, wondering where it was that he thought she might have a phone.

Bob did a circle around her, looking up and down, finally deciding she did not have a phone after all.

Just then, Toby's scent reached Emmie's nose and she started screaming and jumping around. Bob shouted loudly at Rebeca and Toby,

"Get out, now!"

Only too gladly, the teenagers scurried out of the room and down the various hallways, quickly reaching the front desk. The man looked up at them and raised an eyebrow at their hurried departure.

"Gotta go!" called out Toby as they passed him, "We're late! Thank you very much!"

"Thank you, sir!" repeated Rebeca as she followed Toby hurriedly out the front doors which only just opened in time as they dashed out and trotted down the drive where the front gate had already been opened. They jumped in the car, and Joe started to speak,

"What...?"

"Just drive! Go down the road, but turn right and park about four or five houses down. We'll tell you then."

Joe started the car and drove the short distance down the road and around the corner. As he pulled over to park, Toby said, "Turn around and face the other way."

Joe did as requested, and as soon as he parked, Toby recounted their adventure while Joe listened intently. He filled in Rebeca about the part that Bob insisted on going back to the monkey room to get some information for Toby. When he finished, Joe spoke to Rebeca,

"You poor thing! Toby should not have made you do that!" He looked at Toby angrily, but Rebeca defended him.

"I was happy to play my part to try and get Emmie back."

Toby looked at her questioningly, "When you say, 'play your part' does that mean you weren't as terrified as you looked?" he asked.

A huge grin spread across her face, "I was a little frightened, but I pretended to be more so than I was. My heart *was* beating quite hard when I was unclipping the cage and opening the windows. I was not sure what would happen if I got caught. Could we have been arrested and put in jail? I have faced many frightening things in the jungle, Toby. *Bob* did not scare me." She said his name with emphasis.

Joe half smiled and Toby felt his heart warming to this brave Nicaraguan girl. He was beginning to see why Joe admired her so much.

"We just need to wait half an hour," said Toby. "Bob mentioned he needed to go out and get his lunch at 12:30."

"So," began Joe, "You only saw the two men? That is odd, I thought there would be more people around."

"I asked about that," said Toby. "Evidently there is some big meeting that the majority of the staff have gone to. That did and will definitely work in our favour. We got lucky!" He beamed widely, but his smile quickly faded as Rebeca spoke up.

"There is no such thing as luck," she chided him. "God works out everything in conformity with the purpose of His will." She added for emphasis, "Ephesians 1:11."

Toby looked at her, unconvinced. "Do you really believe that NOTHING is random? God cannot have EVERYTHING planned. Didn't He just make the earth and then sit back and let it develop according to everyone's free choice? I mean, why would an all-powerful God care about a monkey anyway? Surely He has better things to do." Toby frowned at the idea that all things in life were part of some great plan that originated before the universe was created.

"God's purposes are beyond our understanding. He made all of creation including Adam and Eve, knowing they would sin and mess everything up. He cares about all of His creation, even little monkeys. His hand is in all things."

Joe smiled, "You sound like a Sunday school teacher," he said.

"Well," began Rebeca, "That does not say much for you two, if you do not know these things."

Joe and Toby looked at each other and said nothing. Just then Toby's stomach growled. "Do we have anything left to eat in the back?"

Rebeca rummaged in a bag on the floor beside her and sighed. "There are cheesies, corn chips, gummy bears and some cans of root beer." She giggled, "I do not know how filling gummy bears are!" She took out some corn chips and a can of root beer before handing the bag over the seat. Joe grabbed it before Toby could take it from her, and a small tussle ensued. The bag ripped and the snacks flew in the air, landing on their laps and the floor, with one can of root beer landing out on the road slowly rolling to the other side. Joe jumped out and picked it up, tossing it on the back seat beside Rebeca. He laughed.

"I think we'd better let than one sit for a while before we open it!"

Rebeca raised an eyebrow, but said nothing, munching on her corn chips with her own root beer firmly in her left hand.

Twenty minutes later, Joe looked at his watch. This Bob guy should be coming out soon. Perhaps we should all duck down a bit. We don't want him to see us and wonder what we are doing parked here."

"Maybe we are just having some lunch before we head home – which we are. Having lunch, I mean, not heading home."

Rebeca curled her lip. "I would not call corn chips and root beer 'lunch'."

Toby rolled his eyes, "Well, he won't know wha …"

"Duck!" called out Rebeca as they saw a car pull out of the road from the research centre. They all hunched over, but Toby peeked over the top of the dash to make sure it was Bob. It was, and after pausing at the junction, thankfully he turned in the opposite direction to where they were parked.

"Okay! Let's go!" called Toby as he jumped out of the car. He helped Rebeca out of the back seat and turned to Joe, "You wait here. Rebeca will come with me and be a look out."

Toby and Rebeca trotted down towards the road and as they turned down towards the research centre, Toby and Rebeca tucked themselves behind the bushes on the left hand side and started quickly walking towards the building.

"Toby!" said Rebeca softly, "You will need to be on the other side. Emmie is on that side of the building."

He looked at her and screwed up his face.

"Are you sure?" As he asked, he immediately remembered how well she could find her way around the jungle without any confusion, and he realised she had a much better sense of direction than him. He nodded to her and they crossed the road, quickly heading towards the building behind the bushes on the other side.

In a few minutes, they were near the back of the building, and Toby looked up at the windows. He could see two that did not look completely shut, and walked towards them.

"Emmie!" he called softly. He turned to Rebeca, "I suppose I could call louder – I could be calling a dog, no one would know!" Before she could reply, he called out louder, "Emmie! Emmie!" He stopped for a moment and the two of them listened, straining to hear the little monkey. Very soon, they heard it:

"Hoo! Hoo!"

"That's it, Emmie! Come on! It's Toby!"

This time it was louder and more frantic, "HOO! HOO! HOO!"

"Emmie! Come on, girl!" Toby shouted louder, and Rebeca scanned around them to make sure no one could see what they were doing.

"HOO! HOO! HOO! SQUEAK! SQUEAK!" This time the teenagers heard the cage rattling as the little monkey tried her best to escape. Suddenly, ever so faintly, they heard a clink, and the rattling stopped. Then a different sound, like a little capuchin scrambling around.

"Come on Emmie!" Toby encouraged her.

"HOO! HOO! SQUEAK! SQUEAK!"

Just then, they saw a little hand poke underneath the window, trying to push it open. Toby bit his lip watching her, wishing there was something he could do to help her.

"Come on, Emmie! You can do it!"

Another hand and a nose poked out as the window moved a little further outward. Toby started jumping on the spot, willing her on,

"Come on, Emmie!"

A head poked through the window, then the teenagers hearts dropped as they heard the deep voice of the large man in reception,

"Hey! You little monkey! Where do you think you are going?!"

The last thing Toby saw was Emmie's pleading eyes looking right at him, before she was pulled back in and the window was slammed shut. He fell to his knees and pounded the ground in anger. "We nearly had her, Rebeca, we nearly had her!" A huge sigh escaped out of him and he knelt there with his head in his hands. Rebeca ran over and knelt down beside him, wrapping her arms around him.

"We will find another way, Toby," she whispered gently, disliking herself for how good it felt to hold him in his despair.

They knelt there for a few moments, until Toby calmed down. Suddenly he was aware of the solace of Rebeca's arms, and when he finally let his hands drop, his eyes met Rebeca's, only inches away from him. A queer pleasant feeling entered him, but immediately his thoughts returned to Emmie and he jumped up. He grabbed Rebeca's hand and lifted her to her feet.

"You are right," he said with determination as they headed back up the side of the building and through the bushes, "we will find another way!"

When they got back to the car, Joe saw their disappointed faces and empty hands, and said nothing. He pulled the car away from the kerb and drove back through the housing estate and towards the highway.

"The man from the reception desk heard her and grabbed her before she could escape," was all Toby could muster as he turned and stared out the window. Joe opened his mouth to say something, then closed it again, focusing on the road in front of him.

No one said anything the entire journey back to Orlando, and when they got back to the hotel, they sat on the beds in the boys' room for a few moments before Toby spoke.

"We were sooooo close, Joe," he sighed deeply again. "I saw her little face and brown eyes. She was pleading with me to rescue her!"

Joe put his hand out to ruffle Toby's hair, then thought the better of it and pulled back. "Why don't we just distract ourselves and watch a bit of tv and cool off for a while? Then we can go get something to eat," Joe suggested as he walked over to the air conditioning unit and turned it up.

"I think that would be a good idea," said Rebeca trying to sound upbeat, "We will rest and we will eat and we will think of another plan." She got up and walked past Toby, stopping for a moment as she placed her hand on his shoulder, and he looked up.

"Thanks for your help, Rebeca." He smiled faintly. "I really appreciate it."

"That is okay, Toby." She smiled, suddenly feeling slightly shy, and headed through the adjoining door. She did not enjoy watching the television. She gave a last smile at Toby as she shut the door behind her. She was happy to lie on her bed and cool down, lost in her own thoughts.

Toby sat there, looking at the closed door, and Joe gave him a funny look.

"What's up, little brother?" he asked, but the uncomfortable feeling of jealousy began creeping through him, as he was sure he already knew the answer to his question.

"It's weird, you know," began Toby as he repositioned himself so he was facing Joe. "I used to think she was just a plain and okay girl. I mean, she is no way near as hot as Gwen." He deliberated as he tried to make sense of this odd feeling inside of him. "And yet …".

"And yet," Joe finished despondently, "there is something really special about her."

"Ya," Toby frowned thoughtfully as he heard the sadness in his brother's voice then turned and saw it in his face. "You DO like her, don't you, Joe?"

Joe's countenance changed in an instant, and he forced out a laugh as he threw a pillow at Toby. "Don't be stupid!" he said defiantly.

Toby did not reply, but he grabbed the pillow and added it to his own two, lying back down on them, his hands behind his head. "We need to think of another plan."

CHAPTER 5

"**G**et up, boy!"

Benito woke up in a cloud of panic, rolling over and trying desperately to gain consciousness before his uncle reached the bed.

SMACK!

Too late, Tadeo's hard knuckles made contact with Benito's arm, and pain shot up into his shoulder, pulsating like an electric shock. He pulled himself to a sitting position, and rubbed his left arm gingerly. He blinked several times, trying to escape the fog of the sleeping pill. He grabbed the glass of water that he had left by his bed, and gulped it all down. Wiping his mouth with the back of his hand, he swung his feet to the floor and tried to wake himself up enough to get to a standing position safely.

"That stupid girl in the pet store sold us a damaged carrier!" He shouted at Benito as if it was his fault. "We'll have to stop there on the way to the research centre, so we need to leave in ten minutes!"

And with that, he turned around and slammed the door behind him as he left Benito, still half dazed, slapping his face slightly to help him gain consciousness. Benito finally felt he was awake enough to walk to the bathroom where he splashed copious amounts of cold water on his face before wiping it dry with the hand towel.

He sat back down on his bed, suddenly thinking of the envelope of information he had stuffed in his jeans, and an idea started to form in his head. He ripped off just the part that had the address. It might work.

True to form, ten minutes and not one second later, Benito was in the truck with Tadeo who drove hastily down the road, still angry that his precision plans had been messed up. He looked at his watch and sighed. He could still make it according to his plans if they did not take too long in the store.

When he pulled into the parking space, Tadeo leaned his arm over the back seat and pulled out the carrier.

"Come on, kid, no dilly-dallying!" They both slammed their doors shut and Benito followed Tadeo obediently into the store.

Benito said a silent prayer to Toby's God as they headed to the tills, and in answer to his prayer, the red headed girl bounced up to them cheerfully. She looked at the carrier as Tadeo held it up to her, his face scrunched in anger.

"Is there something wrong with it, sir?"

"It's broken!" Tadeo scowled at her.

"Oh, I am so sorry! Just you wait there now, and I'll get you another one straight away!"

Benito stood nervously on one foot and then the other, waiting for his chance. Tadeo looked down at him, "Stand still, boy!"

Benito tried, but ended up tapping his toes instead. Tadeo shook his head. Just then, the girl came back with an identical carrier, which Tadeo looked over thoroughly before nodding his head and stomping out of the store.

Benito looked at his uncle, then back at the girl, who was looking at him questioningly. He started to shake, then punched his hand in his pocket and took out the piece of paper.

"Please!" he whimpered.

She cocked her head and looked at the piece of paper.

"Please!" he implored again, pressing the paper firmly in the palm of her hand just as Tadeo turned around and shouted at him.

"Come on, boy!"

Benito trotted after his uncle, but as he headed out, he looked over his shoulder and gave the girl one last beseeching look as the doors closed behind him.

———⇒●⇐———

Pamela looked down at the paper in her hand curiously. How truly odd, she thought to herself as she started to open it.

"Pammy!"

Pamela rolled her eyes – she hated that name and her manager knew it. He was such a dork! She giggled to herself. Did anyone use that word in real life?

"Pammy!" His voice was louder this time, and Pamela sighed as she stuffed the unread paper into her back pocket. The skinny kid was probably just a weirdo – there were certainly many weirdos in the world, she thought as she hurried over to the side of the shop where her boss was standing, hands folded and resting on his enormous belly. He looked down at her and spoke condescendingly.

"Pammy, how many times do I have to tell you we do not give away dog treats." He raised a thick black eyebrow for effect.

Pamela managed to squash the sigh that was welling up inside of her and she smiled up at him sweetly. "But Mr Flatley," she pleaded, "I am trying to use my initiative in making the customers happy! I only give the dogs one or two." She widened her smile even further and cocked her head like a naughty puppy.

"I can't afford to be giving away all our stock!" He grumbled half-heartedly, and he walked away as Pamela shook her head and rolled her eyes again.

———⇒●⇐———

Even though it was now evening, the sun continued to glare down out of the completely blue sky. They drove faster now, and Benito relished the rush of the wind through his open window. The sleeping pill he had taken earlier seemed to resurface, and he drifted off shortly after they left the parking lot. Tadeo drove in silence as he went over his plans.

"Benito!" A harsh voice woke him from his slumber. Tadeo had pulled over in a quiet lane and was rummaging through a bag. He took out a long blond wig with a floppy hat and, placing it on his head, brought the hair around the front of his ears and shoulders, and pulled the hat down nearly covering his eyes, so you could see very little of his face. Then he put bright red lipstick on before rolling the bag up and tucking it beside him. In any other situation, Benito would have laughed, but the sight of his uncle trying to look like a woman only made Tadeo look unhinged, so Benito just stared.

"Stop staring, boy!" Tadeo growled at him and Benito instantly looked away. When his uncle reached in the back seat again and then placed something beside himself, Benito risked a quick glance. It was a large, old fashioned wicker picnic hamper where each side had a flap that lifted up, with a handle in the middle. He wondered what was inside, but dared not ask.

Tadeo looked at his watch, then a few minutes later, he slunk down as low as he could in the seat and still see over the steering wheel. Starting up the truck, he drove slowly forward until they reached the front of the research centre. Tadeo turned the truck around in the turning circle so he was facing away from the entrance and turned off the ignition, throwing the lever into PARK. He sat for a moment, and Benito waited for his instructions.

"Okay," started Tadeo slowly, like he was talking to a four year old. "Listen very carefully, because I do NOT want you to mess this up." He squinted his blue eyes at Benito who stared back in a frightened gaze as though hypnotised, concentrating on every word his uncle said through his shocking red lips. "You are going to take this hamper in and you will collect the monkey." He paused, as though Benito needed time to take in his instructions.

"You will ring the buzzer, and say that you have something to deliver to Fred Barns." Benito nodded, not daring to look away.

"When you enter the building, there will be a security guard who will probably ask to look in the hamper." He paused again.

"You will say that your mom wanted you to bring the hamper to your uncle Fred because it is his birthday. Your mom cannot get out of the truck because she hurt her ankle." He stopped again, trying to think of all the instructions that a kid like Benito would need to keep out of trouble.

"You will be directed to Fred who will give you the monkey, and you will take her out of the building and back here." Benito's gaze wandered towards the metal gates, and Tadeo added sharply, bringing Benito's eyes back to him, "You will NOT speak unless spoken to! Do you understand? Nobody but Fred knows what is going on."

Benito nodded silently and remained still, going over the instructions in his mind, frantically trying to think if there was any questions he needed to ask, but his thoughts were interrupted as Tadeo barked at him.

"Well, go on, get out now! They are watching us through that camera and will be wondering what we are doing!"

Benito jumped out of the truck and took the basket as Tadeo handed it out to him. He swallowed hard and walked up to the gate, pressing CALL on the keypad.

"Yes?" a man's voice answered.

Benito's heart was beating quickly as his mind went blank. The voice sighed and a man spoke slowly and tiredly.

"Not another Knock Knock Ditch kid," the droll voice said.

Benito frowned, confused. "Huh?" He queried, but suddenly the glare of his uncle seared his thoughts and he remembered what he was supposed to say. "I ... uh ... wanted to drop something off ... uh ... f-f-for Fred Barns." he stuttered. Then added, "From my mom."

There was a moment silence, and Benito began to worry that he had messed up, but then the buzzer sounded and the gates slowly swung outwards. Benito walked through them and up the drive to the glass doors that opened automatically as he got near. The large man was still there, sitting with his arms crossed. Like earlier with the others, he stood up and came around the desk, looking down at Benito, intimidating him with the full effect of his height. Benito's legs began to feel weak, but the thought of his uncle's temper spurred him on.

"What have you got in the basket?" The giant man asked with his hands folded across his chest. Benito panicked as he thought of what to say, but the man did not wait for a reply as he opened each side up and looked inside. He lifted up a red cloth to reveal the lasagne, now covered in plastic wrap instead of the cover, making it look home made. It was sitting on a cuddly toy capuchin monkey. Beside those items, there was a bottle of wine, some little iced cakes, the stick of garlic bread, and some serviettes with colourful balloons on them. The man raised an eyebrow.

"It's his birthday today," said Benito, then remembered the instruction not to speak unless spoken to.

The man cocked his head, squinting his eyes at Benito.

"You related?" He asked. "You look like him."

"Uh, yes, my mom is his sister!" He blurted out, looking up at the man nervously.

"I didn't know Fred had a sister," he began, then chuckled. "But then, Fred doesn't talk much." He closed the lids of the basket. Then looked at Benito with a smirk. "Your mom is a bit short for a big truck like that. Can she actually see over the steering wheel?"

"Uh … oh …," Benito stammered, then laughed nervously, "Ya."

The man laughed, and repeating his earlier actions in the day, headed down the tiled hallway, motioning over his shoulder with his hand for Benito to follow him. He opened the same door that Rebeca and Toby had gone through earlier, but this time, there was a very pale, skinny little man with short black hair, in a white medical jacket. He turned as they entered, and looked at the large man irritatedly over his wire rimmed glasses, then saw Benito behind him.

"Ah! Benny! Good to see you young man!" He smiled at Benito in a friendly manner and Benito smiled back.

"Your nephew here has something for your birthday." The man said as he ushered Benito in, then called out as he shut the door behind him,

"Happy Birthday, Fred!"

"Hello, Benny, come on over here! Is that something from my dear sister, Tanya?" he asked, putting his finger to his lips so that Benito would keep silent.

Benito carried the basket over and placed it on the table in front of 'Fred', who opened it up and took out the items, including an envelope that contained a birthday card full of money, which he opened and counted quickly. He looked at the bottle of wine.

"Very nice," he said, "It would appear that my sister has very good taste in wine!" He tucked the envelope in his shirt pocket, and walked over to the cage that held Emmie. Benito's eyes went wide as Fred picked up the now limp monkey. Fred chuckled as he looked at Benito's face.

"She's not dead, just drugged. Should keep her quiet until you get to your destination!" He lifted the lid and placed her inside. He threw the red cloth over her, then handed the basket back to Benito.

"If the guard wants to look inside, just tell him that when I took out the cuddly monkey toy, we noticed it had a ripped seam, so you are taking it back to the store for replacement," he directed. He nodded to the cuddly toy and added, "I'll take the real cuddly toy home with me tonight in my bag." He continued silently to himself, "And I will leave the latch to the cage open, with one window hinge unlocked and hey presto: one escaped monkey!"

Benito stood nodding nervously as he listened, holding the basket in both hands. Fred looked at him. "You can go now, kid." He shook his head and half smiled, turning back to his work while waving Benito away with a flick of his hand.

Benito turned to the door, and breathed deeply as he opened it and headed back to the reception area. The large man stood and began to head around the desk, but just then, the phone rang, and he nodded towards the door, buzzing Benito out as he picked up the phone.

Every part of Benito wanted to run out the door, but he walked steadily down the drive as the gates opened for him to leave. He got to the truck, and opened the door, handing the basket to Tadeo's outstretched arm before climbing in and shutting the door. Tadeo put the basket on the back seat, and headed off down the road, saying nothing to Benito, and letting him wonder how far the journey was to where they would drop off the monkey.

"Pamela! Your dad is here!" At sixty-eight, Colleen was the oldest and friendliest of the staff that worked at the pet shop. She nodded her head towards the window at the police car that had pulled up out front. Pamela made a face.

"Oh, I told him I was going to walk home!" Pamela sighed and bounced her way to the staff room to get her backpack. "Bye, Colleen!" she said cheerfully, then giggled, as she saw her friend duck down behind the till as Mr Flatley headed in her direction.

"Pamela!" he shouted irritatedly. "Have you seen Colleen?"

Pamela gave him a wide smile and tilted her head, "Well, she was here a minute ago!" She turned away, adding with a giggle, "I hope you find her! See you tomorrow, Mr Flatley!"

Pushing open the door, the heat that greeted her immediately made her grateful that her dad had decided to pick her up. It had to be one of the hottest days on record. It was 6:30, but still felt as hot as it did earlier when she went out to sit under a tree to eat her lunch. Pamela opened the back door of the police car and got in.

"Why do you sit in the back, honey?" asked her father, Officer Richard Bartley, who turned around chuckling at her. His thick red hair was cropped short, and his twinkling eyes were exactly the same colour as Pamela's. Along with Pamela's animated smile matching her Dad's, there was no question that she was his daughter.

"I like to pretend that I have committed some evil crime — possibly robbing little old ladies of their last dollars! And you think that you have finally caught me, but in fact, I am soon to escape!" She paused. "I try to put on my most evil face when I look out the window at people, so they wonder what dastardly deed I have done!"

Her dad raised his eyebrows, then laughing heartily, faced forward and drove out of the parking lot. When he got on the main road that would lead them virtually to their home, he looked at her in the rear view mirror, a huge grin on her face – he wondered if she realised the evil look she was giving people was only in her imagination!

"Anything exciting happen today?" He said, as he always did after she finished a shift at work.

"I got in trouble again," she started, "BIG trouble! I think Mr Flatley is going to fire me because I give away dog treats to the dogs that come into the store!" She tittered, "Well, maybe he won't fire me, but he did give me another talking to again! Never mind!"

Just then, they stopped at a red light. A young woman was walking along holding a little boy's hand, and when the boy looked at Pamela, she scowled deeply. He pointed to her and said something to his mom, who looked at her and shook her head. She leaned over and Pamela guessed she was telling her son that he should be careful to always be good so he would not end up like that girl in the police car! A big smile pushed through her frown, and the woman gave her a bemused look. Darn! Thought Pamela, it was so hard to look evil!

"Oh! I had a very miserable man come into the store today to get a pet cage. I think he must beat his son. The son was quite thin and looked terrified of his Dad. I think he probably starves his son, as well. Maybe he keeps him locked in the basement and only lets him out occasionally." Pamela thought of the piece of paper that Benito had given her, and she felt it in her back pocket. She should really tell her Dad. Then again, it could be nothing. She decided to wait until she had gotten home and read it herself first.

"Pamela," her Dad exhaled loudly, "Do you REALLY think the man beats his son? Or is this all in your head? I mean, if you really thought that, perhaps you should have called me, so I could follow it up."

"Well … the kid was definitely scared, Dad, and the man did look like he could hurt someone. But then," she looked mischievously at her dad in the rear view mirror, "you have sometimes given me that very same look!"

Richard shook his head, "Pamela, sweetheart, anyone would think you were ten years old, the way you act sometimes! And what are you going to be next week? Fourteen?" He teased.

"DAD!" she chided him, "You know how old I am!"

"Sixteen?" He winked at her in the mirror as he waited at another red light, "Wait, no! Seventeen?"

"I am going to be a fully fledged adult, and you know it!" She pouted playfully at him. "Next week, I'll be able to do whatever I want and you won't be able to stop me!"

"That thought is rather disconcerting, honey," he said, only half joking. "Hopefully, you will continue to be guided by your faith in Jesus."

Pamela scrunched up her face, "Why do you have to get all serious on me?"

"It's my job as dad to guide you on the straight path, pumpkin."

At that moment, Pamela's dad pulled into their cul-de-sac and parked in front of their large, moss-green house, and she waited for him to get out so he could open her door. As she stepped out, he leaned over and she reached up and gave him a kiss on the cheek.

"Says he who bought the family home because it looked just like the one in his favourite movie, Psycho!"

Richard tilted his head. "You know I was only kidding! Your mom and I loved the house and the yard and it was all just perfect to raise a family in! I just said that about the house looking like the Psycho house as an afterthought."

"Well, a mature adult should not have said something like that to an impressionable eight year old. You scarred me for life!"

He looked down at his eldest daughter with a deep love and thanked God for her and her bubbly personality. "So it's my fault that you are the way you are, huh?" he laughed.

"Absolutely one hundred percent! Nature AND nurturing! The fault is laid squarely at your …" she tittered teasingly, "… Psycho front door!" And with that, she waved her dad good bye as he drove off and she turned up the walk to house, sniffing the air and trying to decide what her mom had cooked for supper.

"Lasagne!" she called out happily as she opened the door. The large entrance opened up on the right into the comfortable and welcoming living room, but she headed straight ahead through the arched entry way into the large kitchen. "And garlic bread! Yippee!" She came up behind her mom and gave her a big squeeze.

Her petite mom turned around and wiped her hands on her apron before tucking a stray strand of blond hair back into the short ponytail.

"Eddie and Sophia were not impressed that they had to wait for you to eat, but I told them that lasagne was something that was best eaten fresh out of the oven! I'm surprised they did not come running when they heard you open the door!" She looked towards the stairs that led to the bedrooms of Pamela's fifteen-year-old sister and twelve-year-old brother.

"I am not surprised!" said Pamela, "Eddie is probably engrossed in his PS4 grand theft auto game that he borrowed from his friend Bobby, and Sophia probably has her earphones in listening to music that you wouldn't approve of!"

Penelope Bartley squinted her eyes at Pamela. "You know I don't like tittle-tattling, honey. I do know what is going on, and I will deal with it after we eat. Now, go get changed and wash up before calling them down."

Pamela turned right out of the kitchen and trotted up the wooden staircase and straight into her bedroom. She took off her uniform and put on some denim shorts and a florescent pink T-shirt – the one her mom did not like because she said it clashed with Pamela's hair. Pamela had told her it did not matter if it clashed – she loved the colour! Sitting on her bed, she took out the piece of paper that the frightened skinny boy had handed her in the store.

"We are picking up Emmie at 7:00 tonight and taking her to the following address." She looked at the address. It was in Louisiana. Hmmmm, she looked at her watch. It was nearly 7:00. Below the address, was a name, Toby, with contact details.

Her mom's firm voice came up from the bottom of the stairs, "Come and eat, now, kids! Supper is on the table!"

Pamela looked back at the paper, pondering it for a moment, but then put it in the top drawer beside her bed before walking contemplatively out her room and then trotting down the stairs to join her brother and sister.

——➤●◄——

"Well," said Toby rubbing his wet hair with a towel, "that didn't help."

Toby, Joe and Rebeca had just come upstairs to their rooms after going for a swim in the hotel pool. Joe had suggested they try to relax and do something fun for a bit in the hope that one of them would come up with a good idea of how to get Emmie out of the research centre. They had all felt refreshed, but nobody had any ideas. Rebeca went through the adjoining door and shut it behind her.

"I have first dibs in the shower!" called out Toby as he grabbed some clothes and hurried into the bathroom before his brother could get in.

Joe changed into some dry bottoms and flicked the television on. He knew Toby would be a while, so he positioned some pillows against the headboard of his bed, and leaned back half sitting, half lying down.

Flicking the remote several times, he finally found a programme he wanted to watch, but he was instantly interrupted by the vibrating of Toby's phone. It lay on the bedside cupboard that was between their two beds. He paused, then reached over to pick it up. Gwen's name was flashing on the screen, so he pressed ANSWER and her face instantly appeared.

"Hey, Gwen!" said Joe, silently agreeing with Toby that she really was 'hot', even though she had just taken a towel off her head revealing her cropped blond hair. Despite himself, he felt a twinge of exhilaration as her perfect coral coloured mouth turned up into a coy smile. Mentally, he shook himself. He had to gain some control or he would make a fool of himself.

"Hey, Joe!" She squinted her eyes provocatively, "I've never seen you without a shirt on, that is one solid chest you have there!"

Joe cringed at the unwelcome warmth that crept up his neck, hoping Gwen would not notice. She really did know how to get to a guy. He was disappointed at himself that he could feel this way when his heart was drawn to Rebeca.

She chuckled as she roughly dried her hair, then tossed the towel behind her. "No need to be embarrassed that you have a great body!"

So much for hoping, thought Joe as he sighed and changed the subject. "Toby's in the shower," he said.

"Oh, that's okay. I was just wondering how you guys got on today trying to find that monkey of his?" Joe filled her in on the disappointing day, and she frowned. "Hmmmm, that's too bad. Have you got any other ideas of what you can do?"

"No, unfortunately not," said Joe, glad at she had switched topics with him. "We thought a relax and a swim in the hotel pool would bring up some ideas – you know how sometimes when you are trying to sort out a problem, if you stop thinking about it consciously, your mind carries on and eventually solves the problem?"

"Uh-huh," she said as she scooped her fingers through her hair and gave her head a shake. The resulting look was quite breathtaking. Joe swallowed hard and chased the unwelcome thoughts away.

"What?" she asked as she cocked her head curiously, knowing full well what was going on inside Joe's head.

"What do you mean, 'What'?" Joe asked innocently.

"You had a funny look on your face just now," she said, smiling provocatively.

Joe felt the uncomfortable heat begin to surface again and quickly carried on his conversation to avoid explaining. "Well nothing came to mind for any of us while we were swimming. We really are quite at a loss as to what to do next."

"I'll try to think, as well," smiled Gwen, "Although I am not very good at coming up with plans and ideas!" A frown appeared suddenly on her face as Joe heard her mom calling in the background. "I have to go. We are having dinner at the neighbours' tonight." She held up a smooth, slender hand with manicured red nails over an exaggerated a yawn. *"They have a very fine son,"* she said in an exasperated voice, and added, *"with a very fine career."*

"Oh?" asked Joe.

"He IS rather dishy! Trouble is, he is sooo boring!" She rolled her eyes. "All he talks about is himself and how impressive he is!"

"He actually says that?" asked Joe.

"No," she smirked, "But he may as well!" Her mom called again, and Gwen sighed. "Oh! How tedious – Gotta go! Tell Toby I called." She smiled and winked as she blew Joe a kiss before hanging up.

He tossed the phone back on the cupboard just as there was a knock on the adjoining door.

"Come in, Rebeca!" he answered.

The door opened, and Joe took a slight intake of breath. She looked completely different with her thick brown, wavy hair hung loose on her shoulders, still damp from the swimming, and wearing a sleeveless turquoise dress that finished just above her knees.

"You look great!" said Joe with mixed feelings.

"Do you really think so?" She asked smiling with pleasure. Joe's heart melted as she sounded like a little child looking for approval. Just then Toby came out of the bathroom and stopped when he saw Rebeca.

"Wow! You scrub up well!" he grinned. Her smile disappeared and Joe frowned at his brother, shaking his head disappointedly.

Toby looked from Rebeca to Joe and back again. "What?" he asked, still grinning with pleasure at the sight of Rebeca dressed to go downstairs for their evening meal. She looked pretty, he thought. How did that happen?

"That does not sound very appealing," said Rebeca slowly. "To 'scrub up well'." She added, "I am not sure that I want to know what that means."

"Gwen called," said Joe, changing the subject.

Toby turned to him, "What did she want?"

"Just to ask how we got on today."

Toby's smiled disappeared as he remembered the disappointment of failing to rescue Emmie, and the three of them were silent. Suddenly, Toby's phone pinged. He walked over and picked it up, frowning.

"That is strange," he said as it pinged again in his hand. "Someone is asking me to accept their call and verify my full name." He walked over and sat beside Joe on the bed, with Rebeca joining them. "Look." He showed them the message.

"T-Rex?" queried Joe and Rebeca together. Toby shrugged his shoulders and his phone pinged again with the same request.

"Maybe it is Benito," suggested Rebeca.

Toby thought for a moment, then shook his head. "He's never asked me to verify my name before." He looked at Joe, "Do you think it is Tadeo?"

"Why would Tadeo contact you?"

"I don't know. Maybe he knows we are in Florida looking for Emmie."

Another PING.

"What should I do?" Toby turned to Joe. No matter what happened between the two brothers, Toby always respected Joe's advice. Joe looked at him, trying to make up his mind as another PING rang out.

"Tell T-Rex your name. They don't know where you are, so what harm can it do? You can always bar him if he turns out to be a nutter!"

Toby typed in, Toby Myers." He looked at his brother who nodded, and Toby hit SEND. The three of them held their breath as they waited.

PING! They all looked at the next message. "Video, please." Toby looked at Joe who nodded again, and clicked on the video symbol. He grinned awkwardly, not knowing who was looking at him. A few seconds later, the screen changed, and T-Rex appeared. The three sitting on the bed exchanged surprised looks.

"Hi there!" beamed Pamela, flashing her braces. "I bet you are wondering who I am! Sorry for making you verify yourself, but you must appreciate that a girl can't be too careful! My dad's a cop. I know all about how people can deceive you to believe they are someone innocent when really they are some crazed psycho or a paedophile!"

Toby, Rebeca and Joe looked at each other, then back at 'T-Rex'."

Pamela giggled, shrugging her shoulders. "I bet you are still wondering who I am!"

"Yes?" Toby encouraged her, completely bemused at who this bubbly girl was with the name of T-Rex!

"Well, I work in a pet store, PetSmart. It's a great place to work! I'd love to have a dog, but I still live with my parents, and they won't let me have one." She frowned in annoyance at the thought. Then perked up, "But people bring their dogs in sometimes, so I get to see lots of dogs. You would not believe the variety of dogs there are! Well, maybe you would; but it is always a surprise to me when I see yet another kind of dog. It's just great, and I do so I enjoy working there. Except for Mr Flatley." She took a breath before adding, "He's my boss. He's always on my case for different things."

Joe pursed his lips and opened his eyes wide at her, "One of those things wouldn't be for talking too much, would it?"

"What?" she asked, then giggled with her hand over her mouth, "Oh, right! Sorry! I do have a tendency to 'rabbit on', as my dad says!"

Toby exhaled loudly, "Look, I don't mean to be rude," he hesitated, "T-Rex…"

Pamela interrupted him with a laugh as she tossed her head, making her red pony tail swing from side to side. "Ya! You were probably expecting some beefy guy!" Laughing, she continued, but not in the direction that Toby was hoping for, "I figure if I have an ID like T-Rex, no one will realise I am just a girl, a kid." A light came into her eyes and she said excited, "Though I am going to be a fully fledged adult next week – the big eighteen!" She sat smiling, pausing for effect, but when she did not get any response, she asked, "So how old are you guys?" She raised her eyebrows in query, waiting for Toby to reply.

The three sat there, looking at this animated girl, saying nothing. Pamela raised an eyebrow, still waiting for a response, but then finally said,

"Oh, ya! Anyway! I was just tidying up a shelf of dog bowls – after someone came in with a bratty toddler, and just let him wander around, messing everything up, throwing things on the floor and moving things to the wrong place, after I had JUST finished putting out some funky new bowls – they are all multi coloured with dinosaurs all over them. Just the kind of bowls I would buy for my dog if I had one." She took a breath, "Do you guys have dogs?"

Toby put his head in his hands and groaned while Joe just sat with a pained look on his face. However, Rebeca smiled back at Pamela patiently, warming to her vivacious, if not frustrating, personality.

"Oh! Where was I? Oh, ya! I was just tidying up the shelf, when a large dark-haired man with piercing blue eyes came in with a skinny kid ..." She tilted her head and looked at Toby, "He looked a lot like you, actually, though his nose and chin were a bit more rounded."

Toby, Joe and Rebeca suddenly became excited, "Yes?!" asked Toby.

"Well, he was a lot skinnier than you, though it is hard to tell how skinny you are, since I can't see your whole body." Pamela screwed up her face. "He looked quite scared, and was trailing behind his dad, who looked like a really nasty fellow. You wouldn't want to meet him in a back alley, let me tell you!" She added, "The dad, I mean, not the kid. Like, who is going to be scared of a skinny kid?" She laughed at her joke.

"What happened?!" Toby nearly shouted at her in his frustration, not correcting her on Benito's relationship with Tadeo, for fear of never hearing the end of the story.

"Sorry! I do tend to take a while to get to the point! Okay, so they buy a pet carrier."

"A pet carrier?" asked Joe.

"Yes, a pet carrier. I guess they have a mongrel. Mongrels are the best, aren't they? When I am older and have a place of my own, I am going to get a mongrel. Anyway, they paid and left, but get this! They came back a couple of hours later because it was broken, so I gave them another. Then, while his dad is at the door, the kid turns to me, and hands me a piece of paper."

"What did he say?" Toby couldn't wait for her to continue the story at her own pace.

"Well, it was weird," she puzzled, remembering. "All he said was 'Please!' and pushed the paper into the palm of my hand before dashing out the door!"

"And what did the paper say?!" Toby nearly yelled.

"I didn't read it straight away, because my boss called me over to tell me off about giving away dog treats – I mean, really, it isn't going to break the bank, is it?" She shook her head, waving her pony tail, "And people really appreciate it. Customers come back if they feel welcome, you know? So really, I think I do a good job in customer relations!" She took a breath and continued, "And then my dad picked me up.

Which at first, I was annoyed about because I had planned to walk home and stop in another pet shop on the way home – they have some new baby rabbits in – but then, when I got outside and I realised how hot…".

"The paper? You did read it, didn't you?" pleaded Toby.

Pamela's eyes brightened and she tilted her head, "Of course I read it, I mean, who wouldn't? Some stranger walks up to you in a store and gives you a piece of paper and…"

"What … did it … say?" Toby tried to remain pleasant, smiling through gritted teeth.

Pamela chortled, "Oh! Well, it was all so mysterious, like a movie and…" Pamela interrupted herself this time when she saw Toby's face turning purple.

She cleared her throat and forced herself to keep on track, "It said: 'We are picking up Emmie at 7:00 tonight and taking her to the following address.' It was an address near Gibson, Louisiana. Below the address, was your name, Toby Myers, with contact details. So, here I am, giving you the information! Who is Emmie?"

CHAPTER 6

After explaining that Emmie was a monkey, Pamela insisted that Toby tell her all about their adventure in the Nicaraguan jungle. She 'oooed and awwwed' and squealed with delight as he recounted the details. While he did, Joe grabbed some clothes and headed into the bathroom to have his shower and change, and Rebeca made herself comfortable on Joe's bed leaning against his pillows that were still propped up against the headboard.

"Oh! How exciting!" Pamela almost screeched with delight and Toby smiled.

"I suppose it was."

"So what are you going to do now?" she asked, her eyes wide.

"Well, it is too late to go anywhere tonight, so I guess we will have a good night sleep and head up to Louisiana tomorrow morning." He paused, "I don't suppose you have any idea how long it will take, do you? Everything seems to be so far away here in America, which in itself feels a bit odd since so many towns and cities flow into one another."

Pamela nodded her head understandingly, tossing her ponytail animatedly. "Well, I am not exactly sure where that address is, but I am guess it will take you about nine or ten hours. It depends on how fast you drive! It is a bit long to do it all in one day. Though if you and your brother took turns driving and you stopped a couple of times to get something to eat and drink, it would probably be all right."

Toby bit his lip, thinking as Pamela spoke. "Well, Joe has to do all the driving, as I am only seventeen. I have my driving licence back in England, but of course everywhere here seems to want you to be twenty-one before you rent a car." Toby smiled at Pamela, "Thanks for the information," he paused, then added, "T-Rex!"

Pamela giggled, then her face fell, "Oh! Is that it?!"

Toby frowned, confused, "What do you mean?"

"I mean, oh, I mean … oh I wish I could come with you! It sounds so exciting! You guys are going off on another adventure and I will just be going back to work in the pet store tomorrow. I love my job and all, but going to chase criminals and track down a stolen monkey sounds like way more fun than I am going to have! It would be amazing if I could come with you."

"You don't even know us, Pamela. I don't think your dad would approve, would he? I mean, you did say he was a cop?" Then a picture of the Mustang with its cramped back seat flashed in his mind. "Besides, you wouldn't fit. There is barely enough room for the three of us and our luggage in the car we rented."

Pamela looked so downcast that Toby felt sorry for her. "Tell you what, we will keep in touch, okay? We'll call you in a few days and let you know how the search for Emmie is going, all right?" he said, trying to console her. Pamela looked slightly comforted.

"I suppose that will have to do, though if you call as soon as you know *anything*, that would be better," she said, pouting. "Nothing exciting every happens to me."

"Of course it does – it did! You met the evil Tadeo, and you are still technically part of our adventure. We will contact you every day and let you know what is happening. Perhaps we can all meet together at some point."

Pamela heaved a great sigh. "I suppose that will have to do." She made a face, then her eyes lit up as an idea came to her. "If you need ANYTHING at all, call me! Maybe there are questions that only a policeman could answer!" Then she scrunched up her face. "But that would mean I have to tell Dad everything. I'll probably be grounded for contacting a stranger ... Still! I am eighteen next week. I can only be grounded until then!" She threw her head back laughing heartily, despite her sadness, and she and Toby ended the call simultaneously.

Joe came out of the bathroom just then. "Let's go get some food!"

Feeling much happier and hopeful after Pamela's call, the three of them went down the stairs to the dining room to a much appreciated meal.

⟶⟫●⟪⟵

Pamela sat for a long time on her bed after she hung up. She tossed her phone down beside her and sat staring at it with a heavy heart. Oh how she would have loved to go up to Louisiana with these guys and help them to track down their monkey friend. How lovely to have a monkey as a pet! Her dad would never allow it. Both her parents would think she was crazy hitching up with some strangers and heading to Louisiana in search of a stolen monkey. Even if they were her own age. Should she even tell her mom and dad? Oh it WAS crazy. But it sounded so exciting!

Pamela heard the house phone ring, and shortly her mom called up the stairs, "Pamela, honey! It is Aunty Ellie on the phone!"

Her heart felt lighter as she headed to her parents' room to answer the phone in there. Aunty Ellie was her favourite aunt, her dad's sister. Pamela laughed to herself. Her dad always said, with a shaking head, how much she was like her Aunty Ellie – maybe that was why she was Pamela's favourite.

She sat on the double bed and answered the phone. "Aunty Ellie! How are you?"

"I've been really busy with my flower shop, which is good! But it means I haven't had a chance to think about what to get you for your birthday, so …" Ellie paused for effect. She knew Pamela would love her idea.

"So, *what*, Aunty Ellie?!" Pamela's heart began beating quickly. Aunty Ellie always had good ideas for presents. Last year, she bought her a three day trail ride on horseback. Her aunt had not been able to go with her because of her commitments with the shop, but Pamela had had an amazing time and met a really nice girl, Joanie, with whom she still kept in contact. Her aunt remained silent, teasing Pamela.

"What?! What?!" Pamela pleaded.

"How would you like to come up and stay with us for a week? Your uncle Caleb is away on a business trip for three or four days, so it will just be us girls for the first half." Pamela could almost hear her aunt's wide grin over the phone.

"Are you kidding me? Really? What about the flower shop?" She stopped, "What about my job?"

"I finally decided to hire a manager," she answered, "I mean, what is the point of developing a successful business if you do all the work yourself?"

"Oh, that's great, Aunty!" Pamela hesitated, "But I don't know if I can get the time off of work."

"Have no fear, my favourite niece!" her aunt giggled like a child, "Ooops! Don't tell your sister that!" Pamela giggled along with her, knowing that Aunty Ellie said that to each of her nieces. "I spoke to a very nice man, called Mr Flatley and …"

"What?!" interjected Pamela, "Mr Flatley, nice??" Pamela didn't wait for a reply before asking, "And? What did he say??"

"I explained to the very nice Mr Flatley, in my most persuasive voice, that I had not seen you for so *very* long, and I absolutely *must* have you to visit me for your eighteenth birthday, and could he not possibly do without you for a week?"

"And??"

"He said yes!" She sounded puzzled as she added, "He mumbled something about saving himself money on dog treats!" She laughed, and Pamela joined her, "Not sure what that was about!"

"When? When?" asked Pamela excitedly.

"Well," began Ellie, hesitatingly, "I hope you don't mind, but I've booked you on an overnight bus that leaves Orlando tomorrow at 8:00 in the evening. So you'll arrive here Friday morning. Is that all right?"

"All right?! Of course it is all right! Thank you so much, Aunty Ellie, it's the best present you could give me!"

"You better get packing, then, as you will still have work tomorrow! Bye, Pamela!"

"Bye, Aunty Ellie! See you in two days! Yippee!" Pamela hung up the phone and hugged herself in delight. She was going to be going to south-east Louisiana after all! "Thank You God!" she whispered, with a very large grin.

———⟴———

Benito drifted in and out of consciousness as Tadeo drove north along the I-75, until around 10:30 when the teenager's stomach growled loudly, waking him with a start. He glanced over at Tadeo who patted his stomach.

"Actually, I think I am hungry as well. Lucky for you, I already decided to stop around here."

Ten minutes later, Tadeo saw a sign for Lake City, and turned off the highway, heading for a Mexican restaurant that he had found on a previous trip through Florida. He remembered the food to be very enjoyable. Pulling up in front of the building, Tadeo was pleased to see it was still open, as he had not been sure what time they shut.

There were only a few people at that time of night, engrossed in themselves. Tadeo took a seat at a table in the corner, then picked up the menus and handed one to Benito, who took it gingerly. He looked at Tadeo, uncertain as to what he could have, and Tadeo grinned widely.

"Have what you like, boy! Tonight I am getting a good reward for my efforts. And this was an unexpected bonus to my work in Nicaragua!"

Benito was not going to argue that it had included his own efforts, as well. He looked at the menu, and his stomach growled so loudly, the heavy set, short brown haired waitress walking by chuckled kindly at him. He looked up and down the menu, while intermittently looking up at Tadeo, who would nod at him.

Finally, Tadeo breathed deeply and said harshly in a quiet voice so as to not draw attention, "I *said* have whatever you want!"

Just then, the same waitress, who Benito now saw on her name tag, was Tammi, came over to them, "Are y'all ready to order?" she asked amicably as she chomped on her gum.

Tadeo looked at Benito, who nodded eagerly, still wary of his uncle's uncharacteristic generosity.

"We'll start with some of your nachos," Tadeo began.

"Will that be two servings?"

"Yes," he said, then added, "then I'll have the Steak and Shrimp Fajita with a side of refried beans, and a glass of coke." He put his menu down and looked at Benito, who hesitated, still expecting Tadeo to change his mind.

"I … uh … I …" Benito gave one last look at Tadeo who was growing exasperated, before blurting out, "I'll have a Chicken and Shrimp Fajita with french fries and a root beer!"

"Great choices!" said Tammi. "I'll leave the menus here, in case y'all want some dessert! I highly recommend the Astel Tres Leche!"

Tadeo leaned back and began swiping on his phone, checking out the address they were going to, and looking at Google directions to see the quickest way there. The waitress soon came back, placing their drinks and nachos on the table. Benito sat with his hands on his lap, silently saying grace while he wondered in trepidation if he really was going to be allowed to eat such a feast. He finished thanking God then waited, watching his uncle until he put down his phone, picked up his drink, took a long swig, and then started eagerly on the nachos.

Benito watched him for a minute, then slowly picked up his own drink, taking several gulps. He had not realised how thirsty he was. He then looked down at his nachos and began slowly eating, all the while expecting his uncle to smack him or yell at him for eating. He looked up nervously, and was relieved to see that Tadeo was concentrating on his own food. Too quickly, the nachos were gone, and Benito finished off his drink, wiping his mouth with the back of his hand.

His uncle scowled at him, "Use your serviette, boy! Where are your manners?!"

Not for the first time, Benito wondered at Tadeo's peculiar ideas that seemed completely out of character for his generally degenerate personality. However, he picked up his serviette and wiped his mouth obediently, just as the waitress came up and refreshed their drinks.

"Your food should be ready shortly."

And true to her word, ten minutes later Tammi brought their main meals and placed them down carefully. "The plates are hot, so be careful!" she warned, then added with a huge grin, "Enjoy!" before taking their empty nacho dishes and disappearing into the kitchen.

After consuming everything on their plates, a couple more drinks, and each of them taking Tammi up on her recommendation of the Astel Tres Leche, which turned out to be huge pieces of sponge cake with lashings of cream topped with strawberries, kiwi fruit and oranges, they left the restaurant and climbed back in the truck. Benito had not eaten so much since he was in the jungle at Rebeca's village, where they had liberal supplies of delicious stew and other good food.

Tadeo headed back onto the I-75, where they drove for only a short while before heading west on the I-10. Benito closed his eyes, rubbing his stomach which was beginning to feel rather uncomfortable. It had had so little in it over the past several days that it had shrunk and was now straining to stretch large enough to contain all that Benito had consumed. However, Benito didn't mind the feeling at all and he smiled silently in the dark to himself as he leaned against the door and drifted off in a contented sleep.

Tadeo looked down at the speedometer and the clock on the dash, then decided to put his foot down hard on the accelerator. He needed to make up some time if he was going to get to his destination by six am.

———⋙●⋘———

"I want to get an early start," said Toby when the three of them were back in the boys' room, "Can you both..." he looked at Rebeca who raised an eyebrow and half smiled, "Okay, I know *you* can get up early, Rebeca!" He turned to his brother who was lying on his bed, rubbing his stomach contentedly. "Can you be ready to go at 8:00, Joe?"

"That means we have to get up at 7:00, if we want to have breakfast before we get packed and ready!" Joe complained. Toby tilted his head and raised his eyebrows. "Oh, okay!" Joe groaned. Rebeca nodded her head and went through to her own room.

The boys stripped down to their boxers before jumping in their beds, and very shortly, Toby was asleep. Joe's stomach began making digesting noises, tackling the enormous meal he had eaten, and he rubbed his belly at the uncomfortable feeling. After a moment, he looked out the window at the sky lit by city lights, that was neither light nor dark, and various thoughts randomly drifted in and out as he thought about the drive and the unknown scenario that awaited them the next day. He thought of Rebeca's words about God and His purposes.

An unexpected thought popped into his head – he should pray. Hmmmm, it had been a while since he had last talked to God, he thought. Joe had slowly been asserting more of his own authority over his life, and seeking God's direction less, but the day he had met his aunt and Benito at the Managua airport and he had learned his brother was lost in the Nicaraguan jungle, that was the last time he had spoken to God, and it hadn't been pleasant. He had been angry with God for letting this happen. How could an all powerful, all loving God have allowed that to happen to his brother? *Why* would He allow it?

But then, thought Joe, it had not even entered his mind to thank God when they had found Toby and again when Rebeca had given his brother the medicine that healed him from malaria. He hadn't given God a second thought, because he had pushed God out of his heart and mind; and, if he was honest with himself, the push had started months ago.

Joe knew the truth, really. He did know why God had allowed such a terrible thing to happen to Toby. He knew why terrible things happened to all sorts of people. They lived in a fallen world. A world that had fallen thousands of years ago when the first man and woman decided to ignore God's commands. But he was not ready to accept that that was okay. His pride was still too strong to accept God's plan for the world, or God's plan for his own life. Especially if it was not a 'nice' plan, one that he, Joe, did not think fit the direction in which he wanted to go. Slowly, he fell into a fitful sleep.

⟫●⟪

It seemed like Benito had only just shut his eyes when he was awoken by the truck stopping. He looked at the daylight and the sun just trying to poke its head above the horizon as Tadeo parked the truck at the back of a building that had an Auto Repair sign on the side. Benito looked at his uncle questioningly, who smirked at him.

"Well, you didn't think we were going to deliver the monkey to the customer's house did you? It IS illegal to have one of those," he nodded to the carrier in the back, "The man is not likely to want us to know where he lives!" Just then, Emmie began making soft noises as the anaesthetic was wearing off. Tadeo lifted the carrier over the seat and placed it between them.

"Right," he began, "that door should be open." He pointed to a back door, "Go in and through to the work area where you will find a red Toyota Camri. On the front seat should be a large envelope filled with cash. Leave the carrier on the seat and bring me the money." He frowned at him before adding, "and don't dawdle!"

Benito opened up the door and got out, before turning around and carefully taking the carrier off the seat.

"It's not a piece of china, boy! Get a move on!"

Benito shut the door behind him and slunk towards the back door, where he tried the knob cautiously. It opened, but the door was heavy as he pulled it towards him. He stepped inside and found himself in an office with windows on the left hand side. Through the windows, he saw the workshop, and the red car sitting in the middle. Turning the handle of the door into the shop, he walked over to the car and opened the front door. On the seat was a large thick manilla envelope. He looked inside and checked it was full of money. He put the carrier down and a little face peered at him through the wire. She made soft little squeaks, and he felt a pang of betrayal as he closed the door.

His heart beat quickly as he tried desperately to think of what he could do. This was the address he had given that girl to pass on to Toby and Joe. What good was it going to be to them? Suddenly, a thought came to him, and he went around to the front of the car. Darn! No number plate. He went around to the back, and as expected, that number plate, too, was missing. What now? He tapped his fingers anxiously against his temple – his uncle would be impatiently waiting for him, and if Benito didn't hurry, Tadeo would be charging in after him. There had to be something. In a flash, it came to him – the VIN number. Each car had its own number! He knew that from the time he spent with Tadeo and his criminal friends. Benito soon found the number, then looked around. He would never remember all those digits.

Quickly, he ran back into the office and rummaged in a desk drawer, finally finding a scrap of paper and a pen, before dashing back to the car and hurriedly writing down the number. He could hear his uncle's angry voice in his head as he ran back into the office and threw the pen back on the desk before bursting out the back door. He trotted over to the truck and climbed in, handing the envelope to his uncle, who grabbed it angrily.

"What took you so long?!" He asked as he opened up the envelope and began to count the money.

"I ... uh ... I thought I heard a noise, so I hid for a few moments."

"And?" Tadeo looked up from the envelope and stared at him through squinted eyes, forcing Benito to quickly come up with a plausible explanation as to what the noise could have been that had frightened him into hiding.

Benito laughed nervously. "It ... uh ... was only a cat."

"Hmmm," said Tadeo staring at his nephew, undecided whether or not to believe him. He finally turned back to the money and finished counting it. "Right then, let's find somewhere to have a nap." He leaned over and put the money in the glove compartment, then put the truck in gear and headed off to find a motel.

An hour later, Benito lay on top of the covers with his hands behind his head, listening to his uncle snoring in the single bed next to him. Having slept most of the night in the truck, Benito was wide awake, staring at the ceiling of the darkened room. Tadeo had pulled the heavy curtains closed to keep out the bright day light that was shining directly into their south facing window. It had the added benefit of keeping their room cool, since the air conditioning did not seem to be working properly.

Tadeo had tucked his phone under his pillow. How was he going to contact Toby now, thought Benito? They would drive all the way up here and it would be a dead end at the auto repair place. Think, think, Benito! he commanded himself. His stomach interrupted his thoughts. It had finally digested all the food and now, having been stretched to an abnormal size, felt like a hollow pit. He got up and walked over to the little fridge in the kitchenette at the corner of their room. Tadeo had continued with his uncharacteristic kindness and stopped at a grocery store before coming to the hotel. He had even told Benito to have some breakfast whenever he wanted, since Tadeo was going to be sleeping for several hours.

Benito took out the milk and some juice, and then grabbed a banana and the box of cereal that sat on the counter. He filled a large bowl to the top with Frosted Flakes and added milk, then poured a tall glass of orange juice before taking them to the table and sitting down. He bent his head, truly thankful.

"God," he began silently, "thank You again for the food I ate last night and for more good food this morning. I don't know how long my uncle's generosity is going to last, but I thank You for filling me with these good things." He started eating his banana, then quietly added, "Help me to contact Toby … and help me to learn more about You and your grace … amen!"

Benito quickly consumed the banana, cereal and juice, and turned to the kitchen, spotting the loaf of bread. He walked over and put a couple of slices in the toaster while he got out the peanut butter. When they were toasted, he slathered peanut butter over both of them and filled his glass with more juice. He grabbed an apple on the way back to the table, and very soon those too, were gone, leaving his stomach feeling very satisfied.

⎯⎯⎯⎯➤●◄⎯⎯⎯⎯

Toby woke early the next morning. He leaned over and looked at the time on his watch that he had placed by his phone. It was only 6:00. He lay his head back down on the pillow, but thoughts of Emmie raced around his mind. She looked so sad, so desperate, when she looked out of that window. They nearly had her! He breathed deeply. She had such human like qualities – did they really have a common ancestor? Weren't they're genes something like 98% similar? He picked up his phone and turned it on. After a couple of minutes, it came to life, and he typed in: what percentage of genes do monkeys and humans share? Hmmm … National Geographic said 96%. That still seemed quite close. Google did seem to bring up options that dismissed God at the beginning of a search for most things, he thought, so he skipped several pages and came across a website, *Answers in Genesis*.[1]

It started off talking about the 98% comparison of many scientists, but went on to say:

… There is inherent bias in these calculations because significant lengths of DNA that are quite different between the two species are omitted from the results. A very simplified comparison would be comparing blue jeans (pardon the pun) with cut-off jeans. The fact that the legs are missing on one is discounted and only the upper portion is compared, with particular emphasis on the comparison of the rivets, buttons, pockets, top stitching, and zipper, but not much comparison on the brand, colour, or the quality of the fabric. In a similar way, gaps or missing portions (like the missing legs on the cut-off jeans) and regulatory portions (like the fabric) from one are typically ignored, and only gene-rich segments of DNA are analysed (like pockets, buttons, and rivets).

Toby read a bit further down:

… it is likely that the 88% similarity number is considerably more accurate than other methods to date.

"Well", he whispered quietly to himself, "what do you know?" He put his phone back down. Still, Emmie had taken care of him in the jungle, like a mother. That was why he had called her Emmie, after his mom, Emily. She had even seemed to scold him when he swore. What did it matter how many genes she was away from him? She was his friend, and she deserved to go back home to her family in the jungle. Even more so, if she *wasn't* related to humans. She needed to be with her own kind.

His thoughts drifted to Rebeca. He had respected her from the moment they had met. She was intelligent and caring, and seemed wiser than her years, but who could not be drawn to Gwen? He had been overawed by her beauty straight away. Maybe that was why Rebeca had looked plain. Gwen had behaved like a spoilt brat at first, but as he got to know her and understood why she behaved that way, he had started to become attracted to her and wanted to protect her. He rolled his eyes. That sounded so corny. And yet, he thought as he blew out a confused breath, it was true.

Now, here he was, having odd feelings about Rebeca. Surely it wasn't the same as the feelings he had for Gwen? Rebeca had become a good, comfortable friend, he mused. Gwen was someone you wanted to date, someone alluring. Just thinking of her made his heart rate increase. With Rebeca, he felt so comfortable and at ease. Surely that was how you felt about friends, he pondered.

It was no good, he shook his head, frustrated. Girls were just too complicated, and thinking about it didn't seem to help. He threw his covers off and grabbed some fresh boxers, putting them on before he chose a pair of loose-fitting khaki shorts and a deep green T-shirt, and put them on.

Looking in the mirror, he ran a brush quickly through his short dark hair. He tossed the brush back in his suitcase just as he heard a light tap on the door.

"Come in, Rebeca," He said just loud enough for her to hear, without waking Joe. Joe was a bear if you woke him too early!

Rebeca was back in the same shorts and T-shirt she wore yesterday, but had left her hair down. Toby greeted her with a warm smile, which she returned.

"I heard noises, and figured you were awake," said Rebeca.

"What noises?" queried Toby.

"Ah," began Rebeca, "You forget that I am well experienced in tracking! A good tracker knows how to interpret sights, smells and sounds, no matter how subtle."

"We are in a hotel, Rebeca, not a jungle."

"It does not matter where you are. If you are a tracker in here," she touched her head with her hand, "you are a tracker everywhere."

"Should we go downstairs and have something to eat? Are you hungry now, or shall we wait for Joe?" Toby asked.

"I can wait. Could we play some more of your card game? I enjoyed that." Toby and Joe had introduced Rebeca to cards, and she had been delighted at this new discovery.

Toby nodded, "Sure!"

He decided to teach Rebeca 'Go Fish' this time, and she was soon playing like she had been playing it all of her life, winning the first three games. She wore a broad smile the entire time, even though she lost the next two. Toby pondered to himself, not for the first time with Rebeca, how she showed him how much he took for granted. There were so many new things for Rebeca, and with each new discovery, Toby felt a renewed appreciation for things that had long ago become mundane.

Rebeca abruptly put down her cards and looked at Toby keenly. "Will we be able to have ice cream today, Toby? I do so want to try it! It was one of the few things my mother missed, being married to my father. She described it to me and it sounds so wonderful!"

Toby chuckled as he nodded his head. It was almost like being with a child – an intelligent, appreciative child. They carried on playing cards until Toby looked at his watch and realised it was 7:05. Joe was snoring happily in the far bed, and Rebeca giggled.

"He does like to sleep!"

"Shall we wake him gently or shall we go for the shock treatment? I'll let you choose," said Toby mischievously.

"The *shock* treatment?" Rebeca asked frowning concernedly.

"Okay, if you say so!" Toby headed to the bathroom with Rebeca trailing after him.

"But I did not say so, Toby, I was merely asking wha ..." She stopped as she looked at Toby putting some water in a glass, then understanding surfaced. She put a hand out to stop him as he went by, but he brushed purposefully past and Rebeca stepped out of his way as he strolled over to Joe who had a faint smile on his face.

"His pleasant dream is about to end!" Toby announced as he quickly emptied the water on Joe's face.

Joe's eyes opened in shock and he sputtered, "What?!" as he looked around bewildered. Rebeca was pleased to see that the cup had not had much water in it. Joe's eyes focused on Toby and he glowered. He leapt out of his bed and threw himself onto Toby, knocking him over onto his bed where they wrestled playfully for a several moments before they both ended up on the floor with a thud.

"Stop!" Rebeca shouted as they continued their play fight on the carpet. They both looked up at her sheepishly. She shook her head disapprovingly. "You really must stop doing that – you might damage something!"

Joe broke into a pained smile as he rubbed his arm, "Like my elbow!" Toby rolled onto his back and they both lay there for a moment catching their breath.

"I would like to have some breakfast soon," Rebeca said, trying to encourage Joe to move. He sat up and winked at her.

"Okay, sweet Rebeca! Anything for you!" Joe got up and went to his suitcase to grab some fresh boxers, then picked up the clothes he was wearing the previous day, before going to the bathroom where he jumped in the shower and had a quick wash before changing into his clothes.

Forty-five minutes later, they had had breakfast, packed up their bags and were in the hotel lobby, checking out of their rooms. That only took a couple of minutes and they were soon all in the car and heading north.

Ten minutes into their journey, Joe pulled off the road as Toby pointed to a sign that said 'Ice Cream'. Joe pulled up to the shop and they all climbed out of the car, then walked into the air-conditioned store. Rebeca was wide eyed as she saw all the different flavours. She walked along the glass front that covered the ice cream, reading all the flavours.

"What is, Rocky Road?" she asked Joe who was standing next to her.

"Chocolate, of course, plus nuts and marshmallows."

"Marsh ... mallows?" she asked hesitatingly.

The man behind the counter looked at her quizzically and Joe explained.

"She's from a small village in Nicaragua, they don't have marshmallows."

"Oh, my dear, have one to try!" The kind man said as he opened a jar and took out a marshmallow with some tongs and handed it to Rebeca.

"Thank you," she said as she put it tentatively in her mouth and chewed it thoughtfully. "What an interesting texture!" Joe grinned at the concentrated look on her face as she savoured the new treat. Finally, she swallowed and nodded. "Oh! Yes, please, I will have a rocky road!" She said enthusiastically.

"How many scoops?" The man asked.

Rebeca turned to Toby who had made his decision and was now standing on the other side of her.

"Two," said Toby confidently. "And I will have two scoops of salted caramel."

"And I will also have two scoops of the triple chocolate," added Joe as he took out his phone and tapped it on the card payment machine.

"Shall we sit down here?" asked Rebeca as she nodded to a little table by the door and pulled out a chair.

"I was just going to drive while I ate mine," said Joe, then added as he sat next to Rebeca, "but I won't take long to devour this!" He took a mouthful with his teeth and Rebeca cringed.

"Is it not cold?" she asked, frowning. "Besides, do you not want to eat it slowly to enjoy the flavour on your tongue?"

Joe laughed, "I always eat my ice cream this way – I enjoy it best if I have a large amount in my mouth!"

Toby joined them and they sat for a few moments in silence, each enjoying the delicious flavours. Five minutes later, Joe was indeed finished. He looked at Rebeca and grinned, as he saw her still working slowly on the top scoop, savouring each lick. Joe stood and glanced at Toby working on the bottom scoop, then gestured to the car.

"Come on, you two can finish in the car, I want to get going. It is a long drive.

⸺⸺⸺⸺⸺

Despite having slept in the car, Benito's satisfied stomach relaxed him, and he lay down on his bed and shortly fell into a deep sleep, beyond dreams and cares. However, after only half an hour, he was startled awake by an angry voice.

"Benito!"

Benito sat up in a cold sweat and turned to his uncle, surprised to find him asleep. He must have been dreaming! Benito lay back down on his pillow, but his heart was beating too fast for him to relax. He began slowly breathing in deeply through his nose and out his mouth, and soon he could no longer feel the pounding against his chest. Out of the corner of his eye, something caught his attention on the bedside table that sat between his and his uncle's bed. The key to the truck!

Benito looked at it fully, wondering if he dare try. If he could get into the truck, he could get his phone and send Toby a message! Tentatively, he reached over carefully, then pulled away and lay back down as his uncle's snoring suddenly grew louder and became a sort of growl. Benito began his breathing exercises again as Tadeo resumed his steady snoring. The minutes ticked by as Benito tried to claw at the courage to try again. This time, his hand reached the key and he lifted it up gingerly, trying his best to be silent.

Once he had the key off the table, he clenched his fist and rolled away to face the door. With painstakingly slow, measured movements, Benito eventually was standing, and then tiptoeing across the carpet, barely daring to breath. It seemed like hours passed, but finally, he reached the door, and turned the handle in a barely visible movement. He jumped at the clicking sound when he reached the end of handle's turn. He stopped dead, and not daring to move, he waited for the next snore, before he pushed the door open. A bright shaft of light pierced the darkened room, but fortunately stopped as it reached his bed. Continuing on tiptoe, he crept outside, still barely allowing himself to breath. He turned around and pushed the motel door to an almost closed position and cautiously released the handle. Still in stealth mode, Benito eventually reached the truck. He looked down at the key and pressed the 'unlock' button. To Benito's horror, a loud BEEP BEEP sounded out from the truck. He stood still, holding the door handle and holding his breath. Then, just as he lifted up the handle, his heart stopped.

"What are you doing, boy?!" asked a harsh voice behind him.

Benito trembled, whimpering like a puppy when it was scolded for chewing its owner's best shoes. His mouth went dry as he tried desperately to come up with an answer that would satisfy his uncle's wrath.

"I asked you a question, boy!" The voice was louder, but still controlled, so as to not attract the attention of the other guests.

All of a sudden, a picture of a bar of chocolate that Tadeo had graciously bought him appeared in his mind, and he turned around slowly. "I ... uh ... I ... f-f-forgot my chocolate in the t-t-truck," he stuttered, "I ... didn't want it to m-m-melt."

He faced back to the truck and opened the door, he shoved the key in his pocket and picked up the very melted chocolate bar in two hands, then closed the door with his shoulder and walked back towards his uncle who was standing in the doorway of their room.

"Give me the key!" Tadeo commanded, angry that he had been woken from a very restful and comfortable sleep. He reached in Benito's pocket and as he pulled out the key, it caught the little scrap of paper on which Benito had written the VIN number of the car, and it conspicuously floated to the ground. Benito's eyes welled up as Tadeo bent over to pick it up. Tadeo looked at the paper and Benito's knees grew weak as Tadeo read the number then looked at his nephew. His eyes grew narrow and Benito shuddered, the anticipation of the punishment terrifying him. Tadeo looked at the piece of paper again, then his eyes grew wide and a huge grin spread across his face. At first, Benito thought it was because Tadeo had come up with a horrific punishment, but then his uncle spoke.

"Well, well," he chuckled.

Benito pinched his eyes shut tight as he stood trembling in the hot sunshine. The waiting was torture.

"What do you know? My nephew is bright after all!" He laughed, then continued, "Come in, boy. Your usefulness to me has just increased, now that you have shown some ingenuity!"

Tadeo took a step towards Benito, who flinched as his uncle put his hand on his shoulder, but Tadeo just forcefully ushered his nephew back in the darkened room, shutting the door with a click behind them.

"You've just increased your value, boy. I think I'll keep you with me a bit longer!" He took the small piece of paper and let it drop in the wicker basket.

Benito stood just inside the door, still shaking, uncertain as to whether or not he should be comforted by his uncle's ambiguous words. Tadeo sat on his bed and shook his head: "Make yourself useful now, and get me a coffee! And a muffin!" Tadeo lay back down on his bed with his hands behind his head, leaning on the pillows. When Benito didn't move, Tadeo growled, "This morning, would be good!"

Benito was startled out of his stupor and hurried over to the kitchenette to get the items his uncle requested. He filled the kettle with water and flicked it on. His hands shook and he spilled some coffee onto the counter as he scooped some out of the jar and into a large mug. He grabbed two large blueberry muffins and put them on a plate, hurrying over to his uncle who had changed to a sitting position, leaning against the headboard, and put the plate down loudly on the bedside cupboard. He jumped at the sound, then scurried back to make his uncle's coffee. As he gave it a final stir, he glanced over to the waste basket, devastated that he had failed.

After he was finished, Tadeo put the key under his pillow and was about to lie back down when a glint appeared in his eyes. He got up, went to the bin and retrieved the paper, then, lifting his pillow, dropped it beside his key and phone, before making himself comfortable once again. Ten minutes later, Tadeo was snoring and Benito was sitting in a crouched position, hugging his knees on his bed and holding back the tears that were threatening to flow.

Benito stayed in his huddled position with tears trickling down his cheeks for some time, then slowly he leaned back. He looked at the drawer underneath the bedside table beside him. Maybe there was something in there to read, like a magazine or something to get his mind off things, he thought. He slid the drawer open quietly and was drawn to the little red book that was on top of some tourist leaflets. He picked it up – Gideon's Bible, it said on the cover. He opened the little book and began to read, "In the beginning ..."

CHAPTER 7

Just after 1:00, Joe turned off the road and pulled into the parking lot of a roadside cafe. The three of them gladly climbed out of the car, each stretching their legs and arms as they walked towards the entrance.

"It looks busy," said Toby as he opened the door. The cool air and hum of amiable chatter welcomed them in. A friendly waitress greeted them and ushered them to a little wooden table covered by a red cloth in the far corner by a north facing window. Toby glanced around as they followed her. It looked like the last table in the place. That was good, he thought, it meant this was a popular, which was a good sign that the food was going to be enjoyable.

The waitress placed three menus on the table then hurried over to the till where another customer was waiting to pay. They sat in silence as they studied the menu cards. It was a standard cafe offering, with reasonable prices, and they each quickly decided what they wanted, just as the waitress came back to take their orders. The food was quickly delivered and after Rebeca said grace for them all, they hungrily tucked in. Joe stopped and leaned back, picking up his iced tea and taking a long drink. He took a deep breath and looked around the cafe. It was already beginning to empty.

"Looks like we got here at the end of the lunch hour rush," he commented, not wanting to hurry his meal. He was quite tired from the drive and was content to make the meal last for a while longer. Toby, who had his back to most of the tables, nodded as he stuck a huge handful of french fries in his mouth and glanced over his shoulder.

Rebeca frowned. "You will choke if you eat like that!"

"You sound like my mom," said Toby irritatedly, then immediately regretted his harsh words as Rebeca's face turned downcast. It was not a comparison she wanted to hear. "Sorry, Rebeca, I am just tired."

Joe raised an eyebrow at him, and placed his hand gently on Rebeca's who had just placed her fork on the table. "Don't worry, Rebeca, with any luck, he *will* choke." He tried to console her with his joke.

She bit her lip and pulled her hand away from Joe's. "I think I need the … what do they call it here?" She turned to Joe.

"The washroom."

When she left the table, Joe scolded his brother in a harsh whisper, "Do you have to keep crushing her like that?" His eyes flashed angrily at Toby who cocked his head at his older brother. Joe couldn't help show his feelings as he defended Rebeca angrily, and Toby smirked at his older brother.

"Don't deny it, Joe. It's obvious you are crazy about her."

Joe hung his head and exhaled loudly, realising he could no longer deny his feelings to Toby. Rebeca's hurt face had actually made him feel a physical pain in his stomach.

"Okay. I am. I think … I know … I am … in love with her. But she wants you; and you are a jerk. And life sucks."

They sat in silence for a moment, each lost in their own thoughts, and Joe felt a kind of relief at finally admitting the truth to his brother. Toby felt a growing unease: ashamed about being unintentionally hurtful to Rebeca. Gwen's beguiling face appeared in his head. And a sadness that he did not return Rebeca's feelings. His feelings were unpleasant.

"It's not my fault," said Toby, suddenly angry at the unbidden burden being laid on his conscience. "I can't help it if I have girls falling at my feet!"

Joe snickered and rolled his eyes, "I wouldn't go that far, buddy. They say love is blind. Maybe I need to get the two girls some glasses!"

Toby snickered back, and after a few minutes of awkward silence, they both continued their meals with less vigour than they had previously. Shortly, Rebeca rejoined them, eyes reddened, and water glistening where she had splashed her face. She greeted them with a forced smile.

"Those ... washrooms ... smell funny. It reminds me of a poisonous plant we have near our village, it has a sweet smell, but is rather unpleasant, as though to warn you to stay away."

Joe and Toby chuckled.

"That will be the air freshener," explained Toby.

Rebeca frowned and turned up a corner of her mouth perplexed. "How can a poisonous plant 'freshen' the air?"

Toby looked at Joe for help, but he just shrugged, and popped the last of his double cheese burger in his mouth, washing it down with his tea.

"Well," Toby began, trying to think up an explanation, then gave up, "It is just one of those weird things in our 'civilised' society that no one quite understands."

Rebeca raised her eyebrows but said no more as she finished her food. A few moments later, they had all nearly finished their meals just as the waitress came back asking if they were interested in dessert. Rebeca's eyes lit up.

"Do you have ice cream?"

Toby and Joe laughed, and the waitress looked at them curiously, but said nothing, answering Rebeca instead.

"We have an ice cream sundae." She smiled, "I would highly recommend it. Ted," she nodded her head towards the kitchen, "is famous for his ice cream sundaes."

Rebeca was slightly bemused, but decided she did not want to ask any more questions, so she just nodded her head enthusiastically. "Yes, please!"

"Make that two," said Toby, chuckling at Rebeca's new-found love of ice cream.

"Three of those sundaes, please!" piped up Joe as he handed his plate to the waitress, who expertly gathered all their dishes and carried them away on one arm. Five minutes later she returned with a tray of three very large sundaes.

"Wow!" exclaimed Toby. Joe and Rebeca just sat there wide-eyed, nodding their heads, unable to speak at the sight of the desserts.

The waitress beamed as she placed the tall glass dishes in front of them. There were three layers of ice cream: vanilla, strawberry and chocolate, interspersed with chocolate sauce and toffee pieces, then topped off with coloured sprinkles, chunks of chocolate, raspberries, nuts and lashings of toffee and chocolate sauce poured over with a single cherry to finish.

"Enjoy!"

When the waitress left, the three of them each stared at the amazing desert in front of them. Rebeca tucked in first, grabbing the long spoon and digging into the ice cream, laughing as the syrup dribbled down her chin. The boys followed suit and for ten minutes, all each of them could say was 'mmmm' and 'ooooo" as they consumed their amazing desserts, despite each having eaten considerable main meals.

Joe finished first and he put down his spoon to grab a serviette to wipe his mouth, exhaling in pure delight. Toby soon followed, and they watched as Rebeca slowly scooped in each mouthful, concentrating on the individual flavours on her spoon, and sighing happily. Finally, Rebeca was finished and the waitress came over with the bill. Joe took it to the counter and paid it, while Toby and Rebeca headed for the door. Soon they were back on the highway and heading towards Louisiana.

At first, Rebeca was wide eyed at all the sights that they passed by, but shortly, the warmth of the day and the motion of the car lulled her to sleep. Toby began to drift off, but Joe gave him a tap on the shoulder.

"You can't go to sleep, Toby, I know I have the GPS, but I still need you to stay awake in case I go wrong somewhere. Plus I need help keeping up my concentration! All that food in my belly is actually making me sleepy!"

They did not talk much as they drove along, each taking in the view around them, and the next few hours passed by quickly.

"Is it very complicated going through New Orleans to get to the hotel?" asked Joe as they drew close to the city.

Toby looked on his phone and found the directions their satnav would be giving them when they reached New Orleans. "No, it looks like we stay on the I-10 until the last 20 kilometres of our journey, when we take the I-310 south."

As they finally reached near the end of their journey, the GPS agreed with Toby's prediction. Fifteen minutes later, Joe let out a deep breath when he finally pulled into the front of the La Quinta Inn and turned off the engine.

"Well, Toby," he turned to his brother, "I think that was way too long of a drive, and when we go back to Orlando for our flight home, we will take at least two days to do it!"

"Ya, sorry, Joe," said Toby guiltily, "I was just keen to get to Emmie. We won't have a reason to rush back." He turned around and smiled at the sight of Rebeca, nearly prostrate in the back with the seatbelt stretched out, head hung sideways with her mouth slightly open and soft snoring sounds that sounded almost like a cat purring.

"Rebeca!" he called out and she jumped, shaking her head and squinting at the bright sunlight. "Wake up, sleepy head. We are here."

"Oh!" she said frowning, rubbing her neck, "I think I must have been sleeping awkwardly."

Toby got out of the car and pulled his seat forward, helping Rebeca out as she turned her head back and forth to loosen up her muscles.

"I do not know how you two can stay awake in a car," she said, yawning. "Every time I get in one, I feel sleepy. I suppose it is the same effect as when you rock a baby to sleep, although we are not actually rocking!" she smiled.

"Well that depends," began Toby, "Joe's driving can seem a little like rocking when he puts his foot down!"

Joe opened the back of the car and Toby grabbed his bag then turned away. Joe gave him a funny look, then lifted up his and Rebeca's and placed them on the ground so he could shut the back and lock the car. He then picked up both bags and headed toward the front entrance. Toby gave his brother a sideways sneer as Joe passed by and lead the way into the hotel.

They were soon in their rooms, this time there was no adjoining door, but the boys were right beside Rebeca's room. Joe opened Rebeca's door and carried her bag in, before he went to his and Toby's room.

"Wow!" exclaimed Toby when they entered and he saw the two queen size beds. There was a microwave and a mini fridge in the corner opposite the bathroom.

Both Joe and Toby tossed their bags on the floor and flopped on their backs on their beds, stretching out and enjoying the soft mattresses under their tired bodies.

"Ahhhhh!" they exclaimed in unison, and for several minutes, neither of them said anything. They had both started to close their eyes when there was a knock at their door. They jerked to consciousness.

Joe called out, "Come in, Rebeca!"

Rebeca had pulled her hair back into a pony tail off her neck, and changed into a loose fitting, yellow sleeveless dress that was fitted down to her waist and then swept out into a flowing bottom that finished at her knees. She stood for a moment looking slightly awkward, but both boys smiled approvingly, and she finally spoke up. "Gwen's mother has been most generous! Never have I had such beautiful clothing!" She giggled as she added, "I guess it would be a waste in the jungle! And it would be difficult to keep them clean."

Rebeca blushed as she realised both boys were looking at her admiringly. She was mildly embarrassed, but it felt good, she thought. If only Toby … she stopped the thought mid-flow, and transferred her thoughts to Joe. Too bad that she did not return Joe's feelings for her; she might be more inclined to feel differently about him if he did not have that bitter edge to his heart; but no, there were too many things she liked about Toby. It was no good, she thought to herself. She must stop being sad about something she could not change. She smiled at Joe, and his eyes widened in response.

"Will we be eating in this hotel?" she asked, her stomach having long forgotten the lunch time feast.

"No, they only do breakfast. I thought we could go to Burger King, it is not far away."

Rebeca made a face, "Do you never tire of eating burgers?" she asked, disappointed that she was not going to be able to find something new to eat.

"We could go somewhere else, but it is only a short walk away, and I don't really want to drive any more tonight," said Joe in a tired voice, and Rebeca was instantly sorry.

"Oh, of course, Joe! That was selfish of me." She looked from Joe to Toby. Both were still sitting on their beds. "Are you ready now? Or would you like time to rest?"

Joe swung his feet over the side of the bed, and Toby followed suit.

"No!" Joe said determinedly, "I could do with a stretch of my legs! Let's go get some grub!"

They were soon at Burger King and shortly were sitting at a table near the back, away from where most people were sitting.

"I was thinking," said Toby after he swallowed a mouthful of burger.

"Did it hurt?" Joe chuckled. Rebeca looked at him confused.

"Ha ha!" said Toby, "You are such a comedian."

"Does what hurt, Toby?" asked Rebeca, concerned.

Toby smiled, "It was a joke. I said I was thinking, and Joe was asking me if it hurt me to think."

"Oh," said Rebeca, not for the first time, unsure of the boys' humour, but deciding again to say nothing more.

"I was thinking, we go do a scout about, tomorrow after breakfast, at this address that Benito gave us. We have no idea what it looks like, so we can hardly come up with a plan until we know what we are up against."

"You do not want to 'wing it' this time?" asked Rebeca, teasing him, and Toby smirked as he shook his head.

"Sometimes it is better to come up with a plan!" A frown clouded Toby's face. "I hope she is all right," he said. "I mean I hope this person who bought her is kind to her." Toby stared out the window, trying to picture what kind of place she had been taken to. Rebeca squeezed his hand gently.

"I am sure she will be treated well," she comforted him, enjoying the feeling of his hand in hers. "The person will surely have paid a high price for her, so he will want to make sure she is well taken care of." Toby pulled his hand away absently and grabbed his coke, taking a sip.

"Ya, you are probably right. Thanks, Rebeca," Toby smiled sadly.

"Come on, buddy! Cheer up!" Joe gave him a gentle punch, "We'll get her back. Before you know it, she'll be back in the jungle swinging with her family."

They were soon finished and headed back to the hotel. Rebeca turned to go in her room, but Joe grabbed her hand. "It is too early to go to bed. Why don't you join us for a while and we can relax in front of the TV?"

When they entered their room the boys jumped on their beds, and Rebeca stood in the doorway.

Joe patted his bed and motioned with his head, "Come and sit here, Rebeca!"

Rebeca glanced at Toby, who was looking at his phone, then climbed up on the high bed beside Joe, who had the remote in his hand. He smiled warmly at her.

"What would you like to watch?"

Rebeca raised her eyebrows and Joe laughed.

"Oh, ya! I guess you don't have any favourites!"

"Wait a second, Joe," said Toby looking up from his phone, surprised at the mild feeling of annoyance at seeing Rebeca sitting beside his brother. He shook it off and continued. "I want to call Gwen and keep her up to date. As her parents are paying for all of this, it is only right that they know what we are doing with their money!"

Joe raised one eyebrow, and grinned mischievously. "Go on, call your girlfriend!"

Rebeca stiffened slightly and Joe looked down at her, but said nothing. Toby tapped his phone and while he waited for the answer, he felt compelled to move over and sit next to Rebeca, holding the phone out so they could all see. Just as he got comfortable, Gwen's face popped onto the screen, smiling widely.

"Oh how wonderful to see you guys!" Her face was heavily made up, though expertly done and she wore tear drop diamond stud earrings and a matching shaped single diamond pendant around her smooth, perfectly shaped neck. They could just make out the top of her silk sleeveless dress that matched her green eyes. "Can you boys come and rescue me, pleeeease?" She batted her eyes and pouted her mouth beseechingly, and Rebeca frowned unintentionally, immediately replacing it with a genial smile.

"From what?" asked Joe, just ahead of Toby.

"From the *very fine* son, Richard." She blew all the air from her lungs through her glossy red lips that frowned unhappily.

"What?" asked Toby, confused.

Joe smirked, and turned to Toby to explain, "I forgot to tell you she was going to visit the neighbours last night and her parents think their son is the perfect catch, but evidently he is the epitome of self-interest and boring company!" He faced back to Gwen who was rolling her eyes. "What's up?"

"He's taking me out to dinner in half an hour." She wrinkled her face, and Rebeca felt slightly comforted. "I tried to refuse his offer, but Mummy insisted!"

"What does your dad think?" asked Toby, feeling jealous that some 'perfect' man would be taking Gwen out for a meal.

"Ah, poor Daddy!" she bit her lip, then realised what she had done. "Oh, hang on, now I have lipstick on my teeth, don't I?" She put her phone down while she found some tissue to wipe her teeth. A moment later she was back. "Daddy just says Mummy knows best." She paused for a moment. "Anything new with you guys? You look like you changed hotels, your rooms are red, now."

"Ya! We had a surprise call from some girl," began Toby.

"T-Rex!" laughed Joe, interrupting his brother, and Gwen looked at them puzzled.

Toby went on to relay the conversation – minus all the verbal detail that Pamela had contributed. Then told Gwen about their journey up.

"So what is the plan?" she asked. "Do you need anything?"

"Well, we are just going to do a drive by tomorrow, and see what kind of place it is. Then we will try to come up with an idea of how to get Emmie out of there. Until we have had a look, we have no idea how to rescue her.

Just then, they could hear Gwen's bedroom door open and a woman's voice spoke, "Gwen darling, I need to do a last minute check! Don't be long on that phone. You have five minutes!" The door clicked shut and Gwen moaned. "I better go, Mummy needs to check that I am presentable." She paused, then added, "I'll let you all have a look and tell me what you think. I haven't chosen my shoes yet, but am I presentable?" She positioned her phone on her dressing table, and stepped back so they could see her. The green silk dress was fitted, hugging her curves and ending just above the knees. The boys gasped in appreciation and, despite herself, Rebeca silently agreed with their sentiment. Gwen walked back to her phone, pleased with their reaction. "I'll take those sounds as approval!" she smiled. Then a sad look appeared in her eyes: "If only I was going out to dinner with you guys!" There was a moment's silence as everyone pondered her curious predicament. "I better go, Mummy needs to make sure I look perfect." Her eyes grew ever so faintly watery, "Call me tomorrow?"

They all nodded, and Joe answered, "Sure Gwen. Have a good time." She blew them a kiss and when she clicked off, the three of them looked at each other.

This time it was Rebeca who spoke. "How very sad," she said with genuine sorrow in her voice, and the boys just silently nodded their heads.

———⟫●⟪———

Tadeo had woken about 4:00, and, feeling quite hungry, decided that he and Benito would go find somewhere to eat. They ate in silence and an hour later were back in the motel where Tadeo positioned himself sitting comfortably on his bed and turned on the television, flipping through various channels before he found something he wanted to watch.

"Get me a coke, boy!" Tadeo grumbled as he adjusted the volume.

Benito walked over to the fridge and took out a bottle of coke for his uncle, and a root beer for himself. He opened the coke and it fizzed up, spilling over the counter and down the side.

"What are you doing, idiot!" Tadeo shouted and Benito grabbed a cloth and quickly mopped up the mess as best as he could. The fizzy brown liquid had gotten everywhere. A few minutes later, he had cleaned up most of the mess, but the coke had wound its way through the side of the wicker waste basket, and he could not wipe it off. Making sure the glass was clean and dry, he took the drink over to Tadeo who snatched it from him, nearly spilling it again.

Benito sat down on his own bed, carefully placing his glass of root beer by his bed. He looked over at Tadeo who was now occupied with tapping the buttons on the remote. Benito assumed they would be heading back to Longwood in the morning, as Tadeo had spoken to someone on the phone about meeting him back at the house the next evening. Tadeo had also spoken to this person about their flight that left the day after that, Saturday.

I'm running out of time, thought Benito, glancing over at his uncle, and picturing the vital scrap of paper under his pillow. How was he going to get it back?

Suddenly, Tadeo glanced over and stared at Benito, as though aware of his thoughts, but then said, "We'll be leaving early in the morning. I intend to be driving off at 7:00, so make sure you are ready." He turned back to the western he was watching, and Benito nodded silently. He turned to the drawer beside him and pulled out the Bible. Tadeo looked at him and laughed, but said nothing as loud gunfire from the television drew back his attention.

Benito found where he had left off, where the Israelites had just gone through the Red Sea that God had parted for them, then closed it back up again and drowned the Egyptians who were chasing them on horse back. Benito tried to imagine how it would feel, to walk through a sea, with water piled up on both sides. How frightening it must have been – how powerful God was! He wondered why God did not do these kinds of amazing things now. Why not just show Himself, then everyone would believe in Him? He put that question aside, as he turned back to the open book in front of him and carried on reading.

Some time later, Benito read, "When the people saw that Moses was so long in coming down from the mountain, they gathered round Aaron and said, "Come, make us gods who will go before us." Benito was shocked as he read about them melting all their gold jewellery into a golden calf. *Why?* He asked himself. How could they worship a gold calf when they had just witnessed God's amazing miracles as He freed them from slavery? He thought of his earlier question and said to himself, *I see it would make no difference to some people.*

He shook his head in amazement. It was a wonder that God carried on loving and taking care of these people.

Benito turned back to the Bible and carried on reading, drawn into this amazing book as though he were actually there, and was startled when Tadeo began shaking him awake.

"Get up, boy! You have ten minutes to have some breakfast!"

Benito's heart dropped. He had fallen asleep! He glanced over at the pillow and his uncle saw him and laughed. Tadeo reached underneath and with a dramatic effect, walked over to the waste bin, and let the piece of paper float down. Hanging his head, Benito walked over to the kitchenette and quickly gathered some breakfast and ate hurriedly, before packing up what few things he had. He stood by his bed, looking at the Bible as his uncle opened the door to leave.

"Come on, boy! Get out!" Tadeo stood by the door, his arm motioning for Benito to follow him and leave the room.

Benito glanced over at his bed. Feeling slightly guilty, the teenager leaned over, grabbed the Bible and stuffed it in his bag. His uncle snorted as he stood back and let Benito pass, then shut the door behind him. They threw their bags in the back and jumped in the truck. Benito stared out the window, thinking about all the things he had read, as Tadeo started the engine and headed south.

Half an hour later, they pulled over and Tadeo got out to fill up the truck with fuel. When he finished, he went inside to pay. Benito watched him pick some chocolate off the shelf, then take his position to pay behind several people who were ahead of him. Benito opened the glove compartment and reached for his phone. His charger was wrapped around it. He looked over to his left, at his uncle who still had four people ahead of him, then across the busy road on his right, to a large shopping mall. He held the phone tightly, as something he had read came back to him, "Do not be afraid, Abram. I am your shield, your very great reward." He glanced nervously over at his uncle who now had three people in front of him, then said to himself, I may not be Abram, but if God can protect Abram, He can protect me, too! With those words to encourage him, he opened the door and jumped out, shutting it quietly behind him. Darting through the traffic, he headed across the road, his pounding heart reverberating in his ears, and dashed into the mall, jogging until he was at the far end.

A few people looked at him curiously, and he stopped, sitting down on a bench to catch his breath. He glanced down at the phone he had clutched tightly in his fingers and pressed the ON button. His stomach sank as nothing happened – his phone was out of charge.

———⇒●⇐———

Joe, Toby and Rebeca all woke early and were downstairs in the hotel having their breakfast by eight o'clock. Soon they were back in the Mustang and heading toward the address that Benito had given them.

Joe made his last turn, then slowed as the satnav advised them they had reached their destination. Toby and Joe looked at each other as Joe stopped the car on the road, opposite the Auto Repair shop. Another car had just pulled up in front of the building, and a man got out and went inside.

"Are you sure you put the right address in?" Joe asked Toby who nodded.

"Yes! I checked twice." Toby curled his mouth, "Do you think T-Rex gave us the wrong details?"

"That is a distinct possibility," said Joe, and Toby nodded in agreement. An old lady walked by with her little white fluffy dog. "I think I'll find somewhere to park, and we'll try to get hold of her."

"Good idea," agreed Toby, as Joe turned the car back onto the road and drove on, pulling up in front of a gas station with a convenience store. He tapped on his phone, and clicked on 'T-Rex'. Rebeca leaned forward.

"This could be a very long conversation," she giggled. Joe and Toby breathed deeply, and waited. Several seconds went by, then Pamela's wide smile greeted them.

"Hi guys!" she called out before they could say anything, "Guess where I am!" She paused for a moment then blurted out, "New Orleans! My Aunty Ellie invited me up here for my eighteenth birthday – she booked a bus and got me off work and everything, isn't that amazing? I mean, who would have thought that Mr Flatley would let me off for an entire week?! Though Aunty Ellie has a way of persuading people. She …".

"Pamela," said Toby firmly, but kindly. "That is great, but we need to check that address you gave us. It took us to an auto repair place."

"Hang on," she said as they were suddenly looking at a ceiling. "I just arrived at my aunty's place and am unpacking my bags. I think I put that paper … hmmmm, now where *did* I put that paper? I knew it might be important to keep it."

They heard more rustling and a bag being unzipped. Several minutes ticked by, and Toby was just about to call out, when Pamela's face appeared on the screen, braces shining and blue eyes dancing.

"Got it!" She opened the piece of paper and put it in front of the screen so Toby could see the address clearly.

"I don't get it," said Toby disappointed, "It can't be the right place. Why would they take Emmie to a garage?"

There was silence all around, then Pamela spoke up brightly, "Maybe that was just where the transfer took place."

Toby looked at her thoughtfully, and considered the idea.

"If you are going to buy an illegal item, you aren't exactly going to invite the seller to your house, are you?" she continued.

Toby found himself surprised at her intelligent answer, and he blew out a deep breath through his pursed lips. "Of course not," he said disappointedly.

There was another pause, then Pamela suggested, "It might be the owner of the garage." She squinted her eyes as she screwed up her face, thinking through ideas. "I doubt it would be someone who worked there, as they would not be earning enough money to buy an illegal monkey. Though, they might have been involved for a fee, of course!"

Toby cocked his head, impressed. His first impression of her had been that she was not too bright. He chided himself for judging her harshly because of her loquacious personality. He smiled to himself as he thought of that word that meant 'talks a lot'. Rebeca had used it for Gwen, but Gwen had nothing on Pamela!

"What are you smiling for?" she giggled. "I bet you thought I was a right airhead!"

Toby's face went red, embarrassed that she had read his thoughts, but the shame of it made him deny it. "Of course not, Pamela." Joe shook his head along with Toby, and Rebeca just smiled knowingly, herself not having been fooled by first impressions.

"Oh, it's okay!" she assured them. "Most people think I am penny short of a dollar!"

Toby chuckled, "I have never heard of that saying, but I know what you mean!"

"Of course you haven't," answered Pamela, "I made the saying up myself! I know how I appear to people when they first meet me. It's okay. It will make me a good detective

– I'll catch people off guard, like Columbo. You've heard of Columbo, haven't you? He is my inspiration!"

"Columbo," said Toby slowly, the name sounding familiar. Joe interrupted him.

"That American detective who always wears an overcoat, no matter how hot it is! Everyone thinks he is a bumbling idiot, when really he is smart and always knows who the murderer is, right from the beginning!"

"Yes!" said Pamela gleefully. She turned her head, "Oh! I must go, Aunty Ellie is calling me. She has made a special breakfast for me and it is ready! Please call me back later and let me know how you got on!" She waved at them like an excited toddler as she clicked off.

Joe and Toby turned to face each other, and Rebeca leaned forward from the back as they discussed how they could find out if Emmie had been passed to someone in the garage.

"Why not do something to your car?" suggested Rebeca. Joe and Toby looked at her questioningly, and she continued, "If there is something wrong with your car, you would take it to an auto repair shop, would you not?" She grinned, pleased with her suggestion.

Joe nodded, "Hmmm, now what can we do that we can still drive it and it will be easily fixed?" He paused for a moment. "I need some chocolate."

Toby and Rebeca raised their eyebrows.

"What? Chocolate helps me to think creatively!" Joe smirked and, opening his car door, got out and strolled toward the convenience store entrance. Rebeca and Toby followed suit, and they spent several minutes choosing various snacks. As they walked to the counter, they passed a section that shelved various items for cars. Hanging on some hooks were various size and shape light bulbs.

"Hmmmm," said Joe picking up one of the bulbs and looking at it contemplatively, "I might have an idea." He replaced the bulb and they carried their items to the counter, where Joe paid for everything.

Returning to their car, Joe pulled out his phone, tapping it a few times until he got to a video clip on how to change an indicator bulb on the Mustang. After watching it for a few minutes he said, "Looks pretty straightforward."

"What are you going to do to the indicator bulb?" asked Toby curiously, "It isn't like you can break it or anything. That would look rather suspicious."

Joe tapped his temple with his finger. "Ah, well now! I can loosen it, though, can't I? Then it will look like it wasn't put on properly and came loose when we went over a bump!" He looked at Toby. "You have a Swiss army knife, don't you?" Toby nodded, picking up his backpack and digging to the bottom. His fingers found the handy tool, and he pulled it out, handing it to his brother.

Joe took the knife and got out of the car. He knelt down beside the wheel and levered off the rivets holding the plastic covering. He pulled it back and reached in to the light bulb, pulling hard. It came off completely, so he pushed it back in, just far enough for it to stay in position. He replaced the cover and pushed the rivets back in before handing the knife back to Toby, then stood up and brushed off the dust from his jeans.

"Okay, let's go to that garage we passed back there and see if they have an indicator bulb that fits our car!"

A few minutes later, they pulled up in front of the garage and Joe stopped the car. "Shall we all get out, or what?" he asked. Toby shook his head.

"No, that would look weird. Just go in yourself."

Joe opened the door and went up to the desk. A stout, elderly lady sat on an old swivel chair, looking at some paperwork, tapping her pen as she did so, frowning deeply as she contemplated the numbers in front of her. She looked up at Joe as he approached her. "Hello!" She smiled broadly, then asked in a friendly manner, "How can we help you today?"

"I've got a problem with my front indicator light." Joe answered. "But we are here on holiday, and I wondered if someone could look at it for me without an appointment?"

"Sure! Just give me a second." The lady pushed herself up from her chair and made a little groaning noise. "Ah! That old arthritis is a nuisance!" She shuffled to the door that led into the workshop, and Joe saw through the windows that there were two men, working on two different cars.

"Lenny!" the lady shouted from the doorway, trying to be heard over the radio that was playing loudly. It was tuned to an 80's station, Joe noted, as he recognised the song blaring out of the portable radio that was sitting on one of the shelves.

The skinny young man, about mid twenties, tossed down the tool he was working with and sauntered over. "What's up, Mildred?" he asked, wiping his sweaty forehead with the back of his hand, leaving a behind a black streak.

"This young man," she nodded towards Joe who was still stood at the desk. "Has a faulty indicator light, and would appreciate you looking at it, as they are on holiday."

Lenny adjusted his navy baseball cap as he stepped into the office and walked towards the front door. Joe followed him out.

"Nice car," said Lenny appreciatively, giving the car a stroke, without acknowledging Toby or Rebeca. "Which light?"

"Front driver's side. It's a rental."

Lenny knelt down beside the wheel and tilted his head, looking by the wheel. "Give me a minute," he said, as he stood up and strolled back into the building. A few minutes later, he was out with a small metal bar with a split end on one side.

He crouched down and wriggled off the rivets, then pulled off the plastic cover as Joe had done earlier.

"So," began Joe, unsure of how to get the information they wanted. "Have you always been a mechanic?"

"Nope!" When I was a baby, I didn't have no job." Lenny spoke in a disinterested manner, and Joe nearly missed the joke. Joe's delayed laugh brought a raised eyebrow from Lenny. "No sense of humour?"

"Sorry, I'm a bit slow at times!"

"Yes."

Joe look at the young man, confused.

"In answer to your question, yes, I have always been a mechanic. Came here as an apprentice, straight from high school. Mr Graham took two of us on, but the other guy didn't like it."

"Mr Graham," started Joe, "Is he the owner of this place?"

"Uh-huh. Turn on your car and try the indicator."

"Sorry?"

"What're you sorry for?" Lenny looked up at him bewildered.

"Oh ... I meant ... I thought it needed replacing," sputtered Joe.

"No," said Lenny as he stood up and walked to the front of the car. The bulb was loose, so I pushed it in tighter."

"Oh!" Joe began to panic, as they had not yet found out anything, and it looked like they had little time left. Obediently, he got in the car and turned on the ignition, then clicked the indicator. Lenny nodded.

"Yup! It's working fine, now. Turn off the engine, and I'll put the cover back on." Lenny came around to the front wheel again and bent down, quickly putting back the plastic cover and re-fitting the rivets in place.

"Do you get much business here?" asked Joe desperately.

"Enough," said Lenny absently as he pushed the cover back in place and began to push in the rivets. "Not enough to make Mr Graham a millionaire or anything, but we are a happy family here."

Joe got out of the car and stood by the back seat where Rebeca sat, out of Lenny's way. He looked at Toby and Rebeca and shrugged his shoulders disparagingly. Rebeca leaned her head over the side and spoke.

"This is a lovely country," she started. "And Louisiana is wonderful – I am looking forward to exploring it more." She grinned at Lenny who had finished and was now standing by Joe.

"Well, I have lived here all my life. Wouldn't want to live anywhere else." He then turned to Joe.

"You're good to go."

"How much will it be?" asked Joe. Lenny shook his head.

"Two minute job – don't worry about it."

"Oh, are you sure?" asked Joe, not wanting to leave, but lost for ideas on how to direct the conversation in the direction he wanted to go. "I feel like we ought to pay something."

"Nah! That's fine." Lenny bent over and picked up the bar he had used earlier.

"Can you give us any ideas where would be a good place to visit? I do not want to see any zoos. I come from a tribe in the jungle in Nicaragua, so I prefer to see animals in the wild. We have all sorts of animals roaming free there." She looked Lenny in the eye as she finished, "Even monkeys; I had a little capuchin monkey that used to come visit me there."

Lenny cocked his head at Rebeca. "Uh, I don't rightly know," he began, "I don't really travel much. If I was you I'd start in New Orleans – there's plenty to see there." He nodded his head at them as he turned away. "I gotta get back to the job inside. Y'all have a nice time here in Louisiana." And with the bar swinging by his hand, he strode casually back in the building and shut the door behind him.

"Hmmmm," said Joe, glancing down at Rebeca, "I couldn't tell if he knew anything or not. Chances are, however the exchange was done, he probably does not know what the man – whoever he is – was buying." He got in the car and put on his seat belt.

"So we are no further ahead," said Toby, disappointed. "And she was probably here. But how do we find out where she is now?"

Joe backed up and drove down the road towards the hotel. Just then, Toby's phone pinged and he pressed ANSWER. Pamela's beaming face popped up on the screen.

"Hi guys! Did you go to the repair shop yet?" she asked expectantly, then saw Toby's despondent face. "What's the matter?"

"It was a total loss. Nothing. No information, absolutely nothing to go on from here."

Pamela scrunched her face, "Oh, I'm sorry. Maybe we could brainstorm together! Aunty Ellie has made a whole pile of Crawfish Étouffée and she's cooking up a pile of Beignets. Aunty Ellie always makes too much food. Uncle Caleb is away on a business trip, otherwise he would help us eat it all. Uncle Caleb is a good eater, but he's not fat, he's just a big man – over six and a half feet tall and about three feet across at the shoulders! If he was here, there would not be enough for Aunty and me, but as he is not, there is too much. I think Aunty just gets used to cooking lots and doesn't know how to cook small amounts." She paused, taking a deep breath.

Toby's eyes glazed over and his face went blank. "Pamela," he said slowly, "I am really glad that you and your aunt are going to be well fed for lunch. But did you have a direction you were headed in this conversation?"

She snickered, putting her hand over her mouth. "Sorry! I can't help myself! Dad says that God combined my DNA with a hamster when He made me, just for a laugh. You know how a hamster runs like a maniac around his wheel? Dad says that is kind of like my vocal cords. He's a real comedian; well, *he* thinks he is a comedian!"

Joe was smiling and shaking his head as he drove, and Rebeca waved at Pamela from the back seat.

"So, will you?" she asked, as she waved at Rebeca. Toby stared bemused, trying to fathom the question.

"Will I *what*?" he asked finally, and Pamela burst out in a hearty laugh.

"Will you all come over for lunch?" She grinned ecstatically. "We're not far at all from where I figure you guys are. On the west side of New Orleans, St Rose. And you guys must be getting hungry now, especially you two guys, because guys are *always* hungry, aren't they? Though of course, I am sure Rebeca could eat something as well!"

When none of them answered straight away, Pamela frowned while still smiling – a rather peculiar look, thought Toby silently.

"Oh, you will, won't you? Pleeeeease! Aunty Ellie loves visitors and her cooking is amazing and we must brainstorm together to come up with an idea to save your little friend!" She cocked her head like a puppy, opening her eyes wide. "They have a HUGE house and a pool! You can have a swim afterwards! Oh, please do!"

Toby looked at Joe and then over his shoulder at Rebeca, who both shrugged their shoulders smiling. "Okay," said Toby finally and Pamela squealed loudly in delight.

"I think that hamster wheel needs oiling!" called out Joe, shaking his head and laughing.

"What?" asked Pamela, then she threw her head back howling, "I get it! The hamster wheel needs oiling! What a hoot!"

"Message us with the address. We'll need to go back to our hotel to get our bathing suits, then we'll head over straight away."

"Yippee!" shouted Pamela. "Aunty Ellie is going to be so pleased! I'll go get the exact address and send it to you straight away! Yippee!" She repeated as she clicked off.

Toby put the phone face down on his lap and glanced over at Joe. Tapping his phone gently with his fingers, he said, "Do you think this is wise?"

"Are you afraid she is going to abduct us?" asked Joe with a smirk, though he knew what his brother was asking.

"How will we shut her up in person? At least I have an OFF button on my phone!"

Joe said nothing, as he indicated and turned a corner, but Rebeca leaned back and smiled, answering, "Maybe she is quite different in person. Perhaps on the phone she feels she has to get a lot of words out before she hangs up."

"That sounds like a very wise explanation," added Joe, chuckling, though not entirely convinced that it was correct.

"Let's hope so!" replied Toby. "I am not sure I could be polite to her, face to face, if she just talks and never stops."

Half an hour later, address programmed into the satnav, Joe, Toby and Rebeca were driving down the road to meet T-Rex in person. They chatted about Emmie and threw ideas back and forth as to what else they could possibly do to find her.

"Maybe I could contact Benito," said Toby thoughtfully.

Joe shook his head, "And how are you going to do that without alerting Tadeo that Benito contacted us in the first place? Maybe Ben doesn't even want Tadeo to know we have his phone number at all."

Toby nodded in agreement, "Well, maybe we could think of some coded message."

Joe smirked, "Coded? Do you actually think that kid is bright enough to figure out a coded message?"

Rebeca scowled in the back seat and leaned forward. "Benito is a frightened boy living with a horrible uncle – that does not mean he is not intelligent."

Joe chided himself silently at Rebeca's rebuke. He would never win her over if he kept showing her the side of him that she did not like.

Finally, they pulled up the drive to the right of the house and Joe remarked, "Beautiful house!" and Toby nodded in agreement.

"Houses in America are so much bigger than in the UK," commented Joe as he turned the car off and got out. Toby and Rebeca followed.

"You put a lot of effort into your houses," observed Rebeca, who had grown up in a simple hut in a small village. "It seems like a great amount of money and time wasted on something that is not necessary. Not that a house is not necessary, but certainly the extravagance of these buildings is not necessary."

Toby considered her words thoughtfully. "I suppose you are right!" he laughed.

"Since I have left Nicaragua, I have heard a few people – including your aunt and uncle – say how little time they had to do the things they wanted. If you had a simple house like mine, you would have much time to do pleasurable things."

Their conversation was interrupted by a petite red headed teenage girl bursting out of the front door. When she stopped in front of them Joe and Toby looked down at her, surprise apparent on their faces.

"I know, you thought I'd be taller, right? And you are probably wondering how a shortie like me can be a police officer! Don't you worry about that, guys, because I will be carrying a gun – I'll be just fine!"

The thought of this little bubbly 'hamster' of a girl carrying a gun was incongruous, if not a bit frightening. Rebeca stepped forward and offered her hand.

"It is good to meet you in person, Pamela." Pamela shook her hand heartily and turned to greet Joe and Toby.

"I'm sooo glad you guys came! Come on in! Aunty Ellie is in the kitchen finishing things off!" Pamela spun around and scurried back into the house with the other three following behind more slowly. They stepped into a large entrance with a wooden floor that opened up to the left into a large living room and straight ahead into another, more casual living room. As they entered the second living room, Pamela turned to the right into the spacious kitchen filled with oak cupboards and granite work tops, with an island in the middle. The counters were filled with various bowls and food and a small woman turned from the sink, drying off her hands as she walked over to greet them. Toby, Joe and Rebeca stared as they saw her face. Ellie laughed warmly.

"I know! Everyone says it – Pamela looks the spitting image of me! Anyone would think she was my daughter instead of my niece!" After shaking their hands, she motioned to her right towards a large wooden table and six chairs with windows behind that looked out into the back yard at flower borders and a lawn surrounding a swimming pool. "Come and sit down! It is all ready!"

The table was laden with food, and they all sat down in wonder at the feast before them. After Ellie said grace, she explained that the stew in the large pot in the middle was a roux with crawfish, herbs and vegetables. There was another dish of rice, a couple of plates with cut up carrots, celery and cucumber with some cherry tomatoes of various colours. There were two baskets of rolls – one held crusty rolls, the other soft ones. A jug of water was at one end, and a jug of iced tea at the other. After admiring the food, they began passing along the various dishes and the boys piled their plates high.

The conversation over lunch was a mix of praising the food as they ate and Toby being narrator of their background and how they came to be in Louisiana. Ellie gazed at Rebeca in a genial manner.

"How strange all of this modern society must seem to you! Are you missing your home very much?"

"I miss my father and grandmother. I have never been away from him for more than a couple of days, and I have never been away from my grandmother overnight. I also find the food very odd," she inclined her head towards Toby and Joe. "Especially the kind of food these two like!" She looked down at her plate, "But this food makes me feel at home – it is very good! This tastes very similar to something my grandmother makes." Rebeca ginned widely at their host. "You are very kind to invite us – especially since you and Pamela do not even know us!"

Ellie dismissed the comment with a short wave of her hand. "Well!" She beamed at them, "What better way to get to know people than over a hearty meal?"

As they were finishing their food, Ellie got up and brought a plate of warm beignets – deep-fried dough sprinkled liberally with icing sugar – and passed it around. Everyone agreed that they were quite delicious! After eating and cleaning up the lunch dishes, Ellie asked if they had brought their swimsuits.

"Yes!" Toby and Joe said in unison, and Rebeca nodded her head.

"That's great!" smiled Ellie, "I'll show you to where you can all change. "There are two spare rooms that aren't in use!" They followed her up the stairs and Pamela turned left towards the room where she was staying, and the others turned right. Ellie pointed to the two rooms. "We'll meet you in the pool!" she said with girlish delight.

Toby tossed his phone on top of his clothes, and the boys went outside to find the girls already in the water. The cool water was very refreshing on their warm skin, and Rebeca commented on how odd it was to swim in such a clear rectangular box of water and they all chuckled at her apt description.

They spent an hour in the pool, splashing each other and throwing a ball around, then Toby asked, "May I use your toilet?"

Ellie giggled, "You can use the whole bathroom, if you like!" Toby smiled at the varying meanings of words in different countries, but said nothing as he got out and towelled himself off before entering through the patio doors. As he passed by the room where his clothes were, his phone caught his eye as it began flashing: someone was trying to contact him. He trotted over and picked it up, his eyes wide as he saw the name, and he instantly clicked on ANSWER.

"Benito! You got your phone back!" Toby smiled and began speaking while the screen was still black, but he frowned worriedly as Benito's frightened face appeared. "What's the matter, Benito, are you all right?"

"I've run away from my uncle! I don't know where I am!" Tears welled up in his eyes. "I've only got a little charge left in my phone. I found a socket in this mall to charge it, but after ten minutes, a security guard came and told me I wasn't allowed to use it. Oh, Toby! Please help me!"

Toby thought quickly as he carried his phone outside to the pool. "What is the name of the mall?"

Benito was silent for a minute as he looked around him. "Give me a second and I will see if I can find a sign." A moment later his face reappeared and he told Toby the name. Everyone was looking at him as they heard Benito speaking, and Toby turned to Ellie to ask if she heard of it and quickly explained that Benito needed help.

"Yes, of course! It is not far. Tell him to meet us at the mall entrance to the Target store."

"Did you hear that Benito?" he looked at his phone to Benito's panicked face.

"Yes, yes! I'll go there now! Please hurry! I have to go, my phone is going to die!" Benito's face disappeared and Toby looked up. Everyone had gotten out of the pool and were hurriedly drying off. Joe was about to say he wasn't interested in going to find Benito, but saw Rebeca's anxious face and thought the better of it. He didn't need yet another strike against his character in Rebeca's mind.

"We'll take my car," offered Ellie. "I know where the mall is, I shop there a lot. It will be quicker if I drive."

Toby unconsciously counted them all and he shook his head. "There won't be enough room when we pick up Benito."

"Have no fear! I have a seven seater!" Ellie trotted past him and hurried into the house with everyone following in her wake.

Ten minutes later, they were all dried and dressed and standing at Ellie's front door as she stood in front of a wooden letter and key holder, running her fingers over the keys. "Now let me see … oh yes, here it is!" She picked a few keys off the rack and retrieved the single key before putting the rest back. "Okay, let's go!"

They all went out the door and down the steps, turning left and to the back of the house where the double garage was situated. Ellie pressed a key pad on the side of the building and the door opened. A green Toyota Sequoia was parked on the right side, and Ellie opened the doors so they could all pile in.

As she pulled out of the garage and off the drive, Toby, who was sat up front in the passenger seat asked, "How come you have a seven seater?"

Ellie turned to him and chuckled, "Well, it is not exactly mine! It belongs to our church, but we had room in our garage to store it when it is not in use! In exchange for letting the church park it there, we are allowed to use it whenever we like." She grinned, "Though I have to admit, this is the first time I have ever had this many friends that I needed to take somewhere!"

Twenty minutes later Ellie turned into the mall parking area and into a space not far from the Target department store entrance. She turned off the car engine and they all clambered out. The door swished open as the entered the large air-conditioned store. Hurriedly, they made their way through one of the larger main aisles, and they had walked half way through Target when Toby spotted the big dark haired man walking towards them. He ducked behind a large display, grabbing Rebeca and Joe's arms, whispering loudly,

"It's Tadeo!"

Pamela joined them and pointed out the man to her aunt, who was standing in the aisle, pretending to look at the display of smoothie makers. Tadeo stopped in the middle of the aisle, only ten metres away, scanning around the store slowly, his blue eyes flashing with anger, then suddenly turned around and stomped in the direction of the entrance into the mall.

Toby pulled out his phone and tapped on it quickly. As soon as Benito's face popped up, he spoke urgently, "Tadeo's coming out of Target in your direction – hide!" Benito's face disappeared.

"Do you think he heard?" asked Pamela, "Maybe his phone died completely."

They waited until Tadeo was nearly at the other end of the store before coming out of their hiding place and walking quickly after him, poised to duck behind another display if Tadeo should happen look over his shoulder. Tadeo stopped dead at the mall entrance, and they all crouched behind a rack of ladies dresses just as he again turned around and did a detailed scan of the store through his angry squinted eyes. A woman with a little toddler walked by the dresses and gave Toby and his friends a funny look.

"He play hide and seek, Mommy!" said the toddler giggling and pointing at Toby.

"Just looking for my friend's earring," Toby nodded to Rebeca who smiled, and brushed her hair over her ears so the woman could not see she did not have pierced ears. The woman and the toddler walked off and Toby peeked around the display of summer dresses to see if Tadeo had left the store, and as he did, the woman glanced over her shoulder and shook her head as she saw Toby's head peering out.

"Coast is clear!" said Toby as he stood up and helped Rebeca to her feet. He held her hand a moment longer than necessary, unsure of why he chose to help her and not Pamela who had been positioned closer. He let go and led them all as they hurried toward the doors. Toby stopped short and everyone bumped into him as he poked his head out, scanning the mall up and down. He saw Tadeo quite a distance away down on his left, walking briskly and constantly turning his head back and forth, searching in each store that he passed.

"Toby!" A voice called out behind a gigantic plastic fern in a tall pot. Benito's relieved face popped out from behind the huge leaves. He glanced past Toby and they all turned their heads to see Tadeo enter a store. Benito jumped out from behind the greenery and they all darted back into Target, trotting down the main aisle that lead towards the exit. Several people glanced at them as they scurried by, but they took no notice of the stares and did not slow down until they were out of Target and in the bright sunshine. They stood for a moment to catch their breaths before darting past several cars and then jumping into the Sequoia. Within seconds, Ellie had started the car and drove quickly out onto the road in the direction of St Rose, everyone remaining silent as though Tadeo might somehow hear them.

Finally, Toby turned around in his seat and looked at Benito, who was sat directly behind him, fear still filling his dark brown eyes. "What happened, Benito? How did you manage to get away from your uncle? How did you get your phone?"

A delayed recollection suddenly struck Benito and he turned around in his seat to face Pamela who had opted for the back seat. He stared at her and a huge grin spread across her face as she realised he remembered her.

"It's you!" he said simply, and Pamela nodded. "The girl in the pet shop! You did contact Toby. Thank you." He pursed his eyebrows together thoughtfully and asked, "But why are you here, in Louisiana? This is certainly some distance from the pet shop!"

Pamela opened her mouth to speak, but Toby, realising if he allowed her to start, the verbal flow of words would be impossible to stop, spoke first. "Tell us your story, first, Benito!" he encouraged. So Benito faced forward and started from where he had met Pamela in the pet shop, and continued on until the point that they had met him in the mall. When he finished, he hung his head.

"But I let you all down. We don't have the car ID. All I have is the make and colour. I don't even know the year."

"I have an idea!" piped up Ellie as she glanced at Benito in the rear view mirror. "Let's go back to that motel, if you remember the name of it, and see if we can find the piece of paper. Maybe the trash wasn't emptied – who knows?"

They all nodded, nobody wanting to say that it was a long shot and very unlikely that the basket had not been emptied in that room by that time in the afternoon, but everyone was desperate to find some clue as to Emmie's whereabouts.

"I do remember the name," said Benito happily, and he told it to Ellie. She gave her phone to Toby as she drove, and he looked it up and found the address.

"Oh, I think I know where that is. I am pretty sure I have driven past it," nodded Ellie confidently, and as she drove, Toby brought Benito up to date on their adventures and Benito's eyes grew wide as Toby explained how close they had been to rescuing Emmie from the research centre.

"I could see her little eyes pleading with me to save her!" said Toby, sadly remembering the little monkey's face staring at him out the window.

Finally, Ellie pulled up in front of the motel that Tadeo and Benito had stayed in. She took her seatbelt off and faced Benito. "Just go to the front desk and say that you lost a piece of paper in the trash and it is very important – can you have a look to see if it is still there. Benito nodded and jumped out of the vehicle. He sighed deeply. He could not see how the paper could possibly still be there at this time of day. He walked up to the front desk but there was no one there, so he tapped the bell. When no one came, Benito tapped it louder and finally an elderly gentleman poked his head through a doorway.

"Want a room?" he asked Benito, raising an eyebrow at the skinny boy.

Benito shook his head. "No. I ... uh ... my uncle and I were here. We stayed last night and left this morning. But I ... uh

… lost a little piece of paper, that is really important and wondered if I could have a look in the waste basket to see if I can find it."

"Rooms have all been cleaned. Trash would have been emptied and in the dumpster out back." He started to disappear back through the doorway.

"Wait!" called Benito desperately. "Can I have a look? Please? It really is very important. Someone was depending on me and I let them down by losing the paper!" Tears began to well up in his eyes and the man took pity on him. He shuffled slowly over to the desk.

"What room was it, son?"

"107"

The man looked behind him at the keys hanging on a board on the wall. He quickly found the one for 107. "Here ya go!" He looked at his watch then back up at Benito, "But don't be long as I got someone coming for that room any minute." He paused as Benito gratefully took the key. "And don't mess anything up!"

Benito shook his head vigorously. "I won't! Thank you! I will be back straight away." Clutching the key, Benito ran out the door and jogged to the room, struggling to open the door in his haste. It finally unlocked and he pulled it open, hurrying across the room to the basket. He looked inside and nearly cried – it was empty. He stood with his hands on his head, moaning, and did not hear Toby come up behind him.

"Are you sure it went in the bin?" Toby asked and Benito jumped at his voice. Benito nodded. Toby went over and picked up the basket, putting his hand around the plastic bag that lined it. Suddenly, his eyes lit up as he pulled his hand out, holding the little piece of paper, now stained brown. Benito's eyebrows raised in disbelief.

"How could it still be there? Our other bits have all gone!"

Toby rubbed his fingers that now felt very sticky. "Looks like you had some coke or something! Some of it must have spilt on the paper and made it sticky! Probably if you only had a couple of things in the bin, they must have just emptied the contents into a main bag." The two boys stood for a moment, grinning at each other, then Toby said, "Come on! Now we need to see if we can find an address to this car somehow!"

Toby went back to the vehicle, and Benito skipped happily back into reception to return the key. He thanked the man profusely, who was surprised but pleased that Benito had found what he was looking for.

Benito climbed back into his seat and Ellie started the car. "Shall we all go back to my place?" she asked. "We can barbecue burgers and hot dogs! You all must be hungry again by now, after all the swimming and all this excitement!"

Benito nodded his head frantically, "Yes please!"

"Then," she said slowly as an idea came to her mind, "We can call Pamela's dad, and see if he can get an address for this car's VIN."

Joe spoke up, "Would he be allowed to do that?"

Ellie grinned impishly, "Well, not officially! But he has a soft spot for his baby sister, so I may just be able to get it out of him!"

Joe grinned, then asked, "How will he feel about Pamela being involved in this?"

Ellie bit her lip thoughtfully, and admitted guiltily, "I may get into trouble for that..." She dismissed the thought with a wave. "Never mind! He's never angry for long!" She giggled, then turned her attention back to driving.

Soon they were back at Ellie's house, and they all piled in the kitchen to help make salads and assist with the preparations for the barbecue, while Ellie went into the quiet of her bedroom to make the phone call to her brother.

Rebeca was helping Pamela make one of the salads, when suddenly, Pamela said to her, "Oh! I have a lovely little red bow that would look beautiful in your hair! I bought it because I thought it was so pretty, but when I put it in my hair," Pamela pointed to her red hair smirking, "you can imagine how it looked!" She hurried out of the kitchen as she said, "I'll go get it, I'll just be a second!"

In a moment, she was back, and clipped the bow in Rebeca's dark hair. "Oh! It looks so pretty in your hair! Come and look." She took Rebeca by the hand to the hallway where a large framed mirror hung on the wall. Rebeca smiled at her reflection.

"It really does. Thank you, Pamela." Rebeca gave her a little hug and they returned to the kitchen to finish off the salads.

A few minutes later, they heard Ellie skip down the stairs and they all turned as she entered the kitchen. She held her phone loosely in her hand, wearing an odd grin with her face screwed up in an expression that said her brother was not at all happy with her.

"Okay, soo…" she began. "How many of you are minors, here?" They all looked at each other, curious, and Rebeca asked,

"What is a minor?"

"Under the age of eighteen. Richie is a bit concerned I am aiding and abetting minors…"

"A … betting?" asked Rebeca, confused.

"Helping young people get into trouble," translated Toby, chuckling and they all smiled kindly at Rebeca who nodded her head in understanding.

"I am nineteen," Rebeca replied.

"I am eighteen," said Benito. They all looked at Toby.

"I am seventeen, but I have my legal guardian here," he said, putting his arm around his brother's shoulders. "And he is a very responsible legal guardian of twenty three!"

Ellie wiped her forehead with the back of her hand in mock relief, then put the phone to her ear again. "See, Rich, I'm fine. We are all fine. Everything is fine!" She paused for a moment, the pained look returning to her face as everyone heard Richard's raised voice stating that he should have known there would be trouble if he let Pamela visit Ellie on her own, since he knew how irresponsible Ellie was. Ellie's eyes twinkled as she attempted to pacify her brother.

"Come on, Rich, I know I am fifteen years younger than you, but I am still a responsible, grown adult." Richard lowered his voice slightly, but they could all hear he was still angry, saying something about it being inappropriate. "Look, I'll phone Caleb now. I'll let him know what is going on, but I am sure he will be okay with it." She rolled her eyes like a teenager as Richard continued less audibly to the others. "It's not like I have invited a man over or any …". She bit her lip, "Richard, I am twenty five years old. I have invited some friends over. I will call Caleb. I promise." She took a deep breath, then spoke in a sweet persuasive voice, "You will find out about that address, won't you? It's important for these kids to get their monkey back home." She nodded as he spoke, "You can be assured of that, Rich. I will most certainly keep Pamela out of it." Pamela frowned and Ellie smiled at her, shrugging her shoulders. "Yes, Rich." His voice now only loud enough for Ellie to hear. "Yes, Rich, I promise." She nodded to something her brother was saying. "Okay. I love you too! Call me first thing! Bye! Love you!" She hung up the phone, and placed it on the kitchen counter, blowing out a loud breath. "Well," she tittered, "That went well!"

"Aunty Ellie!" admonished Pamela, with her hands on her hips. "What do you mean you will keep me out of it? I want to help them find Emmie! You wouldn't stop me from helping them, would you? I know you want to help them, as well!"

"Well," she said, winking mischievously, "We'll just have to think how we can let you help while keeping you 'out of it'!" She glanced around the kitchen, then laughed heartily.

Pamela continued her complaint to her aunt, "Did you tell Dad *everything*? I don't want him turning up here in his cruiser and hauling me back home to Orlando!"

"I told him the important bits. I told him I volunteered to help some young people find a monkey that had been brought into America, because a couple of them were friends with the monkey and wanted to get her back to the jungle where she belongs. He assumed you were from my church, but I didn't bother correcting him. No need to let him know I just met you – he would just freak out. Come on! We have a barbecue to get going!"

They were soon sitting outside in the back, plates piled high with food, and talking excitedly about what they were going to do once they got the address.

"I have an idea!" squeaked Pamela with delight, "Why didn't we think of it already? We can deliver some flowers to the place!"

Joe, Toby and Rebeca looked at each other puzzled; Benito was far too engrossed in his food and was not listening to the conversation at that point. Food had become an important part of his life and he was enjoying every tasty morsel.

"Of course!" Ellie clapped her hands together, nearly upsetting the plate on her lap, and knocking her ice tea onto the grass. She laughed and got up, putting her plate onto her chair as she picked up her empty glass. "I have a flower shop.

We can deliver some anonymous flowers to the address!" She headed into the house to refill her glass, and Pamela nodded happily as she looked around at the pleased faces. Benito looked up and paused as he was about to take a bite of his burger and noticed everyone looking excited.

"Did I miss something?" he asked, and they all howled, shaking their heads. Hurt appeared in Benito's eyes, and Rebeca, who was sat next to him, placed her hand gently on his arm. She was well aware of what it felt like to not understand what everyone else was talking about.

"We have begun plans on how to rescue Emmie," she said kindly, and he nodded, smiling as he continued to eat, chewing thoughtfully and appreciating every mouthful.

As the sun began to set, they gathered up all the dishes, and Toby, Joe, Rebeca and Benito prepared to leave. Joe had called the hotel and booked Benito into the room beside theirs. Ellie and Pamela insisted on giving everyone hugs as they said goodbye.

"I'll contact you as soon as Richard calls me," said Ellie, as she and Pamela stood beside the Mustang while everyone piled in and belted up. Joe carefully backed out onto the road and everyone waved enthusiastically.

They were all tired when they arrived back at the hotel, and Rebeca went straight to her room to go to bed, while the boys went to the desk to get Benito's key. It only took a couple of minutes, then they made their way back down the hallway, and as they reached his room, Benito suddenly turned to Toby and grabbed his hand with both of his, holding on tightly and shaking it firmly.

"Thank you, Toby." His deep, genuine gratitude obvious in his voice and eyes. "Thank you for coming to rescue me." He smiled a shy smile. "You are a good friend." He looked over at Joe, still unsure of how Joe felt about him since he had sent his brother into his adventure in the jungle. "Thank you, Joe." He said softly, lowering his eyes.

Joe, himself, was uncertain as to how he felt about Benito, but as his brother was now safe, the anger that had filled his heart during their time in Nicaragua had dissipated. However, he was not yet ready to forgive Benito, so he just nodded, saying nothing as he looked away and then down at the carpet. Benito glanced back at Toby, not knowing what else to say.

Finally, Toby broke the uncomfortable silence between them, "You're welcome, Benito!" He gave him a half hug, patting him on the back. "Good night. Have a good sleep." Benito opened his door and shut it gently behind him, then Joe and Toby walked over to their room.

Pulling their door behind him, Toby spoke up. "Why do you have to be like that, Joe?"

Joe had stripped down to his boxers and was heading to the bathroom to brush his teeth. He paused with his hand on the bathroom door. "He's a weasel, Toby. What he did to you was inexcusable." And before Toby could respond, Joe shut the door behind him and Toby heard him run the tap and begin brushing his teeth.

Toby climbed into his bed and lay with his hands behind his head staring up at the ceiling and began thinking about his time in Nicaragua while he waited his turn in the bathroom. It all seemed so long ago. And although Joe was only in the bathroom for about ten minutes, by the time he had finished, Toby was fast asleep.

Joe finally came out of the bathroom, having purposefully taken a long time so he did not have to speak to Toby again about Benito. He lay down on his bed, and again, his thoughts drifted to God and how he felt about Him. Joe *did* know suffering and pain and death was the result of a fallen world, but God knew it would happen before He made the world. If only Adam and Eve had not sinned … Joe breathed out deeply as he contemplated it all … would he really have been any different? *Was* he any different? It was all a matter of pride, back to the original sticking point: he didn't want anyone telling him what to do. He wanted to make his own decisions. He soon drifted off, dreaming that he was in the garden of Eden, talking to a snake … .

CHAPTER 8

Despite being keen to get started on their journey to rescue Emmie, they all woke late the next morning, and Toby was surprised when he opened his eyes to discover it was 8:45. He jumped out of bed, calling to his brother as he hurriedly threw on some clothes. "They stop serving breakfast at 9:00, come on!" He hurried out the room and knocked on Benito's door who opened it sleepily. "If you want breakfast, you'd better come now!" He looked at Benito, still wearing the clothes he had on the previous day and smacked his forehead with the palm of his hand. "Oh! I'm sorry, Benito! I completely forgot you did not have any clothes with you. We will pick some up for you today, all right?"

"That's okay," said Benito, who had brightened considerably at the mention of food. He grabbed the key that he had tossed on a counter by the entrance, and shut the door behind him, following Toby to Rebeca's room. She opened straight away, dressed and ready to go. They scurried down the hallway and managed to get to the breakfast room five minutes before the staff began removing all of the left-over buffet, and quickly gathered their desired breakfasts, each of them piling their plates high. They had their pick of tables, as most of the hotel guests had already eaten, and sat down to devour their food.

Toby's phone buzzed in his pocket, just as they were finishing. He took it out – it was T-Rex. "Hey!" he called out cheerfully as Pamela's face beamed out at him. He took a large mouthful of food as she answered, knowing he could easily finish it, and probably another mouthful as well, before Pamela took her first breath.

"Hey!" she greeted him back. "Dad's given us an address, but we are to keep him informed at every turn." Her eyes rolled and her smile faded. "There are some stipulations he has given us in exchange for the information: he wants us to contact the Louisiana police at a moment's notice if there is trouble. We are meant to just see if your monkey is there and then contact the police. He has a friend up here in New Orleans and said the moment you find out if the monkey is there, we need to contact him, and his friend will go and pick her up. Under no circumstances are we to get involved in any kind of rescue ourselves." She sighed in an over-exaggerated manner and rolled her eyes again.

"But what if …" Toby began.

"I know." She said in a pained voice. "He's being a bit of a bother. He has a habit of interfering and spoiling things." She scrunched her face, but then immediately brightened, "But don't worry, I am used to working around his instructions!"

Toby laughed, thinking how difficult a daughter like Pamela must have been to raise. He nodded and accepted her ambiguous reply, feeling certain that they could indeed 'work around' things. "We just finished breakfast. We'll head over to your place shortly." Toby clicked off, and they returned to their rooms to get ready to go.

Soon they were again in the Mustang and Joe started the ignition.

"Do you want directions?" asked Toby.

"Nah!" Joe shook his head. He had a good sense of direction and it was an easy route to remember to get back to Ellie's house.

They were again greeted enthusiastically by Pamela, who burst out of the door as they pulled up on the drive. She ran over and insisted on giving everyone a huge hug. She paused when she got to Rebeca, who wore the red bow in her hair, and gave her a double hug. Pamela led them into the house and called out to her aunt as they entered.

"They're here!" she said excitedly as they followed her into the kitchen where Ellie was just tidying up from their breakfast.

"Would you guys like anything to eat or drink before we head out?" she greeted them with a smile and waved her hand towards the table.

"No thanks, I think we are all good," Joe answered as he looked around at everyone shaking their heads. "We had a good breakfast at the hotel."

"Well, Richard found the man, an Adrian Thompson, and his address is not too far away, a couple of miles past Gibson, where that auto repair shop is." She looked around thoughtfully, then said, "Well then, let's..." Ellie was interrupted by Madonna singing *Papa Don't Preach* from her phone that was on the counter. She giggled in response to Joe and Toby's curious looks, "An apt ringtone for my big brother, don't you think?" She turned her attention to the phone, "Hi, Richard. I assume you are calling with last minute instructions?" Her brother spoke too quietly this time for the others to hear anything. "Yes, Richard, I will." She listened again then spoke, "I called Caleb, Rich, and he was fine. He said he trusted my judgement." She raised an eyebrow at his comment. "Well, that isn't very nice, Richard. I'm hurt — and I'll tell him you said that!" He spoke again and Ellie became impatient. "Don't you have work to do? Someone somewhere is in need of a policeman, I'm sure." Another pause, then, "Okay, 'bye Rich. We'll call you later." Ellie breathed deeply and grinned at the others with an exasperated look as Richard continued to talk. "Yes, Rich, I understand. Okay, I'll call you later, the moment we walk back in the house. Bye Rich!" Ellie hung up before her brother could say anything else, then she turned toward the group who had all sat down on the kitchen chairs waiting for her.

"Let's go!" She stuffed her phone inside her handbag and flung it over her shoulder, striding purposefully toward the front door. She stopped and turned to Toby, "I thought we should do a drive by in the seven-seater, first, to see what we are up against. Then I'll go get a van from my shop. I've already instructed Tina who works for me, to make up a bouquet. It will be ready when we get there." She paused, then added, "Oh! Is that all right with you? Or did you have another plan?" She gave a guilty giggle, "I've kind of taken over. I am so sorry! The idea just came to me and I forgot to okay it with you."

Toby grinned, "That's fine. It's a great plan!"

As they got near the address that Richard had given Ellie, she pulled over to the side of the road and turned off the car engine. "Joe," she said, "I think you should drive the car from here. If the man has money, he most certainly has security cameras. Pamela and I might need to duck, so he can't see us." She got out of the driver's seat and climbed into the back seat that Joe had vacated. Joe started the car and followed Ellie's directions. He stopped as they came to the drive that would take them to the property.

"I'll go up slowly, and see how close we can get. I can just drive like I am not sure where I am going!" He drove steadily up the winding dirt road that led into a deeply wooded area. It was a three-quarters of a mile before he slowed as the area opened up and they began to see buildings in the distance.

"Look over there!" Toby pointed to the right at a wooden building painted green to blend in with the trees.

Joe stopped the car. "Ya, a building, so?"

Toby continued to point. "Look to the left of it, it looks like the edge of a caged area that runs behind the building. Can you see?"

Joe squinted his eyes, then nodded. "You think he would keep Emmie outside in a building with a cage? Wouldn't he have her in the house?" Joe queried.

"He would need to gain Emmie's trust before he lets her loose in his house," piped up Rebeca from the back. "She could cause a lot of trouble in his house if she was scared, and it would be virtually impossible to stop her escaping."

"That makes sense," replied Joe.

They all looked around at the surrounding area for a few minutes, then Joe started the vehicle and drove forward, looking for a place to turn around. Fortunately, they soon came across a little lane on the left hand side that Joe could back into. As he did, they could just make out the edge of a large white house in the distance. A large dog trotted aimlessly around the side then stopped motionless when it saw them. It stared at them for a few moments before deciding to saunter towards them to check them out. Joe hurried to finish his manoeuvre, and sped off back toward the main road where he had to wait a couple of minutes for a break in the traffic. He drove a mile before he found a place to pull over and let Ellie back in the driver's seat.

"Now," began Ellie as she strapped up and looked in her side view mirror. She indicated that she wanted to join the traffic, and a red pick-up truck slowed so she could move into the lane in front of him. "It is only a small vehicle that I am going to use to deliver the flowers. Pamela and I will be in the front but there is only room to comfortably fit two more people in the back. I am assuming Toby is going to be one of those two, since it is his friend we are going to find! Will you want your brother to go with you, Toby? I'll drop off Rebeca and Benito at my place, where they can relax while we go see what we can do about finding Emmie!"

Toby shook his head immediately, "No," he began, and Ellie raised an eyebrow. He turned around in his seat and faced Rebeca who was sat directly behind him. "I would like to take Rebeca," he said firmly. Rebeca smiled back at him, pleased.

"But surely, you would want Joe," protested Ellie, "in case there is trouble? I'm not sure I feel comfortable dropping off Rebeca with you. What if there is a problem? I think it would be wiser to take your brother."

"Emmie knows Rebeca," Toby began, "and …".

"I am perfectly capable of taking care of myself," interjected Rebeca, and Toby grinned at her plucky attitude.

"I'm sorry, Rebeca," apologised Ellie, "I didn't mean to be patronising. I am just not sure it will be safe for a girl. I would not want anything to happen to you. I just think it would be better to have someone stronger …".

"I will be fine," smiled Rebeca genuinely as she patted Ellie on her shoulder. "You forget, I grew up in a jungle. I have encountered many dangerous things – and people – in the jungle! I know how to take care of myself very well."

Ellie nodded her head in acknowledgement. "Yes, you are right." She stopped at some lights and faced Joe and Benito. "I guess I will be dropping you two off together! I was going to suggest dropping you off at the mall, but that is probably a bad idea. I highly doubt that your uncle will still be there looking for you, but you never know!"

Mild worry spread across Benito's face as he looked at Joe. The thought of spending any amount of time with Joe alone set his stomach on edge. It was certainly safer than being left alone with Tadeo, but Benito was still not sure what Joe was capable of.

The lights turned green and Ellie accelerated. "What is the matter, Benito? Your uncle will not be able to find you at my place."

"It is not my uncle that I am worried about," said Benito slowly as Joe's eyes met his. Ellie looked in the rear view mirror just in time to catch Joe's sneer.

"Seriously, Joe, are you kidding me?" She asked in disbelief, "Surely if Toby has forgiven Benito for his actions, there is no reason for *you* to still be harbouring bad feelings towards him?" Ellie frowned and shook her head.

An awkward silence filled the vehicle as Joe turned to stare out the window, saying nothing. He had every right to feel the way he did, thought Joe, and nobody was going to tell him otherwise. Certainly not some self-righteous woman who was only two years older than himself.

"Shall we have an early lunch before we deliver the flowers?" piped up Pamela cheerfully from the back. "I know it is a little early, but we don't know how long it is going to take to see if Emmie is at that place."

"Good idea," said Ellie brightly, "I have some pizzas in the freezer – does everyone like pizza?"

"Yes!" called out Toby. Benito nodded.

"That would be nice, thank you," said Joe quietly but politely.

"I have not had a pizza, yet," said Rebeca slowly, "but I am sure it will be enjoyable."

"I have some Beignets left," said Ellie, then added, "And I have a couple of tubs of ice cream."

Rebeca's face lit up. "I know that I enjoy ice cream very much!"

"Well, then, lunch is sorted!"

When they got back to Ellie's, Joe and Ellie were the last to exit the vehicle. Ellie turned to Joe and spoke softly. "I'm sorry, Joe. I didn't mean to be judgemental. It must have been a very worrying time for you, looking for your brother. I cannot begin to imagine how you must have felt. I understand that this is something that you have to work through yourself." She paused a moment before adding, "Will you be all right with Benito while we go see if we can find Emmie?"

Joe sighed deeply, rubbing his temples as he looked her in the eye. "I'm not going to beat him up, if that's what you are worried about."

Ellie sniggered, "No, I'm sure you wouldn't."

Soon they were once again, gathered around the big table in the large kitchen, consuming copious amounts of food and chattering happily about the afternoon's plans.

Ellie set up the large TV in the living room so that the boys could play some PlayStation games while the rest were away. Joe was not convinced that Benito was going to be much competition playing FIFA, but Ellie said they were welcome to have a swim. They had all left their bathing suits behind and Ellie had washed and dried them, ready for the next plunge in the pool.

As they were leaving, Ellie called out, "Help yourself to anything in the kitchen if you get hungry! Hopefully we'll be back soon."

Ellie's flower shop was not far away and it was not long before Rebeca and Toby were crouched in the back of her small van beside a large display of flowers in a wicker basket with a red bow tied on the handle. Pamela sat up front with Ellie.

"Are you two all right back there?" she called back over her shoulder.

"We're just fine!" answered Toby, and Rebeca smiled, nodding her head in agreement. "I wouldn't want to go all the way down to Orlando back here, but we'll survive to Mr Thompson's place."

Although they had said they were fine, Toby and Rebeca were glad when Ellie finally slowed, since it was not comfortable sitting in the back on the hard floor. Ellie turned off the main road, driving only a short way, just out of view of the highway, before stopping. She opened up the back and the two of them scrambled out of the vehicle, and as they did, something fell unnoticed from Toby's pocket to the van floor with a gentle thud.

"Right," Ellie began, "We'll try to take as long as we can distracting him, in case he can see the building from his house, but we will meet back here, okay? We'll give you a ten minute start before we head further up the drive. Now remember, you are just seeing if Emmie is there. No heroics. My brother's friend at the police was adamant that he would investigate this place and pick up Emmie straight away if she is here. You don't need to worry that there is going to be any kind of delay in rescuing her." Toby and Rebeca began to move away, then Ellie stopped them.

"Wait! We should say a prayer. We need God's help." The two nodded and Pamela got out of the car to stand by them.

"Father," started Ellie, "We should have spoken to you earlier about this. I'm sorry we have rushed ahead without asking Your guidance. If we should not be here, please make it clear before there is any trouble, and keep us all safe. Amen."

"Amen," they all replied.

"Okay," smiled Ellie encouragingly as she took a deep breath. "Ten minutes, then we'll head up the drive."

Ellie and Toby each looked at their watch, then Toby and Rebeca nodded and jogged off the road and into the woodland in the direction of the building that Toby was hoping would house Emmie.

At first, the going was a bit slow as they made their way through the many thin trees with lots of branches, and a thick, grassy undergrowth mixed with a nettle plant that did not sting like the English nettle did. After a little while, Toby grew worried, and stopped, facing Rebeca.

"Are we still heading toward the building? I feel quite disorientated."

Rebeca smiled reassuringly, "Of course we are. The sun alone tells me we are heading the right direction."

Toby looked around him and the heavy vegetation, unconvinced. "I don't see a lot of sun."

"There is enough. Besides, look!" She pointed ahead of them and Toby could just make out where the woodland opened up a bit, and a very small bit of green that looked slightly different to the surrounding trees. It must be the large shed they had seen earlier. They continued on, more quickly, and were soon at a more spacious area where the trees were bigger and the grass was shorter. The large sprawling branches prevented them from growing too close together. Toby thought they looked a little like an oak tree, but the branches hung down more. They stopped at the edge, where the growth was denser, to survey the section of land in front of them. The green building was only about 20 metres in front of them. They came out under the branches of one of the oaks and crept up slowly to the next one, until they were right next to the green shed. They tucked themselves up closely to the wooden walls and edged around until they came to the side of the caged area. As they did, they could see a corner of the house.

"I think we can go a little further before anyone in the house can see us," whispered Toby, and Rebeca nodded.

⸻⸻➤●◄⸻⸻

"Right," said Ellie as she glanced at her watch, "it has been ten minutes exactly. Let's go deliver a flower basket to Mr Thompson. Pamela grinned in the passenger seat and nodded excitedly.

They passed the lane where they had turned around earlier, and continued on as the road curved to the right and the whole white house came into view. It was a rather grand house and on either side of the green double front doors were two large columns that rose to the top of the fascia which ran around the top of the second floor. Out front, the drive went in a circle around a huge patch of grass.

Ellie drove around the curve and stopped at the front door. She turned to Pamela, "Okay now, you stay here. We don't need two of us to deliver the flowers." Pamela's face fell, but she nodded her head as Ellie got out of the car and made her way to the back. She opened the double doors and leaned in to grab the basket that had been placed in the specially made round slot so it would not move as she drove. She shut the doors firmly with a bang, and turned around to head toward the wide steps, but before she could move, she was greeted by a quiet growl. Her heart stopped and she stood completely still as she looked down at the large German Shepherd which was showing her every one of his very large teeth.

"Luna! Leave!" A voice boomed and immediately, the big dog relaxed his stance and wagged its tail. Ellie looked toward the steps to see a tall, slender blond man in a white shirt and cream chinos. He looked at Ellie suspiciously. She hesitated, and the man said in an irritated voice, "He will be as nice as pie now. What do you want?" Ellie regained her composure as she reached out slowly and patted the dog on the head, who responded by giving her a lick, and she giggled. She held up the basket of flowers that had been obscured by the back of the van, and cautiously made her way toward him with Luna following closely at her heels.

"Delivery for Mr Thompson?"

"He raised an eyebrow, still frowning. "Flowers? For me? Who would send me flowers?" He had his arms folded across his chest and stood with his legs slightly apart in a wary stance, his ice blue eyes glaring at her.

Undeterred, Ellie continued to walk closer until she was directly in front of him, a broad grin spread across her face. She held the basket towards him. "Maybe an anonymous admirer, there is no name given. It just says, 'Thinking of you'."

The man made no move to take the basket, and as Ellie stood holding the flowers, her arm out stretched, her muscles in her forearm began to tire. The man stared at her and Ellie widened her eyes and her smile as she moved the basket from side to side slightly, feeling slightly like she was trying to tempt a crocodile with a fish.

"I don't want them." He said simply.

Ellie lowered the basket, debating what she should do. "Perhaps your wife would enjoy them?" She suggested at last.

He cocked his head, his arms still folded. "If I had a wife, do you think she would want flowers from my anonymous admirer?"

Ellie laughed nervously, "Uh, of course not. Bad suggestion." She paused. "Oh, well, it seems a shame to waste them."

"Hoo hoo hoo!" The man and Ellie both turned towards the sound, and Ellie pretended she did not know what it was.

"What a funny sounding bird," she chuckled.

The passenger door of the van opened and Pamela jumped out enthusiastically.

———⟫●⟪———

"Hoo hoo hoo!"

Toby jumped back from the cage as the little capuchin jumped out of nowhere, and landed directly opposite him. She poked her little arm through the wire and grabbed Toby's ear.

"Hoo hoo hoo!"

Toby grabbed her little hand and tried to calm her.

"Shhh! Emmie! Quiet now!" He stroked her little fingers and they curled around his as she began to make little purring noises.

"So we know she is here, now," said Rebeca. She looked at Toby and she sighed deeply as her heart began to pound, realising what she had suspected all along: he was not going to leave without Emmie.

Toby's eyes ran quickly across the cage and found the door. He looked towards the house, and saw that he could still only see part of it, so he turned his attention back towards the door. There was an inexpensive lock over the latch, just so that the monkey could not let herself out. Toby reached in his back shorts pocket and took out his Swiss army knife. He flipped up the small thin tool. Toby was not sure what it was, but it looked like the ideal tool to break into a cheap lock. He held the lock and fumbled for a few moments until suddenly he heard a 'click'. His face lit up and he removed the lock, sliding across the bolt. As he opened the door, Emmie launched herself at him and in her excitement began squeaking loudly.

<hr />

"May I pet your dog, sir?" she asked, smiling up at him innocently. "I do so love ..."

Squeak! Squeak! Squeak!

They all turned towards the sound and Luna, sensing his master's concern, turned back into a guard dog and began snarling. The man turned sharply to Ellie and Pamela, pointing towards the basket.

"Take the basket and leave! Now!"

When Ellie and Pamela tried to stall, he nodded towards the dog who turned his attention back to them. Finally acknowledging defeat, they returned warily back to the van, and Ellie, still doing her best to delay, opened the back and slowly replaced the basket. A wet, grumbling nose touched her leg and she quickly closed the back and climbed into the driver's seat. She tried to fumble with her key to waste time and Luna jumped at the window, barking. Realising there was nothing more they could do, Ellie started the van and slowly made her way around the rest of the circle and crept down the drive.

"I can't see!" Said Ellie anxiously, "What is he doing?"

Pamela looked out her window and stretched her head around.

"He is walking in the direction of Emmie!" She said in a frightened voice. "But he is still watching us. Oh! I'll call Toby!" She quickly tapped her phone, and their hearts dropped as they heard a loud buzzing in the back of the van.

———⋙●⋘———

Emmie had all her limbs wrapped around Toby's head and neck and he pulled her down so he could see, giving her a loving snuggle.

"Come on, Emmie. You're going home!" A dog began barking. "Let's go, Rebeca!"

Toby looked at her confused as she stood still, listening.

"Yes, it's a dog, and he's coming this way." He began moving in the direction they had come and she grabbed his arm. The barking was growing closer and Rebeca shook her head at him.

"The barking, it is echoing around the woods, but it is stronger in that direction." She pointed towards the main road. "He is coming from behind us. We will have to go that way!" She pointed to the right, away from the house and the road, and as she did so, they both began to run.

Toby was breathing heavily and began to slow, listening to the barking. "It doesn't sound like it is getting any closer." He said hopefully.

"They will go to the cage first, and when they see the door open, the dog will easily track our scent. We must hurry!"

Toby did not have to hold onto Emmie at all as she clutched him tightly. The teenagers increased their speed and Toby was ashamed to find himself lagging behind Rebeca, who appeared to be focused on something in the distance ahead of them. All of a sudden, Toby saw it. A little dock leading out onto a waterway, with a small wooden boat moored to the end. Rebeca reached the boat first and hastily untied it, throwing in the rope just as Toby caught up with her, and they both leapt into it at the same time, making it rock in the water. Rebeca held up the oars that were on the bottom and looked at Toby who shrugged, feeling embarrassed that he had never before rowed a boat. Rebeca said nothing, but expertly placed the oars in the oarlocks and immediately began rowing them swiftly away from the dock and along the quiet water.

Toby's heart pounded as he heard the dog barking again and looked over his shoulder, amazed at how far away they were already. The swampy river wound its way around a corner and hid the dock so they just missed seeing the man who waved his fist furiously in the air as he and Luna arrived to find their boat gone.

Toby sighed with relief and concentrated on giving Emmie a scratch on the head as she snuggled herself into his lap contentedly. As Rebeca rowed, the trees grew thicker, and many of them were growing right in the water.

Toby looked at Rebeca nervously. "Where are we going?"

"I thought that it would be best to travel upstream, because when the waters of Louisiana make their way to the sea, there is a wide expanse of swampy area and we will be less likely to find someone to help us.

Toby looked at the still water around him, amazed. "How do you know which way it is flowing?"

Rebeca smiled, "I looked before I got into the boat. The current is so slow that you cannot tell which way it is flowing while we are moving along it."

"So," began Toby, "Is this what they call a 'bayou'?" He asked, and when Rebeca nodded her head, he added, "How do you know so much about this place?"

"My teacher at school was from America. She taught us much about its geography."

Toby suddenly thought of Pamela and Ellie. "I better call Pamela and tell her where we are!" He patted his pockets and groaned.

"What is the matter?" asked Rebeca.

"I've lost my phone! They are going to be worried. We need to find someone to help us soon, so we can contact them!"

Rebeca raised her eyebrows as Toby took in his surroundings and saw that the trees were growing thicker and the water that they were rowing in was getting shallower. "I do not know how much longer we will be able to stay in the boat," said Rebeca as they heard it begin to scrape along the bottom of the waterway.

⸻⸻≫●≪⸻⸻

Ellie parked the van where she had dropped off Toby and Rebeca. As time passed by, Ellie grew more worried. After twenty minutes had gone by, they heard a vehicle coming down the road behind them. The truck they had seen by the front of the house slammed on its brakes and the window rolled down. The blond man called out to them in a hostile voice, his dog stood on the bed of the pick up.

"What are you doing still on my property?!"

Ellie thought quickly. "I think there is something wrong with my battery. I'm waiting for the AA to come." She smiled at him sweetly.

"You better not be here when I get back!" He rolled up the window and sped off towards the highway.

As soon as he was out of sight, Ellie turned the vehicle around on the drive and quickly made her way back to the house. Pamela glanced at her aunt, saying nothing. The second they stopped at the house, Ellie was out of her van. She ran off without shutting her door and Pamela sprinted after her. They reached the cage and Ellie groaned when she saw the open door, shaking her head in despair as Pamela caught up with her. "He took her! No wonder that man was furious!" Ellie looked around frantically. "Where did they go??" Pamela scanned the area, then pointed to the narrow path that led into the trees.

"Well, I doubt they went to the house, or the road. And they didn't come back to us, so the only other option is that way!" This time, Pamela took the lead as they both trotted through the trees. They stopped when they came to the dock, and Ellie covered her mouth. She looked at Pamela and tears of worry welled up in her eyes.

"Oh, no!" Panic spread across Ellie's face and Pamela's heart pounded.

"Where do you think this leads?" She asked her aunt.

Ellie shook her head. "Who knows? Do they know anything about the bayous?"

Pamela shrugged her shoulders and gazed down at the water that was flowing ever so slowly to the left. Just then, she spotted something familiar floating down from the right: the red bow that she had given to Rebeca.

———⟫●⟪———

Toby offered to help Rebeca with the rowing, and he struggled for several minutes trying to get the hang of it. Rebeca giggled as she watched Toby trying to coordinate the oars and get them at just the right angle. They moved along very slowly, and finally Rebeca just smiled and put her hands out to take the oars from Toby who hesitated, but then realised they would move along much faster if he let Rebeca keep rowing, even if she was tired.

The water grew deeper and opened up a little for about a mile, then the trees began closing in on them again, and they could once more feel the boat scraping the bottom of the river.

"Oh, look!" called out Rebeca, pointing behind Toby and he turned in the direction they were headed. They had just rounded a curve in the water and a narrow but long dock came into view. It had a little boat similar to the one they were in, moored to the side. Rebeca rowed quicker in anticipation of finding someone to help them.

As they drew up to the dock, Toby and Rebeca looked at each other. It was a rather rickety piece of construction that looked like someone had just found whatever pieces of wood were available, alternately nailing and tying it together with a strong rope. Rebeca stood carefully as they reached the side and clambered onto the wooden structure, turning to catch the rope as Toby tossed it up to her. She skilfully tied it to a post in one quick movement as Toby climbed up and stood beside her, with Emmie quietly perched on his shoulder. They moved carefully along the dock, testing each plank as they stepped forward, and soon saw why it was so long. Although the water was no longer deep enough for a boat, it was still marshy for about twenty metres. When they eventually reached the end and stepped off onto dry ground they found the beginning of a path that wound its way through the trees and grassy undergrowth. Five minutes later, the path ended as they came to a clearing.

A small wooden house that looked like it was built by the same person who built the dock, stood in the middle on raised stilts with various bushes growing underneath. A thin ribbon of smoke rose from the crooked chimney. On the left was a similar looking shed with a lean-to on the side that held a pile of logs, with various garden tools. A clothes line was strung from the house to the shed and a few bits of clothing swung gently in the warm breeze, while several chickens were pecking the ground as they walked around aimlessly. A rooster crowed somewhere through the trees beyond them.

"Woof! Woof!" Toby and Rebeca jumped as a large bull mastiff trotted around the back of the house and headed towards them. Instinctively, Toby stepped in front of Rebeca, surprising himself at the braveness of his chivalry.

"Pumpkin!" A sharp call stopped the dog in its tracks, but its eyes remained fixed on them. A small, thin dark-skinned woman, who looked in her seventies, followed him from behind the house. Her long, thick wiry hair was a mass of grey unruliness, and she wore a faded green, loose-fitting dress that flowed as she walked. A wide friendly grin revealed uneven, but white teeth as she spoke to the dog, "Friends, Pumpkin! Love them!" The huge dog wagged his tail and hurried towards them, launching himself at Toby, and frightening Emmie who jumped with a tremendous "Squeak!" off Toby and onto Rebeca, just as Pumpkin made contact with

Toby, knocking him to the ground and licking the boy's face with his slobbery tongue.

Rebeca's fear and shock disappeared as she erupted in relieved laughter. Toby covered his face with his arms as he tried to move the heavy animal off of him. When he finally managed to get to his feet, he grimaced as he wiped the saliva from his mouth and eyes.

The woman cackled in laughter as she approached them. "Oh! He likes you!"

"W-what does he do to people he doesn't like?" asked Toby, still wiping his face with his T-shirt and watching Pumpkin warily as he sauntered back to his mistress.

"Ah, well, that'd be tellin'!" She laughed and began scratching the dog's head. She squinted her eyes and walked towards Rebeca. "She is a darlin' monkey!" Emmie began chattering nervously and wrapped her little arms around Rebeca's head, clenching her fingers tightly onto her hair.

The woman stopped a metre from Rebeca and stared at Emmie, making little clicking noises. Emmie stared back as if in a trance when the woman began making odd humming noises at the back of her throat. Emmie relaxed her grip on Rebeca, but remained perched on her shoulder.

She tilted her head as she looked over at Toby and back at Rebeca. "Y'all are hungry. Come inside and have some cajun stew!" She motioned with her hand for them to follow her as she climbed the rickety steps and up to the door that was slightly ajar.

"Uh! Excuse me!" Toby called out as he followed her, "Do you have a phone? I need to contact my friends. We uh ... got lost and I want to let them know we are all right."

"I ain't got no phone, dearie! Come now, sit down!" Toby had to let his eyes adjust as he stepped from the bright sunlight into the dark room. It was a simple kitchen with a few cupboards, an old ceramic sink and a small gas stove. The floor was wood with a large brightly coloured rug in the middle. There was an old fashioned fireplace with a metal bar running across it, and a few logs burning below. Two long wooden benches with sunken seats, covered in a thin fabric, lined the outside walls, and Pumpkin jumped on one, sprawling the length of it. There were two doors leading out of the kitchen on either side of the room, possibly one or two bedrooms, with a slightly smaller narrower door right by the fire. Toby stopped as he saw a wooden table with four chairs. The table was set for three with a large pot of steaming Cajun chicken stew placed in the middle. Toby looked around, but saw no one else.

"I'm sorry, Mrs uh…?"

"Aunt Elena! Everyone calls me Aunt Elena!" she answered, as she waved towards one of the chairs, "Sit! Sit!" Elena turned as Rebeca entered the kitchen and took her by the hand, placing her in a chair opposite Toby. Rebeca and Toby exchanged puzzled looks.

The appetising smell of chicken, onions, peppers and various pungent spices filled the room and Toby's stomach growled. Elena laughed and repeated her command for them to sit. Not wanting to offend the elderly woman, and both being quite hungry, Toby and Rebeca sat down as Elena began dishing out the stew. Thick slices of home made bread were positioned directly on the table beside each bowl. A small pile of figs were next to Rebeca's bowl and Emmie jumped off her shoulder onto the table and began eating them.

"Oh! I am sorry!" apologised Rebeca as she reached over to remove Emmie from the table.

"Leave her eat, they are for her." The woman said simply, and again Toby exchanged a bemused look with Rebeca, but neither of them said anything as they began to eat the delicious stew.

"This is very good, Elena," began Toby.

"*Aunt* Elena," she replied firmly, her smile disappearing.

"Oh, I'm sorry," began Toby, "Aunt Elena." He paused, not wanting to offend her again. "Are we far from town?" He scooped up a piece of chicken and put it in his mouth, chewing while he waited for a reply.

"Town? What do I want town for? Most everything I need is right here." She swept her hand out around her in a semicircle. "And Billy comes once a month and brings me anything else, like flour." She pointed towards the bread.

"Well, we…" began Toby, "We need to find our friends. They will be worried."

"Now you just eat up and stop frettin' about your friends." Elena nodded towards his bowl, and Toby continued eating.

"You can stay here," she nodded towards the two couches. "Billy is due to visit in the next couple of days. He can take you to your friends in his truck."

"But…". Toby started and Elena interrupted him, raising the palm of her hand to him.

"Hush, now. Aunt Elena will hear no more until you have finished your food."

Toby and Rebeca finished their meal in silence. Even Emmie had gone quiet as she enjoyed her feast of figs. When he was finished, Toby placed his spoon on the table, sliding his chair back across the wooden floor, but as he tried to stand, the room began spinning, and he grabbed the table.

"Oh!" He took a deep breath and sat down trying to focus. He looked up at Rebeca who was holding onto the side of her chair, closing her eyes. "I don't … feel … well …".

Elena stood up and slid the carpet in the middle of the floor towards the kitchen sink, then bent over and grabbed a hook on the floor, pulling up a hatch that hid steps leading down under the house floor. She went back to Toby who was swaying on his chair.

"Come now," a smile spread across Elena's face, "Hold onto my arm, and I will lead you to a cool place where you can rest." Toby leaned into her and was surprised at how strong she was as she held him steady, but when he realised she was leading him down steps into the black hole, he tried to fight her and ended up stumbling down the wooden planks. He landed with a thud on a cold, damp ground and immediately, everything went black.

Elena climbed back up the stairs and turned her attention to Rebeca who had turned white and was stood holding onto the back of the chair. Watching what happened to Toby, she tried to scream but nothing came out. Elena reached out her hand and Rebeca tried to push her away, but Elena grabbed her shoulders, shuffling her towards the enclosed area secretly hidden beneath her kitchen floor. Rebeca collapsed onto her knees and grabbed a leg of the table, trying desperately to hold on, but her strength was waning fast and she finally lay helplessly in a heap as Elena dragged her along the floor and down the steps. Rebeca's eyes closed before she landed on the ground beside Toby.

Aunt Elena climbed up the steps and let the hatch fall back down in place before pulling the carpet back over it. She smiled as she looked at Pumpkin who had been watching silently from his perch on the couch. She did an about turn and faced the table where Emmie had curled up in a little ball with a fig held loosely in one hand. Elena tittered to herself as she took the fruit out of the tiny fingers and, cradling the little monkey like a baby, carried her to her bedroom. A pile of clothes lay in the far corner of the dark room, and she placed Emmie on it. Then, taking a pillow case out of a drawer she draped it gently over the unconscious animal. After stroking the animal tenderly on the head, she pulled the pillowcase lightly over Emmie's head and returned to the kitchen.

"I best get these dishes done!" She spoke out loud, and she began clearing the table.

———⇒●⇐———

Pamela knelt down and grabbed the bow as it floated past. Standing, she held it out to Ellie, who looked at her curiously.

"Isn't that the bow Rebeca was wearing?"

Pamela nodded her head excitedly, pointing upstream. "They went that way!"

"Come on! At least we know what direction they went!" Ellie turned and jogged up the path towards the house with Pamela close at her heels.

When they reached the van, they jumped in and Ellie quickly belted up and sped down the drive as Pamela clicked on her seatbelt. They went a couple of miles in the direction that they thought would follow the waterway, but soon grew disappointed as they saw there were no roads leading back off the highway and towards the water.

"It's no good," Ellie said, biting her lip anxiously. "I think the best thing to do is go back home and look at a map of the area. Besides, if they got into a boat and rowed somewhere, chances are they will come upon another house, and will be able to contact us to come and get them." She looked over at Pamela who had an anxious look on her face. She patted her niece's hand and said, more confidently than she felt, "It will be fine, Pamela, they are both capable people. Rebeca does come from a jungle, after all! They'll be contacting us in no time!" She forced a smile at Pamela and turned her attention back to the road.

Ellie went back to her flower shop where they changed vehicles, and then drove back to her house. They walked slowly up the front steps, Ellie silently praying the two teenagers would be all right, and asking God for guidance in telling Joe what had happened.

Pamela and Ellie let themselves into the house and went into the TV room where they had left Joe and Benito. They were still sat there, playing a game. Joe glanced over his shoulder, and jumped to a standing position when he saw the looks on Ellie and Pamela's faces.

"What's the matter? What happened? Where are Toby and Rebeca – and Emmie?" he asked anxiously.

Ellie shook her head, clearing her throat before she spoke. Finally, she said simply, "They took her."

Joe looked at her, confused, "What do you mean?"

Ellie breathed deeply as she answered him. "They were just meant to make sure Emmie was there, but …".

"But what?!" Joe's face clouded over as fear for his brother filled him.

"They must have decided to take her from the cage. She was making a lot of noise and Mr Thompson grew angry. He sent us away, and a little while later he drove off in his truck. We went back up to the house and saw the cage door was open."

"So where are they?!" Joe's voice grew to a shout and Ellie unconsciously stepped back.

Pamela stood beside her aunt and put an arm around her shoulder, giving her a squeeze. "We think they took a little boat belonging to Mr Thompson and headed upstream," said Pamela holding out the bow. "This was floating in the water when we got there." She took a breath and continued, "We tried going back on the highway and driving in that direction, but couldn't find a road, so Aunty Ellie said we would come home and look at a map."

"I should have gone with them!" said Joe angrily. "You should have let me go! I would have kept him in line. I would have stopped him from trying to rescue that stupid monkey!" Joe seethed at the thought of something happening to his brother again, and this time also to Rebeca. "I should have gone with them!"

Ellie tried desperately to calm the situation. "I am sure he will contact us soon."

"Did you try phoning him?" Joe asked and Ellie hung her head, holding out Toby's phone.

"He must have dropped it. We found it in the back of the van." She spoke quietly. "Let's pray, shall we? God will take care of him."

Joe looked at her incredulously. "Pray?! Are you kidding me?? What's THAT going to do? We have to go look for him. That's how we found him last time – God didn't rescue him in Nicaragua, Rebeca and I did!"

When Ellie and Pamela stood motionless, Joe grew furious. "What's the address? I'll go look for him myself! What's the address?!"

Ellie gave him the address and Joe tapped the information into his phone. Striding across the room in a rage, he burst out the front door and disappeared.

Ellie's eyes welled up in tears and Pamela hugged her tightly. "It's not your fault, Aunty Ellie. Toby decided to change the plan. There was nothing you could have done to stop him. He probably wouldn't have listened to Joe, either."

"But I drove him there. I should have insisted that he just look for the monkey." She chided herself and Pamela frowned.

"Now you are being silly! You had no idea he was going to pull a stunt like this. You can't take the blame for someone else being foolish. Come sit on the couch with me, she said, ushering her aunt to the couch to sit next to Benito. "We'll pray. God will take care of him. You'll see."

Ellie pleaded through tears with God for forgiveness for her foolishness at trusting Toby and Rebeca to follow the plan, and for not asking for His guidance in the first place. She begged God to keep Toby and Rebeca safe and to bring them back soon. Pamela and Benito added their amens, and they all sat in silence, each lost in their own thoughts.

———◦●◦———

Joe quickly put the address into the car GPS and pressed START. Turning on the ignition, he backed quickly out of the drive and squealed his tires as he threw the gear shift into drive, swung the steering wheel around, and pressed down hard on the accelerator.

It was not long before Joe heard a siren blaring behind him and he looked in the mirror and saw flashing red lights. Hoping the car was heading to an emergency, Joe pulled over to the side to let it pass but unfortunately, it pulled over with him and stopped right behind the Mustang. Joe let a deep sigh pass through his pursed lips as he opened the dash compartment to find the vehicle information that he knew would be required of him. In Joe's side view mirror, he could see the police car door open and a tall broad man dressed in a blue uniform get out and saunter slowly and cautiously towards Joe. In a hurry to get going again, Joe had the paper work in his hand over the window ledge as the man stopped by the driver's door. The policeman stood with his hands across his chest, making no attempt to take the information from Joe's hand. He nudged his hat up a bit and scratched his brow, squinting at Joe as he spoke.

"Now, this is a mighty fine car and it's a mighty fine day to be cruisin' along with the top down, but I wondered if you could tell me how fast you were going, young man?"

"I don't know. I wasn't looking at my speedometer," said Joe curtly and the officer raised an eyebrow at his attitude.

"Would you mind stepping out of the car, sir?" responded the cop.

"Look," said Joe, growing impatient, "can you just give me a ticket so I can get going? I need to find my brother."

"It was not actually a question." The officer squared his feet firmly below him, and let arms fall to his sides, his right hand resting by his gun.

"It is really important that I get back on the road as quick as possible!" pleaded Joe, then as a too late afterthought, he tried being polite and smiled, "Please?"

"It is really important that I protect the good folk of Louisiana from irresponsible drivers." The officer stepped back slightly so he was in a better position when the door opened, and added in a deep commanding voice, "So, get out of the car. Now."

Joe scowled, opening the door forcefully and slammed it with a huff, only to see another, shorter officer coming from the patrol car in aid of his partner.

"Is there a problem, Doug?" the shorter man asked the officer standing by Joe. The large policeman turned to Joe.

"I don't know. IS there a problem, young man?"

Joe knew if he remained impudent, he could cause himself more problems and a longer delay, but his temper got the better of him. He faced the police officer walking towards him and pointed with his thumb to the larger man who had stopped him.

"I just asked your buddy, Doug here to give me a ticket so I can get going. I am on some urgent business, and I need to go, but he is just being obstructive!"

The shorter officer smiled like an adult trying to pacify a child who is having a temper tantrum, and said in a calm voice, "Now, young man, why don't y'all just tell us about why yer in such a hurry?"

A picture of Toby and Rebeca traipsing helplessly in some marshy bayou, surrounded by alligators flashed in Joe's mind and he exploded in a complete melt down, waving the papers furiously from one officer to another, swearing and shouting, "Do you want these papers or not?!!"

In one swift movement, as Joe's fury was focused on the other man, Doug stepped up behind him and pulling Joe's arms behind his back, slapped handcuffs him. Joe started to struggle, but quickly changed his mind, realising that although he was very fit, Doug was taller with about fifty pounds more muscle than him and Joe was at a decided disadvantage with his hands cuffed behind his back. Besides the fact that he would be even more delayed if Doug decided to slap a charge on Joe for resisting arrest.

"I think you need a little rest in the back of our car," the officer said, as he put his hands on Joe's shoulders and pushed him firmly to their vehicle. The smaller officer opened the back door, and Doug put one hand on Joe's head as he shoved him onto the back seat.

<hr />

"I'm going to call your Dad," Ellie said finally as she looked at Pamela. "Just to let him know what happened. The police will probably not do anything straight away, but at least they will be informed."

Pamela's usually cheerful face looked solemnly back at her aunt as she nodded her head slowly. "That is probably a good idea."

Ellie leaned back on the leather couch holding the phone to her chest and closed her eyes, breathing heavily. Pamela sympathised with her aunt. There had been more than a couple of times she had to confess something she had done wrong to her dad, and it wasn't easy. Finally, Ellie held out the phone and tapped in her brother's number. About four rings in, he answered.

"Hi, Richard, it's Ellie." Pamela heard her Dad's response, and Ellie added, "Of course, you know it's me. I ... uh ..." Her dad's upset voice grew loud as she heard him ask about her, "No, Pamela is fine, she's right here beside me." Ellie patted Pamela on the knee, and Pamela held her hand for support. "It's two of the kids ..." Ellie relayed to her brother the events that led up to Toby and Rebeca's disappearance.

Richard's voice had lowered and Pamela could not hear his question, but Ellie replied, "Well, I ... uh ... don't actually know their parents ..." She scrunched up her face and Pamela heard her Dad utter a few words she did not often hear from him. "I know, but I didn't actually *say* they were from our church." Richard went silent on the other end and Pamela could picture him sat in his cruiser rubbing his temples with his eyes shut tightly. She had invoked that very same response from him on more than one occasion, and she squeezed her aunt's hand in empathy. Finally, her dad spoke very quietly, and Ellie brushed away his query, "Oh well, it's complicated." She smiled painfully at Pamela as she added, "We can talk about how we know them another time. It's a bit of a long story ...". There was a quiet mumble as Richard said a few more things, and Ellie nodded, despite the fact that he could not see her. "Okay, Rich, we'll keep you informed," she paused, listening to her brother, nodding again. "Yes, Rich, okay. I love you too. 'Bye." Ellie quickly tapped OFF before Richard could ask her anything else and she tossed the phone down gently on the coffee table in front of her.

After a long silence, Benito finally spoke up, "Rebeca is amazing at finding her way around in the wilderness." He looked from one to the other anxiously, trying to encourage them, "I do believe she could actually *smell* which way to go to find help." He smiled feebly, but Ellie leaned over and gave him a hug.

"Thanks, Benito. You're quite right. I'm sure Rebeca will soon get them to a house or the main road where they can flag someone down." She patted Benito and Pamela's knees simultaneously, then stood up. "I could do with a cup of tea. How about you guys?" They both nodded and followed her into the kitchen where she got out a teapot and, without asking what kind they wanted to drink, dropped in a couple of chamomile tea bags before filling up the kettle and turning it on.

Nobody said anything while Pamela got out three cups and placed them beside the teapot as Ellie poured over the hot water. She then reached up to the cupboard above her and took out a package of cookies. She took a plate off the draining board and tilted the bag so several Oreos rolled onto the plate and handed it to Pamela who took it to the table. Ellie gave the tea a good stir, then poured it into the three cups. She grabbed two and Benito took the other one as they made their way to the table and they all sat down in silence as they drank the tea.

———⟫●⟪———

Elena washed the two bowls and spoons and put them, along with her clean bowl, back in the cupboard. She grabbed the pot of stew from the middle of the table and lifted it up, carrying it out the door and towards the outhouse that stood at the edge of the clearing behind her little wooden house. Pumpkin followed her, wagging his tail and looking at her mournfully. When Elena had emptied the contents down the hole, she turned and scratched her dog on the head.

"Not for you, darlin'," she smiled as a thread of slobber drooled out the left side of his mouth. He nudged his wet muzzle against her arm as she trundled back around to the front of her house. She glanced over at the chickens and several chicks that had gathered by the entrance to the wired enclosure which encompassed their little wooden dwelling. One of the chickens was off to the side, pulling out a worm from the earth, and Elena looked down at her dog, nodding. "Dinner!" She pointed her thin finger and immediately, Pumpkin bounded over to the unsuspecting chicken and grabbed it between his teeth, shaking it viciously as it's squawks filled the air. The other chickens panicked and ran into their house as Pumpkin clenched his jaws down firmly and began eating his dinner.

Elena went inside to finish tidying. She washed up her pot and put it on top of the stove and, wiping her hands on her dress, she looked thoughtfully at the rug that covered the hatch in the floor. Pumpkin waddled into the kitchen wagging his tail happily at her and she looked down at him.

"They'll be comin' soon, darlin'." She looked out the window towards the path that led down to her dock. "One more thing to do." As she scratched Pumpkin's nose, he looked up at her in adoration and smiled. "Pumpkin, I need your help," she said as she headed out the door and across the clearing. The huge dog trotted after his mistress as she strode purposefully along the path towards the dock that she and Billy had made several years ago.

At the end of the dock, she untied Mr Thompson's little boat and turned to tie the end around Pumpkin, who was stood right beside her. "Pull!" She commanded as she got down on her knees. Pumpkin started backing up and Elena grabbed the boat to direct it sideways and onto the dock as the great dog pulled. Once the two of them got it up, Elena pointed in the direction of her cottage and commanded "home!" Pumpkin promptly turned around and trotted along, pulling the small boat effortlessly towards the house with Elena guiding it so it did not fall back into the water. Once they were in the clearing, Elena guided Pumpkin towards the fire pile she had already started in between her house and the trees. She stopped the dog and untied the boat, then walked over to her shed. Shortly she came out with an axe slung over her shoulder. Within a few minutes, the boat was in pieces, and Elena smiled as she stood with her hands on her hips admiring her work. She tossed the pieces into the wood pile and then went into her house to get some fuel and matches. With a quick splash of fuel over the wood and one strike of the match the pile went up in a flash and Elena lurched back out of the way. Once she was sure everything was burning well, she went back in the house for a last check.

Surveying the kitchen, Elena smiled. "We're ready for 'em, Pumpkin!" Pumpkin sat down in the middle of the floor and cocked his head at her, a faint whine escaping through his panting mouth. "You've been a good help, darlin'," she grinned and lifting the lid off a jar that was sat on the counter, removed a couple of home made dog biscuits tossing them to Pumpkin who caught them expertly. He licked his lips and a sliver of saliva dropped from his mouth landing in a small puddle on the floor.

Elena took the black metal kettle off the floor from beside the fireplace and filled it with water from the tap, silently thinking to herself how pleased she was that Billy had talked her into at least getting water piped into her house. It came from the river and went through a filter before entering her kitchen sink. She had argued with him at first, but finally saw the sense in it. Besides, he wanted water piped into his house, so to be consistent, she really had to, as well. She hung the kettle over the fire and tossed another log on before taking an apple from the bowl by the sink and sitting down at the table. She snickered happily as she bit into the crisp fruit, watching the fire dance under the kettle waiting for the water to boil ... and her visitors to arrive.

———————◆———————

So, now, do you want to explain why you are in such a hurry, son?"

Joe heaved a great sigh and leaned back into the car seat trying to get comfortable with his hands cuffed behind him. He finally accepted that he was not going to be finding his brother anytime soon, so he began to tell the officers what he was doing in Louisiana and why he needed to find his brother.

Ten minutes later, after being interrupted several times by Doug as he asked Joe questions, Joe finished his story where the officer had pulled him over. Doug and his partner looked at each other, deciding whether or not to believe this fellow's story. Finally, Bob picked up the radio and made some enquiries. A woman at dispatch confirmed that an officer Richard Bartley had indeed contacted New Orleans PD regarding an illegal monkey supposedly in the possession of a Mr Adrian Thompson. She gave Bob the address. After a few more questions from Doug, he ended the call and turned around to face Joe who was looking very sullen on the back seat of the cruiser.

Doug raised an eyebrow, "I guess you were speaking the truth," he said to Joe. Joe realised he could not restrain himself from saying anything sarcastic if he opened his mouth, so he just gave the officer a half smile and said nothing.

Doug turned back to his partner. "What do you think, Bob? We are not too far away, I say we have a look for this monkey."

"I'm more interested in finding my brother!" piped up Joe from the back as Bob nodded.

"Well, if we find the monkey, we may find your brother," said Bob. He turned to Doug, "I'll go make sure the car is parked far enough off the road and bring back the keys."

When the Mustang was safely tucked to the side of the road and the keys in Joe's pocket, Doug turned off his flashing lights and signalled to get back into the flow of traffic and towards Mr Thompson's address.

Doug slowed down as he approached the turning and asked over his shoulder, "This the place, son?"

"Yes," said Joe. "It is a long driveway."

Doug turned up the drive and kept a watchful eye as he drove, while Bob was scanning all around. When they came to the house, Doug pulled up in front of the steps and both officers got out. Joe sat forward on the edge of the seat.

"What about me?!" he asked loudly.

"It's probably best you stay here. We will have a good look around, don't you worry."

Bob trotted up the steps and rang the bell, but with no vehicles around, they both assumed that no one would answer.

"I'll have a look around the property, while you check out the house," Officer Doug said to his partner as he headed towards the barn with a caged area outside of it. He walked all the way around, noting the small open door and the faint peculiar smell. He wasn't sure what a monkey smelt like, but

173

the smell was nothing with which he was familiar. There were some slightly unusual faeces droppings on the ground, as well. He took another walk around the building, then headed in the direction where he thought the waterway would be. He glanced over at Bob who was looking in windows, before taking the little path into the trees. Doug was soon at the dock and he stood for a moment, looking up and down the waterway and all around him. After he decided that he could see nothing untoward, he made his way back down the path and over to Bob who was now stood outside the police car. They both shook their heads at each other, then got in the car. Doug pulled out the radio again and asked the dispatcher to look on a map to see which was the first property upstream from Mr Thompson's.

There was a moment's pause as she typed on her computer, then finally she gave them the address. "It's registered to an Elena Brown, I can't tell you anything else."

"Okay, thanks," said Doug, "We'll head over there now."

"Copy that," she responded and clicked off.

Doug followed the circle drive around and headed back towards the highway. He made a couple of turns, then finally turned down a dirt track. He drove reasonably quickly at first, but the road soon deteriorated and he had to slow down to a crawl. The road wound back and forth through a thickly wooded area. The road abruptly ended as it opened up into a wide span and at first, it looked like there was nothing else. However, on the right hand side, there was a narrow footpath. Doug got out first and shut the door behind him before taking the path. Bob told Joe to hang tight, then quickly followed his partner as he disappeared into the trees. The path made a little sweep to the left and quickly ended as the trees opened up to a clearing. A fire was crackling in a fire pit on the left hand side, and he could hear a dog barking in the little haphazard house sat in the middle which Doug was circling around to find an entrance. Bob caught up with his partner just as he tapped on the door.

"Hello!" he called out, and as he did, the barking became interspersed with a deep growl. Both men automatically let their hands drop beside their guns, ready to defend themselves.

"Quiet now, Pumpkin!" An elderly voice said feebly, then, "Come in, officers!" Bob and Doug looked at each other and Doug slowly pulled the door open with his left hand, his right still by his gun. Bob took a step back and Doug rolled his eyes at him, shaking his head. Without warning, the door slammed into Doug who fell back against Bob both landing unceremoniously on the small deck with the huge slobbery dog licking their faces.

"Ah! Will you look at that, he likes you!"

Doug and Bob quickly dislodged the dog and jumped to their feet, brushing themselves off and wiping their faces.

"Come in, come in! Will you have some tea?"

Warily, each with an eye on the dog that now stood beside them wagging his tail, drool dripping unevenly out both sides of his mouth, the men entered the little house to find a thin, elderly woman with a head of thick grey hair, sat at a wooden table with a pot of tea, and a cup in her hand.

"There's plenty in the pot! Come, sit down!" She nodded towards the cupboard above the sink. "You'll find two more cups in there." She rubbed her knee gently, "You'll have to excuse me not getting it myself. It's my arthritis; it's quite painful today."

"Oh, no thank you," began Doug, speaking for both of the officers, "We …".

A loud growl sounded right behind Doug and he felt a wet mouth press against his left thigh. He looked over at Bob who had his hand on his gun, ready to defend his partner, and possibly himself if the dog made a sudden move.

The woman laughed heartily, "Pumpkin doesn't like it when people refuse hospitality. He finds it quite rude."

Doug took a moment in his mind, debating whether to shoot the dog or trust the woman had control over it. "I suppose it wouldn't hurt for us to have a small cup," he spoke finally, and immediately Pumpkin stopped growling, trotted over to the fire, and made himself comfortable on the thick rug that lay on the floor.

"We actually need to get on…" began Bob and a low rumble emanated from in front of the fire. "But I suppose Doug is right, a quick cup would be okay."

Doug took a couple of slow steps toward the cupboard as Bob sat down on a crooked wooden chair. Doug brought two cups over to the table and sat down beside Bob. He poured each of them a half a cup, then looked over at the woman.

"We're actually looking for a couple of missing teenagers," he started. Doug took a small sip of tea. Surprised by the spicy flavour a tiny grimace escaped his lips and placed his cup down on the table. "We think they came up the waterway, and your dock would be the first one they came to."

Elena smiled knowingly at him, "I make my own tea."

Bob looked over at Doug and put his cup down without tasting it.

"It's very good for you. It'll cure all things that ail ya! Even your ulcer, officer." She glanced at Bob, who was staring at her wide eyed. She turned back to Doug and added, "*And* your irritable bowl syndrome." Doug's mouth dropped open as Elena picked up the teapot and filled both of their cups to the top.

"But … how … how," sputtered Doug who was now staring at Bob, who shrugged his shoulders in amazement.

"Never you mind!" Elena interrupted them. "I can see it in yer eyes!" She pushed the cups towards the men and continued, "Now drink up!" She pointed her finger at each of them in turn and, mesmerised, they took their cups and drank until each cup was empty. The officers placed their cups on the table, and neither of them spoke for several minutes. A warm, tingling sensation followed the tea through their bodies and settled comfortably in their stomachs. They looked at each other, wondering if the other had the same feeling.

Finally, Doug shook his head and blinked a few times, trying to clear his mind and remember why they were there.

"So, have you seen anyone today?" He cleared his throat and stood suddenly, going to the door and opening it, breathing in deeply before turning around to Elena. "A boy and a girl, both dark haired. Nineteen and seventeen years old?"

Elena tilted her head and closed her eyes, making a funny little humming sound at the back of her throat. Suddenly, she opened her eyes wide and made the two men jump as she spoke abruptly, "Well now!"She began, "My arthritis has been mighty bad today, and I've been sitting here wondering when my Billy is coming. He is due any day now. Can you tell him that I need some honey? I'm out of honey." She looked down and folded her hands on the table before continuing. "Ain't nobody come and knock on my door today." She nodded to her dog who jumped to his feet and trotted over to her, resting his big head on her lap. "Right, Pumpkin?" She patted his head with affection and he whined innocently. "Nope, I do believe the last person I saw was my Billy, and that was a good few weeks back." She squinted her eyes and looked from Doug to Bob, "You *will* tell my Billy I need honey, now won't you?" She leaned back in her chair, closed her eyes, and promptly began snoring.

Doug was still standing by the door, breathing deeply, but Bob, although feeling like he had just woken from a deep sleep, decided to have a quick look around, opening the one door into a bedroom, then walking across to the other side and opening a door into another bedroom. A smaller door to the side of that, led into a storeroom. Seeing no sign of a couple of teenagers, he sidled past the dog to reach the door, then nudged Doug forward, and once they were out, hastily shut the door behind them.

Once outside, Doug gave a cursory look around the yard, while Bob, still feeling groggy, had a look in the shed. That was filled with various tools, including an axe. He shut the shed then spotted the path in the opposite direction to where they had come.

"You better check on that kid," Bob said, referring to Joe. "I'll just nip down that path and see if it leads to the waterway." Bob sauntered to the path, trying to clear the fog from his brain and remain focused on the job.

"Okay," said Doug, glad to be heading back to the vehicle.

By the time Doug got back to the car, his head had cleared and apart from a mild stomach ache, he felt completely normal. He opened the driver's door, but stood for a moment leaning on it.

"What took you so long?" Complained Joe, "Did you stop for a cup of tea or something?"

Annoyed at himself for being manipulated – or *whatever* that was that had put both officers in a vulnerable situation – Doug snapped at Joe.

"We have procedures to follow, son. You want us to be thorough, don't you?" He was immediately sorry for allowing the situation to control him and he crossed his arms and stood up straight.

"Where's your partner?" Joe asked when Bob did not immediately appear.

"He decided to check something out. He'll be back shortly."

"Well, had the woman seen my brother and his friend?" Joe asked impatiently, anxiety filling him.

Doug breathed in deeply, "No, son, I'm sorry. There was no sign of them."

"Where else could they be?" Joe asked desperately. "Are you *sure* there was no sign of them? Maybe if you let me out to have a look."

"Now, there was no sign of them there, I've told you. I'm sorry. I understand you are desperate to find them." Then, he opened the back door and as he leaned in the car he added, "I guess it'll be safe enough to remove them handcuffs, if ya just lean forward."

Once Joe's hands were free Doug continued, "If you give me a picture of your brother and the girl, I'll put out an APB and have everyone keep their eyes open around here, okay?"

Joe quickly found a picture of Toby and Rebeca on his phone, and sent it to Doug's. Doug sent it in to the station and had them circulate it to all the officers. Just as he finished, Bob came back and opened the car door, sitting down and putting on his seatbelt as he shook his head.

"Sorry, there is absolutely no sign of them here."

They dropped off Joe at his car and sat on the side, silently watching him get in and drive away. Finally, Bob spoke. "What happened back there?" he asked his partner.

Doug pursed his lips and shook his head slowly from side to side. "I dunno, buddy," he began, "but my stomach suddenly feels better than it has for months. Bob frowned.

"Oddly enough, I can't feel my ulcer at all, any more." He smiled, "I reckon I could eat a double hot 'n spicy burrito from Danny's Drive-through and not feel a thing!"

"I wonder what happened to those teenagers?" queried Doug. Bob smirked.

"Maybe they ain't just friends! Maybe they just ran off together! Young kids do that, sometimes." Doug raised his eyebrows.

"You could have something there. More often than not, that's what it's about – kids running away. Nothing sinister happened, they just wanted to leave home."

———➤●◄———

Joe sped off down the highway, this time within the speed limit, trying to decide his next move. *Those police officers were acting kind of odd when they got back to the car, he thought to himself. I wonder what that was about?* He thought about contacting his parents back in England, but he didn't want to worry them. There was nothing they could do over there, anyway. He thought about where he should go next. He didn't want to go back to the hotel. As much as he hated to admit it, there was some comfort in being around other people in a time like this – especially people like Ellie and Pamela. They had caring hearts, and he knew they would do whatever they could to help.

Benito, on the other hand … well, he was a waste of space, but at the moment, he'd just have to accept his presence. He blew a deep breath out through his lips as a spark of guilt singed his conscience. The kid looked constantly wary and the slightest thing set him on edge. Would he really have turned out more confident if he had been in Benito's position? Joe didn't think he would have turned out as spineless as Benito but – who knows how he would have turned out under the circumstances. And, thought Joe, he *had been* brave to escape from his uncle. Joe shook his head and chuckled – he had actually called Benito 'brave'! His thoughts turned back to Toby and Rebeca. Where could they be? *"Please God,"* he began, then stopped. Did he have any right to ask God anything? Would God even listen to him? Why should He when Joe had been behaving so abominably?

Joe was surprised when he found himself on Ellie's drive. He barely remembered driving there. He turned off the car, but remained where he was. Pride was a peculiar thing. It was like putting on a life jacket in a boat because you think it will save you and keep you afloat, but then a storm comes and you fall overboard, only to discover the jacket is actually full of lead and you end up being pulled to the bottom.

Just then, the front door opened, and Ellie stepped out with a sad smile.

"Did you find them?" she asked kindly, even though she could see that Toby and Rebeca were not in the car. He felt one of the knots on his life jacket loosen. Tears threatened to surface in Joe's eyes and he swallowed the lump in his throat. He was overwhelmed with both the fear of losing his brother and Rebeca, and the compassion he saw in the young woman's face.

"Come in," Ellie waved him in, holding the door open as he slowly got out of the car and strode towards her with his eyes cast down. He climbed the steps and stopped when he was directly in front of her.

"Ellie, I'm …".

"It's okay."

Joe shook his head. "No, it's not okay."

"I understand." Ellie stepped to the side and motioned for him to go inside. "I'll make a fresh pot of tea."

Joe gently squeezed her shoulder as he walked in. "Thank you."

Pamela met him as he approached the kitchen. She smiled and gave him a hug. Taken aback, for a few seconds he stood with his arms down, then returned her embrace. Joe stepped back and looked down at the usual bouncy, cheerful girl and gave her a half smile. Rebeca was only a year older than Pamela, but it seemed like she was several years older.

"You're a good, kid!"

Pamela snorted. "Tell my Dad that." She grabbed his hand and led him to the table where she pulled out a chair for him and as she did so, she asked, "So, what happened?"

Ellie came to the table with a fresh pot of tea and placed a cup in front of Joe as he began to recount the previous few hours' events.

"I would really like to go back to that woman, Elena's place." He gazed out the window towards the pool, thoughtfully. "Those two coppers were acting kind of weird when they came back to the car. I don't know what, but something wasn't quite right. I really want to see the place – and the woman – for myself." Looking up at the clock, Joe scrunched his face, "I guess Benito and I will go back to the hotel and I'll head back to the woman's place tomorrow."

Ellie placed a hand on Joe's arm. "Caleb called to say that he had finished his business early and was coming home tonight. He said to invite you and Benito to stay here. Go back to the hotel and get your things ... and Toby and Rebeca's. You and Benito can sleep in one of the spare rooms, it has two single beds."

Joe looked at Benito, squinting his eyes until Benito looked away. Then he turned to Ellie and smiled sadly. "Thank you, Ellie, that is very kind of you – and Caleb." He stood up. "With any luck, Toby and Rebeca will be back before morning." Joe felt a prick at his conscience when he used the word 'luck' and he saw Ellie did not approve, but she said nothing as she walked him to the door.

"There will be some chilli ready when you get back," she said as she closed the front door behind him and headed back into the kitchen to begin cooking.

CHAPTER 9

Toby slowly opened his eyes. He blinked several times and panicked when he could not see anything. Where was he? He couldn't remember anything past being mowed down by a huge dog when he and Rebec … where was Rebeca?

Toby felt along the hard ground beside him as he called, "Rebeca! Rebeca!"

Just as his hand felt her thick soft hair, she spoke in a muffled voice that grew clearer as she turned over, "Here, Toby, I am beside you." She touched his hand that was resting on her head, and he clutched it tightly.

"Are you all right? Can you see?" His head pounded heavily as he sat up, still holding onto Rebeca's hand.

"I am okay, but I feel slightly woozy." Rebeca tried to let go of Toby's hand as she manoeuvred into a kneeling position, but he wouldn't loosen his grip. She held her head down for a moment, then slowly leaned back on her heels, lifting her head slowly as she did so. She drew in a deep breath through her nostrils. "I think we are underneath her house. I can smell various herbs and flowers."

"Oh, then I'm not blind."

"No," said Rebeca slowly, "I do not believe so."

"Why do you sound so clear headed?" Toby asked. Despite their situation, and the fact that Toby could not see her, Rebeca smiled.

"I have been conscious for a few minutes, breathing deeply and moving very slowly. I have learned that it is not good to move too quickly when you have been poisoned."

"Pois … yes, you're right, that strange woman must have poisoned us. But …" Toby interrupted himself, "Wait! You've been poisoned before? Who poisoned you?"

"Me, I did it to myself. Not on purpose, of course. As a young girl, I was curious – and rebellious. I would sometimes try strange plants – just a little amount – even though my father said I must only eat what he had shown me was safe. I had a bad stomach a few times, but most of the time, I was right in the plants that I thought were good. Only twice, did I try something that poisoned me badly. I believe I was unconscious for an hour or two, both times, and I felt like I do now, when I woke up."

Toby shook his head in the dark. He never ceased to be amazed at the things he learned about this young woman. There was a conflict in him in that he felt the need to protect her, yet realised the fact that she was, in many ways, not in need of his protection. So completely different to Gwen, who *had* been very much in need of protection. Still, he held Rebeca's hand in the dark, the unbidden instinct to take care of her, filling his entire being.

"I remember now, a vague recollection of Elena putting us down some stairs, underneath her kitchen floor." Toby spoke reflectively as he positioned himself next to Rebeca who was shivering slightly. Her arm was cold, and he put his arm around her for warmth, startled at the peculiar feeling in his stomach as he touched her smooth skin. It must be the poison, he thought to himself.

"Yes, my head is clearing, too. We *are* under her house," began Rebeca, leaning into Toby as she recalled what had happened. Her heart began pounding heavily, and despite the effects from the poison lessening, it was difficult to think clearly in his embrace. "I ... uh ...". Rebeca cleared her throat, trying to remember the house as they had approached. "The house was about four feet off the ground, and there were thick plants and shrubs all around it. I am guessing this is some kind of room, like a cellar mostly above ground, but still cooler than her house, so she can store food and herbs and keep them fresh."

They sat silent for a few moments, gathering warmth from each other, as they each tried to think of how they could escape.

"I don't remember there being a lock on the hatch," said Toby in a hushed voice as he suddenly realised the strange woman would probably be able to hear them. He stretched out his legs to stand, finally releasing Rebeca as he did so. He waved his hands down low in front of him as he took tentative steps forward. His right hand knocked against the bottom step and he stopped, reaching back towards Rebeca, grabbing her hand again in the blackness. "I've found the steps. Hold onto my waist." He let go of her as her hand touched his back and they crawled blindly up the wooden planks, carefully staying in the middle so they would not fall off.

A few seconds later, Rebeca heard a thud as Toby's head hit the bottom of the cellar door.

"Ow!" Toby cried out softly. He rubbed his head for a moment, then squared his feet, pushing upward with both hands. The carpet added considerable weight to the hatch door, but a faint light pierced the blackness as Toby lifted up the door and saw the moonlight shining through one of the kitchen windows.

"Grrrrrrrrr!" The low rumble stopped Toby from lifting any higher and his heart dropped as Pumpkin's face met his. Even in the dim light, Toby could see the teeth baring and from the left side of his mouth, a strand of drool glistened in the moonlight as the dog stood guard at the edge of the hole. Needing to rethink their escape, Toby lowered the hatch door and sat down on the step, facing towards Rebeca as she knelt below him.

"What now?" asked Rebeca, not really expecting an answer from Toby who responded with a deep sigh.

"She's only a small woman," Toby spoke as he thought things out in his mind, "If we could just figure out how to deal with the dog." He ran his fingers through his hair, adding, "I can't think clearly, I still feel a little funny." Rebeca nodded in the dark and took a sharp intake of breath as she began to shiver from the damp cold surrounding them.

"When you lifted the hatch, I noticed a folded sheet of tarpaulin on the ground in the corner," began Rebeca, "Shall we sit on it? It has to be better than sitting on these stairs indefinitely. Come on." She reached out her hand in the dark and found Toby's knee. Toby took her hand as they carefully crept down the steps. Crawling on their hands and knees with their shoulders in constant contact, Toby let Rebeca lead him to where she remembered seeing the sheet. "Here it is," Rebeca smiled to herself.

"Grab hold of it and I'll try to find us somewhere better to sit," replied Toby. Eventually he found the side of one of the shelves. Between the two of them they managed to open up the sheet big enough for both of them and then Toby sat down, leaning against the shelf. Finally he pulled Rebeca close beside him, wrapping his arms around her for warmth. Again he was startled at the unusual feeling in his chest as she snuggled into his embrace.

Despite their circumstances, Rebeca could not help but relish the close proximity to Toby. She let her head rest on his shoulder, and for a moment allowed herself to believe this was the beginning of a change in their relationship from friends to something more. Gwen's beautiful face flashed in her mind however, and she swallowed hard, exhaling loudly through her nose.

"Don't worry, Rebeca, we'll find a way out of here," Toby squeezed her gently, misinterpreting the sound.

They sat in silence for a while, then Toby spoke: "So, do you think God has His hand in this?" he asked, hating himself for the sarcasm he heard in his voice. Rebeca's body tensed and she pulled slightly away from him at his tone.

"Yes, I do, Toby. ALL things work according to God's plan. Sometimes we will know the 'whys' here on earth, and sometimes the answers will have to wait until we get to Heaven – if that is where we are going."

"You think we might not be going there?"

Rebeca paused, then spoke with concern and humility, "I do not know if YOU will be going there."

Toby's heart quickened, but this time it was not a warm comfortable feeling. "What, so you think you are better than me?" Annoyed, he dropped his arms to his sides. "I'm a sinner and you're a goody goody?"

"No, Toby," she said gently as she turned to face him, even though she could not see him. "We are all sinners. None of us are good enough to get into Heaven."

"You're talking nonsense. First you say you're going to Heaven and now you say you aren't."

Rebeca pursed her lips thoughtfully before responding. "I *am* a sinner, but I *am* going to Heaven because Jesus died to pay the penalty for my sins, not because of anything I have done. It is His gift to me."

"So why do you get the gift, but I don't? There are worse people in the world than me, I've not done anything really bad – I've never killed anyone or robbed a bank or anything."

"Have you ever hated anyone?"

"Sure! Who hasn't?"

"God says if you hate someone, it is murder in His eyes. You may not have robbed a bank, but if you have ever taken anything that does not belong to you, no matter what value it is, it is stealing. God's standard of good is much higher than ours. According to God's standards, I would say that we all have broken pretty much every one of the commandments. We have to understand how sinful we are and how far we are below God's standards, and then repent – begging God for forgiveness and turning away from our sins. *Then* we can accept His gift of salvation."

Understanding began to filter into Toby, but pride pushed it away and he almost huffed as he said, "You sound like some preacher or something. Who do you think you are, and what do you know about my sins?"

Rebeca knew there was nothing more she could say, and an uncomfortable silence settled on them. After some time, they both fell asleep, as the last of the drug worked its way through their bloodstreams.

⸺⸺≫●≪⸺⸺

Joe slowly gathered up all his belongings, then moved onto Toby's things. That did not take him long, as Toby was considerably tidier than himself. He put the two bags on his bed, then went into Rebeca's room. Gwen's mother had said Rebeca could have whatever she wanted when Gwen and her mom took her shopping, but Rebeca insisted she needed very few items. Even then, Gwen chose a few more pieces of clothing for her. Gwen could not understand how someone could need so few clothes. Rebeca was very tidy and only a few items needed to be put into her bag. He took a quick walk around then went into the bathroom again for a last check. He noticed a T-shirt hanging on the back of the door, and as he took it off the hook he unconsciously held it close to his face and closed his eyes. A tear threatened to escape as he breathed deeply, surprised at how he could smell her, even when she did not wear perfume.

"Please God, help us find them," he whispered, and as he voiced his request, again he was he struck by the thought that he had no right to ask anything of God.

It took him two trips to take everything to the car before he went to the front desk and checked out. Soon he was heading down the highway back to Ellie's and, true to her word, a pot of chilli with warm crusty garlic bread was waiting for him on his return. None of them really felt like eating, but they ate the meal leaving plenty left over for Caleb.

After tidying the kitchen, Ellie made some coffee and hot chocolate and they sat down in the living room to discuss the plans for the next day.

"I want to go back to Elena's place in the morning," began Joe. "I didn't actually see the woman, so she won't know who I am. I can either just come clean or I can make something up. I just don't know what would be best."

"Well," said Pamela, "Aunt Ellie" — she glanced over at her aunt — "will probably say you should tell the truth, but quite honestly," she chuckled with worried eyes, "I think you should make up a story. If those cops were acting weirdly and something odd is going on, or if you think something odd is going on, whatever that may be, well — if this Elena knows anything and did not tell the police, then something is fishy and I just don't think you should be honest if something is fishy about her." She took a sip of her hot chocolate, staring at the froth as though she would find answers in it. Joe half smiled at her and nodded his head.

Benito yawned loudly and everyone looked at him.

"You can go to bed if we are boring you, kid." Joe glared at Benito who looked nervously back at him.

"I ... uh ... I ..." he stammered, not wanting to say how tired he was. He felt he shouldn't be tired when Toby and Rebeca were missing and who knew what had happened to them, but he was. Since he had escaped from his uncle this time, he had felt quite relaxed and, although he knew he should be worried about his friends, his selfishness had again taken over and he had actually been feeling happy, not having to worry about what his uncle would do to him.

Ellie put her hand on Benito's shoulder, who was sitting next to her, and spoke softly, "It is okay to be tired, Benito, it has been a long and tiring day. You go on up to bed. Caleb will go with Joe in the morning, so you do not need to be involved in the plans."

Benito looked gratefully at her and glanced once more at Joe who's dark eyes always seemed to grow darker when he had Benito in view. He jumped up and trotted up the stairs before Joe could say anything more to him. Ellie said nothing to Joe, and he sensed her disapproval, but refused to apologise for his attitude towards Benito. *The kid was so difficult to like.*

"So what do you think you could say to the woman?" Pamela broke the silence. "You could tell her you are lost, or maybe you lost a dog, or maybe you ran out of gas; but then maybe she doesn't have any gas, though you could borrow her phone to call for help – which would get you inside her house, which being lost or looking for a lost dog wouldn't." She took a breath, "Unless she had a map so that she could show you where you were, because your phones aren't working so you can't find your position on your phone – then being lost would be all right. But of course you don't know if she has a map, so that wouldn't guarantee you getting into her house."

Joe tried to process all of what Pamela said and decide if there was anything of merit that he could use to incorporate into a feasible plan. Using the phone could work somehow, since he could always say his ran out of battery.

Pamela's eyes lit up. "How about you and Caleb are out walking, and you sprain your ankle? That way you could go in the house to use her phone AND rest while someone came to get you? Though who goes out without their cell phones? Especially if it is *both* of you without one." She wrinkled her face, "I suppose you could always pull the 'I can't get a signal' trick. There are still lots of places where phone signal is bad."

Joe nodded his approval and let the idea mull around in his head as he drank his coffee. Pamela opened her mouth a couple of times like she was going to add something, but then frowned as more ideas popped in her head and then she dismissed them.

"What time is Uncle Caleb going to be home?" Pamela put her empty cup down on the coffee table in front of her.

"Probably not until 1:00 in the morning, honey. You might as well go on up to bed. You've been really helpful." Ellie leaned over and gave her niece a long hug, then kissed her on her cheek.

"Love you lots, Auntie Ellie," Pamela stood up and looked over at Joe, "Goodnight Joe. Don't worry, I'm sure they'll soon be back safely. They probably just got lost and will soon come across a house to get help." She cringed at her platitudes, but felt she needed to say something and didn't think Joe was receptive to her saying she would be praying for them – which of course, she would be doing.

"You need your rest, Joe," said Ellie finally. "You want to be clear-headed for tomorrow."

Joe put his cup on the table beside him and let out a long breath before standing and looking at Ellie. "Thank you, Ellie. You are very kind. Thank you for all your help."

Ellie smiled sadly and reached out to squeeze his hand, then grabbed the cups and walked slowly into the kitchen as Joe made his way upstairs.

Benito was not quite asleep when Joe came in the room, but he kept his eyes shut, even though Joe did not turn on the light. He moved about the room quietly before climbing into the other bed.

Benito's thoughts turned to his mom, remembering Tadeo's threats about her rent, and began worrying about her. He prayed to Toby's God to make her better, and wondered again if He would one day be 'his' God.

Joe began snoring and Benito looked out the window at the night sky that never became completely dark because of the lights of the city. He stared for some time, letting his thoughts run randomly over Rebeca and Toby's whereabouts, his mom and Tadeo, Joe, and these new kind people, Pamela and Ellie. He drifted off but woke for a moment when he heard a car pull in the drive and the front door open and shut, then fell into a deep sleep.

———⟫●⟪———

A bright light streamed down and shone onto Toby and Rebeca who awoke and squinted up as the hatch opened fully. They both ached from lying on the cold hard floor and stretched their limbs as they waited to see what would happen.

"Would you like some breakfast?" Elena's voice called down cheerfully. "I've made some porridge, come up and have some."

Toby and Rebeca looked at each other curiously and Toby stood first, before helping Rebeca to her feet, forgetting the friction between them from earlier. He held her hand as he walked to the bottom of the steps and looked up to see Elena and Pumpkin peering down at them. Elena stood back and Pumpkin followed suit, while again Toby and Rebeca looked at each other, unsure of how to react. Toby, having gone into protective mode again, put his hand out to Rebeca to motion her to wait while he climbed warily up the steps. Finally reaching the top and standing on the wooden kitchen floor, he eyed Pumpkin who had settled back down on the floor again. Toby looked down at Rebeca and he motioned for her to follow. Elena let the hatch door slam shut behind Rebeca and pulled the rug over it. She motioned toward the chairs and table where a pot of porridge was sat in the middle.

"Sit! Sit!" She commanded and Pumpkin let out a quiet growl, encouraging them to do as his mistress commanded. The two teenagers promptly sat down at the table and three bowls were promptly put on the table, along with three spoons, a ceramic jug of milk and a pot of honey. Elena grinned widely as she looked from Toby to Rebeca and then threw her head back as she let out a loud laugh. They looked at each other, then stared worriedly back at Elena, wondering if the porridge would be poisoned.

Elena took a large spoon and scooped some porridge into each of their bowls, then chuckled as she put some into a bowl in front of her. She grabbed the milk and poured it over her porridge, handing the jug to Rebeca, who took it hesitantly, and watched Elena take a few mouthfuls before pouring some into her bowl. Toby's stomach growled as he did likewise. Elena then spooned out a large scoop of honey and handed it to Rebeca. After she and Toby put the honey on their porridge, they locked eyes again, wondering what was happening. They watched and waited until Elena had started eating, then they cautiously followed suit. Toby and Rebeca were silent as they ate their breakfast, but Elena chattered nonchalantly about the chickens and how many eggs she should let become chicks, as though kidnapping two teenagers was a perfectly ordinary occurrence.

"Where is Emmie?" Toby asked looking around the kitchen. He started to get up but immediately sat back down again as Pumpkin pressed his wet nose against his leg, a low growl reverberating in his throat.

"She's resting," Elena said simply, then changed the subject. "The hen house needs cleaning," she said, "After breakfast, I'll show you two how do to it." She took a large mouthful of porridge, then jumped up. "I nearly forgot your juice."

Toby and Rebeca exchanged glances and Toby wondered silently to himself, *she kidnapped us so we could clean her hen house?*

Scurrying across to the counter where a jug of orange juice stood, she bent down, reached in the cupboard, and took out two glasses. She poured the juice where she stood and brought the glasses over to the teenagers who looked at the juice warily. A broad smile spread across the woman's face as she turned around and poured another glass for herself. Again Toby and Rebeca waited until she had consumed some first before they drank theirs. Being very thirsty, they each drank all of juice before they put their glasses down again and turned back to finish their porridge. Elena put down her spoon and gave a penetrating look at Toby and he felt drawn to stare back into her dark brown eyes. Holding his stare, Elena began tapping with her finger nails on the wooden table in a rhythmic pattern: tap tap tap tap, and for the first time, Toby noticed the loud ticking of a clock that hung on the wall above one of the sofas. For some reason, he became totally consumed by the sound, like it was entering his head and ticking inside him as his heart began beating in unison with it.

Elena turned to face Rebeca to repeat her actions. Rebeca was drawn to her stare and the tapping of her nails for a few moments, but suddenly, Rebeca turned to Toby, feeling like she had just entered a dream. She blinked and struggled to remain conscious, but then realised she wasn't falling asleep after all. Elena frowned and tapped her finger against her mouth as she watched Rebeca. After a moment, Elena seemed to come to a decision and turned back to Toby.

"I expect you'll be wanting to do the dishes now," she said simply.

"Of course," agreed Toby, suddenly filled with a need to do the dishes, like it was the most important thing he could do. He looked over at Rebeca, who just looked confused, but she got up when Toby did, and they gathered the dishes and went to the sink. Elena nodded to herself thoughtfully as she watched Rebeca follow Toby.

"There is hot water in the kettle hanging over the fire outside," Elena began, then added, "It is too hot for a fire indoors today."

"Yes," Toby said simply, and headed out the door to the open fire that was burning by the path which led to the boat. Rebeca followed him, feeling light-headed. When they got to the fire, as Toby bent down to grab the kettle, Rebeca whispered.

"We are far enough away from the house. We could make a run for it before the dog notices us going."

Toby turned to her and spoke sharply, "Rebeca! We *must* do the dishes!" And with that, took the kettle back towards the house. Rebeca watched him for a moment, bewildered. She could sneak away by herself and go get help. Rebeca looked at the path then back towards Toby as he walked up the steps and disappeared from the bright sun into the kitchen. A haze settled over her thoughts and as she tried to shake it away, she made her decision. She couldn't leave Toby. She could not guarantee that he would still be here by the time she got help and returned. If she left, most certainly Elena would know what she was up to and leave with Toby to somewhere else. So Rebeca strolled back to the house, trying desperately to keep her mind focused. The woman must have drugged them again, but Rebeca was not sure how.

By the time Rebeca got back inside the house, Toby already had the sink filled with water and soap and was busily washing the dishes. Rebeca stood beside him, grabbed a tea towel that was on the counter and began drying. Elena remained at the table watching them, and when they were done, she spoke in a gentle but firm voice.

"Toby and Rebeca …"

They both looked at her; Toby hanging on her every word, Rebeca untrusting and trying to shake the fog in her mind.

"You know how I have helped you when your families did not want you to be together; how I came to your rescue when you came to me here to hide from them. They want to keep you apart, but here, I will protect you, I will keep you both safe and you will always be together. I've taken you in like you were my own children and I will always watch out for you."

"Yes, Aunt Elena!" answered Toby enthusiastically as he grabbed Rebeca's hand and looked at her lovingly. "They wanted to separate us, but we won't let them." He turned to Elena, "*You* won't let them. We owe you so much!"

Confusion settled on Rebeca as she looked at Toby. She heard his and Elena's words. She knew they didn't make sense, but she was struggling to understand why.

"We will go outside and clean the hen house, my dears."

Toby felt an overwhelming yearning to please Elena. He could not understand how he had thought her evil. She was such a lovely woman and he would do whatever she asked to show his affection as if she was truly his aunt. She really had been so good to help them and he wanted to repay her kindness.

"Oh, yes, Aunt Elena, I do want to help you."

Elena stood up and Toby followed her eagerly out of the house with Rebeca trundling slowly after them. Pumpkin trotted keenly behind, wondering if he would be getting chicken again today for his dinner.

———❦———

Joe woke early and glanced over at Benito who was deep in sleep. A sneer formed on Joe's lips, and for a brief moment, regret washed over him. Why did he feel such contempt for the kid? Why couldn't he forgive Benito for what he had done to his brother? After all, Toby had held no bad feelings towards him. Toby actually seemed to like him.

A faint smile appeared on Benito's lips as he dreamed, and the regret disappeared as suddenly as it had come. How could his brother forgive Benito? How could he like him? Joe let out a deep sigh and went to the en suite bathroom to wash and get dressed.

Ten minutes later, he was downstairs in the kitchen sitting at the table and getting to know Ellie's husband who was sat at the head of the large table, drinking a cup of coffee. Ellie and Pamela were busy at the counter making pancakes and bacon on a large electric griddle, but Ellie brought over a cup of coffee and placed it in front of Joe. She did not ask where Benito was, and Joe assumed she knew he was probably still sleeping and did not want to start off any aggravation with Joe.

Even sitting down, Joe could tell that Caleb was a tall man. Joe was six foot two, and he figured Caleb had to be another four or five inches taller than himself. He had broad shoulders and was muscular – not like someone who worked out at the gym and drank protein shakes, but with a natural, solid physique that spoke of physical work. He had light brown hair and twinkling grey eyes, with a clean shaven, friendly face. Joe rubbed his hand across his stubbly chin. He hadn't shaved in a couple of days, but he didn't have a heavy beard.

Joe discovered Caleb was in construction. He had started as a builder and quickly worked his way up to be a manager and then decided to borrow some money and invest in his own construction company. He had about fifty staff, but he employed someone to be a CEO, as he preferred to continue to work with his hands. He still kept an eye on the business, but on a day to day basis he was on site with the other workers.

Ellie came to the table with a plate full of pancakes and Pamela brought the bacon as they sat down to join the men. Orange and apple juice were in jugs in the centre of the table. Ellie, Caleb and Pamela bowed their heads and Caleb began praying before Joe realised what they were doing. Shame filled him as he realised again how little he had spoken to God lately. After thanking God for the food, Caleb pleaded with God to help them find Toby and Rebeca and to guide them in everything they did.

Joe added his 'amen' to Ellie and Pamela's, wondering why God would again allow something bad to happen to his brother. Of course, he didn't know something bad had happened to them, but he felt certain it had.

"May I have the pancakes, please, Pamela?" asked Joe.

Pamela offered the plate of pancakes to Joe, who took a couple, then passed the plate to Caleb. The same was done with the bacon, then Pamela passed Joe the syrup who took it and looked down at his food with uncertainty.

"Uh, is this meant to go on my pancakes or my bacon?" He asked, and Pamela giggled.

"Both!"

Joe frowned, wishing there was brown sauce, but decided to try the syrup. He poured it over his breakfast sparingly then handed it along to Caleb who poured it over like it was gravy. Joe raised his eyebrows as he watched, but said nothing. He looked back at his food. He really didn't feel like eating, but he began cutting his food as he spoke to Caleb.

"I was planning on heading out as soon as I have finished breakfast. Are you going to join me?" Joe took a mouthful of bacon and pancake and was surprised at the pleasant taste of the sweet syrup mixed with the salty bacon.

Caleb swallowed his food and washed it down with a mouthful of coffee before answering. "Well, it's only 8:00, and I don't rightly believe it's polite to show up on someone's doorstep before 9:00. I'm thinking we'd be better off leaving in about forty-five minutes. Ellie can drop us off and then pick us up again in half an hour or wait until we call her."

"I wasn't too worried about being polite," said Joe curtly.

Caleb ignored Joe's tone and replied, "I just think we don't want to get the woman suspicious, and if we want her to be obligin' in case she might know something, it's best to just act like two polite men out walkin'."

Joe thought for a moment before replying, "I suppose you have a point. I just feel like every moment we delay, it is less likely we'll find them and I don't think you realise how I feel – did Ellie tell you what happened to Toby when that weasel upstairs tricked my brother into ending up in Nicaragua where some terrible things happened to him?" Joe paused, then added, "In fact, you could say he is in trouble again because of that louse, because if Toby hadn't gone to Nicaragua, he would never have met this monkey." Joe stabbed his pancakes angrily with his fork and brought it up to his mouth. "That kid ...".

Caleb held his hand up and looked directly at Joe. "Now hold on there now, son. You ever heard of that sayin': holding bitterness in yor heart is like drinkin' poison and expectin' the other person to die? Besides, don't you know God ...".

"Don't call me 'son' – you must only be a couple of years older than me." Joe put his cup down loudly on the table. He took a deep breath before continuing, "I am really thankful that you and your wife have been so kind to us and that you have offered to help, but I don't need any of your preaching." He looked at Caleb angrily and added, "And I don't actually need your help, either." Joe crossed his arms over his chest defiantly. Pamela opened her mouth to speak but closed it when Ellie looked across at her and silently shook her head.

Caleb took a long drink of coffee before placing his cup gently on the table. Then, leaning back in a relaxed manner, he rested his elbows on the arms of the chair and folded his hands in front of him. The corners of his mouth turned up slightly and a faint twinkle appeared in his eyes as he squinted amiably at Joe.

"So, you're not a believer?" Caleb asked in a humble but purposeful voice, ignoring Joe's other words.

Joe was not interested in a debate with this man, but his anxiousness for his brother and Rebeca bubbled up inside of him and he lashed out. "I believe there is a God up there," Joe pointed upwards, "and I used to think He was in control and that He cared, but these past weeks have shown me otherwise!"

Caleb nodded thoughtfully, keeping eye contact with Joe. "Hmmmmmm ...". Caleb nodded again, but said nothing.

"What do you mean, 'hmmmmm'??!" Joe exploded and Caleb tilted his head, staying completely composed.

"So, your faith is only as good as your circumstances."

It was a statement, not a question, and Joe opened his mouth to retort, but a niggle of acknowledgement prevented him, and a verse from the book of Job came unbidden into his head: "Shall we accept good from God and not trouble?" It didn't make sense; and yet it did. However, Joe was in no mood to engage in a Bible lesson with this fellow, so instead, he stood up, collected his dishes and went across the kitchen to put them in the dishwasher.

"I'll wait outside," Joe said simply and strode outside, plonking himself on a chair by the pool.

He half expected Caleb to come out and carry on the conversation, trying to persuade him that he should have more trust in God. Five minutes later, he let out his breath, relieved that Caleb had not followed him out.

Just when Joe was beginning to get impatient and had nearly decided that he would go by himself, Caleb and Ellie came out the back door. Joe stood up and walked over to join them as they walked around to the front of the house and got in Caleb's metallic grey Golf GTI, with Ellie getting in the driver's seat.

The talk was light on the journey as they went over the plan, then as they got closer, Joe gave them directions. Ellie pulled up on the side as they came up to the entrance of Elena's drive. She put the car in park and started to say something, but Caleb stopped her by leaning over to give her a kiss, then he and Joe got out of the car and headed down the rough road.

———◆———

Toby worked enthusiastically in the small building as he raked and shovelled the dirty straw until the large bucket was full. Elena had disappeared back into the house a few minutes earlier, and Rebeca stood outside the hen house, watching Toby, trying to fathom what had happened to him. Lost in thought, Rebeca jumped as Elena came up behind her carrying three glasses of freshly squeezed lemonade on a tray.

"I thought you would like a drink," she smiled sweetly at Rebeca and called to Toby, "Come now, dear, have a break from your work."

Toby came out and squinted at the bright light, and grinned at Elena. "That is kind of you, Aunt Elena." He took the glass nearest him as she offered the drinks.

Elena turned to Rebeca, handing out the tray. Rebeca looked at the glass that was nearest her, then looked at Elena. Her head was beginning to clear and Rebeca looked at the woman suspiciously, taking the glass that was nearest Elena. Toby had already drank his, and Rebeca stood waiting while Elena took the remaining glass and drank the entire contents. Finally, Rebeca drank from the glass in her hand, surprised at how thirsty she was. Soon, all three glasses were back on the tray and Elena stood watching Rebeca, who suddenly realised she had been tricked as she grew slightly dizzy.

"You are as difficult as the monkey. We mustn't leave it so long between doses for you, I think," Elena said quietly to herself and a determined grin spread across the woman's face as she patted Rebeca on the arm. Instantly, her countenance changed and she spoke loudly and urgently to the teenagers.

"Your brother is coming, Toby! He is coming to take away Rebeca!"

Toby looked frantically at Rebeca and grabbed her hand. "No!" He shouted, pulling her close.

"Shhh!" Elena put a finger to her lips, "He'll hear you!" She looked behind the hen house to where the trees and undergrowth were very thick. "Hurry! Take Rebeca and go hide, now!"

Toby turned quickly and ran into the trees, dragging Rebeca behind him. She was no longer dizzy, but could not remember where she was or what she and Toby were doing. Her heart was beating quickly as she was pulled along by Toby, trying to remember. Remember – why couldn't she remember anything other than Toby? Who else could she remember? Oh, her father! Where was her father? Where were she and Toby? Something was wrong – what was it? Why were they running to hide?

Suddenly, Toby stopped and yanked Rebeca to a halt. He turned around to face the direction of the house, and pulled Rebeca down with him as he threw himself on the ground below some bushes.

"Oh Rebeca, I love you!" Toby whispered in her ear and wrapped his arms tightly around her as he listened intently. Rebeca could not understand. She knew she wanted to hear him say that, but it did not feel right for some reason. Something was wrong – what was wrong? Why couldn't she remember?

A few moments later, they heard a voice. "Excuse me ma'am, I wonder if you could help us?" Toby frowned. That wasn't his brother's voice. Who was that? He got up on his hands and knees and peeked over the green leaves. He saw Joe leaning on a strange man's shoulder, lifting up his right foot slightly. "We were out looking for a couple of our friends that got lost and my friend twisted his ankle. We don't seem to have a signal on our phone to call for help. Can we borrow yours?"

Elena stood with her hands on her hips and Pumpkin was at her side staring intently at the two men. "I don't have a phone," she said simply.

Joe was looking around the area discreetly, trying to see any signs of his brother or Rebeca. "Please, could we just sit inside and rest my foot a bit?" He burst out, and Rebeca's brain cleared for a moment.

"Jo …". She started to call out his name, but Toby turned back to her and covered her mouth.

"No, Rebeca, he's going to take you away from me." He whispered.

Rebeca looked into Toby's dark brown eyes that pleaded with her. *That did not make sense*, she thought. *Joe would not do that. Would he?* Finally, she nodded to Toby and gently took his hand off her mouth.

Joe turned at the sounds coming from the bushes and Elena looked over behind the hen house. "Sounds like that otter's back," said Elena; then, "Come on, I have some herbs that will help your ankle." She waved them along beside her as she made her way into her house. Joe turned towards the sound, but Pumpkin gave a little snarl and Joe could feel the dog's breath on the back of his leg, so he and Caleb followed the woman inside.

"Help your friend over there." Elena spoke to Caleb as she pointed to the sofa nearest them. Caleb helped Joe over to the sofa and Elena went over to her cupboards and took out some herbs. She busied herself mixing some ingredients in a bowl into a paste. She brought the bowl over to Joe and knelt beside him. "Take off your shoe and sock."

Joe complied and suddenly was aware of the fact that his ankle did not look at all injured and thought to himself he should have actually hit it with something to at least make it red. Oddly enough, Elena said nothing as she took the poultice and applied it to Joe's ankle. She took a long cloth and wrapped it around tightly. A heat penetrated Joe's ankle and worked its way down his foot and he believed that if he had hurt himself, this would certainly be healing his injury or at least removing the pain and he responded as such.

"Wow, that is amazing stuff. It feels better already." Joe looked around the kitchen as he spoke, trying desperately to see if he could find any trace of Toby and Rebeca. Elena nodded her head and stood up, taking the bowl back to the sink. Pumpkin came up to Joe and rested his head on his stomach and Joe looked at him curiously. He almost looked gentle, but Joe was certain that one wrong move would show a completely different dog. Joe glanced up at Caleb who was standing beside him, also looking around.

Elena said nothing as she washed up the bowl and put it away. She then made three cups of tea and gave two cups to the men.

"Sit down," Elena spoke firmly to Caleb as she motioned to the kitchen table where she herself sat as well. "Tell me about your missing friends."

"Well, ma'am, they are teenagers, a boy and a girl. They disappeared in this area yesterday around lunch time. We think they might be lost."

Elena smiled at them. "Ah, young love. I remember that." She looked out the window remembering a time long since past. A time when she was sixteen and had run off with her lover. "No doubt after they have had their adventure together, they will come back home." She took a sip of tea.

"They wouldn't do that," said Joe, annoyed, "they aren't like that."

Elena shook her head slowly. "That is what people say all the time. It's always a surprise, but there you go, that is besotted youngsters for you. It's been like that for as long as I can remember." She finished her tea and stood. "I'm sure your ankle is fine to walk on now." She looked over at Joe, and Pumpkin, who had been laying on the floor beside him, stood up and walked towards the door. Caleb took the hint and stood.

"Thank you for your help, ma'am." He walked over to Joe and pretended to help him to his feet.

"It actually feels a lot better now. Thank you." Joe got up and the two of them walked past the dog and headed out the door. The men took one last look around as they walked down the steps and back towards the way they had come, disappointed at the outcome, but both certain that the woman knew where Toby and Rebeca were.

Caleb and Joe walked for five minutes before they felt it was safe to talk, and Caleb reached in his pocket and took out his phone to dial Ellie.

"We'll be back down the lane in ten minutes." Caleb was short and to the point, hanging up before his wife could ask him any questions. He spoke to Joe, "I think we need to go back to the police and insist they search the place."

"That was a woman's voice, I heard in the bushes. And did you hear the whispering? If it hadn't been for that dog, we could have just looked around – she couldn't have stopped us." He looked at Caleb. "Do you have a gun?"

Caleb raised an eyebrow and shook his head. "No, I don't. And if I did, I wouldn't let you go shoot the woman's dog. We don't know for sure that Toby and Rebeca are there. We can't just turn up on someone's property and start shooting – we'll both end up in prison. We'll drop Ellie off back at home and then go back to the police station to see if they can get a warrant to search the area today or early tomorrow morning."

———⊷●⊶———

Rebeca started to get up and Toby pulled her back down. "We need to wait until Aunt Elena tells us it is safe," Toby whispered insistently. He didn't know why, but he felt that she would protect them. He couldn't let his brother take Rebeca away. He wouldn't. He didn't understand why Rebeca was questioning. Couldn't she see what was happening? He looked at her as she scrunched up her face worried and confused, but she remained silent, saying nothing as they waited for Elena to return.

Elena went back in her house after the two men left and headed into her bedroom. The little monkey was awake and huddled between the two pillows on Elena's bed. Elena ignored Emmie and opened the top drawer of her little bedside cupboard and took out the phone. She turned it on and dialled her son's number.

"You have to come today. The boy's brother and another man came today looking for them. They'll be back." She paused as she listened to her son speaking. "I don't know if it is going to work how we planned, but we have to move them to your place immediately. My herb mixture works well, and combined with the hypnosis, it works perfectly on the boy, but the girl is protected by the Great Spirit, Elohim." Elena almost growled as she spoke His name. "I have tried a stronger dose on her, but I do not think it will be feasible to use her. We will probably have to get rid of her and I will change the boy's story for him – his mind is very pliable. Of course we would lose money, but at least we'd have the boy." She paused again, then said, "Yes, I will. We will be ready when you get here." She hung up and tossed the phone on the bed, looking back at the monkey. It would have been nice to keep the little animal – Elena had an affinity for monkeys – but Emmie seemed to have too strong a link to Toby. She sighed, *too bad*.

Elena walked out of the bedroom and left the door open as she went out of her house to find Toby and Rebeca.

"It is safe, now, dears," she said as she approached the edge of the clearing behind the chickens, and Toby immediately got up, pulling Rebeca to her feet. They appeared out of the trees and Elena pointed to the shed.

"There is fresh straw in there, put it in the hen house." She watched as Toby willingly obeyed and Rebeca helped him. When they were finished, she spoke to Rebeca, "There is some feed in the shed, fill up the bowl and make sure they have plenty of water, then lock them all in the enclosure. The rooster is around somewhere; see if you can find him and lock him in with the girls." She then turned to Toby. "Come with me, dear, there is someone who is looking for you." She smiled and Toby followed her inside the house. Emmie was just creeping out the bedroom door and she bounced over to Toby who gave her a loving hug as she jumped into his arms and nuzzled his face. He was always amazed at how she actually seemed to have affection for him.

"Toby, dear, we have a problem with Rebeca." Elena spoke quietly. "You need to convince her how important it is to listen to me. We need to leave and it is important that she does not do anything silly like try to run off. She does not seem to understand that Joe is going to take her back to Nicaragua – you will never see her again."

Toby was rubbing his face in Emmie's fur. He looked at Elena worried, and nodded fervently.

"I have some things to pack up before my son comes to collect us. You go out and speak to Rebeca." Elena shooed Toby out of the house and walked thoughtfully to her bedroom, thinking about what things she would need to take.

Rebeca was just locking the enclosure and she smiled as she saw Emmie sitting on Toby's shoulder with her little hand on top of his head. Toby walked over to Rebeca and took her hand. "I need to talk to you, Rebeca." He sat down on the grass and Rebeca sat down beside him. Emmie jumped off and trundled over to check out the chickens. Toby leaned towards Rebeca, stroking her hair, his eyes looking at her sadly. "Don't you want to be with me, Rebeca?" he asked, bending his head closer to her. She frowned but nodded, trying to pacify him while she struggled to understand what was happening. "I know you don't understand," Toby continued desperately, but we need to listen to Elena. Otherwise Joe will take you back to Nicaragua and we will never see each other again." His face was inches from hers now.

A moment of clarity entered Rebeca at the name of her country. Nicaragua! She opened her mouth to speak, but as she did, Toby leaned down and kissed her cheek. Rebeca became confused again. This wasn't right. She wanted Toby to kiss her, but there was something wrong. What was wrong? His lips met hers and he stroked her cheek, running his fingers through her hair as he pulled her close. For a moment, all Rebeca could think of was the exhilaration of feeling Toby's mouth pressed against hers, his warm breath on her face; then suddenly, she pushed him away.

"No, Toby!"

He sat upright and looked at her surprised, hurt flashing in his confused eyes. "What's wrong, Rebeca?"

Rebeca put her hands over her face, shaking her head. "I don't know, Toby. It just isn't right. My head isn't clear." She spoke as she tried desperately to bring back that clarity she just had. *What was wrong with her?*

Elena watched them through the window and put her finger to her lips. This was not working at all how she had planned. *Maybe if she tried that new herb she had discovered.* Elena opened up the hatch and went down the wooden steps to collect a couple of jars.

A few minutes later, Elena, followed closely by Pumpkin, brought out a tray with two cups of tea to the teenagers who were sat silently on the grass. Putting the tea down beside them she smiled kindly saying, "Have some tea, dears, it is chamomile."

Toby took a cup and immediately drank a big gulp, smiling. Rebeca paused, having an inkling that there was some reason she did not want the tea, but finally brushed away the feeling, took the other cup and had a sip. It tasted delicious and although it was quite warm, she drank it down quickly. She could feel her heart rate drop instantly and a warm comfortable feeling enveloped her.

"Thank you, Elena, yes, this is just what I need." Rebeca smiled at her and placed the cup back on the tray.

Toby nodded, and Elena went back inside smiling to herself. Maybe a different approach was just what they had needed.

———⟫●⟪———

Joe's back pocket buzzed and he jumped. What was that? His phone was in his backpack. Then suddenly remembered he still had Toby's phone with him as well. He took it out and clicked to answer. Gwen's perfect face smiled up at him, but it disappeared the moment that she saw Joe's downcast look.

"What's wrong?"

Joe sighed deeply and explained everything that had happened. Gwen's eyes grew big as he spoke and she covered her mouth with both hands, gasping.

"Where are you now?" she asked.

"At the police station. We are going to see if they won't try and do a proper search of this woman's house and property. I wanted to just go shoot the dog," Joe glared at Caleb, "but Caleb here wouldn't let me." He tilted the phone so Gwen could see Caleb, who smiled in a friendly manner. However, the instant he saw her stunning face with full red lips and amazing emerald eyes, his pupils dilated and he found he had to put his hand on his chin to stop his jaw from dropping.

Caleb's usual calm manner sputtered and he could only manage a weak, "Hi!"

Joe looked at him funny then half smiled to himself. *So the perfect man was not so self-controlled after all.*

Gwen smiled then turned her attention back to Joe. "I'll go speak to Daddy and see what he can do – he might have some friends of influence that can get the police down there more interested in helping out." She blew Joe a kiss and winked at him. "Bye hon, talk to you soon – and keep me updated!"

Joe clicked OFF and put the phone back in his pocket. He chuckled smugly as he looked pointedly at Caleb who was still trying to compose himself.

"She's ..." Caleb began.

"Gorgeous?" Joe finished as he raised an eyebrow at Caleb who could only manage to nod.

Just then, Joe's name was called and the two men went up to the desk where an officer was standing waiting for them.

"Hello, I'm officer Bentley," the short, slight man spoke to them in a sympathetic voice. The man thrust out his hand and shook each of their hands with a strength that belied his small stature. "Look, I'm not going to beat about the bush. The officers that went to Mrs Brown's place to look for your two teenagers said they had a thorough look around and they found nothing that would suggest this woman was involved in any criminal behaviour. They've filed a report and it will be passed on to an investigating officer." He squinted his eyes and looked at the two men compassionately, knowing from experience that his response would not be welcomed.

"But we're a very busy police station and the officers put in their report that they felt that as the two youngsters were committing a crime – trespassing and theft of a boat – the likelihood was that they probably ran off together. It will be investigated, but if they don't feel there is any foul play involved, I'm afraid it isn't going to be on the top of the pile. They are both eighteen, so …".

"My brother is only seventeen!" interrupted Joe earnestly, and officer Bentley looked down at the papers he held in his hand.

"Looks like he's eighteen tomorrow, so that makes them both adults and, well …" He pursed his lips and raised his eyebrows, shaking his head slightly. "I'm sorry."

"You incompetent …" Joe looked down at the man and took a step towards him, but Caleb interrupted him and leaned in, grabbing Joe firmly by the shoulders and pulled him back from the officer.

"Thank you, officer," spoke Caleb politely, taking a sideways glance at Joe. "We would appreciate it if you could get them a bit higher in the pile if it is at all possible." He turned to Joe who had pulled Caleb's hands off of him. "Come on, there's nothing else to be done here."

"We're giving up?!" Joe's eyes were wild and his loud voice was attracting the attention of a couple of other officers standing nearby. "I'm not going …".

"Joe, calm down," said Caleb in a loud but restrained voice. He started to put his hands on Joe to guide him out of the station but decided it would be best to keep it verbal. "The only thing that is going to happen if we stay is that you are going to get arrested." He looked Joe in the eyes and pleaded with him, "Let's go. We'll think of something else."

"I know what I'm going to do!" He turned and shouted at officer Bentley who instinctively stepped back. "I'm going to get a gun and shoot that d**** dog!" The two officers who had been watching them moved directly in front of Joe.

"You better calm down son," the one man said, "and just leave now while you still can."

"Are you threatening me?!" Joe's blood was boiling and Caleb was silently praying about what to do.

Finally, Caleb stepped forward and, trying to appeal to any sensibility left inside of the fuming man, said in a calm, controlled voice, "Joe, if you end up in a cell, we won't be able to find them." Joe looked around wildly at everyone in the station who was watching him, and Caleb tried again, "Joe. We need to go."

Seconds passed, and finally, Joe turned around and stormed out the door to the car. Caleb looked around sheepishly at everyone and walked out after him. He got in the car and put the key in the ignition, looking over at Joe who was sat in the passenger seat with his head in his hands. Caleb started to say something, then changed his mind and started the car, making his way back to his house.

By the time they got back, Joe had cooled down, and when they pulled into the drive he finally spoke: "I don't know what to do," he began. "That officer made me so angry. *You* make me so angry. Benito makes me angry. *Everyone* makes me so angry." A deep breath passed through his lips. "I just want to find them."

Caleb nodded his head. "I know," he spoke quietly, "But God …".

"Stop!" Said Joe sharply, "Please stop with the 'God' stuff!" He looked up at Caleb's compassionate face. "I wish I could trust God like you people do. But you don't have a brother missing for the second time. You don't understand how I feel!" Joe glared at Caleb, the fury building up inside of him again. He felt like he was going to explode.

"Actually," began Caleb quietly. "I *do* understand." He paused a moment, waiting to make sure Joe was listening. "Ellie and I lost a little daughter to cot death when she was three months old. Just under a year ago."

Joe's insides twisted and he was overwhelmed with a myriad of emotions. Caleb's eyes were sad, but there was no condemnation of Joe's attitude or words.

Joe's voice cracked as he spoke, "I'm ... sorry, Caleb."

"It's all right," whispered Caleb as his eyes grew watery, "God blessed us with three special months with her." He swallowed hard. "And one day, we will see her again." He managed a faint smile.

The two men sat in silence for a moment until Pamela poked her head out of the front door. "Are you guys coming in, or what? We want to know how you got on!"

The men sat for a moment longer, composing themselves, then they stepped out of the car and Caleb locked it before he followed Joe into the house. Pamela led them into the kitchen where Ellie had a pot of coffee brewing and a pile of fresh rolls along with various fillings on the table. She gave Caleb a kiss as he came into the kitchen.

"How did it go, honey?" she asked, though from the expressions on their faces, she could assume the answer to her question.

Joe sat down heavily in one of the wooden chairs and poured himself a cup of coffee before speaking. He ran a hand threw his thick hair. "Well, it looks like the police are not really interested. Toby is eighteen tomorrow, and since he and Rebeca were trespassing and stole someone's boat, they think the two of them just went off together somewhere for a while."

Ellie frowned as she put a jug of iced tea on the table and sat down beside her husband. She squeezed his hand gently and frowned. "What now?"

"I still think getting a gun is the best option," said Joe as he took a roll and cut it open, stuffing it with chicken and lettuce.

"What?! You can't shoot the woman!" Pamela's horrified face looked from Caleb to Joe. Benito sat in silence, terrified at the very mention of guns and shooting.

"Not the woman, Pamela, the dog." Joe stuffed the roll in his mouth and he chewed, not really tasting anything, as pictures of the dead dog went through his mind. "The woman would be no trouble at all without the dog."

"But what if *she* has a gun," asked Ellie, worry spreading across her face. "An elderly woman on her own could very possibly have a gun for protection."

The picture in Joe's mind quickly changed to a more sinister one than just a dog lying dead on the grass, and he took a drink of iced tea while pondering the idea. A dog, he could kill. But he was not sure he could shoot at an elderly woman.

"I hadn't thought of that," began Joe. "Do many people have a gun in Louisiana?"

"Well, I think about 40% of households in Louisiana have a gun," said Caleb, filling his roll with sliced ham and tomatoes.

"Is it that high?" asked Ellie, concerned. "I had no idea."

"Yup," answered her husband. "So we need to come up with a better idea than just showing up again and shooting the dog."

The phone on the wall rang shrilly and they all jumped. Ellie got up to answer it. "Hello?" She said. "Oh, Hi, Tess, what's up?" Ellie's face grew troubled as she listened to her friend on the other end. "Thanks, Tess, I'll go turn on the news now." She hung up and headed for the radio sat on the counter. "Tess said that Hurricane Martha has shifted direction and is now heading north – towards Louisiana." She reached the radio and turned it on loudly so everyone could hear.

"... now a category 4, has shifted directions and is now heading north. It is expected to land on Louisiana's shores tomorrow afternoon around one o'clock."

Ellie turned off the radio and the kitchen went quiet.

———◦———

Billy came in the kitchen to find his mother sat at the table with two teenagers who were just finishing some soup. A capuchin monkey sat on the table eating some fruit. He scowled, but spoke as pleasantly as he could muster. "You said you'd be ready!"

"Now, now, son. Two minutes washing these dishes up and we'll be off. Don't be rude now, say hello to Toby and Rebeca."

The two teenagers smiled widely up at the medium height dark-skinned man who had just stomped into the kitchen. They both felt very happy and contented and were completely undisturbed by the stocky man's gruff manner.

"Well, at least they don't look like they'll be any trouble!" He chuckled as he raised an eyebrow at the giddy looks on the teenagers' faces.

"No sir," they spoke in unison, and then giggled at each other. Toby put his arm around Rebeca grinning, as he added, "We'll be no trouble at all, sir!"

Ten minutes later, they were all in Billy's five seater truck, with Pumpkin sat in between Rebeca and Toby, taking up the majority of the seat. Emmie warily made herself comfortable on Toby's shoulder that was farthest from the large dog. Two large bags and some boxes were in the very back of the truck. Within minutes, of Billy driving, the two teenagers were fast asleep.

"How much did you give them?" Billy asked his mother accusingly. "They're no good to me if they fall asleep so easily."

She twisted her mouth. "I told you, the girl was giving me problems. I was trying something different and I need to work on the amounts. Besides, we are making a stop that I don't want them to know about. I want the monkey to 'just disappear'." She gave Billy directions and they were shortly driving up the lane towards Adrian Thompson's property.

"Why are we going here?" asked Billy, curiosity finally getting the better of him.

"Gotta keep the neighbours sweet!" Elena grinned and Billy looked at her confused as they pulled up in front of the large house. Pumpkin growled as Luna trotted towards the vehicle.

"Shush, Pumpkin!" Elena climbed out of the truck and patted the dog on the head. Luna wagged his tail, giving Elena's hand a lick then following her up the steps. Adrian opened the door before she got to the last one, scowling at his dog for not barking. Luna whimpered as he sensed his master's displeasure and trotted off before Adrian could shout at him. Adrian watched the dog trot away, then turned his attention to Elena.

"What do you want?" He raised his eyebrows suspiciously at the woman. He didn't know a lot about her, but he had seen and heard some strange things at her place when he was out walking along the edge of their property line.

"I have something that belongs to you, and thought I would return it." She pointed back to the truck and Adrian looked, but Emmie was snuggled on Toby's lap and could not be seen.

"Why would you do that?" he asked warily.

"Just want to be neighbourly," she winked at him. "You scratch my back and I'll scratch yours." She went back to the truck and took out Emmie who was now as unconscious as Toby and Rebeca who were nearly horizontal in the back seat.

Adrian was thrilled to see the little monkey but he kept his composure and squinted at Elena as he spoke slowly, "Ah, I see. I keep my nose out of your business and you keep your nose out of my business."

Elena nodded, "I knew you would see things clearly, my good neighbour." Her smile oozed pure evil and it made the hairs go up on Adrian's back, but he held his hands out as she handed him the little capuchin.

"What's wrong with her?" he asked dubiously.

"I think she ate a bad fig. She should be just fine in an hour or two!" Elena gave a wave and hopped back in the truck.

"If she doesn't wake up, I'll be visiting you later!" Adrian called out, feeling quite certain that no fig was involved in the little capuchin's unconscious state.

Adrian stood cradling the little monkey, watching Billy turn his truck in the turning circle and drive off, before carrying the little animal to the enclosure.

Twenty minutes later, they arrived at Billy's place. Billy and Elena got out of the truck and Billy grabbed the bags from the back. Pumpkin jumped out as well, and the two teenagers slumped together, still unconscious. Mother and son left the two of them sleeping while they took the bags through the little path that opened up to a setting that looked exactly like Elena's place. Complete with chickens. Pumpkin barked happily and trotted up to the enclosure.

"He's hungry, Billy."

Billy rolled his eyes and opened the enclosure. One keen chicken burst out and flapped itself in front of Pumpkin. Billy glanced over at his mother who nodded her head.

"Yes, Pumpkin, dinner!"

Pumpkin didn't need to be told twice. He grabbed the chicken by the throat and shook it vigorously. Another chicken that had been heading out through the wire stopped when she saw what happened, then turned around and scooted up the ramp and inside the hen house.

"I am, too," growled Billy.

"I'll make some lunch while you get the two kids," spoke Elena as she climbed the steps to the house. Billy sauntered behind the house and soon came back with Rebeca slumped over his shoulder. He stepped into the kitchen and let her fall onto one of the sofas before going back to his truck and collecting the boy.

Soup and bread were waiting on the table for him, along with a cup of black coffee. After dropping Toby on the other sofa, he sat down and began eating. His mother's food was always delicious. Billy was not a good cook and tended to buy ready cooked meals or eat in a little cafe that was only five minutes up the road.

"You've messed me up, ma," Billy frowned at Elena as he ripped off some bread and dipped it in his soup. "The boss ain't expecting them until next week." He wiped his mouth with the back of his hand and Elena grimaced.

"Such manners, Billy, that isn't what I taught you. Here's a napkin."

She came over to the table and handed him a cloth napkin. Billy scowled, but took the napkin and wiped his mouth half-heartedly, crumpling the cloth up and putting it on the table. He dipped in another sizeable piece of bread and stuffed it in his large mouth as some of the soup dripped down his chin.

"There is no reason they can't they stay here until next week," said Elena with authority. "That is the whole point of having our places the same – we can swap back and forth, in case of trouble – while I 'educate' the dears. It's not my fault the boy's brother and his friend came looking for them."

"Actually, it IS your fault," began Billy harshly, then caught himself as he added more meekly, "Why didn't you just 'do your thing' like you normally do?" He put the bowl up to his mouth and gulped down the rest of the soup. Elena smacked him on the back of the head making him bang his mouth on the edge of the bowl and he snarled at her, "Ma! What're you doin'? Ya nearly broke my teeth!"

"Did I ever teach you to drink your soup out of the bowl? Where did ya pick up such manners, boy?!" She grabbed the bowl out of his hands and slammed it on the table loudly, splashing soup on the table. "Now look what y'all done made me do!" She scurried over to the sink and grabbed a cloth, then wiped up the mess. "And I *did* 'do my thing' on the policemen, but then the brother and that man turned up. I wasn't prepared for them." She paused a moment, then looked at him suspiciously, "*Why* can't they stay here until next week?"

A mischievous grin spread across Billy's face. "I got me a girlfriend."

"Aww, Billy, that's wonderful!" She bent down and kissed him on the head.

"Y'all 'r gonna like her, ma!" He finished the rest of the bread and drank the last of his coffee. "But she doesn't know about my people tradin' work, yet. I gotta break her in slowly."

"Well, just don't bring her here, then."

"She's been asking to see my place, ma, I promised I'd bring her here tomorrow. If I say she can't she might think somethin's up."

Elena looked at Toby and Rebeca sleeping peacefully on the sofas. "Well, the boy was easy, he could be placed in a situation straight away. But the girl is going to take a bit more time. We want to get paid for both of them, don't we? There's a big difference between $10,000 and $20,000 – especially when we are splitting the money! Tell your girlfriend you ain't well – you're sick or somethin'." She grinned, "I could give you something to make you sick!" Elena threw her head back and laughed heartily. Billy looked at her worriedly. He felt quite sure his mother would be happy to practise her herbal medicines on him.

"Okay, I'll call her. But it don't matter too much about the girl, ma," he looked over at Rebeca. "We could still be paid for her. The boss could just take care of her like the others he buys. Besides, I got my eye on a couple of homeless teenagers I saw in New Orleans. So if this girl ain't sorted in a couple of days, and you don't want to sell her as she is, I'll get rid of her and we can just sell the boy. I've already spoken to these two others a few times, and I'm pretty sure I can get them to your place by next week."

Elena grinned wickedly. "I've brought some new plants with me I want to try out on the girl. I've been learning a lot about the way different plants affect the mind. I thought I knew it all – my mamma taught me a lot, but she taught me more about incantations than plants. She had her favourite few plants that she always used. I've really enjoyed the chance to experiment. But I do need that money so's I can get me some plants from Africa that I've heard about. Your sister told me about them, but I need to use them quite fresh so they have to come by personal courier and – wouldn't you know it – Trina said they want lotsa money to bring me the stuff over." She scratched her nose and looked out the window thinking about it. "That just fills me with some excitement – I might even be able to grow some of the plants here! Yes sirree – think of the things I'll be able to do!"

"Well, I just wanna buy me a big house on a big piece of property and have some servants – heck! Maybe I'll buy some of the servants *you* produce!" They both laughed at the thought, then turned as they heard Toby moaning, but he still had his eyes closed.

"Aw, son, don't you know – I'd prepare some for free for ya!" She gave him a big hug and stood on her tiptoes to kiss him on the cheek. "Now I gotta mix somethin' special for the girl and we should see pretty quickly if it is going to work. If not, I can't possibly sell faulty stock, but I do know where there is some hungry alligators!" She patted Billy on the back, tittering at herself, and went to work with her herbs, hoping to be finished before Rebeca and Toby were fully awake.

"I don't have a very good signal right here at the house," Billy said, "I'm gonna go stand by my truck – for some reason I get a full signal right in the spot where I park. I'm gonna tell Britney I ain't feelin' well." He moaned as he spoke, "I ain't feelin' so well, mama …". He looked at Elena who smiled.

"That sounds perfect, honey. Remember to tell her you don't know what it is and it may be contagious, so she won't come 'round to see ya. Some young girls wanna take care of their men folk – I don't know why, but there it is!"

Billy nodded as he walked out the door and headed to his truck to call Britney. He almost skipped at the thought of her as he walked – she was one gorgeous lady!

By the time Billy came back, Elena was sat beside Rebeca, giving her some soup and bread. "Rebeca is feeling quite tired," Elena began, "I think she is coming down with that flu that has been going around, so I have made her my special soup to perk her up!"

"I couldn't get a hold of Britney, so I left her a message. You'd have been proud of me ma, I sounded sooo sick!" He laughed and Elena squinted at him angrily as Rebeca looked at him confused. Billy stuttered, "I … uh … I gotta go feed them chickens!" Billy went out the door and Toby moaned again, this time opening his eyes and looking over at Rebeca and Elena. He smiled tiredly at them.

"That smells delicious, Aunt Elena," Toby said as he sat up. He looked over at Rebeca and smiled weakly, his stomach growling.

"Oh! I have something else for you, Toby. Just let me finish helping Rebeca – she is feeling quite weak – I think she has the flu – and I will get yours. Billy had some already and I am keeping it warm on the fire." She gave Rebeca the last spoonful, then stood up and went to the fire to get Toby some soup. She took out some bread and put both on the table for him. Toby sat down and began eating hungrily.

A few minutes later, he looked around. "Where is Emmie?" he asked, and Elena glanced around as if to try and find the little monkey.

"She was here a minute ago. Maybe she just went out to investigate! Monkeys are curious animals."

"Could I get a glass of water, please?" asked Rebeca.

Elena nodded and took out a large glass, filling it to the top with water. Billy's water came directly off the main supply since he lived so close to the city. Elena didn't think it tasted nearly as good as hers. She thought it tasted full of chemicals. Although hers had a little earthy tang to it, she felt it tasted a lot more natural.

Elena handed Rebeca the glass. She took a sip, then stood up gingerly.

"I think I will go outside for a little walk and some fresh air," Rebeca said as she walked across the floor slowly and made her way out the door and towards the chicken house.

Elena decided to ignore Rebeca for the moment and focus on Toby, reinforcing the thoughts and suggestions she had been giving him. He really was an easy subject: it was almost not enjoyable. But then, Rebeca was so difficult! Elena enjoyed a challenge, but she feared she was fighting a losing battle against someone who had protection from the Great

Spirit. Maybe for Rebeca, Elena needed to rely more on the powers bestowed on her by the dark angel, as her mother had done. She would have to find the right balance.

Outside, Rebeca's stomach started churning. Holding her water carefully she hurried behind the hen house and into the bushes. She didn't want to be sick where someone might step in it. She put her glass on the ground and immediately she bent over, falling on her knees and almost convulsing with the force of her stomach pushing up the unwanted contents of her stomach. She took the glass of water and had a sip to rinse out her mouth, then gulped down the rest of the water thirstily, only to bring that up as well, seconds later. She stayed kneeling for a few moments, breathing deeply, and as she did so, memories of her father and her village came rushing back to her. Slowly she stood, holding a tree branch to steady herself. Pumpkin came up to her, sniffing and as his wet nose touched her leg, a flash of Elena's cruel smile appeared in her mind, and Rebeca remembered what the woman was doing to them. She had been drugging them. And hypnotising them – or Toby, rather. For some reason, the hypnosis part of the woman's manipulations did not seem to work on her, and Rebeca wondered why.

"Oh, Father God, help me. Help me to know what to do – please help us," she whispered barely audibly and Pumpkin looked up at her and whined before scurrying away to chase some chickens. Rebeca still felt slightly sick to her stomach and her brain was still slightly fuzzy, but she realised she needed to continue to pretend, for the moment, that she had not just expelled her food, and the drug that had almost certainly been put in it, was now in her system. She went back inside and asked Elena for another drink of water. Elena was busy with Toby, so she did not really pay much attention to Rebeca as she gave her another glassful and Rebeca walked outside with it. She went back to the same spot, downed the glass of water and waited. It wasn't long before the final poisoned contents left her body and she sat down on the grass as her mind slowly cleared, and she began to form a plan of escape in her mind.

CHAPTER 10

"We can still go back tonight," said Joe. "I have an idea." Everyone at the table looked at him expectantly and he continued, "What about we poison some meat? We can drop it on the ground by the house then go off and hide until the dog eats it."

"But the woman still might have a gun," pointed out Ellie anxiously.

Caleb thought about it, and warmed to Joe's idea. "Yes, but if we poison the meat with something that takes a little while to take effect, we can wait until she is sleeping. The dog will be inside with her, so she will feel secure. We'll have a better chance of sneaking up on her and …".

"And what, Caleb? Tackle an elderly woman to the ground before she grabs a gun? What if you hurt her?"

Caleb and Joe looked at her with raised eyebrows.

"We'll be gentle when we tackle her," Caleb smiled childlike at his wife. Ellie was not in the least bit impressed at her husband's attempt to pacify her.

"Perhaps," began Pamela, "You can have a really good look around the place, first. If the dog is unconscious, and the woman is sleeping, you should be able to do that, have a really good look around. You could peek in the windows and in the outbuildings and all around before … before you tackle her … gently." She smiled at her idea and looked at the adults' faces. Two of them were nodding, but Ellie was still not convinced.

"Caleb, I …" she stumbled, "No. I don't like it. One or both of you might get shot. No."

Caleb studied his wife's concerned face thoughtfully. Finally, he made up his mind and, pushing his chair away from the table, stood and strode determinedly out of the kitchen to the front door. "Come on, Joe, we need to find something to poison a dog. I've got some steak in the freezer."

Joe glanced at Ellie's angry face before darting out of the kitchen and following Caleb out of the house. Just as they were about to drive off, Benito ran out of the house waving at them. "Wait! I've got something!"

The two men looked at Benito questioningly.

"I have some sleeping tablets. My uncle gets them for me. I had some in my pocket when I ran away from him – six. Will that be enough?"

Caleb and Joe smiled at each other and nodded heartily. They got out of the car and Benito ran up the stairs to get his pills. He was soon back down and found the men in the kitchen defrosting the steak in the microwave. He looked around the kitchen for Ellie and Pamela, and Caleb answered his unasked question, "They went grocery shopping."

When the steak was defrosted, Caleb took a sharp knife and slit it nearly in half, letting it sit on the plate like an open book. He washed his hands then took the white pills that Benito handed over, and ground them into a powder in a bowl. Then he sprinkled it over the steak 'book' and closed it up before putting it in a small plastic bag. He looked up at the clock.

"I say we wait an hour and go when it is dusk. That way we can get closer to the house without the woman seeing us, plus we don't want the dog to go to sleep too early! Hopefully the dog will smell the meat and forget all about us." Caleb let thoughts run through his mind as he formed a plan. "We'll have to drive pretty much to the house and park where the cops did. If the dog starts to chase us, we need to be able to jump back in the car quickly."

Joe nodded his head in agreement. He looked up at Caleb as he stood beside him, "How tall *are* you?"

Caleb smiled, "Six foot six inches." He stood up straighter and puffed out his solid chest like a cockerel. "Two hundred and ten pounds of solid muscle." He gave Joe a friendly punch on the shoulder and despite Joe himself being a very solid build, he felt a sharp pain at the punch, but refused to wince.

"I could take you down if I wanted to," said Joe casually, "But I need to conserve my energy."

Benito watched the two men curiously, and looked down at his own slender frame. Maybe he should start working out. He wasn't even six foot tall though, he pondered, then suddenly realised both men were watching him.

Caleb smiled kindly. "Don't worry, Benito, boys grow until they are twenty one years old or so. You've still got a few years to go. Then you'll fill out."

It wasn't quite an hour later when Caleb said, "Right, time to go, I think."

He grabbed the steak and Joe was about to ask why he wasn't waiting any longer, then realised Caleb probably wanted to avoid being home when his wife and Pamela got back. Joe had a sneaking suspicion that whatever the outcome, later on that night, Caleb and Ellie were going to have a serious exchange of words between the two of them when no one else was around. Joe didn't envy Caleb. Suddenly, it became clear to Joe what Caleb was doing for him.

"Thank you, Caleb," he said as they got in the car. "I hope you two aren't going to get a divorce or anything." He laughed half-heartedly and Caleb flashed a painful smile.

"We'll be all right. Just put some ear plugs in when you go to bed tonight."

Joe wasn't completely convinced that Caleb was joking, but said nothing as he buckled up. Soon they were driving slowly up the rough lane and Caleb stopped the car half a mile away.

"I don't think I'll be able to run to here before the dog gets to me," said Joe hesitantly.

"Don't worry," began Caleb. "There's a very slight slope this last little way. I'll just coast with the ignition off." When they came to a complete stop, Caleb spoke again, "You're going to have to get out and push the rest of the way."

Joe jumped out and pushed the car which easily moved forward and finally they got to the parking area, facing the car so it was ready to leave. Quietly, the men got out of the car and walked stealthily towards the back of the house, straining their ears for any sound of the dog or the woman. When they reached the house, all they could hear was the quiet clucking of the hens as they pecked around their enclosure. Caleb tried to get the steak out of the plastic bag without making a noise, but it was impossible and he silently chided himself for not putting it in a container instead. However, after he got the steak out of the noisy bag and threw the drugged meat on the ground amongst some low lying bushes, still no dog appeared. Caleb and Joe looked at each other and Caleb shrugged his shoulders. He motioned back towards the car and the two men turned back and climbed in.

"Maybe they went for a walk," offered Joe.

Caleb shook his head. "I don't think she walks that dog."

"Her property must be close to the water, maybe they went fishing or something."

Caleb scrunched his face contemplatively. "Maybe. At any rate, I guess it is safe to start the car from here. I really doubt anyone is home." He started the engine and headed back up the lane.

"What now?" asked Joe, "Go home and wait until she might be in bed?" As soon as he said it, he realised that was NOT what they were going to do. Caleb was not about to face Ellie until their mission was complete.

"I know a really good restaurant," said Caleb smiling as the car bumped along the lane. "Do you like Mexican food?"

"I don't know," said Joe thoughtfully, "I'm pretty sure I've never had it before."

"Ah, well then, you are in for a treat!"

————⟫●⟪————

Rebeca stood for a while, closing her eyes and listening to the sounds of the birds and various animals. Some sounded familiar, but some were strange. She breathed deeply, her eyes still shut as she silently thanked God for His amazing diversity of creation. She pictured her father and her village in her mind, and smiled as she imagined her mother standing there before her. She had been a strong-willed, beautiful woman, but had been completely devoted to Rebeca's father and was the perfect chief's wife. She had balanced her strong will and the honouring of her husband in perfect harmony as God had intended and Rebeca hoped that, one day, she would be able to do the same.

"Rebeca!"

Rebeca opened her eyes as she heard Elena calling. She hurried away from the bushes so Elena would not know she had been sick and guess that the drugs were no longer working.

"Yes, Aunt Elena?"

"Are you all right, dear?"

Elena looked at her and a slight panic rose in Rebeca's stomach as she saw a hint of suspicion in the woman's eyes. She pushed the feeling back down and smiled at Elena feebly.

"Still a little weak, but better than I was. Thank you, you have been so kind to us." She paused, wondering what Elena was expecting the drugs to do to her. "Is there anything I can help you with?"

Elena stared hard at Rebeca for a moment, then grinned widely. "Yes, I have several fish I would like you and Toby to gut and salt. I have a crock pot ready on the side." She motioned for Rebeca to follow her and Rebeca obediently allowed herself to be led inside.

Toby's face lit up as Rebeca came in and she felt great sadness that it was due to the drugs and hypnosis rather than how he actually felt about her. She pushed the thought away as she tried to remain focused on Elena's instructions and how Rebeca thought she should respond. She was not sure she could keep up the act for long.

It did not take them too long and they soon had the pot full to the top with salted layers of fish. Elena opened the storage cupboard and Toby lifted the crock pot and put it on the shelf as Elena instructed him.

"That will stay there for a week, then I will put it in my storage area below. It is cool enough there to store various kinds of food," Elena said as she came out and shut the door behind her.

"I'm getting worried about Emmie," Toby frowned as he went to the door and looked out. Turning to Rebeca, he asked, "Did you see her when you were out there earlier?"

Rebeca shook her head. It *was* odd; Emmie usually did not stray too far from Toby. Rebeca glanced at Elena and nearly frowned, forgetting she was supposed to be drugged.

"Why don't you two go out and have a look for her?" Elena suggested as she busied herself with plans for the evening meal.

Toby grabbed Rebeca's hand and they walked out the door with Pumpkin trotting after them curiously.

"Why don't we see if she's down by the water?" Suggested Rebeca, as she wondered if she would be able to get Toby into Elena's boat and escape.

Toby nodded at her and kissed her hand with a stupefied look on his face and Rebeca suddenly became irritated. It was like being pestered by someone who was drunk on cassava, a fermented fruit that the adults drank – usually the men – back in her jungle village.

When they reached the end of the pier, Rebeca looked around curiously. Something did not feel right. She crouched down and watched the water – it was flowing in the opposite direction. Rebeca tried to imagine what was going on but her thoughts were interrupted by Toby as he crouched behind Rebeca and wrapped his arms around her, kissing her neck.

"Stop it!" Rebeca shouted at Toby and pushed him away. As she did, she unbalanced them both and they stumbled off the edge and splashed into the cold water. It was only a couple of feet deep, but Toby landed on top of Rebeca and pushed her under the surface. Struggling for breath, Rebeca rolled out from under him and stood up, choking and coughing out the water she had swallowed. Toby stood up in front of Rebeca and reached out to her anxiously. She thrust out the palm of her hand in a STOP motion.

"Stop!" She said angrily. "Stay away from me!"

Pumpkin began barking oddly, almost like he was laughing at them. He began jumping excitedly as he barked and seconds later, he too, lost his balance and skidded off the pier and landed between Toby and Rebeca. Just then, they heard heavy footsteps trotting down the wooden planks and the teenagers looked up to see Billy coming towards them.

"What're you two doing? I wouldn't recommend swimming in that – there's alligators around here!" Concerned about losing his 'investment', Billy leaned over and grabbed Toby first, pulling him up and dragging him onto the planks. He then turned his attention to Rebeca and grabbed her hand as she scrambled up as well, anxiously looking around for hungry beasts in the water. Lastly, he grabbed Pumpkin by the collar, but as he was so heavy, Billy could only lift him half way up. Rebeca leaned over and grabbed the dog's backside, helping Billy to hoist him to safety. Pumpkin scrambled to his feet and shook himself off vigorously.

As they came out into the clearing, they met Elena who was walking towards them. She studied Rebeca hard before speaking. "What happened to you two …". She looked at Pumpkin and added, "three?"

"Just messing around and got too close to the edge of the pier – Pumpkin tried to save us." Rebeca began shivering.

"Go on inside and get changed – there's some clothes on my bed for you each."

Toby and Rebeca nodded and scurried inside the house. They grabbed their clothes and Toby turned to Rebeca. "You change in here, I'll go to the other room." He started to stroke her arm and she glared at him. He pulled away, hurt and confusion filling his eyes. "What's the matter, Rebeca?"

Rebeca was sorry for her irritation and she hated to see how she was hurting him. She softened her tone, "I'm sorry, I'm just not feeling well."

He half smiled, still unsure of her, and shut the door after him as he left her to get changed. Toby and Rebeca soon had their wet clothes hanging on the line outside and were standing in front of the outside fire warming themselves.

"Let's go have another look around," said Toby to Rebeca, "and this time we'll stay away from the water." He started to head behind the hen house, but Rebeca took his hand and led him away from where she had been earlier. Pumpkin followed dutifully after them like a guard. An hour later, they were back in the clearing, and Elena was in the hen house collecting some eggs.

"Where have you two been?" she asked, still slightly suspicious of Rebeca and concerned about what she might be doing.

"Looking for Emmie," said Toby, and Rebeca nodded.

"Emmie?" asked Elena and immediately Rebeca knew what was coming next, but let Toby speak.

"You know, my monkey friend," asked Toby, walking to the edge of the enclosure. Elena came out and touched Toby's shoulder, making him look directly into her eyes.

"You did not bring your monkey friend," Elena said, staring at him.

Toby paused for a moment, pondering the matter.

"You left Emmie in Nicaragua, Toby." Elena still locked eyes with Toby, and Rebeca tried to keep a neutral look on her face as she wondered what the woman had done with Emmie.

Suddenly, Elena's eyes flashed and she looked at Rebeca. "Didn't you, my dear?"

Rebeca swallowed and pretended she was believing this and remembering things the way Elena wanted them to remember. She nodded. "Yes, Toby, we left Emmie in Nicaragua – she is with her family now, remember?"

"Remember?" asked Elena; and Rebeca wondered if this was a key word.

"Yes, of course," said Toby, smiling as he remembered – or thought he remembered – leaving Emmie safe in the jungle.

"Come now, you two must be hungry. I know my Billy is hungry! But he has a few jobs to do first."

Elena ushered the two teenagers inside and sat them at the wooden table. Rebeca looked down at the table as she rested her arms on it. It was higher. Was she imagining things? No, the water was definitely running the opposite direction and the trees were not right by the water. She looked out the kitchen window and felt certainty in her mind. For some reason, they were no longer at Elena's, but somewhere else identical. Whatever horrible plan that Elena and Billy had for them, it had been well thought out. And Rebeca guessed that she and Toby were probably not the first unfortunate people who had come across this evil mother and son duo.

Elena had turned her attention towards a pot of stew that was bubbling over the fire. She took two bowls and scooped out the stew with a large ladle, filling them each to the top. She placed them on the counter and took out a clear glass jar from the top shelf of one of the cupboards. She took a spoon and scooped out some of the green flakes and sprinkled some on the steaming stew.

Rebeca watched attentively and Elena looked at Rebeca and smiled, "This is a very tasty herb, but it must be added once you have taken the stew off the heat, otherwise the heat ruins the flavour." She stirred it in and placed the two bowls in front of them. Clearly, she expected them to eat it without question. Alarmed, Rebeca hesitated as she held her spoon in her hand. Toby was already tucking in and eating hungrily. Elena was watching Rebeca intently and Rebeca prayed for wisdom as she strained to smile back at Elena.

"Thank you Aunt Elena." She still held her spoon in the air when suddenly she remembered the bread they had eaten earlier. "May I have some of that delicious bread?" She asked, flashing the most charming smile she could muster.

"Of course, dear," Elena was proud of her home-made bread and was always pleased when someone appreciated it. She got up from the table and went into the little storage room, and as she did, Rebeca held the bowl down for Pumpkin who happily gobbled most of it up. Fortunately, Toby was too engrossed in his own eating and did not see what Rebeca was doing. She brought the bowl up just as Elena came back out. Tapping the bowl as though she were eating hastily, Rebeca kept it tilted to herself so that Elena could not see it was nearly gone.

"This is so delicious; you really are an amazing cook. Perhaps you could show me how to make some of these scrumptious dishes!" Rebeca took a slice of bread and pretended to dip it in the stew before putting it to her mouth and eating hungrily.

When she felt that she had given herself enough time to look like she had eaten most of the stew, she put the dish on the table and took another slice of bread. If she was going to avoid eating these 'special' stews, Rebeca would have to fill herself up on anything else that was offered. She felt certain she could survive on just bread for a few days.

Just then, Billy poked his head through the doorway with a large lump hammer in his left hand. "Come and show me which wood you want me to use for the shingles, Ma!"

Elena stood up and followed him out, and as soon as she disappeared, Rebeca offered the last of her stew to the large dog waiting by her side.

Rebeca jumped as Toby touched her shoulder.

"What are you doing?" he asked her.

"I couldn't resist his soppy eyes – I just thought I'd give him the last of my stew." She stood up and took her and Toby's bowls to the sink, giving them each a rinse under running water just as Elena came back in the house.

"Toby, dear," Elena said, "will you please go and help Billy up on the roof? There's some shingles that need replacing."

"Of course, Aunt Elena!" Toby jumped up with such enthusiasm that he startled Pumpkin who gave a yelp in annoyance. Elena looked at Toby as he almost bounced out of the house and thought to herself she was going to have to change her method of dosing the teenagers. She could not continue to give them the same amount, since Toby needed so little and Rebeca needed so much. At that thought, Elena faced back to Rebeca, squinting her eyes and studying her closely, so she didn't see Pumpkin bouncing out the door after Toby.

"Is everything all right, Elena?" Rebeca asked with a smile pasted on her face, and widening her eyes. She was unsure of how she was supposed to be responding if she had eaten the food. She had watched Toby, and she did not feel like she could mimic his bounce and enthusiasm accurately. However, she hoped that if she aimed for something near to that reaction, Elena would believe she had consumed her stew, but that it had just had a slightly different effect. "What else can I do to please you?" Rebeca spread her wide smile even wider, feeling like a clown, but hoping it would convince Elena that she was indeed, under her spell.

Elena stood for a moment, thinking of something with which she could test Rebeca's drugged state. Rebeca looked into the woman's dark brown eyes and although she kept up the adoration on her face, her heart began to pound heavily against her chest as she realised Elena was not going to make it easy for her.

Finally, Elena's mouth opened into a truly evil grin, and she chuckled. "I know my dear. I know how you can show your devotion to me." She paused for effect and Rebeca tried to control her breathing as her heart beat even harder. "I need you to renounce your love for Jesus, dear. That kind of devotion must be completely focused on me now. *I* have saved you."

Rebeca opened her lips to speak and her mouth went completely dry. She closed her lips to moisten her mouth, and opened them again to try and speak. Elena stood watching her, growing agitated with every tick of the clock that hung on the wall, and Rebeca sought desperately to figure out how to respond.

"Please God, help me," she said silently.

A loud swishing sound ran across the roof. "Ack! Help! Ah!" Then a THUD!

Elena and Rebeca rushed out to find Billy on the ground holding his leg and screaming.

"My knee, Ma! I twisted my knee bad!"

Toby slid feet first down the roof and placed his feet gingerly on the top rung of the ladder. He carefully made his way down and over to Billy. "Are you all right?" he asked anxiously.

"No, you stupid kid! Didn't you just hear me say my knee is twisted?!"

Elena quickly took control of the situation directing Toby and Rebeca to help Billy up the steps and inside by each supporting either side of him. They helped him to the first sofa, and he lay down, crying out in agony.

"Oh! Ma! Do something!"

Elena helped him put both legs up on the sofa as she spoke to Rebeca. "Go in that top cupboard there and get me that small jar on the left hand side."

"This one?" Rebeca asked as she reached up and grabbed a large clear jar with some dark red powder.

Elena glanced up and nodded. "Put a spoonful in a glass of juice and give it a stir."

Rebeca noticed the jug of juice on the side and after putting a spoonful of the red powder in a glass, she poured in some juice and stirred it well before taking it over to Billy who snatched it from her hand and gulped it down. He lay his head down on the cushion and moaned as his mother looked at his leg. She leaned back for a few minutes as she waited for the powder to take effect.

"Don't do ... anything ... that ... will make ... it ...". Billy's eyes rolled back in his head and he went unconscious.

Elena carried on with her examination, finally deciding that although her son had indeed twisted his knee, she could use her poultice on it to bring down the swelling and ease the pain for when he woke up. She stood up and busied herself at the counter with various herbs and made a poultice similar to the one that she put on Joe's ankle. "Hold his leg up, Toby, while I get some cloths to wrap it."

Toby dutifully held up the one leg a few inches while Elena went in the one bedroom and got some cloths, then made a mixture in a bowl in the sink. She had a towel over her one arm as she put the cloths in the bowl and carried it over to where her son lay unconscious. She put the bowl on the floor and placed the towel under his leg before taking out the strips of cloth and wrapping them around Billy's knee, starting just below it and then ending just above it. She looked at Toby and Rebeca who were watching curiously and she explained.

"When the cloths dry, they will be firm but a little stretchy and protect his knee while it heals." She looked down at Pumpkin who had plunked himself down on the floor and was shaking his head slowly from side to side, breathing heavily. "What is wrong with you, Pumpkin? You are acting very strange today. Are you ill, sweetheart?"

Rebeca held her breath, but Elena said no more about it as she turned back to Billy and finished wrapping up his knee. As she finished, she turned to the two teenagers. "Toby, were you done putting the tiles on the roof?" she asked.

"Just one more to replace. I can do it myself," said Toby confidently as he went out the door and climbed the ladder.

<hr />

After their meal, Joe and Caleb drove slowly back to Elena's house, and by the time they got there it was nearly dark.

Caleb did as before, turning off the vehicle and Joe pushed it down the last few metres.

"It's dark," said Joe, looking around.

Caleb raised an eyebrow. "Uh, that was the point – coming back when it was dark."

"No," whispered Joe, "I mean there are no lights over there. I would have thought we would be able to see any lights on in the house from here."

Caleb looked and took a deep breath. "You're right. Come on, let's have a look." He spoke quietly and Joe followed his silhouette through the bushes to the back of the house. Caleb sniffed. "I can smell the meat. It's still here."

Joe's heart sank as the two men walked past the bushes where the meat was now buzzing with flies. They made their way to one of the windows at the back of the house. Caleb gave Joe a leg up, and he looked in and couldn't see anything. Carefully, he took his flash light and shone it into the bedroom. It was empty. Slowly, they crept around the house and did the same at each window. Finally, they crept slowly up the wooden steps and peered into the kitchen window by the front door.

"There's no one here," spoke Joe a little louder. "Let's see if we can get inside and look around." He turned the handle of the door, but it was locked, so they went around the house again checking all the windows. Finally, the last window moved outward slightly. Joe stuck his hand up and unhooked the lever, pulling the window out and hoisting himself up onto the ledge. There was a bed just under the window, so he lifted himself up on his arms and dove down, completing a somersault on the bed just before he got to the edge. Joe turned around and leaned back out the window to Caleb who was standing still, looking up.

Caleb spoke in a whisper, "I think I might wait outside and keep a look out. You never know – the lady and her dog might come back. Besides, I can look around out here and see if I can find anything." Caleb looked around to see in which direction he should head.

"Good idea!" said Joe quietly as he disappeared back inside the dark house.

The moon came out from behind a cloud and shone brightly down on Caleb as he headed towards the chicken enclosure. The crickets sang loudly in the still night while a pack of coyotes howled and barked at each other in the distance. The hens were cooing quietly in their beds and Caleb walked past them to the shed, which he opened up and peered inside. He turned on his flashlight but saw nothing unusual. Caleb crept over to the edge of the enclosure and began walking around the perimeter, swinging his light back and forth through the trees and bushes.

Joe scanned the sparse bedroom and shone his light over various items before heading to the closet and looking inside. There appeared to be nothing other than some men's clothing. He stepped out of the bedroom and jumped as a floor board creaked beneath him. He walked over to the two sofas and had a good look around and on each of them, trying desperately to find something that would indicate that Toby and Rebeca had been there. Joe moved on to the rest of the kitchen and quickly searched the storeroom and the cupboards, not entirely sure of what he was looking for. He soon moved to the second bedroom and he opened the door carefully, just in case there was someone inside. It was empty, but he was met with a peculiar smell. He breathed deeply, trying to place it. For some reason, it reminded him of Nicaragua. Just then, the beam caught a few tiny brown lumps on the floor beside the bed. He was right! They *had* been here – they were little capuchin droppings! His excitement was short lived as he was struck with the next thought –

where were they *now*? He clicked off the light and let out a loud breath, standing still and silent in the dark, and feeling completely helpless.

"God!" he cried out in a loud whisper. "What are You doing? Why have You let this happen? Where *are* they?!"

Joe heard the ticking of the clock. Tick. Tick. Tick. Counting off the seconds, until – what? Tick. Tick. Tick. Closer to the hurricane. He looked out the window at the trees bathed in moonlight – each leaf completely still. Tick. Tick. Tick.

"Joe!"

Joe turned as he heard Caleb call his name through the bedroom window. "Did you find anything?" Joe dragged his feet back to the other bedroom and leaned out the window. "Hang on! I'm coming out."

Joe sat on the window ledge, then twisted around and grabbed the frame as he swung himself to the ground beside Caleb.

"They were here." He said simply.

"Wha…?"

"I saw – and smelled – evidence of Emmie." He pursed his lips angrily. "But they're gone. We missed them." He turned accusingly at Caleb, "We should have brought a gun with us in the first place! We could have shot the dog and the old lady couldn't have stopped us looking for them – I'm sure I heard them when we were here before! With the dog dead, we could have rescued Toby and Rebeca!

Caleb let Joe's temper roll off his shoulders as he spoke quietly. "If you heard them, why didn't they call out to us?" he asked thoughtfully.

"I don't know! The woman is crazy! Maybe … maybe she drugged them or something!" He glared at Caleb.

In the bright moonlight, Caleb could clearly see Joe's face. He looked down at the clenched fist by Joe's side, and he said a silent prayer. He didn't want to fight him, but Joe seemed determined to vent his anger on Caleb. Caleb's father had beaten him as a child, but had left home when Caleb was a young teenager – Caleb did not know where his father was now, and Caleb had sworn to himself that he would not grow up to be violent; however, he had struggled with an unpredictable temper. When Caleb was nineteen, he became a Christian and had had a miraculous transformation. All the hate that had built up inside of him was gone, and he forgave his father – even if his dad did not know it – and a calmness had come upon Caleb that had made its home in his personality. Over the years, he had come to realise that not everyone who became a Christian was changed instantaneously; sometimes it took months or even years, as they journeyed in their faith. Joe was obviously one of those that was going to be changed over the course of the walk in their faith, rather than at the beginning.

As Caleb stood analysing the situation, Joe's anger bubbled to the surface. "What's the matter?! Are you trying to think of another sermon for me?! We should have shot the dog!" yelled Joe.

In an instant, Joe came at Caleb, fists flying. Caleb raised his arms in defence at each punch, his height and strength an advantage, but Joe was strong as well and Caleb winced at every furious swing that made contact. Caleb tried his best to just hold Joe off, but he stumbled backwards and Joe got an upward swing to Caleb's jaw and the pain shot through his head. Caleb threw in a punch to Joe's stomach, and although he did not use full force, Joe gasped and collapsed to his knees. Joe leaned forward, wheezing for a few minutes before he could get a proper breath. Caleb stood watching him silently, worried that he had injured him, but not knowing what to say in case he drew out Joe's wrath again.

After several minutes, Joe's breathing eventually started to return to normal and he rolled on his back and sighed deeply with his hands on his head, as Caleb rubbed his jaw and kept an eye on Joe to make sure he wasn't going to leap up at him.

Finally, Joe leaned back on his elbows and stared up at Caleb. "Don't you *ever* get angry?" Joe scowled at the gentle giant.

"Sure."

"But not like me."

Caleb just cocked his head and smiled, leaning over and offering Joe a hand up.

"Have you always been such a calm person?" Joe grabbed the large hand and stood up, staring at Caleb's serene face questioningly.

"No."

"So how did you manage to tame the inner beast?"

Caleb was not sure what to say. People didn't often like to hear that something they had been struggling with for a long time had been dealt with in an instant by God in someone else.

"It's different for everyone," he offered simply. "Come on, we may as well go back home now. We'll have to contact the police in the morning; see if your … uh … friend got her father to speak to anyone."

Joe suddenly smiled as he winked at Caleb. "She's hot, huh?"

"Smokin'!" Caleb let slip, then frowned as he added, only half joking, "But don't tell Ellie I said that!"

"Hmmmmm …" said Joe mischievously as he patted Caleb on the back, "Seems like I have some blackmail material if I ever need some in the future!"

As they reached Caleb's car, they got in and headed back in silence as the disappointment of the night sunk down heavily upon them.

———⟫●⟪———

Rebeca held the ladder while Toby climbed up to finish the last tile. It did not take him long and soon he came back to the edge of the roof with some tools which he tossed onto the grass. He climbed down carefully on the wooden ladder. Just as he reached the bottom rung, Elena came around the side of the house.

"Is it all done?" she asked.

"Yes," Toby nodded. "We'll just put these tools and ladder away."

"Good. It will soon be dark." Elena turned and went back into the house.

Rebeca helped Toby with the ladder and put it on some hooks at the back of the house. Toby picked up the tools and took them to the shed as Rebeca stood watching him. She took a few steps forward then stopped underneath one of the kitchen windows that was open. Billy and Elena were talking quietly.

"What time is the hurricane due to hit?" asked Elena.

"One o'clock tomorrow, midday. So we'll have to leave in the morning. It will take a couple of hours to get to where we are to drop Toby and Rebeca off. Then we can go over and stay with Trina 'til it's over. Drop-off point is only forty-five minutes from their place."

There was a pause and Rebeca stood on tiptoe, straining to hear as the voices got quieter.

"Well, just you behave around your sister's husband. You know how you rile him up some!"

"Ah, ma! It ain't my fault. Peter is such an awkward cuss!"

"Well, you can keep your mouth shut for two days, can't ya?" Elena's voice grew louder. "Where are those two?"

Rebeca's heart jumped and she trotted over to meet Toby as he was coming out of the shed. Elena poked her head out of the door just as Toby shut the door.

"We have an early start tomorrow!" She grinned widely, "Lots to do! I've made some hot chocolate to help us sleep and we'll all go to bed early!"

Rebeca's mind raced. They would have to escape tonight. She guessed that wherever they were being taken probably was a lot more secure than here.

Their drinks were on the table and the two teenagers sat down. Toby took a swig of his and Rebeca put the cup to her lips, pretending to drink. She felt sure there would be some kind of sedative in it.

"I want some as well, ma!" Called Billy from his bedroom.

"Well come out and get some." Said Elena. "I know your knee is a lot better now, Billy!"

"Please! I'm lying down resting and I don't want to strain it!"

Elena sighed as she poured some into a mug for her son. Toby, still wanting to be helpful, jumped up and grabbed the hot chocolate to take into Billy. Elena looked over at Rebeca suspiciously, and she gave the woman her sweetest smile, continuing her façade of drinking the hot chocolate, all the while wondering how she could dispose of it while Elena was watching her. Rebeca's heart began beating quickly as she tried desperately to think of a plan.

"And I need another pillow, Ma!"

"I have one in my room, just a sec." Elena went to her bedroom and looked over her shoulder at Rebeca as she entered, not trusting that the girl was actually under her influence.

Knowing she only had seconds, Rebeca jumped up and quickly poured the drink into Pumpkin's bowl and dashed back to the table, sitting down just as Elena came back out. Rebeca smiled again and put the cup to her mouth, pretending to finish it up. Pumpkin happily was slurping up the last of the liquid and licking the bowl. Rebeca drew Elena's attention to herself.

"You make very good hot chocolate!"

"It's my secret ingredient," Elena smiled sinisterly then went to Billy's bedroom door and threw in the pillow to Toby. Two minutes later, Toby came out and sat at the table. Rebeca suddenly realised she couldn't let Toby drink his, either. She glanced over at the sink and saw the pot that Elena had used to heat the drink.

"Is there any more hot chocolate Aunt Elena?" She asked, innocently.

"No, sorry."

Rebeca's smile faded, but then, as she had hoped, Toby spoke up.

"You can have some of mine, if you like." Without waiting for a reply, he poured some hot chocolate into her cup, giving her the majority of it, as she knew he would.

Elena tittered to herself. Rebeca was the troublemaker – it was best that she get most of the drug. Toby wouldn't go anywhere without her.

"Thank you, Toby." Rebeca again held the cup to her mouth, making a soft slurping noise. She did this several times, then finally said, "I feel quite sleepy already!" She lowered her eyelids slightly for effect, and Elena nodded approvingly.

"Help me with the blankets, Toby." Elena ordered, and again Toby jumped to attention.

"Of course!"

Elena stood by the doorway keeping one eye on Rebeca as she motioned Toby in, directing him to where she had placed the spare blankets. "No, not those ones. Over there!"

Elena turned and walked a couple of steps into the room, and Rebeca saw her chance. She stood quickly and scurried over to Pumpkin's bowl filling it with more of the sweet drink. She knew she would never make it back to the table, so she started walking quickly to the sink.

"Stop!"

Rebeca jumped at Elena's voice and she stood still. Elena walked over and grabbed the cup from Rebeca's shaking hands, looking inside. Fortunately, Elena was so engrossed in Rebeca's cup, that she did not see Pumpkin happily licking his bowl further across the floor.

"I think you will sleep quite well tonight, my dear." Elena's evil smile spread across her face. "I'll wash the cups and pot. You help Toby put the blankets on your beds." Elena grabbed the cups and filled the kettle with water, putting it on the fire to heat. As she did so, Rebeca surreptitiously slid the dog bowl with her foot, back to where it had been originally, humming as she did so, so Elena would not hear the metal bowl scraping across the wooden floor.

Toby and Rebeca soon had the blankets on the sofas and they each lay down on one.

"I will pick you two up some clothes in town, tomorrow," said Elena.

"Thank you, Aunt Elena," Toby and Rebeca said in unison.

Rebeca soon heard soft little snoring sounds coming from Toby. She wasn't sure if it was due to the little chocolate that he had drunk, or from the other drug that Elena had given him to be submissive. She glanced at Pumpkin who had sprawled out on the middle of the floor and looked completely unconscious. Rebeca closed her eyes as Elena turned away from the sink and came over to check on each of them.

She watched them for a moment, then satisfied that they were both asleep, she went to say good-night to her son. "It's a pity that storm is coming."

"Why is that, Ma? I thought you liked a good storm!"

They both spoke loud enough for Rebeca to hear without straining, and she wondered if they would say anything of any significance.

"I'd like more time with these two. Rebeca has been a challenge, but I think I might be really close to having the perfect mixture of herbs for her. Those folks you are selling them to have no ... no finesse! All they do is get their slaves hooked on common addictive drugs, and then they will willingly work to get more of the drug. My way is a finely tuned procedure. It is a much more satisfying result! And I do believe they would get more work out of the slaves if they weren't worrying about when they are going to get their next hit."

"Your way is more complicated and takes more effort. Theirs is easier."

"But it is like using a broom instead of a paintbrush when painting a picture. Theirs is a sloppy mess, and mine is a work of art!" She paused for a moment. "Or trying to play a piece by Mozart with a set of drums! They have no class."

Rebeca heard a deep chuckle.

"I'll be sure to tell them that, Ma!"

"I would have liked to keep that little monkey," spoke Elena sadly, "She was a sweet little thing. That Adrian does not deserve her. Still, if it keeps him silent, I guess it was worth giving her back to him." Rebeca heard Elena blow out a deep sigh as she turned around and headed toward her own bedroom. She paused in the middle of the kitchen. "Are you staying out here, Pumpkin?"

Rebeca held her breath as Elena walked over to the dog. Just then, the unconscious animal snuffled loudly. Elena chuckled, then made her way to her own room and shut the door behind her.

⸺⸺➤●◄⸺⸺

As Joe lay in his bed looking out the window at the semi-darkness that was typical of a city, he could hear Caleb and Ellie downstairs. They were talking in hushed tones, but he could hear Ellie's angry voice. He felt a slight pang at causing problems between them. He got up and closed the door. Somehow it did not seem right to listen to their argument. He lay back down with his arms behind his head, staring at the ceiling, and thoughts of Caleb and Ellie's little baby floated into his mind. How sad for them. Joe couldn't imagine what it would be like to lose his brother.

In the bed next to him, Benito was breathing heavily as he slept. Joe grimaced. He lay back down and looked at the ceiling, bracing himself for a long sleepless night. *Where are they, God? Please help us find them.*

⸺⸺➤●◄⸺⸺

Someone was shaking him. Toby tried to open his heavy eyes as he heard someone whisper his name. Finally he looked up in the dark night and saw a face looking down at him – was it Rebeca? What was she doing? Where was he? The moonlight shone through the window across from him. It looked like a kitchen. It seemed familiar somehow.

"Wha ...?" he started to speak but Rebeca hushed him.

"You must be quiet," she spoke so softly Toby had to strain to hear her. "Get up!" Her voice was urgent. What was wrong? Where *was* he?

"Where am I?" he whispered as he sat up. He put his feet on the floor and realised his shoes were on. Did he not take them off when he went to bed?

"No time to explain; get up, we have to go now!" Rebeca pulled him to his feet and Toby wobbled as his knees buckled. Rebeca held him up and he leaned on her as they walked to the door. Why was he so tired?

Toby stopped as he spotted a large dog sprawled out in the middle of the floor. Pumpkin! He remembered the dog.

"It's okay," Rebeca spoke almost silently in his ear, "He's had some medicine to help him sleep."

A floorboard creaked and Rebeca stopped. Toby opened his mouth to speak and she put a finger to her mouth, shaking her head slowly from side to side. He couldn't see her face clearly but he felt her body tense and her anxiety transferred to him. What were they supposed to be afraid of, he wasn't sure, but he instinctively trusted Rebeca, and when she resumed walking, he walked carefully so as to not make a sound.

"Grrrrrr...". They both jumped at the sound, but when they looked behind them, Pumpkin was fast asleep, paws twitching, chasing something in his dreams. Finally, they reached the door and Rebeca slid the big iron bolt slowly, holding her breath at the soft scraping sound. Then she carefully lifted up the latch that made a *clink* as it tapped the metal bracket on the top. Very slowly, she pulled the door towards her, praying the hinges would not squeak. Finally it was wide enough for Rebeca and Toby to step through the entrance and out on the steps. It had grown windy since they had gone to bed and the silhouettes of the trees swayed in the moonlight as though dancing to a song that only they heard. Toby watched as Rebeca carefully shut the door behind them, then placed his hand on her shoulder to steady himself as they crept down the steps. The sound of the wind covered any noise they would have made walking across the grass.

Toby wondered where they were going. Elena would be worried about them, he thought to himself, but he trusted Rebeca. She must know something he didn't; some reason why they had to get up in the middle of the night and creep out of the house. Rebeca led him across the clearing and towards the path that led to the wooden dock.

Rebeca picked up the pace the further they got from the house and by the time they got to the little boat that was tied at the end, they were walking briskly. If it had not been for Toby stumbling along, still feeling groggy, Toby thought Rebeca might even have had them at a jog.

Toby was unsure as to whether it was all right to make a noise yet, so he remained silent as Rebeca motioned for him to get in the boat. He held onto her arm while he stepped gingerly down and Rebeca had to stand firm so that he did not pull her in with him as he rocked back and forth with the little vessel. He finally managed to sit down and watched Rebeca untie the rope and hop expertly down with hardly a movement from the boat.

A midnight row, Toby thought, this would be fun! Though he still did not understand why they had to be so quiet. Surely Elena wouldn't mind them having a little fun – she wanted the best for them. He opened his mouth again to speak, and Rebeca held up her hand. He could only see her silhouette as the tall trees were blocking out the moonlight, but he kept quiet as she grabbed the oars and began to row expertly upstream.

As Rebeca silently pulled the oars through the dark water, Toby grew more awake and had a strange sensation that things were not as they seemed. The intense, focused passion he had had for Rebeca began to fade, and when he thought over the last couple of days, he felt like he was remembering a dream. And Elena – was she really trying to protect them? Emmie! Where was Emmie??

"Where's Emmie?" he asked Rebeca anxiously.

"Back with the man who bought her. We will find her again." Rebeca spoke confidently.

"But…".

"We need to get back to Joe and the others to help us," she interrupted as she continued the rhythmic movement with her arms.

Joe! Toby remembered Joe arriving with another man. Why had he and Rebeca hidden from them? His brain desperately tried to sift through the last couple of days and he grew lost in his thoughts.

Finally, after she had been rowing for about fifteen minutes, Rebeca spoke. "How are you feeling, Toby?"

Toby jumped at the sound of her voice, and a picture of him kissing her flashed in his mind and his cheeks began burning. Had he really done that?

"Toby?"

"I … uh … I don't … know." He spoke hesitantly, remembering her pushing him away. "Was I … did I … uh … what happened?" He wasn't sure he really wanted to know the answers to his questions. Actually, he *knew* he did not want to know.

Toby heard Rebeca breathe out slowly as she paused her rowing for a moment. The boat slowed, stopped and then began floating in the opposite direction, so Rebeca resumed rowing as she spoke. "We were drugged – Elena drugged us."

"But … but I … you …" Toby cringed as the faint memories of his being amorous with her and her annoyance at his advances.

"She hypnotised you, as well." She paused. "She tried to hypnotise me, but for some reason it did not work." She was pretty sure why hypnosis had not worked on her, but she did not want to mention it since their last discussion regarding God and faith had not gone well. Sometimes it was best not to say anything, and let God speak in His own way and time.

"Oh," Toby thought about his behaviour and felt ashamed. He couldn't remember it clearly, but it made him uncomfortable. "I … uh … I'm sorry, Rebeca."

"For what?" She looked at him in an odd manner, almost sadly.

"I … I'm not sure, exactly," Toby did not want to admit he remembered any of his behaviour. "I … uh just vaguely remember that I was not behaving well towards you." He took a deep breath. "I hope we are still friends."

Toby looked at Rebeca earnestly, the need to know their friendship had not been compromised, lying heavy on his heart.

Her answering smile was not as reassuring as he would have hoped for, but in her eyes there was a deep honesty as she spoke, "Yes, Toby. We are still friends."

Silence fell on them once again as they each retreated to their thoughts. The rhythmic *splash, splash, splash* of the oars as they entered the water almost lulled Toby back to sleep when suddenly Rebeca's voice broke into his trance.

"We need to stop – the trees are beginning to get in my way."

Rebeca adeptly steered the craft sharply to the side and then let go of one oar, concentrating on paddling on the one side. She stopped for a minute, letting the boat drift and a few seconds later, they stopped with the vessel wedged between two large trees that reached up into the dark sky. She picked up the rope and leaned over to the tree on her right, tying it tightly as the little craft rocked gently in the wind.

"That should do it." She said in a pleased voice.

"What? We're stopping here?" asked Toby incredulously. "Why?"

"I am having trouble navigating in the dark. We have entered into a wide section of the water and I cannot see the trees well enough or watch the water."

"Watch the water for what?"

"To see if there is water coming in from the side of us. That would mean a narrower section of water, which I believe would more likely bring us to solid ground. We will stay here until it gets lighter. Probably three or four hours."

"I'll take your word for it," said Toby slowly, as once again he was amazed at her ability to find her way around a complete wilderness.

Rebeca slid off the bench and crouched down on the hull of the boat. "You may want to make yourself comfortable if we are going to be here a few hours."

Toby nodded, and slid down beside her warm body, surprised that he had not realised how cool the air had become. He started to lift his arm to put it around Rebeca's shoulders, but stopped as his embarrassing behaviour flashed in his mind, and he involuntarily shook his head to rid himself of the horrible images.

Rebeca turned to him. "What is the matter Toby?"

"Uh, nothing. Just a twitch."

"A 'twitch'?" she asked curiously, and he chuckled, despite his uncomfortable feeling.

"Nothing, I didn't mean to."

The leaned against each other for warmth and support as they both fell quiet, hoping to catch a little sleep before they continued their journey.

⸺⊷●⊶⸺

Elena opened her eyes, and immediately sensed something was wrong. She looked at the clock by her bed and gasped when she saw it read 7:00. *Where was Pumpkin?!* He always woke her by 6:00 to be let out. She jumped out of bed and hurried out of her bedroom to find the two sofas empty, and Pumpkin still on the floor where she had left him last night.

"Pumpkin!"

As she called out, he lazily lifted his head and looked at her yawning. He struggled to his feet as she rushed over to him and held his head in her hands, looking into his eyes. Pumpkin decided it was too much effort to stand, so he fell back into a sitting position. Elena squinted her eyes, angrily snarling an obscenity, and Billy opened his bedroom door and looked out.

"What's up, Ma?" he asked.

"Rebeca!" She spit out furiously. "She drugged Pumpkin and the two of them have escaped!" Elena growled loudly with an almost animal-like sound, frightening Billy who took a step back to hide behind his door.

Billy poked his head out, scratching his head and making a face. He wanted to ask how it happened, but he knew it was best to keep his mouth shut until his mother's anger subsided.

"She will pay!" Elena screamed hysterically before turning towards Billy, who was debating if he should shut his door fully as she took a step towards him. "Get dressed! We must find them!" She spun around and slammed her bedroom door behind her. Billy hurriedly got dressed and was out of his bedroom before Elena, his heart beating rapidly. He was annoyed that he was going to lose the money for Rebeca and Toby, but he was more terrified of his mother when she lost her temper. He was standing by the table literally shaking, when Elena stepped back out, her feet barely touching the floor as she flew across the room to him. She stood for a moment glaring at Billy, and he was worried that she would blame him. He felt he should make a suggestion to pacify her, however he wasn't sure how they would go about finding them.

As if in answer to his unspoken question, Elena said, "They probably took the boat, as it would make them harder to find. Go check!" She pointed towards the door with such force that Billy ducked, thinking she was going to hit him. He opened the door and paused a moment as the brisk wind nearly ripped the door out of his hand, knocking him off balance. He steadied himself, then trotted gingerly down the steps, not wanting to injure his knee further. However, as usual, his mother's medicine had worked wonders and he only felt a slight twinge as he hurried along the path to the water. The boat was gone. Billy ran back, not wanting to give his mom the news that would infuriate her more, so he called out before he got inside, "The boat's gone, Ma!" he shouted above the noise of the trees waving wildly.

Elena flew out of the house and down the steps with Pumpkin waddling behind her. She threw the truck keys at Billy, who only just managed to catch them, as she went past him and headed towards the truck. Billy looked at poor Pumpkin who was struggling to keep up.

"I'd hurry up, if I were you, Pumpkin, she won't wait!" He said quietly to the dog as he overtook Pumpkin running towards his vehicle, and managed to press the unlock button just as Elena put her hand on the door handle. She swung around and spotted Pumpkin who had managed to gain some speed as he panicked when he saw that his mistress was running away from him.

"Hurry up, you stupid dog!" She scowled angrily as the dog reached her and clambered awkwardly into the truck before she jumped in herself. "Why on earth did you let her drug you?!"

Billy had no idea how Pumpkin could have known he was being drugged, but he said nothing as he shut his door and started the truck, spinning on the gravel as he put his foot down and sped along the bumpy lane.

Elena bounced off the seat and nearly hit the dash as she reached back and grabbed the seatbelt, clicking it into place as she screeched at Billy. "You idiot! Stop driving like a maniac!"

Billy lifted his foot up off the pedal slightly and kept his eyes in front of him, not daring to speak, as he gripped tightly to the steering wheel.

"Head north when you get to the highway." She paused a moment, gathering her thoughts and trying to picture the lie of the land north of them. She had lived in the area all her life, and knew it well. "Yes, that is the way they will go." She closed her eyes and began her low hum. It never ceased to make the hairs stand up on the back of Billy's neck when she made that sound, and he looked at her worried, wondering if she was going to curse him. He used to have nightmares as a child that she would curse him and something horrible would happen. She hadn't, but he had moved away from home as soon as he was old enough. However, when he met up with the people traders, he had realised that she would be very useful.

Finally, they came to the highway, and Billy indicated to go left. He had to wait a few minutes as the heavy traffic rumbled past him, trying to escape the hurricane. He glanced at his mother nervously, wondering if she was going to get angry because he had stopped, but she seemed oblivious as she concentrated on determining where Toby and Rebeca had gone. Finally, there was a space, and he put his foot down and swung the truck into the flow of traffic. He had only gone a mile, when Elena's eyes sprung open and she shouted loudly, making Billy jump.

"Ahh HUH!"

Billy turned cautiously to his mother and quivered when he saw her evil grin.

"I know where they would have come off the bayous!" she spoke gleefully.

Billy had to hold onto the steering wheel tightly as the truck was buffeted by the approach of the hurricane, and he grew even more worried, as he realised his mother was not going to leave the area before she had found the two teenagers. At first thought, he wasn't sure if he was more afraid of his mother or the hurricane. But as he glanced over at her and saw the evil excitement in her eyes, he knew he would drive straight into a hurricane rather than defy his mother.

———⟫●⟪———

Joe jerked awake and was surprised to see a ray of sunlight shining down on his face. Exhaustion had taken over him and had knocked him out cold. He did not remember even getting sleepy. He looked over at the other bed, surprised to see it empty. Benito wasn't one for getting up early and Joe wondered what time it was. He picked up his phone that lay on the floor by his bed and was surprised to see it read 9:00. He jumped up and scooted into the en suite bathroom to have a quick shower. Ten minutes later, he was dressed and trotting down the stairs toward the sound of people talking in the kitchen.

"I can't believe I slept in!" exclaimed Joe. "One minute I thought I'd be awake for the whole night, the next thing, it was morning."

"You must have been exhausted," said Ellie as she got up and opened the oven door, taking out a large serving plate of pancakes, bacon and sausages and putting it on a hot pad on the table.

"Stress will do that to a person."

Joe sat down in a chair that had a plate and glass in front of it. Across from him, Benito was silently eating his pancakes and bacon, and to his right sat Pamela who gave him a sad smile. Caleb was on her right, at the head of the table, his plate piled high. Ellie sat down and passed Caleb a jug of orange juice.

"Thank you, Ellie," said Joe, smiling at her nervously and glancing over at Caleb who gave him a mischievous grin and wink. Joe assumed they had worked things out between them, and concentrated on filling his plate.

"Your ... friend ... was as good as her word," Caleb's face went slightly pink at the mention of Gwen, and Joe smirked. "Her father contacted some bigwig and the New Orleans PD have given the case to one of their top detectives, a Detective Don Brown. He called this morning saying he was going to go over to that Elena's house. I told him we went there and it looked empty. He was a bit perturbed that we had gone there ourselves, but he understood our actions. He'll let us know as soon as he has any news."

"But I can't just sit here and wait!" said Joe anxiously. "I've got to do *something*."

"We need to prepare for the hurricane," said Ellie softly, looking out the large kitchen windows at the wind that had now picked up considerable speed; and Joe's eyes grew wider as he thought of the added worry.

Caleb jumped in before Joe's anxiety rose to panic level, "If Elena and her son have Toby and Rebeca, they will take them to safety, for their own sake, if nothing else. That is probably why they left." He spoke in a gentle but commanding voice, trying to appeal to any sensibility that Joe might have. "And we need to prepare, as well. There's lots to do before the storm fully arrives."

Joe nodded absently, as the food he had just eaten turned sour. He put down his fork and picked up his glass of juice to try and wash down the pancake that had seemed to slow down on its journey to his stomach. He sighed deeply when he finished. "What do you need to do?" he finally asked.

"To start, we need to get everything out of the garden and into the garage, pull all the storm shutters down on the windows, close the gates and sandbag them," Caleb spoke as he stood up and carried his dishes to the dishwasher. Joe grabbed his plate and scraped the leftovers in the bin, before he did the same, then he followed Caleb out of the kitchen to help him with all the things that needed doing before the hurricane arrived.

Ellie turned to Benito and Pamela. "You two can go out and put the things from the yard into the garage while I clean up the kitchen." She smiled sadly at Pamela. "Sorry hon. Not quite the birthday week I had planned for you."

Pamela embraced her aunt with a tight hug. "Don't worry, Aunt Ellie. After the hurricane, when we have found Toby and Rebeca, there will still be time to have some fun before I have to go back to work." She released her aunt and spoke to Benito, "Come on!"

Benito followed Pamela obediently out the back door to gather the chairs and tables, some of which had already been knocked over by the wind.

"Do you think they are okay?" Benito finally spoke as he carried two folded chairs into the garage and placed them on top of the ones Pamela had already piled in the corner. Pamela let out a loud breath.

"I hope so, Benito."

"Will God protect them?" Benito was still struggling to grasp the understanding of this God of theirs. They prayed to Him, but it seemed they did not always get the answers they wanted. And yet, they continued to pray to Him.

Pamela bit her lip and looked at Benito, "He is with them wherever they are," she spoke slowly, trying to explain what she herself did not fully understand, "and He can protect them from anything." She sighed again as she continued, "But that doesn't mean He *will* protect them from everything. Sometimes He allows bad thing to happen, but we can trust that everything He allows to happen to us is for some good purpose – whether we understand that purpose or not."

Benito raised an eyebrow, confused. "So you trust Him even when He lets bad things happen to you?"

Pamela scrunched her face, "Well, that is the idea, but sometimes it isn't easy. Sometimes it is scary looking at it from our side of things. Like if you try to help a deer that is caught in some barbed wire. It might hurt them as you untangle them and they won't realise you are helping them." Benito looked unconvinced, but Pamela did not have anything else to offer in explanation, as she grappled with her own questions on the matter.

Just then, a gust of wind shook the garage roof and the two of them hurried out the door to grab the rest of the items that the wind was scattering across the lawn. One of the chairs was in the middle of the pool and while Pamela stood with her hands on her hips deciding what to do, a great WOOSH of wind picked it up and threw it towards her. She stepped out of the way as it flew towards the side of the garage and crashed against the brick wall. Pamela quickly trotted over and collected it before it could fly off, and put it in the garage with the others. Benito picked up the last few items and ran inside the garage after Pamela, his eyes wide.

"Will we be all right?" he asked fearfully.

"Sure!" Smiled Pamela with more confidence than she felt. "Come on, let's see if Aunt Ellie wants us to do anything else." They stepped outside and Pamela shut the garage door just as great drops of rain began to fall in a deluge. They trotted quickly across to the back door, but their clothes were already soaked by the time they got inside the house. Ellie smiled as they slammed the door behind them and removed their shoes before stepping off the doormat.

"Go on upstairs and get changed before you do anything else," she said as she nodded up the stairs.

As Benito stepped in his bedroom, he heard a clanking and the room grew dark. He looked up just in time to see the shutter being pulled down outside his window, and his heart began beating against his chest. He flicked the light on and, shivering, quickly changed into some dry clothes. He had never been in a hurricane before and fear was creeping through every inch of his body as he imagined the house being ripped apart and the contents – including himself – flying up into the sky. He shook himself and scurried back downstairs to the kitchen where Ellie was just finishing tidying up. She turned as Benito walked in and she smiled assuredly as she saw his frightened face.

She walked over and gave him a hug as he stood paralysed in the doorway. Taking him by the shoulders she looked into his dark terrified eyes.

"It is all right, Benito. We get hurricanes every year. I'm sure we'll be just fine! Caleb and Joe have sandbagged the front gates and they are shuttering up the windows. We've lived here for five years and the house has been here for twenty. That should tell you something."

Benito thought about his grandparents' small cottage in the country in Yorkshire, England that was over two hundred years old, and was not persuaded that a house standing for a mere twenty years had any meaning at all. He opened his mouth to say as much when Ellie spoke, "Sit down and I will make you a cup of chamomile tea." She motioned towards one of the chairs by the table and Benito obeyed. He was not particularly keen on chamomile tea, but he felt it would be rude to say so, especially since Ellie seemed to think it was the cure for all kinds of ills – including worry.

"Make that two!" Pamela called out as she appeared into the kitchen and took a chair opposite Benito. Ellie filled the kettle with water as Pamela and Benito watched Joe and Caleb at the kitchen windows, rolling down the storm shutters. Ellie clicked on the light as the shutters clunked shut.

Benito shuddered at the sound and again Ellie tried to comfort him with a smile as she handed him his tea. "This will make you feel better!"

He took the cup and had a little sip before putting it on the table to cool. He didn't realise that as he took the sip, he had scrunched up his face, but Ellie noticed it. "Benito, you don't like chamomile tea, do you?"

"Oh, yes, of course I do!" Benito took another sip and smiled, but Ellie shook her head and took the cup from him as Pamela giggled.

"She doesn't bite, Benito!" When he frowned and looked down, Pamela added, "You can speak the truth to us, you know."

"I just didn't want to be rude," Benito began softly, "you have all been so kind to me."

"It's okay to tell me if you don't like something," spoke Ellie as gently as she could. "I would rather you did, then I can offer you something you would rather have." She emptied the tea into the sink and turned back to Benito. "Now, what *would* you like to drink?"

CHAPTER 11

Toby's eyes shot open as a wet drop splashed hard on his forehead. The little boat rocked precariously in the wind and he struggled to climb up onto the wooden seat across from Rebeca who was busily untying the ropes that she had wrapped round the tree.

"Good timing, I was just about to wake you!" Rebeca spoke urgently. "I need you to push us away from the trees as I begin to row."

Still dazed from his sleep, Toby looked around him as the wind whistled and the boat wobbled. How had he slept through this? He must have been really tired; maybe that drug that Elena gave him was still in his system.

"It came up suddenly," she answered as if in reply to his thoughts. "We must hurry and find somewhere safe. I believe a hurricane is coming. Push, Toby!" She slid the oars into the waters and pulled hard as Toby shook himself awake to obey her instructions and push with all his might against the trees. So hard, in fact, he nearly fell into the water and Rebeca had to grab the back of his shirt to steady him.

"Are you okay?" she asked, concerned, as she quickly returned to rowing hard, with the wind at their side.

Toby nodded, feeling rather useless as he watched her strain at the oars. After a few minutes he asked, "Can I help?"

Rebeca raised an eyebrow, and Toby was forced to remember his previous failed attempt at rowing. Just then, a long thin branch floated past them and Rebeca grabbed it, tossing it gently at Toby who caught it and looked at her blankly.

She chuckled and shook her head. "You can help by pushing with this on the bottom while I row."

"Oh, ya, okay." Toby said. How long would it take before he was fully awake and back to normal?

"It should wear off pretty soon, now," Rebeca said, again apparently able to read his thoughts, much to Toby's consternation.

Toby put every effort into his task and it worked quite well as they moved quickly upstream, the rain now falling hard as the wind buffeted them.

Suddenly, Rebeca called out, and pointed to her left side. "There!"

"What?" Toby looked in the direction she pointed and saw nothing but more water and trees.

Rebeca stopped rowing and looked down. "There is a small current coming from that direction." She pointed to Toby's right.

Toby looked where she was pointing, but could see nothing. "I'll take your word for it!" he said, realising that he nearly had to shout as the wind got louder. Fear filled him as he realised that the hurricane must be getting close.

Rebeca adeptly changed course and headed in the direction she had indicated, with Toby pushing hard on the branch. He looked down at the water as he pushed and slowly he saw what Rebeca's keen eyes had seen earlier, an obvious current. He could also feel it as he pushed, and as he saw Rebeca straining harder at the oars, he put more effort into his pushing. Toby may not know how to row, but he could push, and he was determined to make Rebeca's rowing as easy as possible for her.

The scattered drops of rain came more steady now, and both Rebeca and Toby were soon drenched. Toby tried to focus on his pushing, praying that they would soon find solid ground where they could get out of the boat and try to find help. Funny, he thought, he only seemed to pray when he needed something. He supposed God was used to that, but a stab of guilt pierced him and he wondered what it would be like to have a relationship with God, like Rebeca said she did. Someone she could talk to anytime about anything.

"I think we are getting close!"

Rebeca's voice interrupted Toby's thoughts and he looked up. He had been so focused on pushing, he had not noticed that the water had grown narrower into an obvious channel. Rebeca was looking over her shoulders as she continued to row without missing a stroke. Toby thought to himself that once this was all over, he would have to get Rebeca to show him how to row. He imagined it would be quite enjoyable – especially if his life did not depend on it.

Soon there was an actual shoreline on one side, and then on the other and suddenly, Rebeca called out to Toby, "When I say, give your very best push."

Toby nodded and although unsure of what Rebeca was planning to do, readied himself to do as she instructed. How could he be so inept at rowing, he chided himself. Of course, he had never done much rowing, only as a kid, but … .

"Now!"

Toby jerked out of his thoughts and pushed with all his might while Rebeca steered the little boat towards one side, and as she did so, the craft slid part way up the sandy shore and stopped abruptly as its bow lodged itself into the ground. Despite their predicament, Toby was impressed and grinned widely. "Well, done! You are an expert rower!"

The wind nearly drowned out his words, but Rebeca smiled back at him before she stood up and jumped out onto the solid ground. Toby followed suit and stood beside her as she looked in the direction they had just come.

"Look."

Toby followed her gaze and saw what looked like several logs floating upstream towards their boat. "What …?"

"Alligators," interrupted Rebeca, "They are going to find a safe place to wait for the hurricane to pass."

Toby's eyes grew wide and he took a step back. "Shouldn't we run?" Toby called out as his heart began beating rapidly, sending adrenalin racing around his body. He had never seen a live alligator, and he certainly did not want to meet one in the wild. He had heard stories about alligators attacking people.

However, Rebeca smiled and did not move as she watched the animals. "They are not interested in eating while they are looking for somewhere to hunker down to wait out the storm."

Despite himself, Toby raised an eyebrow, "Hunker? I wouldn't have thought you would know the word 'hunker'."

"I have been waiting a while to use that word," Rebeca grinned widely, "I found it a week ago." Rebeca liked to learn new words regularly and would randomly pick a word from the dictionary her high school teacher in Nicaragua had given her, and then wait for an opportunity to use it. She turned around and began walking across the dry ground into the trees. "Come, we must find somewhere safe, ourselves. I believe we are now far enough from the coast to be clear of a storm surge, so we just need to find shelter from the winds. They are already getting quite strong." She bent down and removed the ropes from the boat, shaping them into a loose coil and slinging them over her shoulder as she headed across the dry ground at a quick pace. She strained her eyes as she looked back and forth while she walked.

"Storm surge?" Toby trotted up to Rebeca, panic in his eyes. "That doesn't sound good." He spoke loudly as the winds picked up speed.

"When a hurricane moves onto the coast, it often pushes water from the ocean, onto the land, several miles."

"Are you sure we are far enough from the coast?"

Rebeca bit her lip, "It usually comes before the winds, so hopefully we will be fine."

"You mean," said Toby slowly as he processed her meaning, "it would already have reached us, if it was going to?"

Rebeca nodded thoughtfully as she kept walking, fighting the wind and straining her eyes to find some kind of cover to protect them.

"It all looks so flat around here. Just trees and undergrowth and grass. There doesn't look like any hills or any kind of shelter from the hurricane." Toby looked all around him, his heart racing. There didn't look like any kind of shelter from these winds that he could see. And what if Rebeca was wrong? What if there *was* a storm surge?

———≫●≪———

Adrian opened the front door, the wind nearly ripping it out of his hand as he stepped out into the rain and wrestled it shut before jogging down the steps and over to the wooden building. He unlocked the door and the dim light that shone in, landed on the little monkey squatting on the ground, making distressed chattering noises. Adrian picked up the carrier that he had left on the side and walked slowly over to her. He pulled a banana chip out of his pocket and offered it to her. Gingerly, she took it from him and as she did, he grabbed her and swiftly put her into the carrier. The wind howled outside and, as he began to reopen the door to make his way back to the house, the wind caught hold of it swinging it wide, the hinges straining. He headed out the doorway and leaning on the door he shut and locked it behind him before heading back to his house.

The wind pushed against Adrian as he walked with great effort at an angle, the rain soaking him to the skin along the way. He tried to shield the monkey, but the cage had holes on all the sides and it was too difficult to try and hide it behind his body as the wind nearly ripped the cage out of his hand. Finally, he struggled up the front steps and nearly fell inside, straining to keep a hold of the door as he shut and locked it behind him. He put the carrier on a side table, and as he disappeared from the room to change into dry clothes, a frightened little Emmie sat in a tight ball, large eyes staring through the wire, with the banana chip still held firmly in her tiny hand.

———————

With all the storm preparations done, and nothing left to do but wait, everyone gathered around the table as Ellie put the huge pot on the table.

"Oh, Aunty Ellie, my favourite! Your red beans and rice with turkey sausage is delicious!" Pamela smiled as she put a roll on her plate and handed the rest of the crusty rolls to Benito.

Caleb chuckled as he sat down and pulled his chair closer. "Hang on, Pam, we haven't said grace yet!"

No sooner had he finished praying when the phone rang. Everyone looked up and Joe held his breath, wondering if it was the police. Had they found Toby and Rebeca?

Ellie stood and picked up the phone before the second ring. "Hello?"

No one said a word, and all eyes were on Ellie as she answered the phone, desperately hoping it would be news about Toby and Rebeca.

"Yes, it is." She paused as she listened to the caller. "I see – yes, we really appreciate that – well, I suppose that is kind of good news – okay – thank you very much – yes, all right, thanks for letting us know. 'Bye." Ellie hung up and turned around to the faces looking anxiously at her from around the table.

"That was detective Brown," she began, knowing Joe would be wanting more news than she had to give him.

"And?" Joe interjected, impatient for her to continue.

"Well, he discovered where Elena's son lives, so he drove over to have a look. There was no one there, but it looked like they had left in a hurry – and it looked to him like there had been a few people there, with both bedrooms having been used and bedding on the couches." She looked at Joe. "He said they had probably gone somewhere safer and would most likely return after the hurricane. When the storm has passed, he will go back and keep checking until someone returns."

Joe let out a deep sigh, not realising he had been holding his breath. They had been so close. There was some comfort in knowing that this crazy woman and her son would take Rebeca and Toby and go somewhere safe, but would they have his brother and Rebeca when they returned? What were they planning on doing with them? His stomach churned as various scenarios ran through his mind and he hung his head in despair.

"We'll find them," said Caleb in a determined voice. "We won't give up until we find them." The shutters on the kitchen windows rattled loudly in response and Joe jerked up his head. His eyes locked with Caleb's and a glimmer of optimism seeped into his heart as he saw the genuine concern in Caleb's face.

They ate the hearty meal in a subdued atmosphere as conversation turned to what they would do to entertain themselves as the storm raged its way through; and although Joe did not feel hungry, he ate the meal, surprised that he could appreciate that Pamela had been right – it was delicious.

Soon the pot was completely empty and the only thing left were two rolls.

Ellie stood and looked over at Pamela and Benito. "Do you two want to help me clean up? Caleb and Joe will take one last look around to make sure there is nothing we have missed."

Caleb stood and Joe pushed his chair away from the table. "And then I think a couple of beers or more are in order, don't you think, Joe?"

Joe nodded, thinking to himself that a couple of beers would go down quite well. He needed something to distract him from worrying about Toby.

Half an hour later, the kitchen was cleaned from lunch, the last check had been done, and everyone was gathered back at the table with a game of Monopoly in place of the pot of beans and rice. Joe and Caleb had their beers in their hands while Ellie, Pamela and Benito were drinking iced tea.

"By the time we finish this game, the storm should be over," said Ellie encouragingly.

"That soon?" asked Benito innocently, and Pamela turned to him with a sly smile as the others chuckled.

"You've never played Monopoly before, have you, Benito?"

"Turn here!" screeched Elena and Billy jumped, lifting his foot from the accelerator and slamming down hard on the brakes, jerking the two of them forward forcefully, both being held back by their seatbelts. Pumpkin was not so fortunate, and he was propelled against the dash and slid onto the floor whimpering. Billy's hands were sweating and he tried to keep them from slipping on the steering wheel as he turned off the highway onto a dirt road.

"There was no need for that!" Elena scolded him despite the fact that it was her late direction that necessitated his slamming on the brakes. She gave Pumpkin a scratch on his head, and he decided it would be safer to stay on the floor.

"Sorry, Ma!" apologised Billy, not caring whose fault it was and just wanting to placate his mother. He had long ago learned that an apology, regardless of fault, always came from his own lips.

They drove for about a quarter of a mile when Elena spoke again. "Pull over there." She pointed to a narrow lane. It looked more like a path than a road and it looked dark as it lead into the thick growth of trees.

Billy was not sure that the truck would fit through the gap in the trees, but he steered obediently in the direction that Elena pointed. Branches scratched either side of the vehicle, and Billy silently cursed his mother for making him scratch his paintwork. His truck was his pride and joy, and he washed and polished it regularly.

"Don't you go crying about your truck!" she scolded him, and Billy's heart beat even faster as he contemplated her reading his mind.

"Stop!"

Billy stopped the truck immediately, but this time, as they were going so slowly, they both remained firmly in their seats.

"This is the thickest part of the trees. We'll wait out the hurricane here."

⸺⸺►●◄⸺⸺

"How do you know what direction is away from the ocean?" asked Toby, walking in step with Rebeca, both of them struggling to stay upright.

"All hurricanes north of the equator rotate in a counter-clockwise direction. So the first winds to hit will be heading west. Therefore, if we walk so the wind is generally hitting us on the right hand side, we should be heading north."

Toby grabbed Rebeca's hand as they trudged forward together in the howling winds, the cold rain beating relentlessly down on them.

Suddenly, Rebeca pointed. "Over there!"

Toby squinted through the driving rain in the direction of her finger, but he could see nothing. "What? Over where?"

"A small ridge, like the ground has shifted slightly at some time."

Toby still could not see what Rebeca saw, but he said nothing as they stumbled forward. When they got closer, he saw the ridge, only about three feet high but several feet long – like the ground had subsided at some point. The lower part was north of them, which was why he hadn't seen it right away. When they got to the drop, it appeared as if it had been used by someone – or some animal – for shelter before; a section of the side of the ridge was dug out so that it was concave, creating an overhang just deep enough for a couple of bodies to lie down underneath. Toby motioned for Rebeca to lie down first, then he lay in front of her, facing outward, both shivering in their wet clothes, but holding onto what warmth there was as they huddled together.

"How long will it last?" Toby asked loudly over his shoulder.

"I do not know," she replied, pausing before adding hesitantly, "It could be hours, or it could be days."

"D-d-days?!" Toby exclaimed through chattering teeth. His back had warmed slightly as he leaned against Rebeca, but a cool current of air swirled down and across his wet chest and jeans as the gales soared over the protecting ledge.

"They can do," Rebeca said, not having to speak too loudly as her mouth was right by Toby's ear. "Usually they only last hours, though."

The two teenagers lay there for a while, listening to the great force of the hurricane as it whipped across the land, bending the trees. Toby was amazed that they did not break in half. He supposed it was the bendable trees that stood the test of time in an area that had regular hurricanes. He wondered why someone would choose to live in a place like this.

Suddenly the wind picked up incredible speed and began whirling around randomly in great gusts so loud it almost hurt Toby's ears and he worried that they might get sucked out of their hiding place. "Please God, save us," Toby prayed a desperate silent prayer, feeling certain that Rebeca was praying as well. His body tensed as the winds whipped against him and he felt it tugging at his body while the rain continued to pelt him. Time seemed to tick slowly as his heart raced erratically with the raging squalls and he closed his eyes.

Toby thought about his parents back in England and wondered if his brother had told them he had gone missing. Knowing Joe, he would probably wait a few days so as to not worry them. If it was sunny in England, they were probably sitting on their patio, enjoying an evening glass of wine while his two young sisters galloped around the lawn pretending to be ponies. He hoped Joe hadn't called them yet. He really didn't want them to worry – they had just recovered from finding out about what had happened to him in Nicaragua. *How could someone be so unlucky?* Then he heard Rebeca's voice in his mind, "There is no such thing as luck." *Was that true? Was she right?* If so, then what possible reason could God have to let these terrible things happen to him – not to mention Gwen and Rebeca. *To get your attention.*

Then, just as suddenly as they had started, the wild oscillating winds and the heavy rain stopped. Toby let out a deep breath, amazed at the warm sunshine and the eerie silence that had fallen. He gave an involuntary shiver and flung his arms out to reach the warm sunshine.

"Is it ... over?" he asked hopefully, looking over his shoulder at Rebeca. "That is weird, how that wind just ... stopped ... almost instantly." He started to roll forward, so that his whole body could absorb the sun's welcome heat, but Rebeca put her hand on his shoulder.

"No, Toby. This is the eye of the storm. The middle. As soon as it passes, the great winds will return as quickly as they left."

"Oh," he said with worried disappointment, leaning back into the hollow next to Rebeca.

"But at least that gives us an idea how big the storm is. The next part of the storm should last just as long as the first, and the winds the same strength. Except for the erratic ones that encircle the eye."

"Ya, that was just crazy! I ...".

"Shhh!" Rebeca hushed him and he watched her as she leaned over him, listening intently. Toby listened as well, wondering what she had heard. Finally, ever so faintly, he heard it, a strange sound, like a wave hitting the shore. He opened his mouth to speak to but she interrupted him with a forceful shove forward.

"The surge!" She spoke urgently, Toby rolling forward from her push, and they both scrambled to their feet as the water reached them, grabbing at their ankles. Stumbling forward, they held each other's cold hands tightly as they tried to remain upright while the freezing water shoved them forcefully along through the scattered trees.

"Up here!" She called out loudly.

Rebeca stopped by a large tree and pointed. Toby looked and saw that it was actually two trees that had years ago grown together, and separated about six feet up. The force of the water was strong and now creeping up to their knees. Grabbing a branch, Rebeca launched herself up and scrambled up the tree like a squirrel.

"Come on!" She leaned down to grab Toby's hand as the surging sea tried to wrestle him to the ground. He panicked as he stumbled backwards away from the tree and just as he thought he would be overcome by the wave, a rope swung by his arm. Instinctively, he grabbed it and then he felt himself being pulled back toward the tree. He looked up and saw that Rebeca had positioned herself in the crook so that she had leverage to pull him towards her against the flow of the water. Toby inched slowly forward until he could touch the tree and grab the lowest branch, but as he let go with one hand to reach out, the water heaved towards him and threw him back with such force that the rope was ripped out of his numb hand and he was swept along with the powerful unyielding wave.

"Toby!" Screamed Rebeca, watching helplessly from her perch.

Toby gasped for breath as the water tried to pull him under, pushing relentlessly forwards. He thrashed his arms blindly as he brushed past a tree and he desperately grabbed at it hoping to find a branch, but the merciless bark just scraped his arm like a cheese grater.

"Toby! Toby!"

Rebeca's screams were fading as Toby was propelled forward. He managed to look up just as he was hurled towards another tree that struck his shoulder with a force that shot a stab of pain right through to his toes. Desperately, he tried to roll into a position so he could keep on top of the water as it drove him forwards, but as he started to lift his right arm, electricity raced through to his fingers and he dropped it to his side. Again he was pulled under and he choked as water entered his lungs. Survival instinct tried to kick in as Toby fought with one arm to reach the surface, but again his body began to roll in the icy wave. His heart beat hard against his chest as he struggled to gain control of his movements, but his strength quickly waned as the muscles in his body weakened in the freezing water.

Gasp. Roll. Roll. Gasp. His lungs were burning as he strained to draw in the air as it flashed over his face. Trees battered his body, intermittently halting his roll, but each time, he was thrust forward from the fury of the frigid surge until finally, his limbs grew numb and Toby rolled powerlessly into unconsciousness.

"I'll buy it," said Benito as his tiny metal dog landed on the lightbulb.

Nobody buys utilities," advised Pamela, giggling.

Benito looked at her questioningly, holding his money in his hand. "Why not?"

"It's just not worth buying – you can't make much money on it."

"But if someone else buys it, I will have to pay *them*," continued Benito.

"No one is going to buy it," assured Pamela, grinning.

"But what if they do?"

Benito looked genuinely concerned, and Joe sighed deeply, rubbing his temples in annoyance, and as Benito hesitated, Joe burst out, "Just let him buy the blasted electric company!"

Pamela's smile faded and she lowered her eyes, saying nothing. Joe's anger grew as everyone looked at him, and it was all he could do to refrain from standing up and stomping away from the table.

Finally, Caleb, who was the banker, spoke softly, "You can buy it if you like, Benito, that is fine."

"Good!" He grinned, as though he had made a real purchase.

Benito handed over his money and proudly put the property card in front of him, avoiding eye contact with Joe, who was still breathing heavily. Benito handed the die to Pamela who was sat next to him, and as she rolled, a loud BANG! reverberated through the house.

Ellie and Caleb looked at each other, worried. "Sounds like something hit the back of the house," Caleb spoke slowly and started to get up, but Ellie touched his hand, shaking her head.

"There's no point looking now, honey."

Caleb hesitated, but sat back down in his chair, trying to focus back on the game. "Hey, you got two sixes, Pam!" He smiled at his niece encouragingly.

"Oh! Free Parking!" She squealed delightedly as she placed her little car on the square, and collected the pile of money that had built up in the middle of the board. She rolled again, and got another two sixes, frowning. "Now I'm in jail! How annoying is that!" She parked her car in the 'just visiting' section and smiled. "Never mind! I have loads of money and can bribe my way out of jail!" She placed $50 in the middle of the board.

"I don't think it's meant to be a bribe," smiled Ellie, "It is meant to be bail."

"Well," grinned Pamela impishly, "I prefer bribery and corruption – it is much more exciting than plain old 'bail'! I have bribed the chief of police who needs the money to care for his very ill wife whom he loves so dearly that he has put her in a very expensive hospital with top doctors, on the side of a mountain and a beautiful view of the valley out her window."

"I don't think fifty dollars would go that far," Benito spoke quietly, frowning as he thought seriously about Pamela's explanation.

"It's a game, Ben." Joe glared at Benito who bit his lip nervously. "And if you hadn't already noticed, Pamela here has an extremely vivid imagination. So …".

Caleb opened his mouth to defend his niece, but Pamela jumped in before he could speak.

"Oh, Benito!" She giggled. "It isn't fifty dollars – this 'fifty' here on this paper is just a symbol for fifty THOUSAND dollars, see?" She smiled kindly at him, holding up the piece of paper that said '50'."

Benito nodded, but said nothing, and Pamela passed the die to Ellie who rolled quickly to stop Joe from getting any angrier.

Time passed quite quickly as each took their turn again and again throwing the dice, and intermittently making purchases or following instructions on the cards in the middle of the board. After many rounds, the properties were nearly all sold, and Benito finally felt brave enough to speak again.

"This game takes a long time to …".

Toby's phone chirped. Joe had placed it on the side cupboard so he could check it easily. It was closest to Caleb, so he picked it up and started to hand it to Joe, who stood up,

"I need to go to the toilet, it is probably just Gwen. Click on 'okay', I'll be back in a sec'." Joe headed towards the downstairs toilet, smiling to himself as he went.

"Uh … oh … okay." Caleb stuttered and his face grew warm. Ellie raised an eyebrow as Caleb tapped on the screen.

"Hey there, sexy." Gwen's rose coloured lips smiled demurely at Caleb who continued to stutter.

"Oh, hello, Gwen, I … uh … Joe is … uh … just in the … uh … he'll be back in a minute." He cleared his throat and Ellie reached over and took the phone from her husband, stunned at the beautiful face staring back at her. She paused only a moment before responding pointedly with a jealousy that left a bitter taste in her mouth.

"Oh, no wonder my goofy husband can't speak, you are a very beautiful *girl*." She emphasised the word 'girl' as she tossed a quick glare at her husband, then turned back to Gwen, smiling at her. "I'm Ellie."

Gwen smiled knowingly back at Ellie. She was used to the effect she had on males and the domino effect that had on the women nearby. "Hi, Ellie! I'm Gwen – Toby and Joe's friend. I was wondering what the news was on Toby, and checking if you guys are all right in the hurricane. Has it hit you yet?"

"Yes, we're in the middle of it, but we are all right so far," began Ellie. She then relayed what information they had regarding Toby.

Gwen's face grew serious, but had the confidence of someone who was used to getting what she wanted. "Daddy made it clear to the police chief down there that he wanted Toby found." She paused, her face vacillating with mixed emotions. "And Rebeca," She paused a moment, "she is quite a clever *jungle* girl. If anyone can escape from a crazy woman and find their way out of the Florida bayous, *she* can."

Ellie smiled softly, recognising Gwen's own jealousy. Even the most beautiful had their nemesis, she though to herself. Just then, Joe came back into the room.

Ellie said good-bye to Gwen. "It was nice meeting you," she said politely, as she handed the phone to Joe.

Joe's eyes lit up as Gwen smiled comfortingly at him. "Hi, hon, how are you?"

"Feeling extremely frustrated," Joe sighed. "I just want to be out looking for Toby."

"Well, I think Ellie is right. If they are being held captive, I am sure they will be taken somewhere safe until all this over. Now that the police are making an extra effort, either they will find the two of them, or Rebeca will get them back. You'll see, as soon as this storm is over, Toby and Rebeca will be back safe and sound." Joe made a face; he wasn't entirely convinced, but he appreciated Gwen's attempt to cheer him up, and despite everything, he still felt a twinge of delight at the sight of her perfect face.

"I guess I better say good-bye," said Joe, suddenly realising they had stopped speaking and he was just staring at her. He breathed deeply as he tried to compose himself and she winked at him, making the warmth move up his face. She blew him a kiss and said goodbye, and Joe clicked off before his face was completely red.

"So, who's turn is it?" Joe asked innocently, wishing the warmth in his face would disappear. He really hated the lack of control over his body's response whenever he spoke to Gwen.

Ellie shook her head smiling. "I think it is Caleb's – if he has recovered enough to roll." She raised her eyebrows at him, and he played the innocent card as well.

"I don't know what you are talking about, sweetums," he answered as he picked up the dice and threw them a little too animatedly, sending one rolling wildly and onto the floor. As he hurriedly leaned down to pick it up, he clipped his head on the edge of the table.

"Ow!" he called out in pain, but Ellie just shook her head unsympathetically.

"Good heavens, Caleb! I wish I had that effect on you!" Her voice held a hint of annoyance and she was angry with herself for reacting like a jealous schoolgirl.

Pamela giggled nervously, as she spoke up, "Do you want an icepack on that?"

Caleb looked at her and over at his wife, then back to Pamela. "No thank you, Pamela," he said with a solemn face, "I think I deserve to embrace my pain as my punishment."

Ellie burst out laughing as she rolled her eyes, and Caleb grinned sheepishly at her.

"Get your Uncle Caleb the icepack."

Caleb grabbed her hand and squeezed it. "You know I only have eyes for you, darlin'." He looked so serious, Ellie laughed again.

"You're forgiven. Now roll those dice again!"

Several rounds later, Joe suddenly looked up excitedly.

"What?" Asked Pamela curiously.

"It's quiet! The hurricane must be gone! Do they normally leave that quickly?" He stood up without waiting for an answer and headed out of the kitchen as Caleb called out to him, pushing his chair back as he jumped up to follow.

"It's the eye, Joe! Just the middle of the storm. The next part will be arriving shortly."

Joe paused, with his hand on the back door handle, as Caleb reached him, looking at the door thoughtfully. "Though, we could look outside and see what hit us."

"Just be careful, honey!" Ellie cautioned him.

———⟫◦⟪———

Holding the warm drink in his hands, Adrian sat down on the comfortable leather armchair, opposite the coffee table that held Emmie, as he observed the frightened monkey that sat shivering behind the wire door. Luna plodded over and lay comfortably at his feet, accepting the presence of another animal without question, trusting in his master unequivocally.

After a few moments, Adrian placed the coffee on the table beside his chair, and leaned forward, unlocking the latch and opening the door. Emmie edged away as he did, so Adrian sat back in his chair and retrieved his coffee, not taking his eyes from her, as he slowly sipped the hot sweet liquid. The large grandfather clock that stood by the door ticked loudly in the quiet house as the wind whistled outside, and Adrian waited patiently to see what the little capuchin would do.

Ten minutes passed, and he was nearly finished his drink, as Emmie slowly crept out of the carrier and sat on the edge of the table, eyeing Adrian suspiciously then looking down at the dog curiously, sensing his acceptance of her. She sniffed the air and her eyes rested on the cup that Adrian held. He smiled and cautiously lowered his hand that held the remaining coffee and let it rest on his knee. Emmie sniffed again and she cocked her head, as if analysing Adrian, then suddenly jumped on his other knee and leaned towards the coffee. Adrian tilted it towards her, and the next thing he knew, she had grabbed the china cup and was drinking the now lukewarm liquid like she drank out of a cup every day.

Adrian reached out just in time as Emmie tossed the cup, and as he carefully placed it on the side, Emmie made herself comfortable on his lap, snuggling in to his thick, soft sweater, and closing her eyes. She was a sweet thing, but he would not be able to keep her now; the authorities knew she had been here. They would be back. Within minutes, Emmie was making soft purring noises, and Adrian carefully stroked her head as he lay back, closing his own eyes and soon began snoring in unison with the furry little creature on his lap and the devoted dog by his feet.

———◆———

"An ice cream cart!" Pamela squealed as she pushed her head curiously between the two men who had stepped outside. "It looks smashed up!"

Caleb walked over to survey the damage on the side of his house and Pamela began gathering up the frozen treats that lay scattered around the crumpled cart. Ellie's head appeared through the doorway then disappeared. Within a minute, she had returned with a plastic bag, and relieved Pamela who was screeching as her arms started burning from the frozen 'treasure'. They gathered the last few ice creams, and she looked up at Caleb as he examined the siding.

"Is it very bad?" She asked. Caleb shook his head.

"Not too bad. I can repair it myself." He looked around him as the wind began to whistle. "Better get back inside!" He motioned for Joe to go in, as Pamela and Ellie scurried back up the steps into the house. The wind suddenly picked up slamming the door shut behind them, and Caleb locked it. Ellie grinned and offered everyone an ice cream before taking the rest into the kitchen and stuffing them in the freezer.

Soon they were back playing Monopoly with Benito promptly landing in jail.

———◆———

Rebeca's hair waved wildly in the wind, whipping her face as she sat, tied securely, in the crook of the tree as it bent heavily in the gale. She stared for a long time in the direction that Toby had been swept away, eyes straining as tears ran freely down her cheeks. Her teeth chattered as she began shivering in the driving wind and rain and slowly, she drifted into a fitful unconsciousness where alligators had tied her up and were swimming around her, whistling and shouting in a strange language.

"Miss! Miss! Are you okay!"

The alligators suddenly stood up and ran away, and Rebeca slowly opened her eyes, confusion hanging on like a thick, wet fog. She looked down towards the voice and saw two tall dark-skinned men with guns over their shoulders. Rebeca's eyes grew wide and her heart began beating quickly.

"It's okay," said the one man, seeing her fear, "We've just been looking for a couple of horses that disappeared in the storm." He nodded towards his gun, "You never know what you might meet after a hurricane." He handed his gun to the other man and walked towards the base of the tree, smiling up at her. Rebeca smiled weakly back, her numb fingers fumbling uselessly at the tightly knotted rope. "Here, let me help you!" The man climbed up the tree and untied Rebeca, lowering her down to his friend who grabbed her as her feet touched the soggy ground and her tired legs gave way.

"Easy, now." The man held her up while the blood raced round, warming and strengthening her. "Do you want to sit down?"

Rebeca shook her head and pulled away as she shook her limbs. "Thank you, I just got a bit numb crouched up there in the storm."

"I'm Henry." The man who had climbed the tree, jumped down and landed beside Rebeca. He tilted his head to the other man. "That there is my brother, Mike."

Rebeca nodded solemnly, wanting to be friendly, but her heart breaking for Toby. "I'm Rebeca."

"You get caught out here by yoself?" asked Henry. Rebeca slowly shook her head, her eyes welling up with tears.

"No ... my friend ... Toby," she spoke so quietly, the men had to strain to hear her speak. "He got swept away."

Henry and Mike frowned, and Henry put his arm comfortingly around Rebeca's shoulders. "Mike here will take you back to our house, it's not far. His wife, Bev, is a lovely girl, she'll get you dried off and take care of ya."

"Go steady with her Mike. Come back and help me find those horses once you get her to Bev."

Mike said nothing, but turned to Rebeca, motioning for her to follow him as he walked slowly through the trees, while she trailed behind him, her head hanging down and her arms wrapped around herself to keep warm.

They soon came into a clearing where a large blue bungalow on stilts sat, still wrapped in its steel shutters. Mike helped Rebeca up the steps and the front door opened before they got to the top. A rotund, fair-skinned woman burst out with a blanket and wrapped it tightly around Rebeca, drawing her into the house.

"You poor girl! Did you get caught out in the storm?"

"Rebeca here tied herself into a tree," Mike spoke for her, "poor thing was outside the whole time." He paused before adding quietly, "She lost a friend. He got swept away in the surge."

Bev smiled sadly as she directed Rebeca to a couch positioned by a coal fired stove, and moved across the open-plan house to the kitchen where a large pot was bubbling away on the stove. Without asking Rebeca if she wanted any, she ladled out a large bowl of steaming stew and put it on a tray with a large piece of home-made bread, thickly buttered, before bringing it over to Rebeca.

"I gotta go back out and help Henry find the horses, honey." Mike shut the door behind him without Bev answering, and Rebeca heard him trot down the wooden steps as she took the tray from the kind woman.

———→•◄———

"He's dead, ain't he Ma?" Billy sighed deeply, looking at the teenager they had just discovered lying face down and unmoving. He nudged the body with his foot. He had no compassion for Toby, just disappointment that his investment might be gone and the money he had been counting on would vanish before he even had it in his hand. Elena knelt beside Toby and felt for a pulse in his neck.

An evil grin spread across her face. "Nope! He's still alive, Billy!" She stood up and looked at her son. "He'll need some attention, of course. Pick him up as gently as you can, and put him in the truck."

Billy bent down and tried to lift Toby like a baby, but as he stood upright, Toby slid out of his arms and landed on the grass in a heap, still unconscious.

"You great buffoon!" Elena rebuked her son. "Do you want to damage him some more?!"

"Sorry, Ma! I didn't have a good enough grip of him. Can you help me get him over my shoulder?"

"Hello there! Do you need some help? Is he okay?"

Billy and Elena turned towards the stranger who stepped out into the small clearing. Elena swore under her breath, then turned and smiled weakly at the man, feigning a worried look on her face.

"He's our kin," she began, "we've been looking everywhere for him. He's alive, but we need to get him to a hospital. Can you help my son get him in the truck?"

"Oh! Do you think you should move him? I can call an ambulance." The man got out his phone from his pocket.

"No! That's okay." Elena spoke up sharply. "The ambulances will be busy. It will take ages to get one here. I'm a nurse – I used to be a nurse – and I've checked him over. He's all right to be moved – we can take him to the hospital ourselves, but we need to hurry. I don't know if he has any internal bleeding."

The man nodded, knowing she was right. The ambulances would be very busy. He put the phone back in his pocket as he walked up to them and looked down at Toby.

"Oh!" he said as a thought came to him. "I wonder if this is the friend Rebeca thought she had lost." He looked up at Billy, who was doing a poor impression of a distressed relative as he pursed his lips, wondering how his mother was going to deal with the situation. "Are you missing a girl, as well? Rebeca, her name is."

"Oh! Is she all right? Dear sweet Becky – my only granddaughter, adopted as a wee baby – do you know where she is?"

"Yes, she's at our farm," answered Mike as he carefully helped Billy lay Toby across the back seat of the truck.

Elena thought quickly as she formed a plan in her devious mind.

"How did she seem, mentally?" Elena asked cautiously, frowning deeply. Mike looked at her puzzled.

"Mentally? Uh … well she was obviously distressed about being out in the hurricane and surge, and worried about her friend. Come on, I'll show you where she is," he said.

"No," said Elena firmly. "I'm worried that her psychosis will have returned with this trauma. Just a minute!" She turned to Billy, "Get my bag out of the box."

"What psychosis?" asked Mike as Billy leaned over the back of the truck and opened the box that was fitted across the width of the vehicle. He grabbed a bag and gave it to his mother, who turned her back on Mike as she reached into the bag and pretended to look for something. Quickly, she wrote Rebeca's name on the label that looked like a prescription, and stuck it on the bottle of powder as stood up and handed it to Mike, looking directly into his eyes with her hypnotic gaze, humming the strange sound. Mike tried to look away, but a queer sensation buzzed through his head. After a few moments, Elena smiled and stepped back.

"Poor Becky had a mental breakdown a few years ago and was consumed with the idea that we had kidnapped her as a baby. Every now and again, she has another episode. She usually takes medication, but she stopped recently. If you dissolve two of these pill of in a warm drink, it will relax her. Don't let her see you – she might think you are in on the kidnapping, poor dear." Elena shook her head. "I'll wait a little while, then will come in the house when she is relaxed. Billy can take Toby to the hospital and he will come back for Rebeca and me."

Mike looked at the bottle in his hand with Rebeca's name on it. He still felt the strange buzzing in his head and he shook himself as he turned away, heading in the direction of his farm, while Elena hurriedly grabbed another bottle out of her bag and shoved it at Billy, who promptly put it in the back of the truck.

"Drive down to the place where he waited out the hurricane," said Elena hurriedly. "Put two spoons of this in some water, Billy. Try and get Toby to drink it all. I'll call you when I am ready for you to come back and get me." She picked up her bag and gave it to him as well, before she turned and hurried after Mike.

Mike looked back over his shoulder to see if Elena was following him all right. "Tell me if I walk too fast. My wife always complains about that."

"No, I am fine," answered Elena as she hurried closer to him.

Billy threw the bag back in the box and jumped in the truck. Pumpkin looked up at him from the floor where he was still sat, as if to ask where Elena was. Billy looked down at him. "Don't ask, Pumpkin. I don't know myself!" Billy started the truck and drove off.

Elena followed Mike for about five minutes then stopped as the blue house came into view. "I'll wait here. It takes about twenty minutes for the medicine to start to relax her. She's been through enough already, poor thing." Elena spoke as she eased back a few steps to hide in the trees in case Rebeca happened to look out a window.

Mike nodded and climbed up the steps slowly. The buzzing had stopped, but it had left a strange fog lingering in his head. Turning the handle, he walked inside. Rebeca was curled up on the couch under a blanket; an empty bowl and plate on the coffee table.

Mike clutched the small bottle in his hand as he went into the kitchen area. "How are you feeling?" he asked, as he flicked on the kettle.

"All right, thank you," She answered weakly. "Bev has been most kind."

"Where is Bev?" he asked. He didn't want to have to explain to Bev what he was doing.

"She said she had to sort some laundry."

Mike nodded his head as he turned his back towards Rebeca and grabbed a mug from the cupboard. He glanced over his shoulder, but Rebeca was just gazing sadly at the fire. Quickly, he opened the bottle and shook out two pills, dropping them in the cup. He put the lid back on and dropped the bottle in his pocket before reaching for the hot chocolate powder and putting a couple of heaped teaspoons into the cup. A minute later the kettle had boiled, so he poured it over the mixture and pills, stirring thoroughly. Just then, Bev came into the kitchen carrying a basket of clean dried clothes on her hip.

"Hi, honey! I'm just going to pop these 'round to Mama and make sure she is okay." She turned to Rebeca. "My mama is quite arthritic, so I do her laundry for her."

Rebeca nodded, not looking up, and holding the blanket tightly around her shoulders. Mike opened the front door for Bev before going back to Rebeca's drink. He gave it another stir and then walked over to Rebeca, standing beside her. When she didn't look up, he held out the mug and said, "Here, hot chocolate is a little bit of comfort for the soul, Bev always says."

Rebeca smiled faintly and took the cup from him. He stood for a moment as she just held the cup, looking at it.

"You have to drink it for it to comfort you," he said with a compassionate smile.

Rebeca took a sip, then put it on her lap with her hands wrapped around it. Mike waited a moment, then felt awkward just standing there, so he said, "I ... uh ... gotta go back and help Henry. Will you be all right by yourself for a bit? Bev will be back soon, and she will help you contact your family."

Rebeca didn't answer, so he spoke again, "Will you be all right until Bev gets back?"

"Yes, thank you," answered Rebeca, who took another couple of sips. She looked up at him. "Thank you, the hot chocolate is very nice."

Mike nodded and went out the front door. He walked down the steps, looking around for Elena. Suddenly she stepped out of the trees and he jumped back. He spoke hurriedly, wanting to get away from the woman. "She's drinking some hot chocolate now. Here are the pills. I gotta go help my brother, if you don't mind, ma'am."

"That's fine, you go on now. You've been very helpful." Elena smiled at him, and Mike nodded as he walked off to find Henry.

Twenty minutes later, Elena crept up the steps and quietly opened the front door. Rebeca was lying back on a pillow with her eyes closed. Elena tapped in Billy's number on her phone and he answered after one ring.

"Come now!" Elena commanded firmly but softly.

"Yes, ma'am!" said Billy and hung up without saying goodbye. When his mother said 'now', that was exactly what she meant. He started up the truck and headed back to where they had found Toby. Elena was stood there waiting for him, and as soon as the truck stopped, she motioned for him to get out and follow her as she hurried back to the house.

"We don't have much time. I may have managed to manipulate that man, but I don't know how his wife will respond. She is gone for a little while," she said over her shoulder as she scurried through the trees.

They reached the house and Billy trotted up the steps after Elena who opened the door. Billy stood for a moment looking at Rebeca, then decided the fireman's lift would be easiest, so he leant over and Elena helped him to get Rebeca over his shoulder. He turned around slowly as he positioned Rebeca more comfortably on his shoulder, and Elena went ahead to open the door. He took his time down the steps and Elena scolded him.

"Hurry! We don't know when either of the men will come back. I don't want any more questions!"

Billy hurried his pace and as he felt a faint pain in his knee he panicked, stumbling down the last step and swaying slightly. Elena grabbed his arm to steady him, then they moved as quickly as they could through the trees. Soon they reached the truck and Billy unceremoniously dumped Rebeca on the front seat before climbing in the driver's side. Elena climbed in and fastened her seatbelt as Billy shuffled Rebeca over so she was lying across Elena's lap. Rebeca let out a quiet moan as Elena repositioned her. Pumpkin was still in the foot well, and he gave his mistress an unhappy whine. Hurriedly, Billy turned the ignition, throwing the truck into first gear and putting his foot down, immediately regretting his action as the truck bumped over the uneven road. He let his foot up slightly, but continued as quickly as he could, as he tried to find the smoothest part of the dirt lane.

Finally Billy reached his house and he stopped the truck. He got out then leaned back in to get Rebeca but Elena reprimanded him.

"No, Billy! She'll be just fine for a while. We need to get Toby in so I can patch him up!"

Billy pulled his seat forward and leaned into the back to grab Toby, manoeuvring the boy onto his shoulder. He was not a whole lot heavier than Rebeca, but Billy was not very strong and he grunted as he walked with the heavy weight, slipping on the sloppy ground that was still saturated from the surge water. Finally, he struggled up the steps and inside the house where Elena helped him get Toby onto the couch. She shouted instructions to Billy as she ground, soaked and cooked various herbs. When she got each of them into separate bowls and hung the cloths that Billy had collected over her arm, she barked at him to help her bring everything over. Finally Billy sat on the kitchen chair, watching his mother clean Toby's wounds then stitching up the gash on his head before placing some of the herbs on it and wrapping one of the cloths firmly around his skull. He had to admit it, his ma did know how to get people better ... *and* worse. Her skills were very impressive to watch.

Elena stood up and turned to Billy. "Grab his arm here."

Reluctantly, Billy got up out of his chair and sauntered over to the couch. He sensed she was going to ask him to do something unpleasant, but Billy grabbed where she pointed, waiting for further instructions.

Elena moved Billy into position and then commanded, "Okay, when I say so, pull hard."

Billy's face went pale and he let go of Toby's arm. "Aw, ma, no!" He winced at the thought of what she had asked him to do. He took a step back, and Elena grew angry.

"I can't do it myself, now get back here now!"

Billy stepped forward and put his hand back around Toby's arm, breathing heavily and closing his eyes tightly in disgust.

"Now!" Ordered Elena.

Billy yanked hard and felt his stomach heave when he heard the loud crunching noise as Toby's shoulder moved back into place. Billy stumbled back then scurried into his bedroom and slammed the door behind him as he curled up on his bed trying to control his stomach. Pumpkin lay in the middle of the kitchen and raised his head curiously at the sound of the door banging, then lay back down again with a big sigh, glad to be back on solid ground that did not move or throw him against hard surfaces.

Elena just shook her head and carried on with her work. She felt along his other arm, and decided some ligaments were just badly strained, so she put some of her poultice on it, and wrapped it securely with some more cloths to support it. She took another thirty minutes to sort out all his other wounds, then she called her son.

"Billy, you coward! It is safe to come out now."

A few minutes passed before the door creaked slowly open and Billy poked his head through the opening. When he saw his mother at the kitchen cleaning up her bowls and Toby still unconscious on the sofa, Billy crept cautiously out.

"Go get the girl from the truck, Billy. We need to decide what to do with her. Stick her under the house for now."

Billy obediently went out through the door and soon came back with Rebeca over his shoulder. Elena nudged Pumpkin over with her foot and moved the carpet, then lifted the hatch so Billy could take the girl down the steps. Elena heard a moan as Billy dropped her carelessly on the damp ground.

Coming back up, Billy let the hatch down with a crash. "She's gettin' to be a real pain, Ma, don't ya think?"

"Yes, I believe we will just have to get rid of her." Elena sighed deeply. "It is very disappointing, but she is going to cause much more trouble than she is worth. I really thought I could succeed with some of my newer herbs. If only we had a little bit more time." She scrunched her face. "It's no good, we'll have to dispose of her. I just have to think of the best way to do it."

Just then, Toby mumbled, "Best way to do what?" he said softly.

Elena looked over at him and saw that his eyes were still closed. She filled a cup with the soup that was boiling in the pot and walked over to the couch, sitting down beside him. She spoke encouragingly, "Toby, darlin'; Toby, open your eyes. I've got some soup that will make you feel better."

Toby's eyelids fluttered, then he opened them, blinking slowly and squinting. "Wha...?" he started to ask, but Elena lifted his head and placed the cup to his lips.

"Drink this. You have been through a terrible ordeal. This will help you get your strength back."

"It's some *real* good soup," chuckled Billy and Elena shot him a warning glance.

Toby lifted his head higher, and with great effort one little sip at a time, Toby eventually finished the warm nourishing liquid and then he collapsed back on the couch with a heavy sigh and closed his eyes. *Where am I? Am I still in Nicaragua? Who gave me the soup?* "Rebeca?" He called out feebly and opened his eyes, startled to see Elena's face. She smiled back at him pleasantly, but an uneasy feeling crept through his whole body.

Something was terribly wrong.

———⟫●⟪———

"Well it's about time, Mike, where ya'll been?" Henry scowled at his brother as he appeared through the trees. Henry had managed to find one of the horses and held the wet, frightened animal with a rope attached to its halter. "Buster needs wiping down and settling in a warm dry stable." He handed the rope to Mike who took it without answering. His face clouded over. Suddenly, now that his head had finally cleared, what he had done now seemed completely wrong and his heart beat heavy against his ribs. *What HAD he done?*

"What's the matter with ya?" Henry frowned at Mike, who still felt helpless to answer.

Mike shook his head, unable to speak; not knowing what to say, since he couldn't explain his actions. He led the horse away in silence and Henry watched him for a moment shaking his head, puzzled, before heading off to find the other horse.

The surge had not quite reached their farm, so the stable was still dry. Mike vacantly added some fresh straw and took a pitchfork to spread it evenly before he turned to Buster with a towel, rubbing him down until he was satisfied that Buster was dry enough to be comfortable. He unhooked the halter and flung it over the hook, closing the stall door. Sliding the bolt shut, he headed up to the house, where Bev greeted him with a confused look. Mike looked down at his shoes, then back up at Bev, realising he would have to tell his wife.

"Where did Rebeca go?" she asked.

Mike stood at the entrance, looking at his wife, then his eyes caught the television screen beside her. It was a news bulletin saying that the police were looking for two missing teenagers, believed to have been kidnapped. Rebeca and a boy's face filled the screen. It was the boy who had been unconscious on the ground. Mike stared with his mouth open and Bev looked behind her to see what had caught his eye. She looked slowly back at Mike.

"Where *is* she, Mike?" Bev asked slowly, fear filling her. "Where is she?!"

"Oh, Bev!" Mike said, panicked. "Oh, Bev! I've done something awful!"

Speaking so quietly that Bev could barely hear him, he haltingly relayed the events beginning from when he found the man and lady looking down at the boy unconscious on the ground. Bev covered her mouth, horrified. When he finished, he added, "I've never been hypnotised, Bev, but sure as an angry wasp will sting ya, that must have been what happened! I can remember the licence number clear as day, it was a personalised one."

"You have to call the police, Mike!"

"What am I gonna say, honey?! I aided and abetted a kidnapper??! Who's gonna believe I was hypnotised??"

Bev thought frantically. "They said you could leave information anonymously, Mike."

"But what if they track my phone number?"

Bev twisted her lips, frantically trying to think of an idea. Surely there was some way they could call without being traced. It was difficult these days with all this modern technology. They had said you could call anonymously, but you never knew with the authorities, especially if they thought you had something to do with the crime. They might still try to track you down.

Finally, Bev spoke, "What if you use mama's old phone? I think there is still some credit on that! When you're done, we'll chuck it in the bayou. If anyone traces it back to mama, we can just say we lost the phone. She hasn't used it for a couple of months since we bought her that new one. She won't want it back."

Mike thought for a moment, then nodded, and Bev rummaged through a kitchen drawer, pulling out the old phone and thrusting it at Mike. He stood silently, looking at the phone in his hand.

"Go, Mike!"

Mike shook himself and flew out the door running down the steps two at a time, and jumped in his truck. He didn't know much about phones, but he felt that they could probably still trace his location while he spoke, so he sped off down the drive and onto the highway. Ten minutes later, he pulled over and dialled the number he had seen on the screen.

His call was picked up on the second ring, but before the person could speak, Mike launched into the speech he had planned on his drive.

"I got information on those two teenagers the police are looking for."

Sensing he was not going to let her speak, the woman on the end of the phone just said simply and hastily, "Can I take your details or do you wish to give information anonymously?"

Mike paused for a moment, swallowing hard. The receptionist was about to repeat her question, when Mike finally spoke.

"Anonymously. I saw the two of them with a young man and a lady in a truck and I've got the number..." Mike hurriedly described the man and woman and gave the licence number of the truck, then hung up. He turned the phone off and pulled out the battery. Then he sped off down the road to where he knew he could get near to the bayou in his truck. He tossed the phone and battery as far as he could, then jumped back in his vehicle and headed back home, his heart racing wildly.

———⇒●⇐———

"I think we should declare Pamela the winner and go see what needs cleaning up outside." Said Caleb placing the dice on the board and leaning back. They all looked at Pamela, who clearly had more money than anyone else, and whose properties had considerably more hotels than any of them. They all nodded in agreement, everyone tired of the game and wanting to move about. Caleb and Joe were the first to stand.

"Come on, let's go see if there's been any flooding, then open all the shutters," said Caleb, looking at Joe.

Joe was anxious to be doing something productive and he stood up eagerly, following Caleb out the front door into the bright sunlight. Benito and Pamela helped Ellie tidy up the game and put it away, then went out the back door to see if anything besides the ice cream cart needed cleaning up.

"Get the telephone number off the cart, Pamela, and give the company a call. They may want it back for parts or something. It doesn't actually look as bad as I first thought. The hinges on the lid are twisted and the wheels are broken off, but it might be repairable. I don't know how much these things cost. It might be cheaper to fix it," Ellie instructed Pamela as she and Benito began clearing the debris that had been deposited in their backyard.

———⇒●⇐———

Elena closed her eyes as she stood in the middle of the room. *They're coming*. She looked over at Toby who was growing more conscious, but also had a frown of concern. She quickly made him a 'special' drink and gave it to him. He held it in his hands, unsure.

"Come now," she smiled sweetly, "drink this down. It will help you feel better. You have lots of injuries and this will help take away some of the pain." She looked at him directly in the eyes and Toby felt compelled to do as he was instructed, despite his misgivings. When he was finished, Elena grabbed the cup and tossed it in the sink.

"Billy! We need to go. Take everything you want to keep." She scurried into her bedroom and began packing, leaving a confused Billy sat at the table eating his soup and bread. There was no point in questioning his mother, so he scoffed down his meal and rushed into his bedroom to pack his large suitcase.

Twenty minutes later, the back of the truck was full of suitcases, boxes and bags. They walked back to the house and Elena stood with her hands on her hips, planning her next move. "Get Toby into the truck, and wait for me there. I'll deal with the girl."

Not wanting to know what his mother was going to do, he again heaved the now sleeping Toby over his shoulder and staggered out to the truck.

"Wait there," said Elena needlessly.

Pumpkin sat by the open door and watched his mistress as she pulled the couch over the hatch. She was sure that Rebeca would not wake for another few hours, but she did not want to take any chances. Then she took the large tongs by the fire and proceeded to pick out the burning logs one by one and placed them on the couch and the floor, then tilted a wooden chair back so it was half in the coals and over the hearth onto the floor. The floor began smoking and the blanket on the couch began to burn. Pumpkin whined as he slowly backed out the door. Elena paused for a moment until she was satisfied that she had done enough, then walked casually out the door with Pumpkin at her feet. She walked towards the truck, then turned around and waited until she saw the glass on the kitchen window shatter and the flames begin to consume the house.

It wouldn't take long. The burning house would soon collapse on the girl and she would be burned to death. If someone found her, they could deny all knowledge. They were at her daughter's house, waiting out the storm. Her daughter lived in the country. No one would know when they arrived. The girl must have sought refuge from the storm in the house and accidentally set the place alight as she lit a fire to keep warm.

After one last look, Elena trotted to the truck and opened the door, letting Pumpkin jump on the seat before she climbed in herself. "Drive, Billy!"

———⟫●⟪———

Rebeca's eyes opened slowly. *What was that noise? It sounded like a hurricane. Wasn't the hurricane over? Did it come back on itself? It felt so warm. Why was it so dark?*

Slowly, her eyes adjusted to the dim light, and she smelled the familiar smell of the herbs in the store area under the kitchen. She sniffed again – she could smell burning. Rebeca climbed up the steps and tried to push against the door, but she pulled her hands away at the intense heat. Why was it so hot? Smoke drifted down to her nostrils. The house must be on fire! She crawled back down and huddled on the damp floor. All of a sudden the ceiling caved in at the top of

303

the steps as some large burning object crashed down and tumbled towards her. She stumbled back into a corner away from the flames, but they were quickly dancing towards her. Rebeca screamed as she felt the heat around her intensify.

"Help! Somebody help me!"

CHAPTER 12

In a little over an hour, the two groups had cleaned up Caleb and Ellie's yard and it looked almost like it had before the hurricane had arrived. They gathered in the kitchen for iced tea and Ellie began making supper.

"I think I'll head over to that woman's house and see if she is back." Said Joe as he stood and began to leave the kitchen. He stopped when Ellie spoke.

"But the police said that they felt the last place Toby and Rebeca were at had been the son's place. We don't know where that is."

"You never know, they might go back to Elena's. Who knows? I gotta do something!"

"The police said they would keep an eye on both places, Joe," said Caleb, realising as he spoke that he would not be able to stop Joe from going anyway. Caleb stood as well, and followed Joe. "I'll come with you."

"Afraid I'll stop off and buy a gun on the way?" asked Joe, as he headed to the car smirking.

"I thought I would keep you company." Caleb was not counting out anything, but he just smiled and climbed into the passenger seat, clipping on his seatbelt as Joe backed out of the drive and turned the vehicle towards Elena's house. They were both silent on the drive. Joe was lost in thought, thinking of how he could deal with the large dog. Caleb was praying, asking God to help them find Toby and Rebeca, and also for guidance on how to hold Joe back from doing anything rash, without making him angry.

Joe stopped the car when they reached Elena's property. The two men got out and gave a cursory look around. They both turned towards the way they had come when they heard a vehicle. It was a police car. When it pulled slowly up beside

Joe's vehicle, and the two men got out, Joe groaned: "Not you two," he said with disdain.

"What is *that* supposed to mean? Are you disrespecting New Orlean's finest?" Doug said, squinting at Joe.

Caleb looked at Joe, confused, and Joe blew his pursed lips apart with a deep breath. He didn't want to have to explain to Caleb about any other incidents that showed his impulsive, bitter heart, so he said simply, "These are the two policemen who originally came to investigate Elena's house." He paused for a moment, choosing his words thoughtfully. "I'm not sure how thorough their investigation was, though, because when they came out, they both were acting kind of weird, like they'd had some kind of strange encounter or something." The two policemen looked sheepishly at each other for a moment, then Bob spoke up defensively.

"Look, you two need to leave. We've been instructed to do some surveillance – which, to you two civilians, means hiding so that the person doesn't know you are there. We'll have a quick check around then move our vehicle down a bit and in the trees."

"But I ..." Joe began, but Bob spoke firmly.

"If you stay, I'll arrest the two of you for obstructing a police officer." He stepped closer to Joe, and folded his arms in front of his chest, in the same manner that Joe had first encountered him.

"We'll let you know if anyone arrives." He continued in a firm tone, and pointed back down the lane. "Now leave."

Joe stared at him for a moment, clenching his fists that hung at his sides and fighting the urge to swear at the police officer. Caleb watched, saying nothing, but again praying for God to control Joe. After a full sixty second stare down between the two men, Joe swung around and climbed back in the driver's seat with Caleb quickly getting in the other side.

Caleb only just shut his door when Joe put his foot down and gravel spun under the wheels as he sped off down the lane.

⸻➤●◄⸻

Suddenly, a bright light shone on Rebeca from the other side of the heavy wire that wound around the base of the house amongst the plants and bushes. Rebeca called out frantically.

"Help! Oh, help me please! I can't get out!"

"Go as far back as you can, away from the wire. We'll cut you out," said a deep, calming voice. Rebeca obeyed and crawled back as far as she dared.

"Oh hurry! Please hurry!" Rebeca pleaded as the fire inched closer to her. She couldn't see what the man was doing as she had to look away from the bright light. She closed her eyes, praying that God would spare her. What seemed an hour later, though only a couple of minutes, she felt someone grab her arms and drag her out from underneath the burning house, and as he did, water sprayed on her from the hose with which the other men had been spraying the house. The large man picked her up and carried her like a child, trotting away just as the house collapsed.

⸻➤●◄⸻

"Billy, you need to drive faster! We need to get off the interstate and onto a quiet road to get to your sister's."

"Ma," said Billy slowly, not wanting to upset his mother. "If I drive faster, the police will pull me over."

Just then, flashing red lights turned on behind them. Elena looked over her shoulder, the patrol car was several vehicles behind them.

"Foot down, Billy!" She ordered.

Immediately, Billy put his foot to the floor and, gripping the steering wheel tightly, began weaving in and out of the traffic. The police car weaved as well, passing a couple of cars, and getting uncomfortably closer.

"Take the next exit, Billy, but stay in this lane until the last minute. I'll tell you when."

The exit was coming quickly and Billy started to move over.

"Not now! Wait until I tell you!"

Billy started breathing heavily as he clenched the steering wheel tighter, and his heart was pounding against his ribcage. They were nearly at the exit, and Billy held his breath as he stayed in his lane until … .

"Now, Billy!"

Billy yanked the steering wheel hard to the right and the car beside him screeched his brakes. He heard a loud BANG as the truck behind slammed into it, but he didn't look back as he took the slip road at ninety miles an hour. Elena held onto Pumpkin, but she heard Toby slide off the back seat onto the floor. She was about to scold Billy, but then she looked back and cheered. The police car following them could not make the turn safely, and sped on past the exit. Elena patted her son's shoulder and he lifted his foot up and slowed to sixty.

"No, Billy, we need to go faster. We need to find a secluded road and hide for a few hours. Until they give up looking for us."

Twenty minutes later, Elena pointed. "There!"

"Wha …?" The turn was so close Billy thought he misunderstood where she was pointing.

"Now, Billy!"

Billy slammed on the brakes. He hadn't see the lane until they were nearly on top of it. He slipped off the road and headed into the thick growth of trees, driving until his mother told him he could stop.

"Stop!" She called out and Billy obeyed immediately, wiping his sweaty palms on his jeans and breathing heavily. "Over there, it looks like a small cabin. Go have a look to see if there is anyone there. Knock on the door first, and if someone answers, just tell them you are lost and need some directions."

Billy jumped out of the truck, but Elena instructed him to get Toby off the floor first, so Billy leaned in to lift Toby back on the seat, before he sauntered over nervously to the wooden building. He wasn't a quick thinker, and he was worried that if there was someone home, they might ask him something he didn't know the answer to. He stopped and looked back at the truck. His mother scowled and waved him on. As he got closer, he saw there were no cars parked outside, and the area surrounding the house was quite unkempt. Eventually, Billy reached the small cabin and noted the broken roof slates. He climbed up the wooden steps, taking care to avoid the broken planks. Lifting open the door screen, which was hanging only on one hinge, he reached in and knocked firmly on the door.

After a few moments, Billy knocked again, but this time, instead of standing and waiting, he walked across the veranda and looked in the window. He could see a kitchen table and four chairs, but there was nothing on the counters to suggest anyone was there at the moment. He walked back and down the stairs, making his way around the side. There was a fire pit, and some rickety looking chairs – two of which were broken – suggesting that no one had sat in them for a long time. He took one of the chairs and placed it under a window and looked in. A bed with no sheets and a chest of drawers with a thick layer of dust. It looked like someone had tidied up and left a long time ago.

Billy made a quick walk around the cabin and decided it would definitely be a safe place to hide for a while. He suddenly realised his mother would be wondering what he was doing, so he trotted quickly back to the truck to the passenger side where his mother was waiting impatiently with her window open.

"No one there, Ma! Doesn't look like anyone has been there for some time now. There are a few bits of old dusty furniture, but that's it."

Elena nodded and opened her door. Impatiently, Pumpkin jumped over his mistress and scurried into the bushes to do his business. Elena got out of the truck and walked to the cabin while Billy jumped back in and drove the truck up to the sad-looking building.

Elena carefully climbed the dilapidated steps. The screen door was still leaning open as Billy had left it. She turned the door handle, and was surprised to find it locked. She stepped off the old faded mat and lifted it up, shaking her head as she saw the silver key. It was amazing how many people actually stored their keys there in real life. It was not only foolish people on television.

"How did you know the key was there, Ma?" Billy asked, as he stood behind her with Toby slung over his shoulder again, but before Elena could answer, Toby began moaning softly. Billy followed her in the house and tossed him on the couch gently, so his mother would not scold him. Toby's eyes slowly opened and he looked around confused.

"Wha...?" He tried to sit up, then collapsed back down again, causing dust to escape from the old pillow in a cloud that hung in the air. Elena coughed and waved at the dust particles.

"You had a nasty tumble in the surge waters, and we found you and patched you up, dear." She smiled pleasantly down at him, but Toby frowned, trying desperately to remember the past couple of days. "Don't you worry, son," she added as she saw Toby's questioning face. "I'll get you some soup and you'll feel better real soon!" With that, she swung around and commanded Billy to get some supplies out of the truck. "This looks like a fine place to hunker down in for a while!" She called out as cheerfully as she could be, now that the police were after them. They'd stay there a few days, until she came up with a plan. Elena looked around her and twisted her mouth. If they were going to stay a while, she better get Billy to give the place a dust and clean while she made some of her special soup!

⸻

Joe's heart began beating quickly as he pulled into Caleb and Ellie's drive and saw the police car parked at the kerb. He threw the car into park and flew out of the car, racing up the front steps, with Caleb following closely at his heels.

Ellie was sat in the kitchen drinking a cup of coffee with a policewoman. She looked up and smiled when she saw the two men come in.

"They found Rebeca! She is in a hospital. She has a bit of smoke inhalation, but we can probably collect her tomorrow!" She paused, realising it was not all good news, and the police officer continued for her.

"Someone reported seeing Elena's son's truck and remembered the licence plate. There was a dark-haired teenage boy with them. One of the patrols found the truck, but when they took chase, the truck got away."

Happy. Angry. Frustrated. Hopeful. Joe was overwhelmed with a myriad of emotions and he dropped into a chair beside the officer, exhausted from the stress.

"Are you the brother?" she asked kindly. Joe put his head in his hands, breathing heavily, and he nodded. "We'll find it again. Don't worry. They won't get away." She patted his shoulder as she stood. "Thank you for the coffee ma'am. We'll let you know the minute we spot the truck again." She tipped her head as she exited the kitchen. "Bye, folks!"

Ellie stood and went to the stove where two large pots were bubbling. She gave them a stir and turned to Caleb. "Will you set the table, honey? Then put these pots on the table." She turned to the counter and opened a large plastic bin, taking out a bag of crusty rolls, which she placed in a basket and then put the basket on the table before she sat down.

Caleb said grace, thanking God for the food and for Rebeca's safe return and praying for her complete recovery and then pleading with Him to help them find Toby and soon bring him safely back to their home.

———⇒●⇐———

Tadeo squinted his blue eyes, as he watched the policewoman get into her car. He was parked on the opposite side of the road, a few houses down. No one was looking for him here. The police lost him when he left Nicaragua. He had various passports and easily made it into the US. Losing Benito had made him very angry. He shouldn't have left him. But then, he hadn't thought the boy had it in him to try to escape. Thankfully, the kid was foolish enough to not realise Tadeo could track where he was by his phone. If he had had any brains, he would have dumped the phone. Still, Tadeo wasn't complaining. Now he had to decide how long to wait. He had just heard on the radio that Rebeca had been found and was now in the hospital. Presumably she would be just overnight, as they said they were just taking precautions. He thought for a moment. The fewer people in the house, the better. He guessed that at least two people would go and get Rebeca in the morning, that would leave two people and his nephew. He could handle that.

———◦●◦———

The next morning dawned clear and hot. Joe felt sweaty and uncomfortable before he even opened his eyes. Although he was sleeping on top of the blankets in his boxers, the warmth was still oppressive. He looked over and saw that Benito was already up. Joe jumped off the bed and had a quick, cool shower to freshen up, then quickly dressed and hurried downstairs. He was greeted by the smell of bacon and coffee and his stomach growled as he walked in the kitchen. Despite that, he couldn't wait any longer.

"If you give me the address of the hospital, I'll go and get Rebeca," he said as his stomach gurgled in protest. Ellie smiled, as she held the mouthful of pancake in front of her. Caleb's plate was full of bacon, eggs and pancakes, and he was busy slicing everything up.

"Sit down, Joe. It is only 8:30," began Ellie, "I've called the hospital and they won't be able to release her until 10:00 after the doctor has checked on her. It is only a ten-minute drive to the hospital. Sit down – it sounds like that is what your stomach wants to do!"

Reluctantly, Joe stepped towards the table. The free chair next to Benito was the closest, but Joe walked around to the far side and plunked himself down beside Pamela. She smiled up at him as she grabbed her orange juice and took a large gulp.

"Any news on Toby?" Joe asked hopefully.

Ellie didn't want to dampen his spirits, but she shook her head sadly. "I'm sure they'll find him soon. Now they have the licence plate number, the police can track them easily."

"Oh, yes! Of course!" Chirped up Pamela.

"Number plates can be changed," said Joe curtly, automatically changing the American terminology to the British.

Joe stabbed a piece of bacon but stopped before it reached his mouth. Grace. He hadn't said grace. He didn't often say grace any more. He didn't often thank God for anything these days. A conflict began in his mind, but when he saw Caleb looking at him, he placed the bacon in his mouth and began chewing. He wasn't going to say grace just because Caleb expected him to. Though, he had thought of saying grace before Caleb even looked at him. Joe blew out an exasperated sigh through his nose as he looked down at his food and continued to eat.

An hour later, Joe could stand it no longer, and he asked Ellie for the address of the hospital. Caleb stood up. "I'll go with you."

Joe raised an eyebrow. "I'm not a child, Caleb," he said abruptly. "You don't have to keep an eye on me. I've managed my life perfectly well without you so far." He knew it was a lie. His temper seemed to be becoming more and more of a problem lately. *But then*, he defended himself, *he had every right to lose his temper, what with all the trouble there had been lately. Who wouldn't be losing their temper if they had been through what he had been through with his brother and Rebeca?* An unwelcome thought rushed in unbidden – Caleb wouldn't.

"Joe," Ellie began, wanting to defend her husband, but Caleb put a hand on her shoulder and spoke firmly.

"I don't think I have to keep an eye on you, Joe. But if we go in my car, I can drop you off and drive around until you and Rebeca get out. Hospital parking is really expensive."

It did seem to be a reasonable idea to Joe, though he was still dubious as to Caleb's motive. He stood motionless thinking it over, then decided it was a good idea; whatever Caleb's reasoning. He nodded at Caleb, and the two of them walked out of the front door.

At the hospital, Caleb pulled up to the kerb. "I'll wait here for as long as I can, but if I get moved on, I'll just drive around and keep passing by."

"Okay, thanks," said Joe as he climbed out of the car and up the concrete steps of the hospital. He stopped at the reception to find out where Rebeca was, and within minutes, he was stood outside her room. She was sat on the side of the bed, looking out the window thoughtfully. Joe's heart melted as he watched her. She turned around and smiled, then frowned, obviously full of mixed emotions just as he was. He swiftly walked over and as she stood, he threw his arms around her and held her tightly. She hugged him back, but he could feel it wasn't the same. He bent down and let the smell of her hair drift up and into his memory. Suddenly, he realised he had been holding her too long and he let go, stepping back and looking at her face.

"Has there been …" Rebeca began, and Joe shook his head.

"No, not yet. But the police will find him."

"Yes," she said, "when he took my statement this morning, the policeman seemed pretty confident they would." Rebeca looked up at Joe, and saw the emotion in his eyes. She smiled faintly. Once again it pained her to see how much he thought of her when she could not return his feelings. And also accepting that Toby could not return hers. But then, she was struck once again with the thought that she could not have a romantic relationship with someone who did not love God. So it shouldn't matter to her that Toby did not care for her in that way. How could love be such a miserable thing?

"Come on, let's get out of here," said Joe finally, as he took Rebeca's hand in the most platonic way he could muster.

—➤●❰—

Tadeo waited ten minutes after the two men drove off. Finally, he got out of the car and left it unlocked. He didn't want any delay on his leaving. He looked around, but there was no one paying attention. Anyone who was outside was busy cleaning up the mess around their house. Tadeo walked quickly, while trying not to look suspicious. He paused for a moment deciding whether or not to knock. Finally, he tapped on the door and Pamela's smiling face appeared. Panic quickly wiped away her happy face as she recognised Tadeo and he stepped through the door pulling his gun out and pointed it at her. She automatically raised her hands as she stepped back, her eyes wide with fear.

"Where is he?" he growled softly. He turned as Ellie came out of the kitchen.

"Who is…?" Ellie froze as she saw the gun pointed at her niece.

"Get over there!" Tadeo ordered Pamela as he waved his gun towards Ellie. Quickly, Pamela obeyed.

"Wwwhoooo?" asked Pamela loudly, hoping that Benito would hear and not come down from the bedroom.

"Benito!" Tadeo hollered, making Pamela and Ellie jump.

Up in his bedroom, Benito's world became black and the air became heavy as he struggled to breath. He sat on the bed and couldn't move. How had his uncle found him? He looked down at the phone in his hand and closed his eyes. How could he have been so stupid? Of course his uncle would have a tracking app on his phone.

"Benito! I know you're here! If you don't want me to start shooting your friends, you better appear in three seconds!" Tadeo's eyes flashed in anger.

Benito only had to think for one second. He was terrified of his uncle, but that new found bravery he had experienced when he had escaped, although weak, was still there. He could not let him shoot Pamela or Ellie. He flew down the stairs and skidded to a stop directly in front of Tadeo.

"I'm here, uncle!"

"If you call the police, I'll kill him!" threatened Tadeo, as he ushered Benito out of the front door, hiding the gun back in his trousers under his shirt. He shut the door behind them and pushed Benito down the steps and across the road towards his car, shoving him in the passenger seat before rushing around to the driver's side. A second later, his foot was on the pedal and they were speeding off down the road.

"What are we going to do, Aunty Ellie?" asked Pamela as the two stood in the hallway where Tadeo had left them. They both jumped when the phone rang. Ellie hurried into the kitchen and picked up the receiver.

"Hello?" she said. "Yes," she paused as she listened to the person on the other end. "Oh, well that is good news. What is going to happen to her?" Another pause. "Oh. Okay, I'll tell them. Thank you for letting us know." She hung up and turned to Pamela.

"Uh," Ellie was still dazed at what had just happened. She shook herself. "That was the police. Someone turned in the little monkey. Someone left her on one of the chairs in the reception – there was a note. The person had his hood up and kept his face down, so they couldn't see who it was on the CCTV."

Pamela rushed over to her aunt and gave her a long hug. "I'm so scared, Aunty!"

Ellie hugged her niece back tightly. "So am I, Pamela, so am I." She took a deep breath and blew through her mouth. "But God will take care of him."

"But he doesn't *know* God!"

"It doesn't matter. God knows *him*." Ellie thought for a moment. "Benito's searching, Pamela. He asked me some pretty good questions when no one else was around. I think he was worried that his questions would sound dumb. They weren't. He trusted me enough to ask and I answered as best I could. It's up to God, Pamela. He's the one who draws people to Himself. You can't push them. We can't do anything."

Pamela smiled. "You always know how to make me feel better, Aunty Ellie."

———⧫———

Toby opened his eyes with a start. It was just light enough for him to see his surroundings. He sat up and looked around. He began to remember the last few days. Rebeca! Where was Rebeca? She was in a tree. And he – he was in some musty old house – he glanced out the window – in a forest somewhere. How did he get here? They'd been drugged ... that was what Rebeca said before the hurricane ... by that crazy woman and her son ... *they* had brought him here ... why? He had to escape!

Toby slowly stood, then looked down when he felt the bandage on his arm. It hurt. His hand went to his head, which also hurt, and he felt the bandage wrapped around his skull. He felt wobbly and sat back down, breathing deeply. Waiting five minutes, Toby tried again, this time feeling stronger. He walked slowly towards the door. When he finally reached it, he put his hand on the door knob and turned it carefully, trying not to make a sound. When it finally clicked open, he paused a moment, looking over his shoulder to see if anyone had heard. Silence.

Cautiously, Toby pushed open the door. He could hear his blood pulsing in his ears as it raced around his body. Surprisingly, the door did not make a noise. However, the outside deck creaked as he put his foot down. He stopped for a full minute before moving forward. Slowly, inch by inch, he made his way across to the steps and down, relieved when his feet finally landed on the quiet grass.

He began to walk quickly now, and started to run, but his head began spinning and he had to slow back down to a painstakingly slow pace. Finally, he could see the highway, and he picked up speed once more, only to feel dizzy again. He walked with determination, but the road seemed so far away. He began wandering from side to side down the lane until finally he fell onto his hands and knees. His vision was getting hazy. *Which way was the highway? Surely it was the direction where it seemed lightest. Oh! What was that? Was that tarmac? Had he reached … ?*

Toby blinked his eyes open and his heart sank as he realised he was back on the couch and Elena was stood looking down at him, shaking her head.

"Who is a naughty boy?" she said as though scolding a toddler. "After all I have done for you, you want to just leave? Besides, you are not well, surely you realise that. I'll get you feeling better in no time!"

Toby's head hurt. He put his hand up to the bandage and when he brought it back down again, he saw blood.

"Look what you've done! You've opened that wound! I am going to have to re-dress it. You just lie back now and I'll get my supplies."

Toby had no choice but to obey: exhaustion consumed him. He stared up at the ceiling, drifting in and out of consciousness.

"Hey ho, who's the escape artist?" Billy called out loudly, jerking Toby back awake. "Thought you could get the better of us, huh? No sirree! I wasn't about to let you go!"

"Billy, shut up!" Elena scolded him sharply, and Billy cowered, lowering himself into the armchair furthest from his mother. "There's nothing to escape *from*, Billy, Toby wants to be with us." She turned to Toby, "Isn't that right, dear?"

Toby looked at her confused. It all seemed so clear earlier. Just then, he heard it. The tick tock tick tock of a clock. Tick … tock … tick … tock … He lay back down on the cushion, closing his eyes and holding his head. *Why was everything so foggy now? What was wrong with him? No, no, no! It was all so clear and now … nothing was clear … nothing made sense. He was locked back in that weird nightmare where Elena was in control. Or was she? He* wanted *to do what she asked. She had done so much for him. What had she done for him??*

Elena placed a chair next to Toby and sat down, carefully unwrapping his bandage to have a look. "Look what you've done, now Billy! Poor thing thinks we've kidnapped him or something – he looks frightened, poor soul!" Elena spoke in a soothing voice, as she took off the last of the bandage and rolled it up, throwing it on the floor. She wiped off the fresh blood, and put on more herbs, then took a fresh bandage and wrapped it around tightly.

Tick … tock … tick … tock …   Toby closed his eyes but it didn't help. *Was he asleep or was he awake?* Tick … tock … tick … tock …

Caleb smiled as he watched Joe help Rebeca out of the car and stick by her side as she walked into the house.

"Somebody is smitten," Caleb said quietly to himself.

As they walked in the house, Ellie rushed up to them, giving Rebeca a hug before turning to her husband. "Benito's uncle has taken him away!"

"Wha…?" Began Caleb who was interrupted by Joe.

Joe snorted and they all looked at him disapprovingly, and he responded in a defensive tone. "What? I always told you he was a snivelling low-life with no backbone."

"Actually," burst out Pamela, "He was upstairs in his bedroom. He could have hid up there, but he came down because Tadeo had a gun pointed at Aunty Ellie and me!"

Caleb embraced his wife at the news. "Are you all right? Did he hurt you, sweetheart?" He stepped back and looked her over as though looking for bullet wounds.

"I'm fine – we're both fine, but Pamela is right, Benito gave himself up for us. It was a very brave thing to do."

"Very!" Pamela nodded her head vehemently, then launched into an explanation even though the two men did not ask her for the details. "Someone knocked on the door and when I opened it, there he was – Tadeo – pointing a gun at me. I recognised him immediately from when I saw him in the store. You can't forget those piercing blue eyes, you almost feel like they could hurt you by piercing you themselves. Which of course they can't! But you *feel* like they can hurt you. But of course, he did have a gun, which *can* hurt you." Pamela sucked in a breath before continuing, "Then Ellie came in and he told us to stand together and asked where Benito was. I tried to pretend I didn't know who he was talking about and spoke loudly, so Benito would know to hide but his uncle shouted for him and said he was going to shoot Aunty Ellie and me if he didn't get down in three seconds, so he did." Pamela breathed again before ending the affirmation of her new friend, "Which was *very* brave indeed!"

They all looked at Joe who, although agreeing, did not want to say it out loud. However, as they continued to look at him, and Rebeca stepped away in disappointment, he got angry.

"There's no need to be judgemental about me! So the kid did one brave thing, that doesn't mean he's now completely changed!"

Realising that was the best apology they were going to get from him, Caleb turned to his wife. "What did the police say?"

"Oh! We haven't called the police yet. Benito's uncle said he would kill him if we called the police." Ellie frowned, "We didn't know what to do."

"But the police called us to say that Toby's monkey was handed in. That's something!" Pamela blurted out, wanting to say something positive.

"I think we should still call the police. I'm sure they get that sort of thing all the time and know how to deal with these situations quietly." Caleb didn't wait for an answer as he walked to the phone in the kitchen to make the call, while the others sat in the living room. Immediately, Ellie stood back up again.

"Would anyone like some tea or coffee?" she asked.

"Can I have some hot chocolate?" asked Pamela, "I think hot chocolate is very comforting when you are stressed about something."

"I would like some of that chamomile tea, please," asked Rebeca politely.

"Coffee, please," said Joe quietly as he sat in the far corner of the room, idly swiping at his phone so he did not have to look at anyone.

Ellie came back into the room and was handing out the drinks when Caleb came in and sat next to Rebeca.

"Evidently they knew about Tadeo," Caleb began as he took the coffee Ellie gave him and sipped a mouthful before putting it on the coffee table in front of him. "The police in Nicaragua had a tip off that he had escaped into America on a passport with a different name, Ed Parks. They are going to send someone to come by this afternoon and take your statements." He looked at Ellie and then Pamela and tried to reassure them. "So, he won't know you called the police, as they were already looking for him. They just now know for sure that he is in America, and that he was here an hour ago. That will be very helpful."

The phone rang and they all jumped, looking in the direction of the kitchen expectantly. Ellie jumped up and hurried to answer the phone.

"Hello?" she asked anxiously. Then in a disappointed voice, said, "Oh, well that is good. Yes we will be home ... that's fine, no problem ... okay, goodbye." She came into the living room, but everyone realised by the tone of her voice that it would not be important information. "It was the ice cream cart company. They are coming by after lunch to pick up the cart." She looked at her watch, then added, "Speaking of which, I should make some lunch."

Caleb grabbed her arm as she turned to leave. "Sit down, honey. I'll order pizza." He pulled her down to sit on the other side of him and she picked up her coffee.

"That sounds lovely." She smiled up at him and he gave her a deep kiss and hugged her tightly.

"Yuck! – PDA! No kissing, please!" said Pamela screwing up her face.

"What is P ... D ... A?" asked Rebeca, confused.

"Public display of affection!" smiled Caleb as he continued to gaze lovingly at his wife, then kissed her again, brushing a lock of hair away from her eyes. "I have immunity, due to the trauma experienced by my beautiful wife."

"Oh, yuck!" squealed Pamela as she jumped up. "I'll order the pizza!" Halfway to the kitchen, she shuffled awkwardly backwards, reaching out her hand with her back facing Caleb so she didn't have to watch. "I need a credit card."

Toby drifted in and out of consciousness after Elena re-bandaged his head, and it seemed only minutes later when Elena came back with a stew of finely chopped vegetables.

"Rebeca!" said Toby, "We must find Rebeca!" He closed his eyes, trying to remember. Yes, she was in a tree.

Elena patted his hand comfortingly and handed him the bowl. "She was rescued, dear, but she was rather traumatised and she wanted only to see her father, poor thing. He was all she could talk about. So she went back to Nicaragua."

Toby looked up from the bowl at Elena, unsure. Rebeca didn't seem to be the type of girl to get traumatised by anything, but maybe he didn't know her very well. Maybe she wasn't as tough as he had thought she was. He suddenly felt sad.

"She didn't say goodbye," he said thoughtfully to himself as he stared at the bowl of stew that was now in his hands. He could hear the clock somewhere in the cabin ... tick ... tock ... tick ... tock ... .

"Ah, well, sometimes you think you know someone when really, you don't. I'm afraid she just wasn't as fond of you as you thought." She smiled brightly at him, "Eat up! I cut up the pieces small, so it would be easier for you to eat, dear. You need to eat this up and rest some more. By tomorrow morning you should feel well enough to go catch some catfish with Billy. We had to leave quickly when the hurricane came, so I didn't have time to pack many supplies. According to my calculations, the water shouldn't be too far away." She said smiling, as she handed him the stew. "A mile at most."

Toby suddenly wondered why he felt sad, then he looked up at Elena, confused. "Isn't this your cabin? Don't you know the area?"

Confident that Toby would eat his soup, Elena stood and spoke as she left the room. "It's a cousin's house. They said we could stay here until it was safe to go home. I've never been here before."

Toby accepted her explanation as he began to eat, mesmerised by the tick … tock … tick … tock …, mouthful after mouthful, … tick … tock … tick … tock … .

"Aunt Elena," he said weakly as he scooped out the last bit of the stew. He had hoped to feel stronger from the nourishment, but instead, he felt the energy draining out of him.

Elena came in the room and strode over. "Are you finished, dear?" she asked as he handed her the bowl and she looked inside. "Would you like some more?"

"N-n-no," he struggled as he tried to keep her in focus. "I thought I would … feel better … after the stew, but I…" Toby's voice trailed off as he lay back on the cushion and drifted off into a deep sleep.

Elena smiled. He really was too easy to manipulate – it almost wasn't any fun.

Elena and Billy busied themselves around the cabin, cleaning and fixing things that they found were broken. Both weary from their efforts, that afternoon they each finally headed to a bedroom, both of which, fortunately for them, still had a bed with a mattress. Elena even managed to find two blankets and one pillow. She decided Billy could sleep without a pillow. Pumpkin followed Elena to the back of the house where he fell asleep on the bed with his mistress snoring loudly beside him.

Some time later, Toby's eyes jerked open as a narrow beam of light pierced the darkness in the room, and he looked around. It was night. He must have slept through the rest of the afternoon and evening. He crawled slowly off the couch, still feeling a little woozy, and carefully leaned on the arm to straighten himself up to a standing position. He froze as the front door gradually opened and he squinted as the beam of light shone in his face and a voice whispered.

"It's the police! Are you Toby?"

Shocked, Toby could only nod silently, standing still, unsure of everything. He still didn't know if he was dreaming. He could hear the clock … tick … tock … tick … tock …. *Should he call Aunt Elena?* He opened his mouth, but no sound came out … tick … tock … tick … tock ….

The next thing he knew, a strong man had a gloved hand over his mouth and was dragging him out of the cabin and down the front steps. As the man pulled him behind a police car and told him to get down, he heard the man's radio click on.

"Go! Go! Go!" A loud whisper broke the quiet of the night. He heard shouting and footsteps running around the wooden floors inside, and a dog barking loudly.

"They won't hurt Aunt Elena, will they?" Toby asked the man who looked down at him compassionately. They had been told that the woman was very good at hypnosis. She had really done a number on this kid.

"No, son, I'm sure they won't," said the man who wasn't sure at all. He guessed if the woman relied on hypnosis and drugs, she probably didn't need a gun, but the son might have one. And if people tried to use guns against arresting police officers, it often did not go well.

Joe woke as he heard the phone ring in Caleb and Ellie's bedroom. He rolled over and looked at his phone: 7:00. Who rings at 7:00 in the morning? He sat up and swung his feet off the bed. The police! Maybe they have news on Toby! He started heading out his bedroom door then stopped. It wasn't really appropriate for him to be going to Caleb and Ellie's bedroom in his boxers. He sighed. It wasn't really appropriate for him to be going to Caleb and Ellie's bedroom at all. He quickly put on some clothes and sat on his bed with the door wide open. His heart was pounding heavily and he could barely breath. It *had* to be the police at this time of day.

After an agonising ten minutes where he could hear Caleb speaking, but not what he was saying, he heard him hang up and then he heard their bedroom door click open. Joe jumped up and stood in his door way, nearly colliding with Caleb who had just reached it. He had a big grin on his face, but Joe wanted to hear it out loud.

"Tell me!" he almost shouted.

"They found him! He's in the hospital but he's okay. They just want to keep an eye on him for a day or so." When Joe looked confused, Caleb continued, "Let's go downstairs and get a cup of coffee and I'll explain exactly what the police said."

When they got to the kitchen, Ellie was already turning on the coffee pot and opening up cupboards, deciding what to make for breakfast. She gave Joe a hug as he entered. "Isn't it fantastic?" She smiled broadly as she returned to her ingredients. "The coffee will just take five minutes."

Caleb and Joe made themselves comfortable and Caleb opened his mouth to speak as Pamela squealed into the kitchen.

"Did I hear you say they found Toby?!" She didn't need a reply as the three of them were grinning from ear to ear. Delighted, she gave Rebeca a hug as she came up beside her, then proceeded to hug the others as she danced around the kitchen before plunking herself in the chair next to Joe. Smiling happily, Rebeca sat in the chair next to her.

"Right," began Caleb. "One of the patrols came across them in the truck on the highway, but they sped off when they realised they were being followed. They gave chase and I guess they were going quite fast, then suddenly the truck pulled off, but the police car couldn't manage the turn safely enough. They lost them for a few minutes, then they had another sighting, but lost them again. So they scoured the area and came across some tire marks on the road, at a turning down a little lane. It looked like someone had stopped quickly, so they decided to have a look around, just to check things out, and they found a small trace of blood on the road."

Joe's face grew concerned, so Caleb quickly continued. "Toby had a cut on his head, but he is fine, Joe, don't worry. I guess he had tried to escape, but was groggy from drugs and collapsed as he reached the highway, and left some blood where his head landed. The woman's son found him and took him back to a cabin they had found down this lane." Caleb looked at his wife who was handing him the first cup of coffee and took it from her, "Thank you, sweetheart." He took a sip, and placed the cup on the table in front of him as he continued: "The police investigated and found the truck parked in front of the cabin and saw Elena and her son wandering around the cabin, so they waited until night-time, when everyone would be asleep. They watched the entrance to the lane to make sure they didn't leave, then they went back in the dark and one of the officers saw Toby asleep on the couch. He quietly got Toby out before they stormed the placed and managed to arrest Elena and Billy without incident."

"So why is Toby in the hospital?" asked Rebeca, still concerned even though Caleb told them not to be.

"Well, he sustained considerable injuries when he got swept away from you in the surge, which was where he got the wound on his head. The woman managed to patch him up, but they want to make sure that she did everything properly. I guess it appears at first check that the woman knows how to heal people well, but they want to do some x-rays and run a few tests just to make sure." Caleb took another sip of coffee as Ellie came over with a cup for Joe, along with a jug of juice and some glasses, to which Pamela and Rebeca promptly helped themselves.

Joe looked at him expectantly. "You said they need to run tests – what else do they need to check?"

"Well," Caleb continued taking a deep breath, "as you know from what Rebeca told us, Elena used some drugs and hypnosis on both of them. Although the hypnosis didn't work on Rebeca, it worked extraordinarily well on Toby for some reason. But they have a psychiatrist coming to see him today to give him a thorough check. We can go get him this evening, providing the check goes all right, but they expect the psychiatrist will still want to see him again after he's left the hospital."

Ellie placed some bacon, eggs and toast on the table and Caleb bowed his head. The others followed suit as Caleb thanked God for His great mercy on Toby and bringing him safely back to them. He prayed that God would heal Toby completely, both physically and mentally. And he prayed God would keep an eye on Benito, that the police would find him, and that Benito might finally be free of his uncle and allowed to live his own life. There were some hearty amens as Pamela giggled.

"You forgot to thank God for the food!"

Caleb smiled and they all bowed again, "And thank You for the amazing food before us, amen!" Caleb finished, before he began piling up his plate.

Joe just looked at the food. "I think I am too excited to eat."

"Ah, said Caleb, squirting ketchup over his food, "You may think that, but I bet your stomach disagrees."

Joe laughed, and filled up his plate as Ellie sat down and they all chatted happily, enjoying the good food as they asked Rebeca to explain, in more detail this time, all that had happened to her and Toby while they were with Elena and her son.

The day turned out to be hot and sunny, so they spent their time outside in the pool and also inside in the air conditioned house introducing Rebeca to Monopoly. Though they all spent the day relaxing and enjoying the time as they waited to hear from the hospital, they all – except one – had a little niggle in the back of their minds about Benito.

At 5:00, the phone rang and Ellie scurried in the kitchen to answer it. "Hello?" She paused as the person on the other end of the line spoke, "Oh," she said disappointedly, "No, I understand. We'll come first thing in the morning." She came back to the table where Pamela was explaining to Rebeca how she was bribing the police to let her out of jail. Ellie shook her head chuckling.

"I'm afraid the psychiatrist wants to see him one more time in the morning before they release him." They all looked disappointedly back at her, but each was happy that the doctors were being so careful with Toby.

Joe didn't think he would be able to sleep that night when he went up to his bedroom at 10:00, but the worry over the past few days had exhausted him, and he was asleep before his head hit the pillow.

When he awoke the next morning, he couldn't believe it was 9:30. He had a quick shower and hurriedly dressed, before he realised he would probably have to wait until 10:30, as he had had to do for Rebeca. He trotted down the stairs happily to join the others for breakfast, but when he saw they were all nearly finished, he felt the need to defend himself. "I don't know what happened to me! I never sleep this late."

Ellie stood up and patted him on the arm. "Your body was happy not to be worrying any more, I expect!" She walked to the stove as she continued, "Don't worry, though we've left some for you, Joe, sit down."

It was decided that Caleb would drive again, while Rebeca and Joe accompanied him, as they both were anxious to see Toby. So once again, Caleb pulled up to the hospital while Joe and Rebeca climbed out of the car. The two of them walked into Toby's room together, but Rebeca held back, unsure of how he would respond to her coming. Toby was lying down but he swiftly sat up when he saw Joe who quickly strode over and embraced his brother in a huge bear hug.

Toby moaned at the pain in his shoulder from his brother's enthusiastic squeeze. "Oh, easy, Joe!"

"It's so good to see you, Tobs." He couldn't resist rubbing his brother's hair before giving him another hug, despite his brother's cheery protest. Toby's eyes drifted to the side to see Rebeca.

"Rebeca, you're still here. I thought you had gone back to Ni…". He frowned and closed his eyes. "Of course," he sighed. "Elena lied to me so I wouldn't question what happened to you." Toby stood up as Rebeca walked awkwardly toward him, but when he opened his arms to her, she rushed towards him and hugged him gently, not knowing what had hurt when his brother had embraced him. Toby held onto her as he breathed in deeply, burying his face in her hair. "It's so good to see you."

Joe stepped back, and once again felt the grief of a broken heart; this time even more acutely as he saw something begin to awaken in Toby's face. After a few moments, they stepped away from each other and Joe piped up, "Come on, let's get you out of here! Caleb is waiting outside."

"Have you called Mom and Dad?" asked Toby, "and Gwen?" He paused for a moment before blurting out, "What about Emmie?!"

Joe shook his head sighing heavily, "I'm not sure what we are going to tell Mom and Dad, yet! Fortunately on your birthday, they sent a message via someone else saying their internet was down and the next day they and the twins were off somewhere. We'll make the calls when we get back to Caleb and Ellie's place. And the little monkey has been found."

"Where is she?" Toby persisted.

Joe quickly explained about Emmie, then added, "All the loose ends have been tied up …". Joe's voice trailed off as he realised that wasn't the truth and he felt a heavy guilt in his heart that he had not given any thought to Benito.

When they got to Caleb's car and got in, Caleb leaned over the back seat and spoke to Toby.

"Good to meet you, son!" He smiled, then a shadow fell across his face. "I'm afraid that Benito's uncle turned up and took him away again. The police are looking for them. He shouldn't be able to get out of America."

Toby's face fell at the revelation. "America is a very big place – how will they find them?"

"They are pretty sure that Tadeo will try to leave the country. They'll catch him at an airport, probably." Caleb said confidently.

Toby suddenly felt very tired, and he leaned back in the seat, falling asleep against Rebeca's shoulder just as they pulled up on the drive. Rebeca nudged Toby awake, and the others followed him up the steps, with Joe putting an arm around Toby's shoulders to steady him, "Let me help you, buddy. Perhaps you should have a little nap or something."

Toby nodded, "Good idea." So after Ellie and Pamela greeted them at the door, Joe helped his brother up the stairs to lie down on the bed that Benito had slept in, which was now covered in fresh sheets.

At 12:00, Ellie produced another pot of her special Crawfish Étouffée along with the Beignets that they had enjoyed the first time the had eaten there. They had all sat down, when Toby came silently into the kitchen. "What's this? Are you guys going to eat without me?" He smiled, refreshed from his nap and feeling better than he had for several days.

He sat down beside Joe, but just then, Toby's phone pinged and he looked down at it. He glanced at Ellie, then Caleb. "It's Gwen, do you mind if I answer it?"

Ellie tittered, "Just don't let Caleb see her again – he might choke on his crawfish." Toby looked confused as the others laughed, while Rebeca nodded her head thoughtfully in understanding.

Toby clicked 'answer' and her beautiful face instantly appeared, but somehow, for the first time, he wasn't worried about embarrassing himself. "Hi, Gwen!"

Joe leaned over to say hello and was immediately sorry. She looked absolutely stunning, oozing femininity. The familiar warmth began pervading his entire body this time.

"Hi, Gwen!" he said quickly, then sat back down, trying to concentrate on his food.

"Hi Toby! It's so good to see you! My dad's friend in the police down there just told us you're finally home. Are you all right? Oh, you have a bandage on your head! Is it a serious wound? Are you recovered from that hateful woman and her son?"

Toby smiled at all her questions. "I'm fine, Gwen. Thank you so much for all your help. By the sound of it, if your dad hadn't gotten involved they would never have found us. I don't think they were going to even bother, as they had some dumb idea that Rebeca and I had run off together."

"That *is* a dumb idea!" Gwen smirked, then stopped herself when she remembered Toby didn't like her criticising Rebeca. "Not that Rebeca isn't a girl you would want to run off with ...". She trailed off as she was unsure what else to say regarding the police. "Well, you are safe now! And looking ever so rugged with your bandage and all your scrapes!" She winked at him and he chuckled. Then his face went solemn.

"Did you hear that Tadeo got Benito? He pointed a gun at Ellie and Pamela, and threatened to shoot them if they didn't hand him over!"

"So they did?" She raised an eyebrow.

"No! But Benito heard them being threatened and gave himself up."

"Wow! Will wonders never cease!" They heard her mom call in the background and she groaned. I have to go for a gown fitting. Mr Perfect is taking me to a ball next week." She rolled her eyes. "I have to get my make up on."

"You have to wear make-up for a dress fitting?" asked Toby.

"Mummy won't go out in public with me if I'm not wearing makeup, remember. She says we have to maintain a *standard*." She made a face, then batted her eyes at Toby. But I know you prefer me without, so I thought I'd call you first!" Toby grinned – she certainly looked beautiful without make-up, that was for sure. He heard her mother calling again and she looked over her shoulder.

"Hang on mother, five more minutes!" She turned back to Toby. "We also heard about the monkey, so I wanted to let you know that Daddy has arranged for you and Rebeca to take the little thing back to Nicaragua. You'll need to go soon, as they don't want to hang onto the monkey. Just give me a call when you know, and Daddy will book the flights and arrange the travel. I said you probably wouldn't want a hotel as you would want to stay in the jungle for a few days visiting Rebeca's dad." She made a face when she mentioned the jungle. It was certainly a place to which Gwen would never want to go again.

"Thank you, Gwen, that is too fantastic of you!" responded Toby.

Gwen smiled, "Nothing is too much for my parents to do for you and Rebeca!" She paused a moment. "I'll speak to Daddy about Benito and see what we can do. Gotta go, honey!" She winked and blew him a kiss. "Tell that hunky brother of yours that there is no need to be shy!" She clicked off before Toby could say goodbye.

Toby put his phone down and looked at Joe who was decidedly way too focused on the food in front of him. Everyone laughed and continued to eat their meal.

CHAPTER 13

"It will be wonderful to see my father again," said Rebeca, half to herself as she unbuckled her seatbelt and looked out the window. She turned and saw that Toby was looking at her and she smiled happily at him. "It seems like we have been gone for months instead of a couple of weeks!"

"I know, so much has happened, it is hard to imagine it was such a short time ago we were here."

Although they were both keen to get Emmie and take her home, they waited a few minutes while most of the other passengers stood to retrieve their items from the overhead compartments and then stand, waiting for the door to open so they could start filing out.

Soon they were amongst the others, walking down the aisle and stepping off the plane and down the metal steps. It was a small airport, so it did not take them long to go through security, but the bags were slow to arrive on the belt.

"You wait here and watch for the bags, Rebeca, I'll go over to that desk and see if Emmie is off yet."

Toby made his way through the crowd to a desk that was below a sign that had something written in Spanish, then underneath in smaller letters it read: Large or unusual baggage claim.

A short dark-haired man with eyes so dark they were almost black, stood behind the desk writing something in a book.

"Excuse me, do you speak English?"

"Si," he laughed then added, "yes," with a broad grin. "How may I help you, sir?"

Toby handed over the papers to claim back Emmie. "I was wondering if a monkey has come off the plane yet?"

The man glanced through the papers and nodded vigorously. "Of course, señor! All animals are put on last and taken off first. Give me one moment and I will go find your monkey." He went through a door behind him, and shortly came out carrying a cage. He looked at the ticket that Toby had handed over and looked at the one on Emmie's cage, nodding. "Everything is okay! Here you go!" He put the cage on the desk in front of him and Toby looked inside. Emmie was sleeping, curled up on a soft blanket he had put in. Toby grinned broadly.

"Thank you, sir!" He nodded to the man and carried the carrier back to where Rebeca had put her backpack on and was holding out Toby's. He put Emmie gently on the floor and put on his backpack, before picking up Emmie again and heading towards exit where a car was waiting at the kerb to take them to the helicopter. A small dark man got out and opened the back before he turned to Rebeca to take her backpack. Toby already had his off by the time it was his turn, and he put his bag in himself. The man looked at the monkey, but Toby shook his head. "She'll be on the back seat beside me." The man smiled and nodded as he shut the back and they all got in the car. It was only a five minute drive, and Toby thought they could have walked, but it was easier this way, since the man knew where he was going.

When they got out by the helicopter, Toby paused when he saw the pilot. It was the same man that had dropped him and Tadeo off when Tadeo had first taken him into the jungle. The day his life had gone from dull to extraordinary in one fell swoop. The man did not appear to recognise him as he took their back packs and threw them unceremoniously in the back. Toby reached in and placed Emmie on the floor before climbing into a back seat, while Rebeca got in the front beside the pilot. They thanked the car driver and two minutes later, they were in the air – the pilot still seemed to be in as much of a hurry now as he was back then!

By the time they landed at the clearing, Emmie was beginning to wake up. Rebeca and Toby jumped out, and Toby grabbed their bags, handing Rebeca hers, and placing his on the ground as he opened the cage and carefully scooped out Emmie. He shut his door then leaned into the front.

"Thank you! You can …" he started speaking loudly to make himself heard above the blades which were still whirring around, but he quickly shut the door and jumped back as the helicopter began to rise before he could tell the man he did not want the cage back.

Emmie clung to Toby's neck at the sound of the helicopter, but she soon relaxed as she began to take note of her surroundings, perched happily on Toby's shoulder. He put on his pack, while Emmie expertly sat undeterred, and followed Rebeca as she happily strode towards her village.

"I can't remember where I met up with Emmie," said Toby as he came up beside Rebeca.

She grinned. "Don't you worry, she will know exactly when she is home!"

The heat began to overwhelm Toby as he began sweating under his pack, but Rebeca did not even seem to notice. He swatted at a mosquito and stopped. "Hang on, Rebeca, I need to spray myself!" He dug in the side of his pack and pulled out his spray which he squirted liberally over himself, much to Emmie's consternation, who jumped to Rebeca's shoulder. She giggled.

"I do not believe Emmie wants to be sprayed! Monkeys have their own mosquito repellent. She will find some millipedes and rub them over herself if she needs to! You should try it – they are very effective!"

Toby made a face and asked, "You don't use millipedes, do you?" Rebeca laughed and opened her mouth to speak, but Toby stopped her as he closed his eyes at the thought. "No, don't tell me! I don't want to know. I am not sure I could ever hug you again if I knew!"

Emmie jumped back on Toby's shoulder, but then she began sniffing him and began squeaking loudly. Rebeca and Toby both laughed as she jumped back over to Rebeca and rubbed her little nose in Rebeca's thick black hair.

A little while later, Emmie stood up and began sniffing the air. Then, just as they passed under a large tree, she squealed and jumped up several branches. Toby and Rebeca stood and watched her for a moment. They couldn't see the troop, but they could hear them chattering excitedly as Emmie scampered further up towards them.

Toby frowned sadly. "Oh, she isn't even going to say goodbye."

Rebeca started to laugh, but when she looked at Toby and saw his face, she walked up to him and gave him a hug. "Monkeys do not say goodbye, Toby. She is with her family now, and that is what we both wanted for her. She is happy."

Toby half smiled. "I guess it is better than the long tearful goodbye you get with people. It is just over," he snapped his fingers, "like that. No messing, no last words, not even a 'bye! After all we have been through together, she disappears without even looking back."

Rebeca rubbed his back comfortingly. "She is home, Toby."

Toby shook himself and smiled broadly, "You're right, what am I standing here sulking for? This is why we went to go find her – to bring her back home. Let's go get some of your grandmother's amazing stew – I'm hungry!"

With that thought in mind, they both picked up speed and it was not long before they arrived at the edge of the village. Rebeca slid off her pack and crept up to the old woman who was instructing some children which items she wanted to go into the pot. The woman looked up just as Rebeca reached her and her smile seemed to reach across her entire face as she held open her arms.

"Pequena!" she shouted happily, and everyone looked on as Rebeca and her grandmother squeezed each other tightly. Then the children and all the other villagers came up to Rebeca talking excitedly in Spanish.

Toby stood where he was, enjoying the scene as Rebeca's family welcomed her home enthusiastically. Eventually, one of the children noticed him and she called out, pointing to him.

Rebeca's laughter was almost musical as she called out to Toby, "Come, Toby, they want to welcome you, too!" Just then, Rebeca's Dad came out of his hut, and he paused at the entrance, grinning at her happily. Rebeca squealed like Emmie, and she ran to him almost knocking him over as they embraced. He steadied himself, then swung her around like a child.

"Rebeca! Rebeca!" He kept repeating her name, overwhelmed by the emotion of seeing his only child, whom he thought would never return. Although it had only been a couple of weeks, the whole tribe had thought they would never see her again, and Toby suddenly felt a grief well up inside him. This was Rebeca's home. Just like Emmie. Was he now going to lose her when he had just realised how much she meant to him?

Rebeca startled Toby out of his thoughts as she grabbed his hand and pulled him over to be mobbed by her grandmother and the children. The other villagers were not so sure of him. Last time, he came with that evil man that made them very nervous. Rebeca shouted out something in Spanish, and many of them smiled and nodded their heads, then she led him towards the hut that he had been in before, so he could put down his pack and have a rest in the cool while they waited for the stew to be ready. Rebeca returned to sit by her grandmother, father and villagers as they all chattered happily, presumably – since they spoke in Spanish and Toby could not understand – Rebeca recounting what life was like outside of their jungle.

Over the next few days, Toby enjoyed living the life of a villager with Rebeca. They caught fish, hunted deer, foraged for food, and Toby learned to prepare it all. Rebeca taught Toby how to row almost as well as herself. They swam in the river in the day and sat around the fire dancing and singing in the evening. Toby enjoyed every minute, but the thought that Rebeca might want to stay behind when it was finally time to leave, cast a dark shadow over every minute they spent together.

Finally, the day arrived. Toby sat on his mat and pulled the satellite phone out of his bag. He switched it on and held it in his hands. It bleeped it was ready, but Toby just sat staring at it. He jumped when it pinged loudly at him. It was a message from Gwen: Looking forward to your call!

Toby sighed heavily. How quickly his feelings had changed. Then a thought struck him. If his feelings changed that quickly over Gwen, how did he know they wouldn't change quickly over Rebeca as well? If she chose to stay, couldn't he just forget about her and let his feeling go? He looked through the open doorway and his eyes landed on Rebeca in a bright pink simple flowing dress. She was talking to her grandmother and laughing. Even from here he could see the intelligent sparkle of life in her eyes and her character that oozed out into a beauty that went far deeper than Gwen's. Gwen was stunningly sexy, there was no doubt about it, but she couldn't hold a candle to the warmth that radiated in every direction to anyone who got close to Rebeca. He sighed again and looked away, focusing on the phone. He pressed Gwen's number and waited for her to answer.

"Oh, hi, sugar! How are you? Are you ready to get out of that hideous jungle and back to society?" She laughed and he imagined her sat on her bed, running her long fingers with bright red polish through her cropped blond hair. He imagined she would have the same red on her pouty lips and if she could see him, would be batting her eyes at him.

He cleared his throat and tried to speak cheerily. "Actually, I've had an amazing time, Gwen. I've learned how to hunt and skin a deer," Gwen gagged as he smiled and continued, "and how to row, and we've had loads of fun singing and dancing by the fire."

"Oh," Gwen said simply with an obvious touch of disappointment.

"But ya, it's time to leave. If you could send the helicopter tomorrow, that would be great. Just send a message with the time and also with the details of the flight back to London."

"What about jungle girl?" Gwen said unkindly out of her jealousy.

"I don't know yet. I'll ask her this afternoon and message you back quickly." His heart was so heavy he could not keep the sadness out of his voice, but he had reached a point where he didn't care if he hurt Gwen's feelings. All he could think about was Rebeca.

"Okay, hon," Gwen said quietly and clicked off.

Toby sat for a moment pondering what to say, and finally stood and waved at Rebeca through his doorway. "We need to talk, Rebeca!" He knew they should have had this discussion earlier, but he was so afraid that she would decide to stay that he didn't want to ask and risk spoiling the time he had left with her. He had decided it was best to pretend they were both leaving together, in case her answer was not what he wanted to hear.

Rebeca lowered her eyes and her smile faded slightly as she turned and walked up the steps and into his hut, stopping opposite him. He looked down at her and opened his mouth a couple of times to speak, but nothing came out. Finally, she answered his unspoken question.

"I am staying, Toby."

Toby could feel his heart banging against his chest and his breathing quickened, sounding loud and laboured in his ringing ears.

"I have had my adventure," said Rebeca simply. Then smiled, adding "I have tasted ice cream." Still Toby couldn't speak, and Rebeca began to look confused. "What is the matter, Toby?"

He reached out and stroked her softy shiny hair, then pulled her towards him as he leaned down and kissed her softly. Her lips tasted of strawberries – real strawberries, not lip gloss strawberries like Gwen's, and he smiled despite himself. He broke away, but kept her face held in his hands as he looked deeply into her dark brown eyes. He never noticed before that they had flecks of gold sprinkled through them. He had never seen such beautiful eyes. He actually felt a deep stabbing pain in his heart.

Rebeca was stunned. She had been wanting him to kiss her, without hypnosis, for so long – and it felt so good. But it was not right. After much soul searching, she knew that now. Her mind was racing in several directions. "I thought you liked Gwen, Toby." Though that didn't matter now, since she had come to accept that something far more important would keep them apart.

"Gwen is stunning, and sexy, sure." Rebeca looked at him bewildered as it sounded to her like there was a 'but', however how could anyone match Gwen? "But she's not *you*, Rebeca!" He pulled her close and held her tightly as he buried his face in her soft hair, breathing in deeply. "Please Rebeca! I can't leave you here, not now that I have finally discovered ...," his voice trailing off, not wanting to say the words so that he could pretend he didn't really feel it.

Rebeca's resolve was quickly disappearing as she was overwhelmed by the exquisiteness of being held by someone you loved with all your heart. While she still had the strength of will, she took a step back, holding him at arm's length and looked up at him.

"No, Toby, I am sorry. I realise that no matter how much I love you, I cannot have a relationship – other than friends – with someone who does not know and love Jesus." Rebeca's lip quivered as she spoke. It felt like it was the hardest thing she had ever said.

"But I can change, Rebeca, I can become a Christian!" Toby pleaded with her.

Rebeca half smiled as she shook her head. "It does not work that way. You have to understand your own sinfulness and need for God's gift of salvation. You have to do this for yourself. You cannot just 'become a Christian' to make someone else happy. It is an understanding between you and God."

"W ... well ... what if I change and want to ...?"

"Toby," Rebeca began, "I will be here if you do."

Toby became desperate. "But what about Benito?? Don't you want to find Benito? You know only you can find him. No one can track like you do. Please, Rebeca! I need your help! I can't find him on my own!" When he saw the hesitation in her face, he added, "And after we find him and get him help, you can come back home, and I won't say another word. Pleassssse! For Benito!"

Rebeca realised she was being manipulated, but she did want to help find Benito and get him to a permanent safe place, with his uncle in prison. It was a good cause. "Okay," she said finally, "but you must not kiss me again, and we may hug only if someone else is present." She smiled sadly. "It is too difficult to step back on my own strength."

Toby smiled hopefully, pleased that at least they would be together for another couple of weeks. They had spent much time together as friends, he could do it again. But then, surely in that time he could get her to change her mind. He reached out to touch her cheek and she took another step back.

He nodded. "You better get out of here, otherwise I may just kiss you again!"

Rebeca rolled her eyes and strolled off to speak to her father and grandmother, while Toby turned to the satellite phone. There was another message from Gwen. Tadeo and Benito had managed to get back to England on a new passport of which the authorities were not aware. Gwen was going to meet Toby and Rebeca in London as the 'very fine man with the very fine career' was beginning to grate on her nerves and she needed a break.

Toby supposed it was a good thing. With Gwen around, he would be able to be more self-controlled around Rebeca. He glanced up to see she had picked up a little toddler and was laughing as she swung him around and made the little boy giggle frantically. He took a deep breath – but it was definitely not going to be easy.

⟶➤◆◀⟵

THE END

ENDNOTE

1. https://answersingenesis.org/answers/

Printed in Great Britain
by Amazon